NO HEAVEN *for* GOOD BOYS

No Heaven
for Good Boys

A Novel

Keisha Bush

Random House
New York

Published in the United States by Random House, an imprint and division of Penguin Random House LLC, New York.

RANDOM HOUSE and the HOUSE colophon are registered trademarks of Penguin Random House LLC.

Grateful acknowledgment is made to Random House, an imprint and division of Penguin Random House LLC, for permission to reprint seven lines from "The First Elegy" from *Selected Poetry of Rainer Maria Rilke* by Rainer Maria Rilke, edited and translated by Stephen Mitchell, translation copyright © 1982 by Stephen Mitchell. Used by permission of Random House, an imprint and division of Penguin Random House LLC. All rights reserved.

Library of Congress Cataloging-in-Publication Data
Names: Bush, Keisha, author.
Title: No heaven for good boys : a novel / by Keisha Bush.
Description: First edition. | New York : Random House, [2020]
Identifiers: LCCN 2019054027 (print) | LCCN 2019054028 (ebook) |
ISBN 9780399591969 (hardcover ; acid-free paper) |
ISBN 9780399591976 (ebook)
Subjects: LCSH: Senegal—Fiction.
Classification: LCC PS3602.U8388 N6 2020 (print) |
LCC PS3602.U8388 (ebook) | DDC 813/.6—dc23
LC record available at https://lccn.loc.gov/2019054027
LC ebook record available at https://lccn.loc.gov/2019054028

Printed in Canada on acid-free paper

randomhousebooks.com

9 8 7 6 5 4 3 2 1

FIRST EDITION

Half-title page, title page, chapter opener, part opener images: copyright © iStock.com / © Mellok, © ulimi

Book design by Andrea Lau

For the Talibé and vulnerable children everywhere

Every angel is terrifying.
And so I hold myself back and swallow the call-note
of my dark sobbing. Ah, whom can we ever turn to
in our need? Not angels, not humans,
and already the knowing animals are aware
that we are not really at home in
our interpreted world.

—RAINER MARIA RILKE, "THE FIRST ELEGY"
(Stephen Mitchell, translator)

I.

I.

Ibrahimah slumps against the trunk of an ancient baobab tree and sets his red tin can between his feet. The tree's gnarled, flowerless branches twist and bend over a wide, empty road with only a single white line running down its middle. It is late morning and the road is quiet, free of people, traffic, houses, or businesses. Just dry, parched earth stretching as far as the eye can see, with a scattering of baobab trees. Above, the sky is overcast and gray, but the air is warm. While his cousin Étienne and the other boys from the daara debate how to spend the afternoon, Ibrahimah's eyelids hang heavy and his thoughts drift to his mother. The warmth of her touch, the sound of her voice, and the scent of her skin exist now only in memory.

Just as his daydream is about to take full possession of his consciousness, a ball of fire streaks toward him, landing on his knee. His slack muscles spring tight and his almond eyes stretch wide as teacups—the apparition is a tiny red bird cocking its head, as if to get a good look at him. Not knowing whether to shoo the bird away or call for his cousin to witness the spectacle before him, he watches quietly and hopes that it is some kind of fairy, like the one his sisters told him would come for a tooth beneath his pillow.

"Fairy godmother?" Ibrahimah squeaks in Wolof.

The creature shakes its small head.

"You can understand me?"

The bird moves its head up and down.

Ibrahimah's mouth forms a circle and his eyebrows arch.

"Are you here to help me?"

The bird tilts its head back and sings a melody that the boy has heard before. He sees his village, Saloulou, and his mother flipping small pieces of lamb on the grill. His sisters chase one another, pulling the pigtails they can catch, and his father carries a box of vegetables from their farm. The image of home gives way to the small red bird's fleeing tail feathers. Ibrahimah's eyes linger on his knee, where the bird had landed, then he turns toward his cousin, who stands beneath another tree several feet away, out of earshot.

"Étienne! Did you see?" Ibrahimah yells, jumping to his feet.

Étienne turns away from the conversation he is having with Abdoulaye and Fatik, two other boys from their house. "See what?" Étienne shouts back.

"The bird! On my knee! He could understand when I talked." Ibrahimah races over to explain.

"So do you want to go or not?" Abdoulaye asks.

"Go where?" Ibrahimah asks, his mind still focused on the bird.

"The zoo!" Abdoulaye says, scratching at a patch of eczema on his bald scalp.

"You should have seen the bird on my leg! It talked to me!"

A silver Mercedes Benz passes by, its tires sticky against the newly paved road. Ibrahimah turns his head, but the car is going too fast for him to ever have a chance at begging from its occupants.

"Cousin, the day is passing, and once people get out of school and work, they may not let us in," Étienne says, impatience lurking at the corners of his mouth.

Ibrahimah's eyes drift back toward the empty sky. "You missed it," he mumbles, following behind the three older boys.

Ibrahimah stands below the chipped blue arch that poses as the entrance to the Parc Zoologique in Hann Mariste, on the eastern rim of Dakar. The zoo is a little over an hour away by foot from Marabout Ahmed's house in Ouakam, but the boys rarely abandon their normal route unless they hear of a good opportunity like free food, or a chance to make money. Excursions like this take too much time, and as the Americans like to say, time is money. But with Marabout gone, the hours from sunrise to sunset belong to the boys, and not even Étienne has been to the zoo before in the five years he has lived in Dakar. Ibrahimah's cousin walks up to the window now and strains his neck to speak to the woman sitting on the stool inside the booth.

"*Niaata* for four boys?"

The young woman looks down at Étienne.

"Six cent."

Étienne begins to count out six hundred francs from the coins in his palm, but the young woman slaps her hand on the counter to get his attention.

"No, just go in," she says, pointing to the black gate that spontaneously clicks open. Étienne looks up at her in surprise. She replies with a wink of her eye.

"Give them a tour. The rush won't arrive until later, when school is out," she calls over to a man standing on the other side of the gate, wearing a dark-green park uniform.

The man pulls the gate further open. Excited, Ibrahimah pushes past Abdoulaye and Fatik and bumps into the slim, dark-skinned park ranger. Lush tall trees sit behind the man, and a dirt path. It doesn't look like anything exists inside. Ibrahimah is curious to see what lies within.

"Are you ready?" the man asks.

"Yes!" Ibrahimah squeaks in excitement.

"Have you seen lions before?"

Ibrahimah shakes his head no. The others mimic him.

"Pumas?"

"No."

"Gorillas?"

The boys look at one another.

"Hyenas?"

Silence again. The man chuckles and motions for the boys to follow him.

"What do I smell?" Ibrahimah asks, scrunching up his nose after taking a few steps.

"The chimpanzees," the guide tells him as they come upon a large metal cage to their right.

A large chimp gazes at the boys in boredom.

"Wow, it's a monkey!" Ibrahimah says, moving closer to the cage to stare at the animal. He has seen small monkeys climbing in the trees back home, but he did not know they grew to be so tall and fat.

"Dance, dance," the man instructs the animal, clapping his hands.

The chimp stands up and flaps its arms, then flips over backward and swings itself toward them, sticking his arm through the fence. The man hands Fatik, the boy standing closest to him, a piece of banana from the bucket near Tiki's cage. Fatik pops the banana into his mouth and chews without a second thought. The chimp screams at them, jumps up, and bangs its hands against the fence.

"No, no!" the man says, stepping forward to hand the chimp a chunk of banana. "You're supposed to give Tiki the banana after he dances. He dances for the food."

Fatik's eyes open wide with embarrassment as Ibrahimah, Étienne, and Abdoulaye fall into a fit of laughter.

"Dance, dance," Ibrahimah instructs Fatik.

"Shut up." Fatik pouts.

The man digs out an additional four bruised bananas from the bucket and hands them to the boys.

"These are for you to eat."

Ibrahimah sets his banana in his red tin can for later.

"Dance, dance," Ibrahimah shouts to Tiki.

The chimpanzee stands up, flaps his arms, does a half flip, and then swings his body over to the gate and shoves his arm out, palm facing up. Ibrahimah accepts a chunk of banana from the guide and passes it to the animal. Tiki's palm feels cold and rough, and he meets Tiki's eyes for a second before the monkey swings away again. The guide ushers the group along, with Ibrahimah bringing up the rear of the pack.

He whispers the word "chimpanzee" to himself as the guide winds them down a narrow dirt path hugged by trees and plush grasses. The low growl of a beast rises up from behind a small group of park rangers and Ibrahimah's heart beats faster in anticipation. Within another cage, this one smaller than the chimpanzee's home, is a large four-legged golden-brown animal. Its skin is smooth and taut, its square jawline similar to Fatik's face.

"This is a lion. He is Lion King. King of the jungle," the guide says to the astonished faces of his group.

"Oh!" Étienne says.

The lion paces back and forth about ten feet, the length of its mosaic-tiled home, in a hurried manner.

"Why does he do that?" Étienne asks.

"He is restless," the guide says. "*Calmez-vous*, Lion King. *Calmez-vous.*"

The lion growls, then releases a deep sigh of resignation and plops his large muscled body onto the floor.

"He is sad," Ibrahimah whispers.

"Why?" Étienne asks.

"This is not his home, just like Dakar is not our home," Ibrahimah says, and walks away leaving the group and the beast behind.

The guide tells him to hold on and wait for him, but Ibrahimah continues to walk; he is too impatient to wait. He wants to see everything, right now. His sisters would love to see all of these wild animals. Fatou, his eldest sister, would surely be able to identify each of them from her studies in school, and Binta, the youngest girl, would be scared, with Aisha somewhere in between trying to be brave like Fatou but really feeling scared like Binta.

Ibrahimah approaches a cage with a golden-brown beast standing inside its metal-and-ceramic holding pen. This animal does not have a large furry sprout of hair framing its face; instead it's got a bald head, like himself and Étienne. He wonders if this creature is as unhappy as the Lion King. When the group catches up to Ibra-himah he turns and asks the guide, "Is this the Lion Queen?"

The man raises his eyes in amusement.

"Not quite," the ranger says, "but you are a smart one, young man. This is a female lion. She does not have the large mane as the adult male lion does. Her name is Nala."

Ibrahimah steps closer to the cage, and the lion lets a low growl escape from the back of her throat. Before the guide can stop him, Ibrahimah grabs onto a bar of her cage. She looks at him, her head tipping to the side for a fleeting second before she approaches.

"No!" the guide yells out.

The lion licks Ibrahimah's fingers and he giggles. He lifts his hand from the fence and sticks his arm inside, petting the creature's head with the light touch of a child. The lion turns her head into his arm and licks his wrist. The guide snatches Ibrahimah away from the cage.

"That is not safe, young one. You have to behave or the tour will end early."

Nala roars and jumps up onto the fence, standing on her hind legs, front paws resting on the bars.

"This is not your baby," the ranger says to her, motioning toward Ibrahimah as he pulls him away from the cage.

Nala roars again, louder.

Ibrahimah turns his head as the man pulls him away and catches the lion's eye. She drops down from the fence and watches him before slinking away.

"The animal likes you, Ibrahimah!" Étienne exclaims, resting his arm across the back of Ibrahimah's shoulders.

"She does!" Ibrahimah says as he peels his banana. He offers Étienne a piece but his cousin shakes his head no.

"But I guess you should be careful like the man says. Life would be much harder if you only had one arm," Étienne says.

Ibrahimah gasps but then sees that Étienne is joking. Still, he cannot deny that his cousin is telling the truth.

"Remember when that dog attacked the boy?" Étienne asks.

"Yes, what about it?"

"That's what I'm talking about. The lion is much bigger than the dog."

"Ton-ton, can a lion eat a dog?" Ibrahimah asks the guide.

"Like that," the guide says with a snap of his fingers.

Perhaps the animals are spirits here to protect Ibrahimah, because the lady lion surely was not interested in eating him. The next cage they approach has an animal that looks like Nala but has dark spots.

"This is an African lion," Abdoulaye proclaims with authority, mimicking their guide with a puffed-up posture.

"How do you know?" Étienne asks.

"His skin has black dots on it."

That does not make sense to Ibrahimah. The lion's skin would have to be the color of all the dots to be African.

"No, no, little ones," the tour guide interjects, "all of these animals are African, and this one is a cheetah. He is a fearsome beast. He runs faster than any animal alive. He can get to top speeds faster than most cars."

The animal walks around his small pen in a slow methodical manner. If only Ibrahimah had the power of a cheetah, he would return home and nothing could stop him.

"How did you capture this cheetah if he's the fastest animal alive?" Étienne asks.

"The only way man knows," the guide tells them. "With guns. They shot him with medicine so strong that he fell to the ground. One minute he was king, and the next he was like the rest of the animals here. At the mercy of mankind."

"Does he ever get to run?" Ibrahimah asks.

"If we let him out, he would run and never return. But he has been away from his home so long that he would just terrorize the people of Dakar, because he has no way of finding his way back to South Africa."

South Africa is as far away as America. Two years ago, his sister Aisha drew a map of the world at school and brought it home to put up on the wall in the bedroom that he shared with his three sisters. He would gaze at the picture, amazed at how many other places existed in the world. One day, Fatou showed him where South Africa was on the map, although he was more interested in learning about America. His mother was always talking about a girl from America who had lived in their village many years before.

"The girl was so nice," his mother would say.

His mother would be proud of him and the new things he learned today. Soon, he will return home, and when he does, he will tell her everything he saw, how the lion licked his hand, the cheetah couldn't outrun its captors, and the red bird sat on his knee.

II.

The morning air is cool against the nape of Ibrahimah's neck; his body aches in symphony with the churns of hunger that assault his belly. Marabout Ahmed has returned from his travels, and the lazy days of the week before, and the visit to the zoo, are but a distant memory. Across the street, nestled beneath the shade of a large tree, sits a vendor with a bounty of fruit at his wooden stand. Ibrahimah salivates at the sight of the bright-yellow bananas and plump, juicy mangoes. He does not have enough money to buy any food, as he has yet to meet his daily quota of three hundred francs for Marabout Ahmed. He assesses the vendor; the man seems nice enough to possibly give him a piece of fruit for free. His eyes linger on the colorful ensemble of food, but before he can ask, someone calls out.

"Boy!"

Ibrahimah turns his head in the direction of the voice. Two older Talibé boys are running toward him and his heart stops a moment; they aren't brothers from his house. With mouths wide, baring teeth, he knows these boys are determined to take what he's got— even if it's not much. He flees, turning down Rue Deux, a quiet residential street lined with single-family homes, but the two boys are not far behind, their legs are longer than his. Clouds of dust trail behind him as he crosses over asphalt to dirt roads. Pebbles and stones scrape at his callused soles.

"Stop now and we won't beat you!" one of them calls out.

Clutching his red tin tomato can in one hand, a twenty-five-franc bronze coin in the other, Ibrahimah dashes across the busy road with nary a glance to check for oncoming cars. A moment's hesitation would give the boys the gain they need to catch him.

The four sugar cubes that he'd been saving in his can fall out of it. His heart skips another beat as he questions whether to stop and pick them up. Marabout takes four cubes with his morning café, but gifts don't replace his daily quota of three hundred francs. Money is everything. Ibrahimah doesn't stop.

The billowing dust sticks to his sweat-drenched body. His oversized T-shirt, his only piece of clothing, is filthy and plastered to his frame, but he's lived out on these streets too long to be ashamed of what he looks like. He glances behind him once more to check on the boys. To his surprise they've stopped to pick up the fallen sugar cubes. With a bolt of strength, he pushes his body harder and takes the next bend in the road, disappearing behind La Piscine Olympique.

A quarter mile later he stops, on Rue PE Vingt-Trois, to catch his breath behind a navy-blue Peugeot, parked up on the sidewalk beneath the shade of a tree. Wedged between the car and the cement wall that caches its owner's house from passersby, he replays his narrow getaway in his head. He peeks out to see if the two boys are still in pursuit, but after several minutes pass, he's convinced the coast is clear. He abandons his quiet hideaway in search of rich people and his cousin, who was supposed to come back and get him.

The wide one-way street, lined with two-story houses, soon fills with the sound of young Wolof men dragging their plastic-flip-flopped feet across the pavement, calling out the inventory of the wares they have for sale. The aroma of hot shawarmas and fresh-baked chocolate croissants from Les Ambassades entices anyone within thirty feet of the restaurant. Cars honk their horns incessantly with impatience. Sizing up the pedestrians, Ibrahimah spots a young white woman bouncing along to a separate beat all her own. Checking the road to make sure there are no other Talibé around, he approaches her.

"Money for my marabout," he mumbles in Mandinka.

When tired, Ibrahimah reverts to his native tongue without even realizing it. The young American woman looks down at him. She doesn't need to understand the words. No one can mistake the sight of a Talibé: the economy-sized red tin tomato can, bare callused feet, shaved heads patched with eczema, skinny bodies, and faces of children without love.

"*Je n'ai pas d'argent*," she says, looking straight ahead as if he isn't there.

"Money for my marabout," he mumbles again, this time in Wolof, the widely spoken dialect in Dakar. If he accepted every refusal he received, he'd never raise any money. His legs do triple time to keep pace with her long-legged strides.

"*Va-t'en!*" she snarls.

He'll follow her to her destination if necessary. Foreigners don't like to be followed, and just as he expects, within moments she heaves a sigh of exasperation and digs through her straw bag with the letters J C R E W at the bottom. Ibrahimah doesn't know what the letters say but he assumes it's English, because that is what Americans and British people speak.

She drops a hundred and fifty francs into the red tin can, ignoring his outstretched hand. Without thanking her, Ibrahimah turns to the next person on the street, but the young Ivorian college student with the armful of textbooks walks past him in the direction of Dakar University. A ghost among thieves, beggars, and vagabonds, Ibrahimah is months past the hurt of being ignored. He walks farther down the road and approaches a Senegalese woman selling peanuts on the sidewalk beneath a tree that offers her thin shreds of shade. Her dark, smooth skin is taut and healthy; she looks like the women in his village. She offers him a small packet of peanuts. He takes it and offers her one of his coins but she tells him to keep it.

"Thank you, ta-ta."

"What village are you from?" she asks.

"Saloulou," he says, proud that he remembers his home.

"My village is near there. You remind me of my son when he was your age."

Ibrahimah sits down on the curb near the base of her table, eating the nuts. It's high noon and the sun beats unrelentingly against the earth. Pedestrians and cars alike are few on the road during lunchtime. When the packet is half-finished, he twirls the plastic closed and sets it in his can. With a quick survey of the area to ensure that no Talibé are lurking nearby, he takes his money out of his can. He has three small silver franc pieces and a big bronze coin—almost enough for Marabout. Ibrahimah remembers back when he was just a baby and did not know anything about money. He just liked how shiny the coins looked. Now he knows the value of a franc. He squints up at the sky and smiles. Soon he won't have to care about money or his marabout. Ramadan is near, marking his seventh birthday. "One year," his father told him before he left for Dakar with Marabout Ahmed. Just a year and then he can return home.

"Ibrahimah!"

He looks over to his right to see Étienne bounding down the road toward him.

"Étienne!" he cries, and jumps up from the curb.

Étienne slings his arm across Ibrahimah's shoulders. "Where'd you go? I was looking all over for you."

Ibrahimah relays the story of his narrow getaway to his older cousin.

"You're lucky you run fast!"

"I ran faster than a cheetah," Ibrahimah says, smiling.

"You can't wander off like that. You were supposed to stay at the parking lot of On the Run. I can't protect you if I don't know where you are."

Ibrahimah nods while keeping pace with Étienne's longer legs. He got distracted thinking about his family, Marabout, and food. His mind goes to sleep during the day sometimes and when it wakes up everyone is gone.

They pass by a woman getting ready for the lunch rush and Ibrahimah tugs on Étienne's arm. She has a table set back from the road and a small grill. The smell of roasting meat fills Ibrahimah's nostrils, and his mouth becomes wet.

"Maybe," Étienne says.

A dirty white hen runs by screaming as a rooster chases it around in circles, cock-a-doodle doodling. Étienne approaches the woman.

"Ta-ta, money for my marabout, or food?"

Étienne's eyes wander to the sizzling grill behind her. The short, stout woman wears a colorful head wrap that matches her green-and-yellow ensemble perfectly. Her round face is pleasant and her eyes twinkle when she speaks.

"You're the first person to ask me for food today. This is my *teranga* for the day," she says, handing Étienne a meat patty.

Étienne motions to Ibrahimah, who lingers behind. Noticing the tiny boy for the first time, the woman calls him over and also hands him a patty. Ibrahimah takes it and begins to devour it. The meat burns his mouth but he doesn't care. Étienne nudges him in the side.

"Say thank you. A rude Talibé is a hungry Talibé."

"Yah," Ibrahimah says with a mouth full of patty, the flavor of the perfectly seasoned ground lamb reminding him of his village. "Thank you, ta-ta."

The woman bends over and touches his cheek.

"Eat it slow to make it last." She turns back to her makeshift kitchen to flip the meat over. On a separate fire, hibiscus leaves are boiling. They will leave a dark-red tea that's sweetened and served on ice. An old blue sheet hangs above her table to protect hungry patrons from the piercing sun and suffocating car fumes.

The boys sit down behind a car, hidden from the street.

"I can eat these all day!" Ibrahimah exclaims, the flaky crust of the patty flying out of his mouth.

"Me too."

Ibrahimah's face turns solemn. "I don't like Marabout."

Étienne stops eating and looks away. "Marabout takes care of us."

"Let's go back to the village. It's better there."

"We can't go back. Our papas have sent us here. We belong to Marabout Ahmed, he's our teacher. You think about it too much," Étienne says.

"I didn't do anything bad. I don't have to stay! My father said I can come home after a year. When Ramadan arrives again."

Ibrahimah hits the ground with his free hand to make his point, but drops his meat patty in the process. Diligently picking the flaky food up with both hands, his panic passes once he resumes eating.

"We're not here 'cause we've been bad," Étienne says, looking down at the last smithereens of his fataya. "We're good Talibé. Marabout says good Talibé go to Paradise and we'll get seventy-two virgins."

"Twenty-seven what?"

"No, no. Seventy-two virgins. Good Muslims go to Paradise when they die."

Ibrahimah frowns. "What's a virgin?"

"A girl."

"How many is seventy-two?"

"More than the Talibé at Marabout's house."

Ibrahimah scrunches up his face in disbelief. He does not want to live with seventy-two girls in Paradise. He and Étienne barely find enough food to feed themselves now. How is having to share food with seventy-two girls a reward for being good?

"Where's Paradise?"

"In the sky." Étienne points up to the cloudless blue space above them.

"Paradise! Where airplanes go?"

"Yeah," Étienne says, as if he himself had planned it that way.

"I don't want seventy-two dirgins. Would you be in Paradise with me?"

"It's virgins. Yeah, I'll be in Paradise with you."

Ibrahimah looks over at an old abandoned truck set upon four cinder blocks, its wheels long gone.

"Why is everything so hard," he whines, "and expensive?" Ibrahimah pops the last of his meat patty into his mouth, dusting his hands on his dirty shirt hem.

"I don't know." Étienne furrows his brow in thought. "It was like this before we got here."

Ibrahimah stares blankly at the tire of the old car that hides them from any passersby and inquiring Talibé. He recalls standing in the kitchen with his mother and sisters, the feel of the flour on his fingers as he spread it across the counter before his mother slapped the wet dough down. The heat from the oven leaving his body sweaty, his belly always full of something good to eat.

"God must not like us."

"Don't say that, he loves you," Étienne says, frowning.

"If he loved me, I would be in my village with my family. My mother and father love me. My sisters love me. Marabout doesn't love me."

"How can you know what God's love is supposed to look like? God is bigger than Marabout. His love is stronger," Étienne says, looking at Ibrahimah quizzically.

He rarely disagrees with his cousin, but there is nothing Étienne can say to change his mind. If God is so mighty, then he will return Ibrahimah home; until then it seems Marabout has an edge on God, and so believing in God is like believing his empty red tin tomato can will somehow produce food out of thin air and protect him from Marabout's cane.

He gets up from the ground and surveys the road for the direction with the most opportunity. He had stopped depending on God months ago.

"Give me money," Ibrahimah says to the passenger in the taxi, already scoping out the passenger in the next car. His red tin can presses against his chest in a tight hug.

Étienne nudges him.

"*Allahu Akbar,*" Étienne starts, reciting a verse of the Quran in Arabic while holding his hand out, palm facing up.

Ibrahimah picks it up about halfway in, mumbling over most of it. He doesn't really see the point in trying to learn them, or recite them for that matter; people are going to give, or not, regardless of how much of the prayer he knows. With a friendly face and an in-viting smile, the British man searches through his satchel and hands each of them a hundred-franc piece, along with a banana for Étienne and an opened pack of cookies for Ibrahimah.

Over the next five hours, Ibrahimah follows Étienne's lead, re-peating the same script coupled with empty thank-yous and tepid smiles. When the sun begins its descent, after a long day of work, the sidewalks fill with students, cashiers, errand boys, and street vendors walking four, five, and six miles home from downtown Dakar, forgoing the bus fare of one hundred fifty francs. By the time dusk finally settles, Ibrahimah, Étienne, and some of the other Tal-ibé brothers from their house gather in the parking lot of the On the Run Gas Station & Food Plaza, one of the popular hangouts in mid-town Dakar. The South African–owned plaza offers one of the few options for pizza and burgers in the neighborhood of Point E. For-eigners, university students, and locals fill the tables located on the outdoor covered porch to eat beef and chicken burgers, pizza, and calzones for dinner. A mini market sits between the two fast-food restaurants and offers a larger selection of yogurt, juice, soda, and other groceries than the local boutique does.

Cars line up to fill their tanks at the gas pump while hip-hop music plays over the parking lot. Those taking their pizza and bur-gers to go navigate through the bodies of Talibé boys and the scat-tering of Mauritanian and Senegalese women, begging with outstretched palms while the other hand straddles a toddler to their hips.

Étienne, a Talibé for more than five years now, taught Ibrahimah that he's better off getting someone's leftovers rather than spending the money he makes on food. Every coin earned is essential for sur-viving the day with Marabout. But right now, Ibrahimah would rather sleep than eat or beg for more money. He lies down on the sidewalk, next to the computer shop that sits directly across the street from the action in the parking lot of On the Run, and nods off to sleep.

"Boy. Get up. You shouldn't sleep on the curb like that," someone says, shaking Ibrahimah awake.

Ibrahimah opens his eyes. Above him, the wide, shiny face of the computer-store clerk looms just inches from his own. The pavement scratches at his cheek.

"Are you okay?" the clerk says, his eyes feigning concern.

Ibrahimah sits up. He doesn't remember falling asleep. He rubs at his eyes and looks around before catching sight of Étienne, who beckons at him now in a hurried manner from across the street.

"Thank you, ton-ton," Ibrahimah, still groggy from his nap, mumbles to the clerk.

He remembers to look both ways before propelling himself across the road.

"Come quick!" Étienne urges, once Ibrahimah is within earshot.

Étienne leads him to the far end of the parking lot, behind the food plaza, out of sight from the Rue de Ouakam, where they find several boys and a small bowl of rice. At the sight of food so near, his senses reawaken. He and Étienne wiggle their way into the circle, pushing and shouting as they clamor for a few handfuls of rice and fish bone. In just moments the bowl is scraped clean. Ibrahimah stands up, hungrier than before, when Étienne reaches into his can, and grabs a big shiny coin.

"No! Don't take my money! Give it back." Ibrahimah hits Étienne's arm.

"No, Ibrahimah, we share," Étienne says, holding it up above his head. "I gave when you didn't have enough, remember? Don't be a baby. You have enough."

Étienne pushes Ibrahimah's hands away, warding off his cousin's flailing arms. Ibrahimah lunges at his cousin, his lips in a defiant pout.

"Marabout will beat me!"

"But I don't have enough."

"Give me my money. Here, I'll give you these peanuts," Ibrahimah says, shoving the half-empty packet of nuts at Étienne.

"Look"—Étienne waves the peanuts away—"I'll buy you a Coca."

Ibrahimah raises his eyebrows, his fist suspended in the air. A Coca is just what he could use right now.

"How much money do I have now?"

Étienne looks into Ibrahimah's can and grabs the coins, counting.

"Two hundred fifty."

"I need three hundred for Marabout!"

"I have even less—Marabout won't be mad if you're short. You're the baby. But if *I'm* short, I'll get beat. Plus, I'm sure you'll find more money before we get home, it's only *vingt-un heures.*"

Ibrahimah snatches his can and stomps off. During the hour-and-a-half trek back to the two-room shanty Marabout rents in the working-class neighborhood of Ouakam, Ibrahimah contemplates how to get his money back from his cousin. Passing by a boutique, he stops short.

"I want my Coca!"

"Aye! Wait. I promised him Coca," Étienne calls out to the boys walking up ahead.

The group turns back and gathers in front of the boutique, waiting for the customer at the counter to finish.

"Give me a big coin," Étienne says, holding his hand out.

"What?" Ibrahimah asks, frowning at Étienne.

"I'm buying you Coca. Give me the money for it."

"No. You said you were buying me Coca after you took my big coin. Now do it! I can't give you more money!"

"Well, I don't have enough to buy you Coca, so I guess nothing for you."

"You're a liar. Give me back my coin!" Ibrahimah yells, pushing Étienne.

"No, you already gave it to me."

"You took it. You lie. No!"

The two cousins stand off like two rams ready for a showdown when the customer ahead of them, a light-skinned black man dressed in a dark-blue suit, crisp white shirt, and a crimson blood-red tie, turns to walk past them. His dark-brown leather shoes are shiny even on the sandy walkway. Étienne rushes up behind the man, leaving Ibrahimah with dried snot crusted on his upper lip and a frown.

"Bonsoir, monsieur, l'argent, s'il vous plaît," Étienne says.

"I want Coca!" Ibrahimah yells at Étienne.

The man turns around and looks down.

"Bonsoir, petit gars, qu'est-ce que tu veux?" he asks with an American accent.

"L'argent, s'il vous plaît," Étienne says to the man again.

The man runs his hands over his flat pockets. *"Pour manger?"*

The other boys have crept in closer to hear the exchange and sing out a unified *"Oui!"*

"Oh! It's a group of you," the man says in English, laughing as the boys circle around him.

"Give the man space! Don't harass my customers!" the clerk behind the counter scolds in Wolof, though the boys ignore him.

"Okay then, *qu'est-ce que tu vas manger?"*

"Coca!" the boys yell out in unison.

"Coca-Cola? You all look pretty dehydrated to me."

The blank expressions on the faces of the boys remind the man to revert back to French.

"Tu ne veux pas de l'eau?" he asks.

"Coca!" they scream out again, giggling.

"Why is this man talking about water? I want Coca," Ibrahimah grumbles.

"He'll buy us Coca, don't worry. He's nice, I can tell," Étienne assures, looking the man up and down.

"If he doesn't buy us Coca, you better give me my money back!" Ibrahimah threatens.

Ibrahimah looks around at the other boys pushing up against his small body. He's not convinced they'll get what they want from this man. He inches over to Étienne, who is distracted with the lure of food, and slides his hand into his cousin's can. Étienne moves before Ibrahimah can grab the money inside.

Laughing, the customer takes several sodas out of the lukewarm refrigerator and hands them over to the boys with the instructions to share. He starts to pull money out of his pocket, then stops and grabs several yogurts, placing them on the counter alongside seven plain madeleines. He pays with a bright crisp ten-thousand-franc note. The clerk smiles at the man and thanks him for his kindness.

The boys gather outside by the entrance of the boutique, filling their bellies with Coca-Cola, French pastry, and sweet-flavored yogurt in plastic tubes that they can suck out.

The clerk behind the counter scolds them again about their bad manners. They yell out in thanks after the man, and he turns around in time to see them reciting prayers while cupping their hands in front of their faces. He smiles and waves before turning the corner.

"See, Ibrahimah?" Étienne says between gulps of Coca-Cola. "You shared your money with me and you get more in return. You have Coca, cake, and enough money that Marabout won't be too mad."

Ibrahimah's cheeks are too stuffed with cake to argue. Maybe Étienne is right.

Dingy white walls greet him inside the two-room house. Ibrahimah lines up with the other boys in two rows, his can clasped tight to his chest. His sugar high from the soda and cake is tempered by what is to come next.

"Diatu! Bring me my water," the woman next door yells at her daughter. The walls are so thin she sounds like she's standing right next to Marabout Ahmed. Ibrahimah hopes his teacher is in a good mood.

"You're back early. I assume this means everyone is successful," Ahmed says.

Ibrahimah stares at the man in front of him and hopes someone else will approach first, but no one budges. He glances at a Quran sitting on the shelf above Marabout's head. A thick layer of dust blankets the dark-green book.

"Don't stand there looking stupid. Bring me my money!"

Nine-year-old Abdoulaye steps forward and drops three hundred francs into Marabout Ahmed's hand. Marabout counts it carefully, and when the amount is confirmed, he grunts in approval. Abdoulaye then hands him four sugar cubes and a packet of raw peanuts. Ahmed motions for the boy to drop the expensive little white cubes in a bowl beside him and waves the peanuts away. Abdoulaye stifles his smile, walking over to the far corner of the room to stuff the raw nuts into his mouth. No other boy in the house dares try to steal them from him with Marabout in the room.

Ibrahimah loathes the evenings. None of the walking or begging he does all day compares to the pain he experiences every time he hands his hard-earned money to the ugly, sweaty man in front of him. His heart races in fear as Marabout counts the dirty coins before placing them in the long black stocking he keeps with him at all times.

"Where is the rest?"

Ibrahimah would never share his extra food with Marabout; the man is fat enough, with his big bloated belly.

"It's all there," Ibrahimah says in a small voice, wishing he hadn't dropped the sugar cubes earlier that morning.

Marabout Ahmed wears the same dull, black boubou every day, the traditional African robe, purposefully designed three times the size of the person wearing it. His boubou has lost its luster after so many washes, yet it never loses the scent of the strong oils he wears to mask the smell of his sweat. Ibrahimah still finds his teacher stinks.

"You're missing fifty francs," Marabout Ahmed says, ignoring Ibrahimah's assurances.

Ibrahimah drops his head.

"I thought I counted right. I'm so stupid. Please have mercy on me, Teacher."

Ibrahimah sneaks a peek over to Étienne, who is looking down at his feet. Ibrahimah stands there for several moments, his body clenched tight in anticipation of the wooden cane. Without warning Ibrahimah's stomach gurgles loudly into the quiet room and Marabout laughs out loud.

"Get out of my face," he says with a wave of his hand.

Ibrahimah does not need to hear him twice. He heads out of the house before any of the other boys. Outside, the streets are pitch-black but for a lantern or candle flickering inside someone's small shanty. Ibrahimah stands at the bottom of the front stairs while his eyes take a moment to adjust.

"One day I will be a marabout," Abdoulaye states, bounding down the stairs.

"That's stupid. Marabout is lazy and mean," Ibrahimah says, turning to look at his friend.

"Lazy, mean, and rich."

Ibrahimah broods over this a moment. Étienne exits the house with Fatik close on his heels.

"You'd beat your Talibé?" Ibrahimah asks.

"I don't know. I haven't thought about that," Abdoulaye says.

"Would Talibé work hard if they didn't get beat?" Étienne asks, walking past Ibrahimah and motioning them to follow him out onto the road.

"Maybe," Abdoulaye says.

"Marabout is wicked," Ibrahimah says.

An awkward silence falls upon the small group.

"I'm going to play football for Senegal!" Fatik interjects.

Eleven-year-old Fatik's face is hard and weathered and he doesn't tug the heartstrings of adults as easily as Ibrahimah, the youngest boy in the house. Stepping on a stone, Ibrahimah yells out in pain.

"Be careful!" Étienne says, grabbing his elbow.

"I'm okay."

"I play football better than you," Abdoulaye challenges.

"What? You play stupid. I beat you every time!" Fatik exclaims, slapping at Abdoulaye's shoulder.

"How will you play for Senegal, eh? You're just a Talibé, nobody cares about you," Abdoulaye says, pulling a few steps away from Fatik's reach.

"How will you be a marabout?" Fatik asks, his lips pursed in doubt.

With only a sliver of moonlight present the boys walk in silence down the wide streets of Ouakam, in a loop around their block, as Ibrahimah ponders the major question in their lives. What do Talibé become when they grow up and Marabout no longer wants them? He shakes the thought from his mind. He's going home soon; his parents *want* him back.

Back in front of the two-room house they spot the rest of their brothers, the last seven of the houseful of twenty-one boys, entering with hunched silhouettes and tattered clothes. They arrive late every evening and within moments Marabout's voice can be heard from inside.

"I house you, feed you, and teach you the Quran! All you have to do is bring back money to make this possible. What am I to do with one hundred francs! You play all day, not work!"

The sound of Ahmed's cane pounding against the body of a boy travels out the front door and into the street where they stand.

"He doesn't feed us or teach us the Quran. He does nothing," Fatik grumbles.

Abdoulaye shushes him for fear that Ahmed will hear them.

"He can't hear us out here, he's too busy with that stupid boy who eats his money and gets beat every night," Fatik says, louder this time with more confidence.

An hour after the candles are blown out and the boys are ordered to go to sleep, Ibrahimah stares out into the dark and sinister space before him.

"Ibrahimah!" Ahmed calls again, from the cracked bedroom door. Ibrahimah's eyes well up with tears of dread. Rising to his feet he starts toward the voice. Fear grips at his stomach and his bare feet skim the cool tiled floor when a thought flashes across his mind and he turns back to his mat.

"Étienne," he whispers.

"What?"

"You go. It's your turn."

"What? No," Étienne whispers back.

"You took my money today and I didn't have enough."

"But he called *your* name!"

"I'm sick. I poo-poo everywhere," Ibrahimah says, giving his cousin the lie to convey to their marabout.

"Don't let me come out there!" Marabout threatens from his bedroom doorway.

Ibrahimah lies back down on his mat, his arms crossed against his tiny chest. "You want me to share my money so you don't get beat, you go."

Étienne gets up with a sigh of resignation and maneuvers through the gridlock of bodies on the floor.

"Where's Ibrahimah?" Ahmed asks, annoyed at the sight of Étienne. "He was short my money so he makes it up to me tonight."

"He's sick," Étienne says. "He poos everywhere."

"Eck. Leave him then. Shut the door," Ahmed says, spitting out the shell of a sunflower seed onto the floor. The candle on the night-stand casts dancing shadows across his sweaty face and long white dashiki.

The low rumble of Marabout's voice can be heard outside the closed door as Étienne's howls of pain diminish to grunts, then a low whimper. Twenty sets of eyes are open as the boys lie on the ratty pieces of cardboard. No one makes a sound or moves an inch in the mosquito-infested room. One boy throws his hands up to cover his ears, and begins to murmur something under his breath. He receives a frantic jab in the ribs from the boy lying down beside him.

"Shut up!" the boy hisses.

Ibrahimah lies there quiet, too afraid to breathe or blink. He's filled with relief that it's not him with Marabout tonight, but know-ing that Étienne is inside bearing the pain alone leaves him no peace. With tears in a free-fall down his dirty cheeks, fatigue over-takes his tiny body. He falls into a fitful sleep as he runs from the devil, fast on his heels.

When the five o'clock morning prayer call sings out across the dark sky from the nearby mosque, Ibrahimah notices Étienne sound asleep next to him. The memory of evening rushes back and he touches his cousin's arm, thinking back to the day he left his village.

"When Ramadan comes again it will have been a year and you will return home to me and your mother. It will come faster than you know," his father told him that morning as he pulled Ibrahimah into a hug before Marabout Ahmed grabbed his hand and dragged him away, complaining that they were already late.

Ahmed comes into the room with his dark-brown wooden cane and hits at the sleeping bodies. The sun has yet to rise.

"Get up or I'll beat you awake," he mutters.

Ibrahimah pokes Étienne awake and the two boys hop to their feet before Ahmed can make his way over to them. Having already performed his ablutions out back, Ahmed returns to his room and lays his prayer rug down on the floor. The boys scuttle out to the back of the house to the basin, filled with day-old water, pushing and shoving one another as they try to scoop out enough water to splash onto their heads, hands, and feet. They quickly return to the room and fall into formation, following Ahmed's lead through prayer. Afterward, Ibrahimah lies back down; he's not ready to be awake.

"Meet me out back," Ahmed instructs them.

The line of boys begins at the basin, stretches through the house and out the front door. One by one Ahmed shaves each of their heads with a razor. Bald heads lessen the risk of fleas and lice.

With the sun fast on its ascent, the twenty-one boys prepare to go out. They stack their cardboard mats up against the back wall and grab their red tin tomato cans. And by seven o'clock in the morning they spill out of the house wearing the same dirty clothes they had on the day before. Maids, mechanics, errand boys, security guards, and other faceless strangers join the large gang of Talibé in their morning commute. Ibrahimah lags behind everyone and notices that Étienne is walking with a slight limp.

"Étienne, you okay?"

Étienne doesn't reply.

"I'll find us mango for breakfast," Ibrahimah says, trying to sound hopeful for his cousin.

Once they make it to the Rue de Ouakam the large group splits into three packs of seven, and Ibrahimah and Étienne break off from their group in search of breakfast. They work better alone.

III.

A week has passed since Marabout has called either Ibrahimah or Étienne into his room, but as life would have it though, when one thing is going well for a Talibé, something else goes wrong.

The boy who jumped him punched him several times in the face and chest before Étienne could come to his rescue. And now in the palm of his hand was a bloodied tooth covered in dirt. Ibrahimah stares down at the lone tooth, torn from his body. If he loses any more teeth in another fight, he could be left with none at all, and won't be able to chew. The aroma of pizza from Le Régal, across the street, fills his nostrils. Without teeth he'll starve to death.

"What's wrong?" Étienne asks as he assesses the damage.

"My teeth fell out!" Ibrahimah sobs.

"Let me see." Étienne pushes his head back to get a better look at the gaping hole in the front of his mouth, bloody and raw.

"You lose all your teeth already?"

"What? I don't know. No. I want to keep my teeth!"

"You'll grow new teeth. Stop crying."

"Really?"

"Yes. When you're small all your teeth come out one by one, then new ones come," Étienne says.

"How do you know?" Ibrahimah challenges, his bottom lip no longer quivering.

"Because I do! You're a baby, you know nothing. All of my teeth fell out before and look."

Étienne opens his jaw wide. Ibrahimah stands on the tips of his toes to get a good look.

"Wait, I'm still looking!" Ibrahimah protests when Étienne closes his mouth.

"They're all there. Don't question me."

Étienne puts his hands on his hips the way grown-ups do. Ibrahimah inspects the lonely tooth in the palm of his hand.

"But what about old people? Old people have no teeth."

"You lose your teeth again before you die, but when you're young they grow back. Like hair," Étienne says.

The sand billows up around them as they walk across the dirt road like miniature soldiers. It's only noon, their energy hasn't abandoned them yet.

"You lost your tooth but you still have your money. When your tooth falls out the fairy brings you luck," Étienne adds.

Ibrahimah places the tooth inside his red tin tomato can; it dances about, making a dull clanking sound against the coins and sugar cubes at the bottom. The same sound his grandfather's mutton would make when walking around their village right before sunset. The rope around its neck had an old rusty bell and Ibrahimah would sometimes follow the animal, petting it or poking it with sticks until it ran away from him. Binta, who is only two years older than him, would tell on him, and his grandfather, Papa Yoro, would scold him for being so naughty, then give him Laughing Cow cheese because it was Ibrahimah's favorite. Ibrahimah would sit on his grandfather's lap and listen to stories about his grandfather's early days of growing up in the village, how Papa Yoro would work on the farm with his father and how he built his house, the one he stills lives in, with his own two hands.

"You remind me of myself when I was a young boy," Papa Yoro told him one afternoon. "And you look just like I did."

Papa Yoro showed Ibrahimah an old, faded photo of a young

five-year-old boy. Ibrahimah did not know what he looked like, but he was pleased that his grandfather believed they were much alike. Papa Yoro was wise and smart, and everyone in the family loved him; Ibrahimah wanted the same.

"Let's go to the ocean," Ibrahimah suggests to his cousin Étienne. Their grandfather loves the ocean as much as he does.

"Later. We have to work first," Étienne says as they walk a half mile farther, down to Les Voies d'Alternance, until they find a Talibé-free spot on a small island set between east- and westbound traffic, where they play Red Light, Green Light with the cars with the opposite rules of the actual game. Étienne taught Ibrahimah the game months ago. He doesn't know where his cousin learned how to play, but it's fun. For all their effort Ibrahimah raises only an additional hundred francs and a chunk of melted cheese, which barely tickles his appetite.

Ibrahimah's stomach gurgles loudly.

"I'm hungry," Ibrahimah whines. His body is covered in sweat.

Étienne agrees, "This spot wasn't so great after all."

They abandon the island for the quiet, tree-lined streets of Sacré Coeur Trois, where all the houses are white, multistory, and adorned with colorful flowers, gardens, and expensive cars, and head toward Baobab, where all the NGO employees like to live, when they come upon a group of boys.

Spotting them from down the road one of the boys yells out, "Aye, boy! Come!"

Étienne walks up, unsmiling, to the kids standing in the middle of the street. Ibrahimah hangs back two steps and braces himself for a fight.

"What do you want?" Étienne demands of a clean-cut boy in blue shorts.

"Play football with us. We need two more for our team," the boy says.

A boy from the other team shouts, "You play like old men, now you ask Talibé to help you."

His teammates snicker.

"Our other players went home," the boy in the blue checkered shorts says. "We're beating them, don't listen to him."

Étienne turns back and looks at Ibrahimah with raised eyebrows. Ibrahimah's eyes light up. He's never been included in a football game with the older boys before, and he hasn't played with non-Talibé boys since he arrived to Dakar. In his village he was like all the other children; here in Dakar he is something to be ignored and avoided, less than the other kids because he begs all day, the worst anyone can be in life.

"What's your name?" Ibrahimah shyly asks the boy in the checkered shorts.

"Moustapha. And yours?" the boy asks.

"Ibrahimah."

"I'm Étienne."

"Cool. We can play a fairer game now. Mohamed will go up front, I play middle, and you two cover the field," the boy informs his new teammates, pointing to where he wants everyone to go.

Étienne and Ibrahimah put their tin cans down at the side of the road, within sight.

"Where's the ball?" Ibrahimah asks.

"Over there, see," Étienne points to the white, black, and gold soccer ball.

Ibrahimah can't believe his luck, he's really playing football. He sticks his chest out a little further; he's one of the big boys now. The boys in front fight to position the ball on opposite ends of the street. Ibrahimah is caught off guard as the ball cuts across the air, heading directly toward him.

"Ibrahimah, kick it!" Étienne shouts, catapulting his body toward his cousin.

"Kick it!" the other two boys on his team scream.

Jumping into action, Ibrahimah pounces toward the ball. Surprising himself, and everyone else, he blocks the ball with his chest. Étienne jumps in, takes the ball to the front of their offense, and attempts to drive it down the middle of the opposing team. Ibrahimah is basking in his accomplishment when the boy wearing a football jersey with *Italy* written across the chest yells at Étienne.

"You fouled me!"

"No, I didn't," Étienne retorts, waving his hand dismissively at *Italy*.

"Yes, you did. He fouled me," the boy screams to the other boys, pointing at Étienne.

"I didn't. You whine like a girl!"

"You cheat, Talibé! You fouled me. My brother plays for Italy! I know!" The boy yells, shoving him. Étienne pushes the boy back.

"No fighting. We're friends," a boy from team *Italy* says, coming between the two angry players.

"I'm no friend of dirty Talibé!"

"Étienne!" Ibrahimah yells, running up to his cousin and pulling on his arm.

"Who cares about Italy? This is Dakar, stupid," Étienne says, rushing toward the boy to punch him.

"Be cool," Moustapha says.

Étienne's teammates pull him away.

"Ignore him. His brother doesn't play for Italy, he carries their water." Moustapha snickers.

Étienne laughs. Tempers calm as the boys on the other team talk *Italy* down, and in a few moments the game continues on until, one by one, each of the boys is called for lunch as a different maid appears from the row of beautiful multistory houses on the tree-lined street.

"Hey, Talibé," Moustapha calls, "come eat with me," he offers, grabbing his soccer ball.

Étienne and Ibrahimah hang back.

"I'm hungry," Ibrahimah mumbles, eyeing Moustapha as he heads in the direction of the big house.

"Bring us the food. We'll eat out here," Étienne replies.

"Okay," the boy says.

Moustapha's house is behind a high cement wall and he disappears through a white metal door. Tomato cans under their arms, Étienne and Ibrahimah wait out on the street.

"Look at my teeth now."

"It looks good. You get a wish when you lose a tooth."

"I want to go back to my village."

"One day, maybe. But right now, you were hungry and now we get food."

"Oh." Ibrahimah's face falls in disappointment.

"Don't be ungratitude. When you're unthankful Allah takes away the good stuff you have."

"But Allah doesn't give me anything I *want*. What do I have that's good?"

"We're about to eat!" Étienne whacks Ibrahimah.

The boys are horsing around when the large oversized door groans open. A neatly dressed young maid appears.

"Get over here," she says with impatience.

They scramble over obediently. She yawns, steps to the side, and waves them in. The boys move quietly onto the manicured lawn. The heavy door closes on its own, locking automatically. Ibrahimah looks around the space. It reminds him of the zoo, but instead of animals there are trees and flowers everywhere. The young woman spreads a vinyl tablecloth onto the grass, placing a heaping platter of thieboudienne. Ibrahimah is overcome with joy at the sight of the flavorful fish, rice, cabbage, and onions.

"Don't steal the plate, eh! These people are being nice to you!"

"Yes, madame," Étienne says.

"Mademoiselle," she says, cutting her eyes.

With large fearful eyes, Ibrahimah looks up at the woman, who is more than twice his height. Being around adults for more than a few seconds makes him uneasy.

"And what do you say?" she demands.

"Thank you," Ibrahimah mumbles.

The maid grunts, turns on her heels, and bounces her hips in that slow I-don't-have-anywhere-to-go-in-this-lifetime gait of a Senegalese woman.

Ibrahimah sets his can down and kneels in front of the food, shoving the oily rice into his mouth with fervor. Étienne breaks apart the perfectly grilled fish, placing an equal amount on both sides of the plate. They eat in silence. Speaking would take up too much precious time. They could be kicked out of paradise at any moment, the food gone forever. Handful after handful, the rice and fish disappear.

With the bowl wiped clean Ibrahimah stands up first. Grains of rice drop from his chest to the tablecloth. He wipes the back of his hand across his mouth, smearing additional oil and rice across his cheek. His small protruding belly is full of gas and food. His tongue probes around his mouth for any stray bits lodged away.

"Let's go. We need money."

Étienne looks up at him.

"Wait. We should give the plate back first."

Étienne hands the platter to Ibrahimah to hold as he folds the tablecloth as best he can. They walk toward the back of the house, where most second kitchens reside, and Étienne points to a large blue basin where there are several dishes immersed in the water. The basins remind Ibrahimah of his mother and sisters.

"Put it there," Étienne says, pointing while he lays the tablecloth on the back of a white plastic chair.

"Ramadan will be here soon," Ibrahimah says.

Étienne is quiet.

"Maybe Marabout will let you go back to the village with me. I can ask my papa for you."

A look of pain flashes across Étienne's face before he turns away. Ibrahimah drops the platter into the basin, causing the water to splash up against his ashy legs. He's about to step his foot into the basin to make an even bigger splash when a different, older maid walks out of the house.

"What are you doing?" she demands.

"Returning the plate," Étienne replies. "Thank you, ta-ta."

"Finish already?"

"Yes," they say in unison.

"Okay, good," she says, leading them back toward the front yard.

The woman looks up and down the street to see if anyone is watching. The street quiet and deserted, Ibrahimah and Étienne leave the premises with a wave; she returns it.

The late-afternoon sun burns Ibrahimah's skin. He has just enough money to meet his quota tonight, but, once again, Étienne does not. They make their way over to Casino Sahm, the super-marché on the Rue de Ouakam, where a box of American cereal costs five thousand francs and they find exactly what they need for success—traffic, foreigners, and lots of pedestrians. The busy inter-section houses a small open-air market of vendors selling cheap goods along the Boulevard de la Gueule Tapee. It's here that the Rue de Ouakam ends and the continuing road becomes Avenue Blaise Diagne leading into downtown Dakar, drawing scores of Car Rapides, sept-place taxis, and other forms of transport for passen-gers traveling to the numerous villages outside of the capital. They also find, as they walk up, Fatik, Abdoulaye, and several other boys from their house. The boys have been out there for a few hours al-ready hitting up the wealthy locals and Western shoppers who pre-fer the supermarché over the local open-air markets.

"Étienne, let's go. Lots of cars!" Ibrahimah calls, looking toward the exit of the lot, where cars are waiting to merge back into traffic.

"No, Ibrahimah, wait," Étienne calls out as he approaches Fatik.

"You all find good money?"

"Yeah," Fatik says. "Where did you and Ibrahimah go?"

"Just working." Étienne casually brushes his mouth to make sure there's no rice stuck to it. "We didn't find much."

"Foreigners are greedy." Fatik shades his eyes, searching for his next mark. "They never give easy. It's why they're so fat and ugly!"

Ibrahimah starts off toward the busy intersection; he doesn't have time to stand around talking. If he gets any more money, he'll give it to Étienne. He doesn't want his cousin to have to deal with Marabout's wrath tonight.

A woman screams at the sound of tires screeching across hot asphalt. Bang! Metal crumples as two cars collide. As a taxi swerves to avoid the wreck it races toward him and a flame of red appears before his eyes. The red bird screams and flaps its wings wildly. Ibrahimah reaches out to touch it. Brakes screech. Tires skid across hot pavement. The ground trembles. There's no place to hide.

I'm going to die.

Images of his family flash before his eyes; the times they spent on his father's farm harvesting the crops; the days of laughing together; his mother planting kisses on his forehead before bed; his father reading the stories of Moses and Noah after dinner.

Just before the yellow taxi crashes into his body, the sunlight fades and everything turns black.

IV.

Maimouna stares at the warped image in the mirror. Her eyes are red and puffy, the pain in her chest undeniable. She looks out of the window. The world beyond the village continues as if nothing has happened. No tragedy has passed. Life is nothing but joy and carefree winds.

Maimouna clutches the sides of the dresser for support. No woman should have to experience the death of a child. A piece of her has been removed by force. Neighbors whisper outside her bedroom, clucking their tongues. Shaking their heads in pity. Have another child, her sister-in-law suggested. She and Idrissa can barely make ends meet to feed their five children now. Tears well up in her eyes. Her shoulders slump forward. Their four children.

She picks up the baby rattle, a gift from the American girl who had lived in their village years ago. A sweet girl from the Peace Corps. The purple-and-white toy, with stripes on the bottom half and stars above. Each of her children enjoyed this toy as a baby. At night, she dreams of them growing up to be important doctors and lawyers, living in America or Europe. The American toy had been just the beginning, handed down to each new baby in the family, from her eldest, Fatou, to Aisha, to Binta, to Ibrahimah, and finally to Aisatu. She clutches the rattle to her chest and moans a low howl.

"Mama."

Butterflies flutter about in her stomach, rising up into her chest. She holds her breath, turning toward the bundle of innocence barreling toward her. Ibrahimah wraps his small arms around her legs and clings tight. The pressure of his six-year-old grip brings her back to the present.

"Do you remember this toy?" Maimouna wipes her cheeks.

"Yes, it's mine," he says, reaching for it. She holds it up out of his reach.

"No, it belongs to your sis—" Her voice trails off.

Ibrahimah looks up at her, waiting. Maimouna sits down on the edge of the bed, holding the rattle.

"Yes, my chou-chou, the rattle belongs to you."

Ibrahimah leans up against her.

"Mama."

"Yes, Ibrahimah."

"I'm sad Aisatu die."

Maimouna wraps her arm around Ibrahimah's small frame, pulling him closer. Maybe if she had paid more attention she could have picked up on some sign. She thought it a blessing that the child was quieter and slept more than her other four children. She got so much done with such a peaceful toddler. This was all her fault.

"Mama! I can't breathe!"

Ibrahimah wiggles to get out of her death grip.

"Ya Allah, Ibrahimah, I'm sorry, my baby."

She strokes his cheek.

"Please, forgive your mama. It was an accident; Mama would never hurt you."

"It's okay. I still love you, Mama." Ibrahimah cocks his head to the side. "Will I die too?"

"What? Of course not! Don't talk like that!"

Ibrahimah's eyes well up with tears.

"No, no, my baby, don't cry. Mama didn't mean to yell. I'm sorry.

Nothing in this world will ever take you away from me. You hear? You'll always be with me."

She strokes the back of his head, kissing his cheeks until he calms down. She hands him the rattle. The baby of the family again, he's barely six years old. Healthy and vibrant. If she gets it right with him, then perhaps, perhaps all can be good again. Ibrahimah turns his attention back to her.

"Why so many people visit us?" Ibrahimah shakes the rattle.

"To pay respect for Aisatu. They pray her soul goes to Paradise."

"I'll pray too. Papa said Aisatu is in Paradise." Ibrahimah shakes the rattle again.

"Ibrahimah, give it to me," she says, reaching for the toy.

"But it's mine!" he whines as he jumps back, out of her reach.

"I'll give it back to you. Come sit next to your mama first. Please, my baby, just come back to Mama."

Ibrahimah climbs up onto the bed. Maimouna takes him onto her lap and cradles him in her arms like a baby. She hums a tune she learned from her grandmother, who learned the tune from her great-grandmother, and so on.

Maimouna fed Aisatu for the last time twenty-four hours ago and the pressure hurts so much it feels like it will burst through her engorged breast. The leaking milk has soaked yet another shirt. It was when she went to nurse Aisatu that she found the toddler cool to the touch and unresponsive.

Maimouna closes her eyes in an attempt to clear the image from her head. This is just a bad daydream. She forgot to feed Aisatu. That's what this is all about; the pain, the pressure, the sadness. She'll feed Aisatu and the pain will subside, like it always does. She reaches into her shirt, lifts her tender breast out, and places the nipple at Ibrahimah's mouth. He looks up with surprise, studying his mother's face for a moment before grasping her breast in a familiar manner, only his grip is stronger now, his hand bigger. Parting his lips, he takes the nipple into his mouth. Maimouna looks across the room and waits with distracted patience. He begins to suck and sweet milk rushes through her ducts into his mouth. Her face contorts in pain then relaxes after several moments. The fury of the day morphs into the remnants of her bad dream. Fatou walks into the bedroom.

"Mama, people are arriving—" Fatou stops in her tracks. Shock dances across her face before disappearing behind a masked cloud of indifference.

"Papa said it would be nice if you came out for a moment. People are offering prayers."

Maimouna rocks back and forth, humming quietly. She closes her eyes. Fatou's voice is a soft whisper.

"I'll be out soon, my daughter. I'm almost done nursing Aisatu."

Maimouna looks down at Ibrahimah.

"Are you done?"

He tightens his grip on her breast, increasing the flow of milk. He grunts and closes his eyes.

"Tell Papa, I'm coming."

Fatou nods in response and starts for the door, glancing over her shoulder for another look before leaving the room. A sense of calm envelops Maimouna. Ibrahimah pulls harder on her breast.

"Come," she says, motioning him toward her other breast.

He switches position and latches on. Outside, the carefree winds and melodies of birds float across the room. She looks down at Ibrahimah. Everything will be okay. Life will continue on.

"You're mama's baby again. You'll never leave me, will you?"

Ibrahimah shakes his head no and continues to drink the sweet, warm milk.

V.

"Fatou! Aisha! Binta! Let's go. It's almost two-thirty. Your father is already at the mosque and we don't want to be late!"

"Na'am!" Fatou calls out from the bedroom she shares with her siblings.

"Come now, Ibrahimah, we have to go."

She pulls her breast from his mouth and nudges him away. Milk dribbles down his chin.

"I'm not done."

Maimouna wipes his face with the hem of his shirt.

"No, we have to go."

The afternoon prayer call fills the village with melody and a feeling of duty, and belonging. Just a few sandy paths away from their home, La Grande Mosquée du Saloulou stands taller than any of the mostly one-story houses populating the small village.

She enters the mosque and slips off her sandals. "Bismilla-Hir-Rahma-Nir-Rah'im," she says quietly, before washing her hands and wrists. Next, she washes her face from ear to ear, and then her arms and elbows, passes her damp palms over her covered head, and then rinses her feet last. The pipes are hot from the sun, and so the typically cool water runs warm across her smooth, dark skin. Flanked by her children, they mimic her moves in perfect sequence.

Inside the large carpeted hall, she greets her neighbors, *"Salam-alaikum."*

"Malaikumsalam," Madame Touré replies, touching her arm with a smile.

Maimouna's sister-in-law approaches the two women before Maimouna can begin a conversation with her dear friend in earnest. "Will you make us a batch of your fatayas for tomorrow afternoon?" she asks.

"Good to see you, sister." Maimouna smiles. "Of course."

With a click of her tongue, her sister-in-law looks down at Ibrahimah. "When are you going to allow him to grow into a man? He should be up front with his father."

Madame Touré rolls her eyes and walks away into the main hall.

"Ibrahimah isn't feeling well, and I want to keep an eye on him. If he's in front and gets ill he'd be a distraction," Maimouna replies, pulling Ibrahimah closer.

"Hmmm," her sister-in-law replies, scanning the hall to see who else's business she can meddle in.

Maimouna takes a deep breath, and the scent of the traditional incense she and her neighbors burn at home fills her nostrils. She takes her sister-in-law's silence as the end of the inquiry and ushers Ibrahimah into the main hall behind Madame Touré. Large white cement pillars litter the airy, grandiose space and give way to several skylights.

She and Ibrahimah hurriedly whisk by several marabouts wearing dark sunglasses, crowding the first row of the men's section. Only holy men can be trusted to shield their eyes from Allah. In the past week alone, two marabouts have asked to take Ibrahimah on as a student of the Quran; Idrissa staunchly refused both men, against his father's advice.

In the women's section, located behind the men, Maimouna lowers herself onto the floor with Ibrahimah by her side. A sliver of sunlight bathes her covered legs. Fatou sits behind her with Aisha and Binta. When the call to prayer ends, everyone settles down within the large hall, and for a moment a vacuum of silence takes command of the space where so much sound had just been.

The imam sits in the front of the room and recites the opening prayer. In unison, everyone prostrates head to floor, two times. Sitting back on their heels all heads turn to the right, then to the left. Maimouna smiles as Ibrahimah follows the prayer with ease. When the prayer is complete, the imam rises up from the floor to stand at the podium, and speaking into the microphone, begins to read a passage from the Quran about the evils of pride and ego.

The sound of the imam's voice fades and Maimouna ruminates on the anxious feeling that has yet to loosen its grip on her, since the death of Aisatu. Between the marabouts circling like vultures and Idrissa's father and brother, Maimouna feels like she is battling an all-out attack to take her only son. Ibrahimah's cousin, Étienne, is currently a student of a marabout at a daara in Dakar, but this happened years before the rumors began circulating throughout the villages. Now it feels as if every week there are new stories of abuse, forced begging, and neglect of children at the hands of these marabouts. Maimouna's brother-in-law, Idrissa's older brother, brushes the stories off as false—he believes his son is in God's hands, but Maimouna questions why anyone would lie about the ill treatment of children.

Maimouna sighs. It's been two months since she lost her youngest child. She has to trust that Allah will protect her family. She pulls Ibrahimah closer to her and he snuggles into her side, quietly dozing off to sleep.

Like every Friday, at four-thirty, the mosque empties its inhabitants out into the world; for Maimouna, each Friday afternoon feels as if the sun shines brighter, the birds sing sweeter, and worries evaporate into the forgotten memories of yesterday. Men meander home in deep discussion amongst themselves as women rush to finish preparing dinner. Children romp and play. Local stores and markets reopen. Maimouna and Idrissa talk quietly as Ibrahimah and his sisters walk up ahead.

"Do you think it may be time to wean him off the breast?" Idrissa asks quietly.

"The milk will help keep him strong. Remember when he got sick last winter? I was afraid we would lose them both, and now he is our youngest. I think perhaps one more year. Just to be sure."

"My brother thinks he is too old."

"Other women have breastfed their children well past six years old, and older," Maimouna says with reproach.

"Who?"

"You men shouldn't concern yourselves with the affairs of women caring for their children," Maimouna says curtly.

"My love, he is my child also, and I am also his caregiver."

Ibrahimah stops short, turns around, and tells his mother, "I want to go to the ocean."

Binta's and Aisha's eyes light up.

"Can we, Mama?" Binta asks.

The children encircle their parents with pleading eyes, and Maimouna smiles. "Only if you promise to watch Ibrahimah close."

"We promise!" the girls squeal.

Before Maimouna can say another word, Ibrahimah and his three sisters run off down the sandy path.

"I run faster than you, Binta!" Ibrahimah shouts.

"No, you don't. Follow in my shadow!"

Ibrahimah pumps his legs hard trying to keep up with his eight-year-old sister.

"Ibrahimah!"

He slows his pace at the sight of his friend Moussa, letting Binta tire herself out as she continues sprinting down the hill.

"Where are you going?" asks Moussa.

"Down to the beach. You want to come?" Ibrahimah says, catching his breath.

"Look at what I got." Moussa pulls a five-hundred-franc coin from his pocket.

"What's that?"

"Money, my uncle gave it to me. I'm *rich*."

"Really? I want to see."

"Here, take it. It's nice. I can buy anything."

Ibrahimah smiles approvingly and hands the money back to

Moussa. He thinks about what he would buy if he had money. For a brief moment he cannot think of anything he wants. Then he remembers, Coca! Soda is a treat, and Coca is the most expensive treat of them all.

"Ibrahimah, come on!" Fatou calls out, now several yards ahead of them.

"Come, Moussa, let's go," Ibrahimah says.

The two boys run down to the shore, passing Ibrahimah's three sisters as they charge into the froth. The salty breeze hits his face, slips through his parted lips, and lands on his tongue. There is nothing in the world better than the ocean. Unable to resist, Ibrahimah kicks at the water, splashing Moussa along with his three sisters.

"You better not wet me! If you do, I'm taking you home!" Fatou screams.

"I'll tell Mama it was you who ruined our clothes," Aisha adds, folding her arms across her chest.

Ibrahimah shoots a look of defiance at his sisters. Binta stifles her laughter. She wants to be taken seriously by her older sisters. The boys race up ahead. Once a safe distance away, they continue their water fight.

"Let's find treasure," Moussa says, suddenly switching interest.

Ibrahimah kicks up one last great splash. The water is so warm and inviting, he's tempted to immerse himself, fully clothed, into the sea. He glances down the shoreline and sees his sisters talking and giggling.

"What kind?" he asks Moussa, returning to the beach.

"Pirates from far away buried their stolen treasure on the beaches here in Africa long ago. My brother tells me no one has found them yet."

"How much?" Ibrahimah asks, his interest piqued.

"A lot. In big trunks."

"What's that?" Ibrahimah asks, pointing toward the sand.

"It's a shell, nothing good," Moussa says, dismissing it with a wave of his hand.

Ibrahimah picks up the broken shell and flips it over in his hands. The two boys walk along slowly, their eyes scouring the dry, sandy beach. Ibrahimah's stomach grumbles with hunger, but the thought of treasure compels them to scour more of the shoreline.

"Look!" Ibrahimah says, scrambling over, with Moussa in tow, to an object sparkling in the sand. The girls have caught up and peer over their shoulders.

"What did you find?" Aisha asks.

"It's a key," Fatou says, plucking it from Ibrahimah's hands.

Ibrahimah grabs for the shiny bronze object. "Maybe it can open a treasure?"

"The key to a treasure chest would be old and rusty," Fatou says. "This one is new. I bet it opens nothing important."

Ibrahimah, satisfied by this logic, hands the key to Moussa and walks off in search of something better. Passing by a small hill of sharp black rocks that are hugging a sand dune, he sees a patch of tall grass growing on the rear of the beach. He can hear Binta and Aisha talking to Moussa, and looks over his shoulder to see an older boy walk up to Fatou. The boy says something that makes her laugh. Looking back at the grassy patch of beach, Ibrahimah is convinced he will find something more interesting than seashells.

A mélange of orange, yellow, and purple hues reflect off big cumulus clouds as the sun rests on the horizon. The small crab Ibrahimah has been toying with turns to him, its claws set to attack. He calls out to Moussa to come see, but gets no response. He looks up. His friend is nowhere in sight. When he looks back down, the crab is gone. He could hear them all talking just a while ago off in the distance, but all that fills his ears now is the incoming tide. He stands up to see if Moussa is crouching down somewhere, but the beach is empty. The path in front of the rocks and the dune he had crossed earlier is now completely swallowed up by the sea. He is the only one there.

"Moussa!"

Nothing.

"Aisha!"

Silence.

"Fatou! Binta!"

The tide is coming in fast. He looks up at the sky and frowns. His body begins to sweat even as the cool ocean breeze washes over him. Being on the beach at night brings bad luck, and it's getting dark. The beach is the only place evil spirits can sneak onto land without being seen; they can walk right along beside you without you even knowing it, his father once told him.

Ibrahimah looks to his left. The dune looms high above him. He looks to his right. The coast stretches on for what seems like eternity. If he goes in that direction, he would be walking farther away from his village, and he's never been down that end of the beach before. In front of him lies the rocky wall that encases the coast. The tide slaps at the back of his ankles. He walks forward and tries to climb the dune, but his feet sink into the soft sand and he slides down the steep incline. Trying again, he drops down to his knees in an attempt to crawl, but he ends up facedown, clutching handfuls of soft earth. He lies sprawled out on his stomach in defeat.

"What are you doing?" A voice rings out through the noise of the crashing waves.

Ibrahimah rolls over to find a man standing behind him. He had just looked down the coast and hadn't seen anyone before.

"Didn't you hear me?" The man shifts his weight. "Answer up, boy."

Ibrahimah stands and looks up at the man wearing a black boubou, his head wrapped in a matching turban.

"I'm trying to get back home."

"Where do you live?"

Ibrahimah points toward the dune.

"Come with me. I'll show you the way back."

The man turns to head down the coast, away from his village. Ibrahimah doesn't move. He doesn't trust the stranger.

"If you stay here, the tide will gobble you up and you'll live out the rest of your life as a fish, running from the fisherman who wants to eat you."

The swelling tide, angry and aggressive, crashes against Ibrahimah's legs. He looks toward the dune one more time, hoping to see Moussa or his sisters, but he knows they are gone, so then turns and follows the man down the beach.

"What's your name?" the man asks.

"Ibrahimah."

"How old are you?"

"Six." Ibrahimah holds his hands up, fingers spread wide.

"That's a good age."

They walk for what feels like a long time before reaching a set of deteriorating cement steps leading to the top of the cliff.

"Be careful," the stranger says, standing aside for Ibrahimah to ascend first.

Ibrahimah uses both hands to climb the tall stairs, relieved to see the crest of roofs in the distance. The two of them walk toward the unfamiliar small village of quiet, tin-roofed shanties to the main road.

"I'm sure your family must be worried about you by now. Let's find a taxi to get you back faster, huh?"

The man hails a horse-drawn wagon. He lifts Ibrahimah onto the back and then hoists himself up. Ibrahimah's body bounces to the rhythm of the horse trotting across the dirt road, the smell of manure lingering from the day's errands. Hay scratches at the backs of his legs. He looks up at the man, but with the evening settling in he can only make out the silhouette of his face. His eyelids hang heavy but are shocked open with every rock the wagon stumbles over. Ibrahimah jumps to attention at the sight of the mosque his family attends.

"I live here!"

The man shouts to the driver to stop. Once his feet are planted firmly back on the ground, Ibrahimah runs down the sandy path all the way to his house. Barreling through the front door, he's greeted by a chorus of relieved voices.

"Ibrahimah! Alhamdulillah! My baby, where have you been?" his mother exclaims.

"Where did you run off to?" his sisters ask over one another.

"We thought you were with us. Moussa said you were together and then when he looked up you were gone. Don't do that again!"

"The water got really high, I couldn't get to you," Ibrahimah says, on the verge of tears.

"Fatou! Don't yell at your brother. You should have kept a closer eye on him! The one thing I ask you to do. Just one thing. Watch your brother!"

"But, Mama, I *was* watching him," Fatou says with a pout.

Maimouna rushes over to Ibrahimah and scoops him up into her arms before he can respond. Binta wraps her arms around him and their mother. Aisha joins in, roping in a begrudging Fatou.

"I was so frightened, I thought you had drowned!" Binta exclaims, ever the drama queen.

"Don't talk like that, Binta!" Maimouna says.

Idrissa walks into the house then, and his face lights up at the scene before him. The stranger from the beach trails behind.

"Ibrahimah!"

"Papa!" Ibrahimah says, reaching out to his father from the hive of women enveloping him.

"That's who brings me home," Ibrahimah says, pointing to the man behind his father.

"Your father was searching all over for you, my baby," Maimouna says.

"Well, we have this gentleman to thank," Idrissa says.

"Oh, monsieur, thank you! We owe you everything we have for bringing our only son back to us. Please, join us for dinner. It's the least we can do. Fatou, my love, get our guest something to drink, quick."

Fatou sighs and exits the room.

Maimouna sets Ibrahimah down and the family ushers the stranger into the living room, offering him the best chair in the room. Fatou brings a cup of bissap and sets it on the coffee table in front of their guest, chastened.

"Ibrahimah, my baby, come to Mama so we can get you into clean clothes before dinner."

"My kind sir, what is your name?" Idrissa asks as Maimouna leads Ibrahimah by the hand to go bathe.

Ibrahimah looks up at the stranger in the light as he passes; the man's face is greasy with sweat, his eyes cloudy and dull.

"Marabout Ahmed," he says with a quiet smile.

Ibrahimah follows his mother out of the living room.

An hour later, his plate cleared of any remnants of the grilled mutton or the bed of fried onions and petit pois that it sat within; Marabout Ahmed wipes his mouth with the white cloth napkin.

"Dinner was *nekh.*"

Maimouna smiles at the compliment.

"It's the least we can do, after all that you've done for our family." She rises to prepare the children for bed.

"I should get going," Ahmed says, standing.

"Where are you staying?" Idrissa asks.

"I'm a guest of the N'Diaye family. I'm here for a few days."

"Well, please let me know if there's anything I can do for you while you're here. My family is at your disposal."

Ahmed smiles as Idrissa walks him to the door. Before stepping into the night, he spins on his heels.

"Actually, there is something I would like to request of you," Ahmed says.

"Oh? What is that?"

"I have a daara in Dakar and I'd like Ibrahimah to return with me. We talked the whole way back from the beach. He'd make the perfect student. His cousin is a student in my daara. Ibrahimah is just the kind of disciple I'm looking for. I believe our meeting was Allah's will."

"Or perhaps, my brother's will," Idrissa says, looking at the empty doorway that held the silhouette of his wife just a moment ago.

VI.

Walking out of the door to work the next morning, Idrissa tells Maimouna about Marabout Ahmed's request, but before she could respond Madame N'Diaye appears at their front door, blurting, "My daughter is getting married!"

Maimouna stares after the retreating figure of her husband.

"The wedding is scheduled for tomorrow!" Madame N'Diaye continues, needing no encouragement.

The twenty-two-year-old girl will be the third wife of a rich Senegalese businessman. Madame N'Diaye cannot believe her family's luck. Already, the girl has received a dowry of two and a half million francs, along with an abundance of jewelry, perfume, housewares, and other gifts.

"My daughter is such a good girl," Madame N'Diaye boasts. "She's given me several gifts already."

Maimouna shifts her gaze and her attention to the pressing task in front of her. She has twenty-four hours to make three hundred fatayas, her ever-popular meat-and-fish patties, her secret being a local Guinea spice that her husband is able to procure for her from a vendor that specializes in spices, at a market located down by the Casamance River, more than two hours away. Maimouna is happy for her neighbor, but Marabout Ahmed's request hangs heavily on her mind. She thinks back to Friday's afternoon mosque. She did not see Marabout Ahmed there, nor had she ever met him. She thinks back to her sister-in-law's comment. Perhaps, her in-laws had been planning this all along. She rubs the back of her neck and walks into the kitchen.

"Binta! Aisha!" Maimouna calls from the back of the house. "Go fetch water from the well. Fatou, start mixing the dough. Ibrahimah, my baby, stay close to me. I don't want you out of my sight, you hear?"

Maimouna welcomes the distraction of cooking. Flour is poured into a large metal industrial bowl. Another bowl is filled with spices while Fatou cleans the meat and then uses a meat masher to decimate the tough muscle of mutton. Buckets of water appear, and Aisha and Binta sit rinsing the onions, peeling and then cutting them. Everyone knows their task and so the day passes quickly, and the familiar choreography that has preceded so many past village occasions takes command of Maimouna's home. Ibrahimah picks up a cooked patty that has fallen on the floor, and then sprinkles flour on the table before his mother lays out the dough.

"Ibrahimah! Are you eating the fatayas again?" Binta exclaims.

Ibrahimah looks up at his sister with big owl eyes and puffed-out cheeks.

"Binta, leave your brother alone. Here, take this finished batch and put them over by the door. Be careful, they're hot."

"Fatou, how is dinner coming along?"

"Almost done."

Fatou, having long since finished mashing the pile of meat, has started grilling the fish for their own meal that evening.

"My goodness, you all are busy!" Idrissa exclaims, arriving home from work and entering the kitchen.

Maimouna looks up from the large bowl of spices and ground meat she's mixing together.

"How was your day, my love?" she says over her shoulder.

"Good. I harvested eggplant and tomatoes. There should be enough for the week."

"I need a break from these onions," Binta says with tears in her eyes.

"Well, go see if Fatou needs help," Maimouna replies.

"Ibrahimah, what are you doing in the kitchen with the women?" Idrissa quips.

Ibrahimah looks up at his father from the floor, his cheeks puffed out, full of more fataya.

"Let us be. We have much to do. As a matter of fact, my strong husband, perhaps you can go fetch two more buckets of water for us."

Idrissa kisses Maimouna on the cheek before walking out of the house to do her bidding.

Having worked through the night, with a short break for dinner and to put Ibrahimah to bed, Maimouna and her daughters bring the last batch of fatayas to Madame N'Diaye by noon. The bride's festivities are just beginning. Pleased with herself, Maimouna places the generous payment inside her brassiere. Two-thirds of the money will go toward the freezer they're saving for, since the miniature refrigerator they have now is no match for the twelve-hour rolling power outages the village experiences on a regular basis. The remainder of the money will buy extra rice, oil, eggs, and bread for the month.

She catches a glimpse of Marabout Ahmed sitting in the foyer; he'll bless the bride and groom later in the evening, but Maimouna goes outside. She has nothing to say to him. She regrets allowing the children to go to the beach on Friday, and curses her lack of foresight—she should have been keeping cowrie shells under Ibrahimah's bed for protection, especially after her dreams.

Maimouna sits down beneath the canopy. Guests arrive in Saloulou from as far as Touba and Dakar, both of which are more than a thirteen-hour drive away, depending on which route one takes. Women wear long silk flowing tops with traditional ankle-length wrap skirts to match. Overstarched boubous in elaborate designs saunter by. Pointy-toed, high-heeled shoes sink without mercy into the loose earth. Layers of expired makeup from France and America give the women washed-out skin tones that remind Maimouna of Morticia from *The Addams Family*. The entire village has been invited. A wedding is not celebrated in any other way. Everyone is there to see, and be seen.

Idrissa cannot afford to buy Maimouna the most expensive materials for the latest fashions, but he works hard to give her and the children a life to be proud of; her girls go to school and don't have to work as maids to bring in extra income for the family, and this year Ibrahimah will start school with his sisters. After spending a respectable amount of time enjoying the festivities, she bids her neighbors goodbye; she has to finish preparing dinner. As with many traditional men, Idrissa only eats food cooked at home by his family.

She puts the rice onto the fire and fries a small piece of meat. The crackling sound of the oil reminds her of the days when she lived in Dakar with her uncle Youssef. She remembers watching the American television shows *The Cosby Show*, *The Addams Family*, and *Dallas* during her free time, her aunt's shrill voice interrupting Bill Cosby's jokes; her constant demands of Maimouna neverending. It amazes her how she ever came back to live in the country that stole her youth; how she left her mother and Guinea a second time, fourteen years ago. She hears the feet of her children bounding through the house.

"Ibrahimah!"

"Na'am!"

"Come, my baby."

Ibrahimah appears in the doorway.

"You want to drink?"

"No. I want to go play with Moussa."

"Where are your sisters?"

"Outside."

"Stay with me a while."

"But Mama! I want to go play!"

Ibrahimah stomps his foot in defiance, his face contorted in displeasure at Maimouna's request.

"Ibrahimah!" Fatou calls out from the front of the house.

"Fine, go with your sister. But don't wander far from her. Fatou!"

"*Na'am!*"

"Ibrahimah is coming. Don't let him out of your sight!"

"*Na'am!*"

Her two children trample out the front door and the house is quiet.

Maimouna thinks about their options as she flips the meat. They are indebted to Marabout Ahmed, that much is true. He found their son, and now he wants the very thing he'd just returned to them, but Ibrahimah is the one thing she's unwilling to give up. She cannot bear the thought of parting with another child. She pushes the guilt of Aisatu's death from her mind. The toddler died in her sleep. There was nothing she could have done to save her. Maimouna has to focus all of her energies on Ibrahimah and her three girls, and the boiling rice before her.

When Maimouna first moved to Dakar she was eight years old and her uncle Youssef promised her mother he would take care of her and send her to school. Her first summer there, the city was hot with barely any rain. Maimouna gave her all, learning to cook the traditional Senegalese dishes, cleaning and running errands for her aunt and uncle. She had dreams of living in a house like the one she saw on *The Cosby Show*. She would go to college in America, find a rich husband, and become a lawyer. When the month of August arrived, she could barely contain her excitement, even while dusting the living-room furniture while her aunt read a magazine.

"What are you so happy about these days?" her aunt asked.

"School. I can't wait! I will buy pencils and notepads. I will study hard and get the best grades. Mama will be so proud of me. When I become a lawyer in America, I will call for Mama and we will live in a big, fancy house."

"*You*, go to school?" Auntie folded the magazine against her lap. "Where did you hear that?"

"Uncle is sending me to school. It is why I've come to Dakar."

"Well, that's news to me," her aunt said, picking up the magazine again, which had Whitney Houston on the cover. "We have no money to send you to school. Youssef is still searching for work. We can't afford it. You watch too much television. This is your reality—go start dinner."

"But if I'm not going to school, why am I here?"

"You're here because your mother is too poor to feed you, so now you're my burden. If you want to avoid living in the streets and prostituting for food, you'll earn your keep around here. Now go start dinner before I send you back to that shanty in Guinea."

Maimouna was running out the front door into the street before she knew what she was doing.

"Maimouna, get back in here!"

With the unforgiving sun on her back, Maimouna's dreams sank into the earth beneath her feet. She looked around, a scared and clueless eight-year-old. She could hear the ocean off in the distance and ran toward it, determined to run until she found Guinea, and her mother.

"Something smells good," Idrissa says, leaning over to kiss her.

She closes her eyes at the touch of her husband's lips and smiles.

"Come with me," she says, covering the rice and setting it to a simmer.

In their bedroom she takes off his shoes and rubs his feet. Idrissa closes his eyes, leans his head back, and grunts in appreciation after his thirteen-hour day on the farm.

"How was your day?" he asks her, lifting his head.

"It was good. I got all the fatayas done in time and received several additional orders from the neighbors and visitors."

"Wonderful."

"I think we'll have enough to buy the freezer this month."

Idrissa forces a smile. He looks at her quietly as she rubs his feet. The silence is heavy between them. She knows what she has to ask him, but says something easier instead.

"Are you ready to eat?"

"When am I not ready to eat, my love? I'm a lucky man," he says.

She brings him a plate and sets it down in front of him on the coffee table.

Join me, he gestures.

"I can't."

"Try, it'll do you good."

"What are we going to do?"

"We cannot refuse," Idrissa says, rolling a ball of rice with his fingers and plopping it into his mouth.

"We cannot send him away. I can't survive the loss of another child."

Maimouna sits down next to her husband.

"You wouldn't be losing him. It would just be for a little while."

"I couldn't live a day without him."

"My family will not back us up on this. You know my brother's son is already one of his students, and although Ahmed is not *our* marabout, to refuse would be an embarrassment to my family. My brother could take back the land my father had him lend me."

"You are my husband, his father. Protect us."

"My love, I am trying the best I can. Only Allah has the power to ignore familial and societal obligations," Idrissa says.

Maimouna falls silent and Idrissa uses the remote to turn the television on. Her mind slips back to the time she tried to run away. Hunger and fatigue sent her back to her uncle's house two days later.

"Ton-ton, is it true? Am I not going to school?" she asked.

"Maybe next year, my niece, I just can't afford it right now. But continue to be a good girl and do as my wife tells you. The rewards will come. Wait and see. Allah will bring plenty of blessings for you, *Insha'Allah.*"

Later that evening, stepping out into the warm night, the sandy floor gives beneath her feet. Idrissa slaps his arm, killing a drunken mosquito. Blood splatters across his arm and hand.

"Eck!"

Maimouna fishes a tissue out of her purse and wipes the gore off his arm. The lights beneath the canopy shine bright, welcoming a new wave of freshly dressed attendees. Ten hours since the festivities began and the food and drinks still flow. The drummers have calmed their beat to a mellow fever, considerate of neighbors who may wish to sleep. The groom has yet to arrive to claim his bride.

Idrissa's brother comes by to greet him. *"Salamalaikum."*

"Malaikumsalam."

"How goes you, little brother?"

"I am at Allah's will. And you, big brother? How goes it with you?" Idrissa asks.

"Good, good."

Maimouna and her sister-in-law follow the men inside Madame N'Diaye's house. A constant flow of guests moves in and out of the room with monetary offerings for Marabout Ahmed, who sits in the corner of an oversized sofa with dark sunglasses on. Idrissa and his brother sit down next to him while the women sit across from the men and Madame N'Diaye buzzes about the room offering everyone food and drink.

"I leave for Dakar tomorrow," Ahmed says.

Idrissa does not respond. Maimouna's heart skips a beat; this cannot be happening.

"My Étienne has been Marabout Ahmed's pupil for five years now," Idrissa's older brother says.

"And a fine young man he is turning out to be," Ahmed says.

"Yes," Idrissa replies, "I'm sure he is, but we're not comfortable sending Ibrahimah to Dakar. Ibrahimah is our only son. He's just turned six, too young to be so far away from home."

"Too young? No man is too young to learn the Quran and the responsibilities of life."

"I agree with you, brother," Idrissa states in a quiet tone. "That is why my children learn the Quran with me already."

"You're just a farmer, what do you know of the Quran?" his brother snorts.

Maimouna's sister-in-law sits nodding in agreement with her husband.

"We have a house full of girls. We just lost Aisatu. If something should happen to Ibrahimah . . ." Maimouna says.

She pulls on her wrists as sweat trickles down the side of her face. The walls of the room look garish and menacing, the air smells of bleached skin and cheap perfume.

"Aisatu passed months ago," Maimouna's sister-in-law says, finally opening her mouth, "and this is different. You are young enough. Have more children like I suggested before. You're too attached to these children, it's not healthy."

"I know enough of the Quran that I don't need to send my son away, brother. We're not beggars. We work hard to teach our children to have dignity," Idrissa says.

"Are you calling *me* a beggar for sending Étienne to Dakar to live as a Talibé?"

"No, my brother, that is not what I mean," Idrissa says.

Maimouna sits unblinking, her back is stiff; the glare of the light pricks at her eyes.

"Hard work will teach the boy humility. Desire for ungodly things is corrupting our people. Living the life of a Talibé ensures Senegal will have a legion of men devout to Allah and his word, able to overcome obstacles and the influences of the wicked," Ahmed says.

"We've heard stories of how difficult life is for the Talibé in the city. It is unnecessary. We don't want that for our son," Idrissa says, looking his brother in the eye now.

"Marabout Ahmed is a man of the highest esteem. How could you even imagine he does not care for the children as you?"

"Because no one will love and care for my children in the same manner as Maimouna and myself. No one can replace a father's love for his son," Idrissa retorts, harsher than he expected.

"Your children do not belong to you; they belong to Allah, and Marabout Ahmed is a man of God. Giving our sons to him is the same as giving them to God himself!"

Maimouna looks at her brother-in-law, whose face is now contorted in anger, with the same distrust she learned in her youth. Year after year she worked day and night as her uncle's unpaid servant. Cooking, cleaning, washing their laundry, and taking care of the ever-increasing number of children her aunt continued to birth, trapped in the house all day with the miserable woman while her uncle traveled through Mauritania and Mali looking for work in construction. In an attempt to save her sanity, Maimouna concocted a plan to get out of the house, at seventeen years old.

"You work? Ha! I have more use for you here in the house," her fat aunt snorted.

"I will still come home and cook afterwards. You always complain Uncle doesn't send enough money to cover the monthly expenses. I can help."

Her aunt was silent, as if she had not heard Maimouna.

"I'll give you everything I make."

Her aunt turned away from her favorite soap opera, *Dynasty*, and looked at Maimouna with soft eyes for the first time in nine years.

"You're a good girl," she cooed before her eyes hardened again. "If you can find work, then you can do it."

Maimouna looks around the room with disgust. Idrissa is still in deep conversation with his brother and Marabout Ahmed. Her sister-in-law is now talking to whoever will listen to her. Nothing about this is right. The dread she felt creeping up her spine yesterday morning rises up, wrapping its tentacles around her neck. She looks at Marabout Ahmed sitting without expression, his eyes hidden behind those stupid sunglasses. Ibrahimah is a sheep about to be devoured by a wolf, and there is nothing she can do about it. She looks to Idrissa, her eyes wide with fright.

The conversation continues to circle around her when a commotion rises up from outside the living room. The groom has arrived, having left the festivities in his family's village home more than two hours away in Casamance, to claim his bride. The older man, dressed in a slim knee-length sage tunic with gold embroidery on the torso, saunters into the room and hands Marabout Ahmed a wad of cash. Ahmed, quite finished with the conversation about Ibrahimah, welcomes the gentleman and beckons him to sit. Understanding the meeting has come to a close, Idrissa ushers Maimouna from the room. The festivities have calmed, the drums having come to a close now that the groom has arrived, and a slow trickle of guests begin to leave.

Back at home she and Idrissa prepare for bed in silence. She pulls back the sheets. Idrissa lights the mosquito-repellent coil and places it on the floor at the foot of their bed. The flame from the candle on the dresser casts dancing shadows across the dark room. The spirits are restless.

"We don't have to send him."

"It's not in our control."

Idrissa sits on the edge of the bed, his shoulders hunched over.

"But it is. We don't have to follow the lead of what everyone else thinks."

Idrissa does not respond.

"Will we allow pride to overshadow the well-being of our children? No one will care in a year. We can go back to Guinea with my mother."

"We can't leave. Our life is here. My inheritance. If my brother disowns me, we have nothing. I already pushed him much harder than I should. I couldn't live if you and the girls had to work in someone else's house just to make ends meet. I said I would take care of you."

"Husband, please, I beg you."

"Faith in Allah will lead us down the righteous path, my wife. Marabout Ahmed has agreed to keep him only a year and then Ibrahimah will come home. The time will go by quickly, I promise."

The next morning Maimouna wakes to find Idrissa and Ibrahimah gone. Marabout Ahmed left for Dakar before sunrise.

VII.

Étienne turns around to a panoramic view of the calamity. Several cars have crashed. The front end of a yellow taxi sits on the trunk of a black car, which is sandwiched into the rear end of a green hatchback, which has flipped on its side.

"Whoa! Look at that!"

"Étienne!"

Étienne looks back at Fatik who stands frozen in his steps and then back at the woman screaming with her hands clutching her chest. The taxi driver, visibly shaken, looks around in confusion from his car, suspended in the air. Where is Ibrahimah?

"Fatik. Ibrahimah? Have you seen—"

"Étienne!" Fatik yells, pointing to the accident.

Étienne drops his tomato can and takes off running toward the mangled cars.

"Ibrahimah!" Étienne yells, running into the mass of spectators forming around the plumes of smoke and wreckage.

"The boy is dead!" the woman on the side of the road screams.

The crowd swells with curious onlookers. The driver of the black car walks in small circles with his hands cupping his ears. The inhabitants of the hatchback remain inside the car, motionless. The taxi driver swings his car door open and the crowd swoops back as two men run forward, urging him to sit still and wait for the police.

Étienne fights his way to the front of the crowd, his eyes darting around the cars' edges.

"Ibrahimah!"

He looks at the cars but sees nothing. Someone tries to hold him back by the shoulders but he shrugs them off and reaches the wreckage.

"Ibrahimah! Where are you?"

"Help!"

"Ibrahimah! I'm coming!" Étienne drops to his stomach, crawling within the small space beneath the taxi that sits atop the trunk of the black car.

"I lost my can," Ibrahimah says.

"It's okay. You hurt? Are you bleeding?"

"I—I think I'm okay."

"The boy is alive!" a man shouts out from behind Étienne.

"Give me your hands! I'm going to pull you out."

Étienne grabs his cousin by the wrists and pulls him a bit, then scoots back while trying to pull Ibrahimah with him. Ibrahimah calmly waits for Étienne to free him. Hearing their exchange, a man slowly begins to drag Étienne out from beneath the wreck by his legs. Another man joins in. Ibrahimah is free.

A joyous shout rises up from the crowd.

"He's a prophet!"

"Alhamdulillah!"

"Touch the boy; he'll bring you good luck and fortune!"

Ibrahimah squints up at the people touching his face, arms, and back. Several policemen push the crowd away so that they can talk to Ibrahimah.

"Talibé, you get hit by the car?"

Ibrahimah looks up at the officer, still in a daze.

"Are you hurt? Do you need to go to the hospital?"

The officer lifts up Ibrahimah's arms and touches his back in search of any lacerations or broken bones.

"Who is your marabout? What's your name?"

"Marabout Ahmed. His name is Ibrahimah," Étienne interjects.

The officer writes the names down. A petite woman approaches them and hands Ibrahimah his red tin tomato can, miraculously unscathed; it had merely rolled to the curb in the ensuing chaos. When he grabs it, she caresses his arm and smiles.

"Well, tell your marabout if anything goes wrong with the boy, he should bring him to the hospital right away."

Étienne cradles his arm across Ibrahimah's shoulder and leads him away. People stare and whisper before turning their attention to the wreckage.

The officers turn to the driver, still pacing around the scene as the paramedics arrive and begin extracting the unconscious driver and passenger from the hatchback.

Étienne and Ibrahimah walk back over to the other boys.

"Am I dead?" Ibrahimah says, assessing his body.

"Ibrahimah! You're a miracle. You got hit by a car, and you're alive. You'll be rich one day!" Fatik says, running up and patting him on the shoulders.

"Come, I touch you for good fortune!" Abdoulaye says, rushing forward.

Abdoulaye tickles Ibrahimah, sending him into a fit of giggles. Ibrahimah runs behind Étienne, even as he enjoys the attention.

"What happened?" Fatik asks.

"The car comes, *brrrrrrr,* like that, and I see it come right at me! I scream, *'Ah!'* and I go to sleep. Then I hear Étienne say, 'Ibrahimah! Ibrahimah!' When I wake up, I'm under the car and people yell! Then Étienne saved me!" He does not know why he omits the fact that he saw the red bird again, but he does.

Ibrahimah's adrenaline rushes forward again and he kicks his leg out. "Ouch!"

"What's wrong?" Étienne asks.

"I'm okay; just my leg hurts a little bit."

"You were scared?" Fatik asks.

"Me? No!"

"Yeah, you were!" Fatik challenges.

"I wasn't!"

"You went to sleep?" Abdoulaye asks.

"He fainted," Étienne says.

Ibrahimah laughs as he grabs Étienne's arm. "Étienne saved me like this!" Ibrahimah sticks his hands up in the air.

"Étienne the hero!" Abdoulaye jokes.

Étienne kicks at the dirt on the ground.

That evening Étienne counts the coins several times to make certain they both have enough before heading to Ouakam with the others. The moonless sky kisses the city as rolling power outages leave the streets void of color. The large group of boys traipse through the vast darkness. Ibrahimah drags his feet. He's exhausted.

"Ibrahimah," Étienne whispers.

Ibrahimah's feet fall hard against the ground as his pace doubles to keep up with Étienne's voice.

"Yeah."

"You okay?"

Ibrahimah nods, although Étienne cannot see. They approach a lit section of the road sandwiched between black sheets of night. Sisqó's "Thong Song" bumps from behind the entrance door of a club as the motor of the generator growls nearby. Instant chatter rises up from the group of boys.

A Senegalese woman approaches the entrance dressed in tight jeans and a silky shirt that exposes her smooth, taut back. Her big ass and curvaceous hips strain the seams of her jeans, her dark chocolate skin is hidden behind layers of makeup and a stiff multicolored weave. The eyes of the men in front of the club ogle her body from head to foot. The white Frenchman with her walks with his chest poked out and a swagger in his step. The other men look at him with envy; women like her don't bother with poor men.

Several boys run up to the woman, bombarding her with demands for money. Waving the woman and the Frenchman inside, the bouncer shouts at the boys for crowding the entrance of the club. Before disappearing behind the curtain, the woman reaches into her small knock-off Gucci bag and throws a handful of coins in the direction of her hungry audience. Like an angry coastal wave, the boys dive for the fallen coins. Ibrahimah starts forward to join the chaotic fury, but Étienne holds him back.

"We have enough. Leave them."

"No! I want more money."

"No, leave them!"

The mass of boys tussle on the ground for the change.

"They look like tigers fighting in the wild!" a bouncer yells out, laughing.

Another patron follows suit and a shower of one-hundred- and five-hundred-franc coins floats across the night air onto the sand, chiming right at their toes as if inviting them to join the scrum, upping the stakes. Ibrahimah is unable to resist the bounty landing within inches of his feet. Two boys see Ibrahimah picking up coins and lay their hungry eyes on him, sniffing out an easy kill. Étienne stands in front of Ibrahimah shielding him from the threatening duo.

"Leave him," Étienne says.

"Get out of the way, boy," Caca threatens. His real name is Abba, but after an embarrassing bout of diarrhea the nickname stuck.

Étienne stands his ground as Ibrahimah cowers behind him. Caca swings at Étienne and the two of them go to blows. The boy with the scar running down his face, from temple to chin, steps to the side and grabs Ibrahimah.

"Leave me alone!"

"Give me that money. You think you're special after a stupid car crash. I'm going to take what you got. Now I'm the miracle."

"No!"

He catches a glimpse of Étienne fighting with the other boy. The bouncers do nothing to stop the fray. Scarface pushes Ibrahimah down to the ground. Ibrahimah flails his arms in the air, but he is no match for the stocky ten-year-old boy. He tries to curl up into a ball, but the boy throws sand in his face and rips the money from his hands. Ibrahimah yells out for help, but no one comes.

"Don't just watch them. Break it up! They're not animals," a man approaching the club says in Wolof.

Ibrahimah can hear feet scraping against the dirt, grunts, and yells.

He tries to open his eyes but sand cuts at them, the pain unbearable.

"I'm blind! Étienne! I can't see!"

"You have sand in your eyes," Étienne says.

Someone pulls him to his feet. Ibrahimah rubs his eyes hard, making matters worse, and cries out in pain.

"Lean back, boy," an adult instructs.

Ibrahimah begins sputtering and gurgling as fresh water runs up his nose and everywhere else. He wipes his hand at his eyes and then opens them. Standing next to the man, Étienne is looking down at him with worried eyes, as if he hadn't just been brawling himself.

"He'll be fine," the older Senegalese man says.

"My money!" Ibrahimah cries, his eyes burning as he searches the ground.

"You should be ashamed of yourselves," the man scolds the bouncers.

"They're only Talibé, but they fight meaner than a pack of mad hens in a chicken coop!"

The man sucks his teeth in disgust and enters the club.

"Get out of here, you little pieces of shit! You're bothering the customers."

"We don't have to go anywhere. We're working for our marabout!" Fatik shouts.

"Fuck your marabout. I could care less. Get, before I beat your dirty little asses straight back to the village!"

Fatik and some of the others throw sand at the men. The bouncers start after them, but the boys' small feet run fast into the shadows of the night.

Sore and bruised, Ibrahimah limps alongside Étienne while they slowly walk up the dark road. His entire body hurts. What is he going to do? He has no money. So much has happened today it feels like a week has passed by since just this morning.

"I'm so sleepy I can lay down right here," Ibrahimah says.

Étienne pushes him on; if they are not accounted for tonight it will be hell to pay once they finally do show up. Before entering the house, Étienne hands Ibrahimah the extra money he has.

"You are slow tonight," Ahmed says when they walk through the door. "Come give me my money."

Still sore from the night before, Étienne hands Ahmed his money. Shaken and afraid, Ibrahimah hands Ahmed one hundred fifty francs.

"Where is the rest?"

"Ibrahimah got hit by a car today. Then Cheikh and Abba stole his money," Étienne says, pointing.

"Cheikh and Abba stole your money?" Ahmed asks.

"Yes," Ibrahimah says in a small voice.

"You were hit by a car?"

"Yes."

Ahmed stares at Ibrahimah. A flash of concern disappears behind the squaring of his jawline.

"You need to learn to be a man and protect my money. How am I to teach you and give you shelter if you return empty-handed?"

"But I had the money. Talibé brothers beat me up and took it."

"Well, then perhaps if I beat you well enough, you'll know next time to fight harder."

"But Marabout, I try. He throws sand in my face."

Ibrahimah backs away from the man looming over him, and his bladder gives. Hot urine trickles down his naked legs. Ahmed grabs the stick from beside his chair and brings it down heavy. Ibrahimah's cries fill every corner of the house.

"But Teacher—" Étienne steps forward.

"If you have something to say, you can share his fate," Ahmed growls.

Ibrahimah stiffens his body against the blows of the cane. Pain sears from the initial impact and reverberates down through the muscle to his bones. His mother's face flashes before his eyes and the smell of ocean air fills his nostrils. The cane lands on the middle of his back and he buckles to the floor. Rolling onto his back he gets a glimpse of Marabout's face. The monster is in a blind rage. He wonders if he can die from a beating. He turns and scratches at the floor in an attempt to crawl away, but he's dragged back by his leg. Again, and again the cane comes down on him. The cane whines under the pressure, threatening to crack with the force of each swing, but he can no longer feel the blows. If he stops crying out, it will probably make Marabout angrier than he already is, so every time the wood slams into his body, Ibrahimah cries out on cue. His voice becomes hoarser with every blow.

VIII.

The pain is everywhere. A large gash sits across his forehead. Raised welts zigzag his face, back, and arms. Marabout didn't emerge from his room this morning, so they did their prayers alone, facing the closed bedroom door. Étienne left Ibrahimah to sleep until the moment before they had to leave the house.

"Don't cry," Étienne consoles, staring at his cousin.

"Mama!"

"Next time listen to me! Do what I say. I will protect you!"

"Étienne! You come?" Fatik asks, stepping outside the house.

"No, later," Étienne says, waving the boy away without turning around. The morning sun is still cool and so he needs to figure out the best plan for the day because Ibrahimah is not well enough to work like he normally does.

Étienne holds Ibrahimah's can as the two boys walk down the street toward the main road. The open wound on his forehead oozes a mixture of blood and clear liquid that keeps running into his eyes. The morning air is crisp, but his body feels hot. The sun is bright but distant, the sky a cool azure. Étienne motions for him to sit down on the ground and approaches the fruit vendor whose stand sits outside of the embassy of Burkina Faso.

"What happened to the little one?"

Étienne barely shrugs. The man searches out two small overripe mangoes and hands them to Étienne.

"Thank you, ton-ton, may God be with you."

Étienne walks over and hands Ibrahimah the larger fruit.

"You should have helped me tell Marabout," Ibrahimah whines.

"I tried. You don't listen to me."

Ibrahimah takes the fruit. The mango is heavy. The taste of sweet juice on his tongue perks him up, thinning the fog in his brain, but his body refuses to cooperate. He lies down and watches Étienne weave in and out of the morning rush-hour traffic like a football player. The memory of last night's beating repeats itself over and over again in his mind. Every once in a while, he'll bang his can on the sidewalk when someone walks by. He's gotten two coins so far. Étienne is talking to a man in a car and then turns to point at Ibrahimah. The man hands Étienne money before driving away.

"Ibrahimah," Étienne says, running over to him, smiling, "I make good money! Try to look like you're almost dead!"

Ibrahimah attempts to frown, but it's too painful. He doesn't find Étienne very funny at all.

"Perfect!" Étienne says before running back into the street.

High noon approaches, and the sun is too much to bear. In a slow two-man procession they walk down a quiet street off the main road. Ibrahimah spots a group of children his age playing in a schoolyard, walks up to the gate, and stares through the white metal fence. Inside, children laugh and play with one another. A boy in a blue shirt kicks a red ball across the yard and a girl picks it up and throws it back to him. Ibrahimah grips the fence. He could throw like that if he had a ball. A girl in a pink shirt and two pigtails runs up to the gate and stops short in front of Ibrahimah.

"Hi!" she says.

"Hi," Ibrahimah says.

The girl frowns. "What happened to you?"

Ibrahimah lets go of the gate and steps back. He glances over at his cousin, who is talking to a foreigner who is shaking his head no.

"Wait! Don't go. Here. Take this," she says.

She thrusts her hand through the gate. A yellow crayon sits in her open palm. He hesitates. If he's not asking for money, he really doesn't know what to say.

"Take it. You can draw the sun," the girl says, pointing up at the sky.

"Fanta! Come back over here," a woman calls out from across the yard.

"*Na'am,*" she replies, flashing Ibrahimah a big toothy smile before running off.

Ibrahimah flips the yellow crayon around in his hand and looks up toward the fiery orange ball of gas until his eyes begin to burn. He drops the yellow Crayola crayon into his red tin can and follows after Étienne, turning back every few seconds to glance at the children behind the metal fence.

They turn the corner and find a tall, light-skinned Mauritanian woman dressed in expensive clothes exiting a silver Mercedes Benz. A grandiose house looms above, with a spray of purple and pink flowers, and dark-green plants adorning its second-floor terrace.

"Fancy car," Étienne says, looking up and down the deserted street.

The woman needs no coaxing; she gives them a bounty of eight hundred francs. They duck down behind a parked car to rest.

"We each have enough for Marabout. Pay attention, so you don't lose out like yesterday. You have to listen to me!"

Regret sits heavy across Ibrahimah's shoulders.

"You hungry?"

His hunger is not a priority. Never again does he want to be without enough money for Marabout.

"I want to work."

"We'll look for lunch first, okay? Then find more money after."

It hurts too much to argue. But after twenty minutes of walking around with no success Ibrahimah has to sit down. Étienne's stomach grumbles with hunger but Ibrahimah only cares to close his eyes. Everything from the top of his head to the bottom of his feet hurts.

"Let's go see the boy from before. He lives just over there," Étienne says, pointing in the direction of the neighborhood of Bao-bab. Ibrahimah scrunches up his face at the thought of walking another step, but the memory of him blocking the goal during the last game motivates him and he gets up. The gash across his forehead has stopped oozing and a soft thin scab is attempting to form.

"There he is," Ibrahimah says, pointing as they turn down the street.

"Aye, boy!" Étienne calls out.

Moustapha looks up from his conversation with two other boys. He raises his hand and waves them over. Étienne runs up ahead and he and Moustapha slap hands in greeting. Moustapha introduces him to the other boys and a game of football is suggested. Étienne and Moustapha form a team; the two other boys are the opposing team. Étienne turns around when Ibrahimah finally catches up.

"Ibrahimah! I almost forgot. You want to play?" Étienne asks.

"No," Ibrahimah says, pouting. He limps over to the curb and sits down.

Étienne and the other boys yell, laugh, and push, likening themselves to the professional players of France and Spain, champions of the World Cup Title. Ibrahimah's mouth sits in a pout. Marabout beats him, the bigger boys steal his money, and he's in too much pain to play football. He hates Dakar.

A gray car honks at the boys for blocking the road. Ibrahimah strains his neck to see who's inside and notices Moustapha doesn't look at the driver at all. Reaching into his red tin tomato can, Ibrahimah grabs the yellow crayon and draws circles on the sidewalk. He'll make lots of suns. That way night will never come and he'll never have to go back to Marabout. He draws arms and legs onto one of the circles. He likes the girl who gave him the crayon. She can live in his world with all of the suns and they can be friends. He looks up toward the sky and squints against the light. It is the same sun his mother and father see. He wonders if his mother is looking up at the sun that very moment and thinking of him.

"Ibrahimah! Watch out!" Moustapha yells.

Ibrahimah looks up to see the ball fly through the air with fire behind it. Before he can react, the ball makes direct contact with his chest, knocking him flat on his back.

Étienne and Moustapha run over to him with wide, fearful eyes.

"Ibrahimah!" Étienne yells, casting a shadow over a prone Ibrahimah as he leans in to see.

"Is he okay?"

With the wind knocked clear out of his body, Ibrahimah struggles to purchase a gulp of air.

"I'm a-alive," Ibrahimah says.

"Thank Allah!" Étienne exclaims, jumping up now.

"We would have been in big trouble if we killed you!" Moustapha jokes.

"I'm a miracle. I don't die," Ibrahimah says, "just hurt."

Étienne helps him sit up. The rest of the boys stand around with arms akimbo, kicking rocks while Moustapha retrieves the ball for them. Just then, a pretty foreign woman comes to the gate and calls Moustapha over to her. After a brief conversation he returns and bids the other boys goodbye.

"I have to go home. My mom wants me to start my homework."

They give the white-and-gold-and-black ball back over to Moustapha and then disband, moving down the street.

"Talibé!"

Étienne and Ibrahimah turn back to Moustapha.

"My mother wants to know if you're hungry."

"Yes," Étienne says, speaking for both of them before Ibrahimah can respond.

"Come in. My mom will have Aria get you something to eat."

They follow Moustapha and his mother inside the gate like last time, but stop short at the doorway leading into the house. There are very few places Talibé are welcome, and Étienne knows that Moustapha's house is not one of those places.

"It's okay. Come in," Moustapha says.

Inside the house the floors are cool against Ibrahimah's bare feet. He lags behind Étienne, his eyes perusing the magnificent foyer. Everything is four times his size; the large vases with flowers; the potted plants; the big chandelier hanging from the high ceiling, its crystals glistening with the sunlight dancing through the sky-light. The walls are decorated with gold trim and weird designs. Moustapha is so rich he has trees inside his house. Ibrahimah's mouth forms a circle and his eyes open nearly as wide.

"Aria, viens ici s'il te plaît," Moustapha's mother calls out over her shoulder.

The older woman comes into the foyer and looks at the scene in front of her with raised eyebrows.

"My husband does not need to know," she says in English, look-ing the boys over.

"Monsieur n'aimerait pas, madame," Aria says, recognizing Étienne and Ibrahimah.

"I don't care if my husband doesn't like it, this is my house too and they need a bath. The little one has wounds that need care. Af-terward, give them something to eat."

"Oui, madame."

A tall, slim woman walks into the foyer and places herself di-rectly in front of Ibrahimah and Étienne, blocking their path to Aria.

"Dear, are these little wretches Talibé?"

Moustapha's mother does not respond. Aria rolls her eyes and looks to her employer for direction.

"Your Senegalese husband would kill you if he knew. You know the locals don't play. They don't mix with the lower classes unless it's to employ them." The foreign woman tilts her head to the side to get a better look at Ibrahimah and Étienne.

Ibrahimah is tempted to ask this woman for money but ques-tions whether that would be a good thing or not. Something tells him it would not be okay. He looks over at Étienne, who is staring down at his feet. Whatever the tall woman in her fancy dress and sparkling bijoux is saying, it seems asking her for money is not the thing to do right at this moment in his friend Moustapha's house.

"They're children, how can anyone leave children in the street to beg, no shoes, dirty, and hungry. It's child abuse," Moustapha's mother says.

Aria cuts in front of the friend and takes the hands of Ibrahimah and Étienne and guides them over to the stairs.

"One of my mother's friends she has tea with every morning while I'm at school. I think they knew each other when they were in college back in America," Moustapha whispers to Ibrahimah and Étienne.

"My dear, every society survives by its rules."

"You sound like a hypocrite right now," Moustapha's mother says.

"Some rules, of course, are to be broken, but you can't go around breaking them all! You follow some rules to cover the ones you break. Did your mother not ever teach you that one?"

"No," Moustapha's mother says, holding the door open for her friend.

"C'est la vie, ma belle petite."

Her friend plants a kiss on the corner of her mouth and takes her exit.

"Moustapha, go start your homework, once the boys are cleaned up you can have a snack with them," his mother says.

"Yes, Mom," Moustapha replies, running upstairs to his room with Aria and the boys coming up behind him.

Everything in the bathroom is new, like downstairs. Aria runs water in a large white shiny tub. The water rushes out fast and impatient. Ibrahimah can see his reflection in the chrome faucet. He moves around, watching his reflection change shape. First his face is wide, and then it is long. Aria drops sweet-smelling oils into the rising water. At her command Ibrahimah takes his T-shirt off and is ready. He stands there naked and dirty, his small penis shriveled and raw from abuse suffered at the hands of his Marabout.

After big rainstorms, pockets of water can be found throughout the city where the streets and sidewalks are uneven. When Ibrahimah and Étienne can find a pool of water that does not smell like sewage, they will bathe themselves in it, along with the other boys. It's their only option for keeping clean. But since it is the dry season it hasn't rained in months. Ibrahimah looks at his naked cousin standing opposite him and giggles.

"What's so funny?" Étienne asks.

Ibrahimah fills him in on the joke.

"That's stupid. I don't look like caca! Take it back!"

"Now, now, boys, that's enough," Aria interjects, "nobody looks like caca; you are both very handsome. Step inside; I'll leave the water running until the bathtub has filled."

Ibrahimah climbs inside. He oohs and ahs at the first sting of hot water against his feet and legs. Étienne joins him and they sit down opposite each other. Aria takes a washcloth and rubs soap onto it before softly wiping his back. She cups her hands and scoops water up onto his scalp. The water runs down his face, making haphazard paths along the contours of his body and eczema-ridden skin, side-stepping open wounds and fresh welts on its journey back down into the tub.

The last time Ibrahimah was given a bath with such care was by his mother after Marabout had helped him find his way home from the beach. Just like Aria, his mother would run the rag over his back and wash him in all his "stinky places" as she would call them, teasing him. He misses her.

Aria rinses his feet gently. His soft baby feet, callused with clumps of damaged tissue and skin, ingrown nails, fungi, and dirt. The sight of them causes her to turn away a moment before she can continue.

When he gets out of the tub Aria pats him dry with a big soft towel and slathers him down with pure shea butter mixed with fresh lime. Eczema medicine is applied to Étienne's skin. Ibrahimah wiggles with annoyance as alcohol is applied to the gash on his forehead. Once the burning calms, Aria applies two bandages to cover the area, hands him two white pills with a cup of water, and tells him to swallow.

"This is a shame," she mumbles to herself.

"Thank you, ta-ta," Étienne says, his head hanging low.

Ibrahimah follows his cousin's lead and thanks Aria. He hugs her thigh in the same manner he would cling to his mother, his head arched back, gazing up into her eyes. Aria clears her throat, her eyes glistening like the chandelier downstairs. She looks away a moment and tells them to follow her into the guest bedroom, where Moustapha's mother has laid out clothes.

"Slow down, the clothes are not going anywhere," Aria says to Ibrahimah, laughing, as she pulls the shirt over his head.

Ibrahimah cannot believe it, new clothes. He walks around in a pair of underwear with cartoon characters on them, imitating an airplane before Aria grabs ahold of him and slips him into a pair of pants. The clothes feel foreign and strange, constricting, but warm. He can't remember what happened to the clothes he was wearing when he first arrived to Dakar from his village. The throbbing on his forehead has dulled to a whisper.

"You boys look great!" Moustapha's mother says.

Ibrahimah stops and looks up at the woman with hesitation. Maybe she's upset and wants him to take the clothes off. He grabs Aria's hand.

"Don't worry, little one, the madame thinks you look very nice," Aria says in Wolof, patting his cheek.

"You speak English?" Étienne asks.

"I understand it from working with Americans, but the madame prefers I speak French to help her learn." Aria turns to Moustapha's mother. *"Oui, madame, les vêtements leur vont bien, mais ils n'ont pas de chaussures."*

"Oh! I forgot about shoes. I don't know if Moustapha has any old shoes around here."

"Les chaussures en plastique qu'ils vendent à la boutique sont très bien pour eux."

"Oh, yes. In America we call those sandals jellies."

Moustapha's mother hands Aria a five-thousand-franc note.

Decked out in a green short-sleeved shirt, khaki pants, and a light blue sweater tied around his waist, Ibrahimah saunters around the kitchen downstairs like a king.

"Étienne, look at me. Look at you! We dress rich."

Étienne smiles at his cousin, touching the fabric against his skin.

"You boys look like models in a Ralph Lauren ad," Moustapha's mother says.

Why doesn't this woman speak Wolof to him so he can understand what she wants? Ibrahimah stops playing and sits down. Aria walks into the kitchen with a black plastic bag and reminds her employer the boys don't understand English.

"Oh, I keep forgetting," she says, throwing her hands up in the air. *"Désolée, mes petits chéris! Vous êtes très beaux!"*

"Merci, madame," Étienne replies.

"Merci," Ibrahimah says, smiling. No one in Dakar has ever called him handsome.

Aria shows Moustapha's mother the shoes she found.

"Those are fine."

Moustapha's mother starts to leave, then turns on her heels.

"Aria, how old are the boys?"

"Le grand a douze ans. Le petit a environ six ans, je crois."

"Six years old. Who would send their baby out in the streets begging at such a young age?"

"C'est notre tradition," Aria whispers.

Ibrahimah looks down at his feet, pretending not to understand. Étienne seems occupied with his own thoughts.

Moustapha comes down from his room and the boys snack on cookies while they watch television. *Tom & Jerry* is on. Ibrahimah cracks up laughing as the colorful characters run across the screen torturing one another. They jump, flip, slide, and do all the things he would like to do. When something is said in French that he doesn't understand, Étienne or Moustapha translates it into Wolof for him.

This is the best day he's had since leaving his family. He looks around the room. The sofa is soft against his skin and bigger than any piece of furniture he's ever sat on. Ten boys could sleep on it and have more than enough room to move around. No mosquitoes or flies are buzzing around his head. Cool air blows into the room from the air conditioners mounted high up on the walls.

"Étienne, we found Paradise."

Étienne looks over at his cousin and then turns his attention back to the cartoons. After an hour Aria comes to deliver the bad news.

"No! Let them stay a while longer. Mom!" Moustapha yells, running out of the living room in search of his mother.

"We have to go?"

"I think so," Étienne says.

A few moments later a somber Moustapha returns.

"I have to finish my homework, but come back tomorrow, same time."

"Okay."

Étienne and Ibrahimah get up. Ibrahimah stretches his arms wide and heaves a sigh. He feels different. Better than before.

"Where's my can?" Ibrahimah asks.

Aria appears with the two oversized red tin tomato cans, scrubbed clean. The outer red color shines like the day they left the manufacturing plant. Inside each can is a piece of fruit, some cookies, and an extra five hundred francs.

Étienne's and Ibrahimah's eyes light up when they discover the money. The boys wave goodbye before turning and walking down the road.

"We have so much money," Ibrahimah says, shocked at his good luck today.

"Life is easy like for Marabout today. No work. Sit, eat, get money," Étienne says.

Ibrahimah falls into a fit of laughter. He laughs so hard his stomach hurts, and he bends over to lessen the pain. That is the funniest thing he's heard in a long time. Étienne joins in the laughter for a bit, but then stops abruptly, his face serious. He puts his can down, takes Ibrahimah by the shoulders, and looks him straight in the eyes.

"Ibrahimah. We can't tell anyone about the money, the food, or where we find the clothes. Understand?"

Ibrahimah grins from ear to ear.

"Cousin, if anyone ever finds out about Moustapha, we can never come again. Too many Talibé to share. Not even Fatik or Abdoulaye."

Ibrahimah stops smiling and looks at his cousin's face. No money means beatings. No food means hunger.

"I won't say anything."

"Promise you do what I say? These are rich people. They don't want lots of Talibé in their house, eating their food, wearing Moustapha's rich clothes."

"I promise, Étienne."

"Okay. If the others ask, say Christians gave us the clothes. Marabout doesn't care what Christians do."

Later that evening in front of the pizza shop, their house brothers are shocked to see them.

"Look at you!"

The group encircles Ibrahimah and Étienne like a swarm of bees to a hive. Dirty little hands reach out and touch Ibrahimah's arm.

"Allah brings us good fortune, *alhamdulillah*," Étienne replies.

"Allah gives to *you*?"

"Yes," Ibrahimah says.

"Why Allah bring good for you and not me?" Scarface demands. He pushes the other boys out of his way and stands in front of Étienne with a scowl on his face.

"I'm a miracle!" Ibrahimah says, smiling.

Étienne steps around the boy and hands Fatik the packet of vanilla cream cookies Aria gave him. Fatik takes two cookies and then hands them off to the other boys.

"Thanks," Fatik says, patting Étienne on the back.

Étienne grabs Ibrahimah by the arm and they lean up against the lamppost, watching the others perform the routine evening dance: run up to foreigner, get ignored, turn to chase the other customer leaving with hot food, get swatted away, turn back to start again from the beginning. Like Tiki from the zoo, they dance for food and money. Scurrying across the parking lot, trying to get what they can get, as fast as possible. Worry begs at the back of Étienne's neck.

It was when Étienne first came to Dakar with Marabout Ahmed, while walking the streets alone beneath the scorching-hot sun one day, that he came upon an old man drinking tea beneath a large shady tree.

"Boy, why are you beaten so bad? Where are your pants? Your shoes?"

"Someone took them from me."

The man spit the remnants of chewed-up bark onto the ground.

"Boy, remember what I'm about to tell you. It will save you grief one day. If a man claims to be a true Muslim and he tries to take something Allah has given you, he is damned to hell. No man has the right to take anything that Allah has not given him directly. You understand what I say?"

Étienne stood there with his head hung low. What did this old man know about being seven years old and losing one's family, clothes, money, food, and happiness?

"Listen to me, boy. You suffer because you don't listen. Who gives you that red tomato can?"

"My marabout."

"Allah willed your marabout to give you that can. Meaning, Allah has given you that can. If someone comes to you and says, 'This can is mine!' you immediately state in a loud, clear voice that Allah himself gave you that can. A *true* Muslim has no argument against you. Allah is almighty. If he wants a can, he now has to wait for Allah to give him one. If his heart is true, he won't take your tomato can. If his heart has no truth, make sure you have witnesses to influence his behavior. Take this advice and you will see.

"Do you want some tea?"

So, Étienne sat with the old man, drank tea, and listened. He instructed Étienne to return the next day, and when Étienne arrived, the man gave him a new pair of shoes. Week after week Étienne would stop by the large shady tree, bringing the old man sugar cubes and listening to him talk about life, the Quran, and Allah. He taught Étienne prayers and passages from the Quran and how to read. As the years passed Étienne grew stronger, taller, and more poised. One day he arrived only to find several men in the old man's spot beneath the tree.

"Where is the man that sits here each day?"

"He died last night. What's it to you?"

"Nothing," Étienne replied, kicking the sand up to hide his approaching tears as he walked away, the familiar pain of loneliness creeping up into his chest. The next day Ibrahimah arrived in Dakar with Marabout Ahmed.

Étienne looks over at Ibrahimah, posturing in his new clothes, an easy grin on his face as he talks with Fatik. Night spreads across the sky in the absence of sun. Ibrahimah reassures Fatik that he and Étienne received everything from Allah. But Étienne knows the real challenge will be convincing Marabout of this.

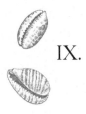 IX.

Suspicious of his good mood and fancy clothes, Marabout slaps Ibrahimah across the back of his head, accusing him of cockiness. Ibrahimah's hand shoots up to the spot that now stings in pain, and turns around to face Marabout, his mouth in a defiant pout, but before the situation can escalate, Étienne grabs his cousin by the arm and drags Ibrahimah out the front door. When they get down to the main road, the cousins ditch their Talibé brothers as they have been doing, and spend the morning working, before heading to Moustapha's house for lunch and play.

"Maybe they're not home," Étienne says, ringing the bell again.

Ibrahimah shifts from one foot to the other with impatience. He has never visited a house where *no one* was home—but rich people like Moustapha are different. He imagines his friend off doing something fanciful, like eating in a restaurant or enjoying the rides at Magic Land, the only amusement park in Senegal.

"Let's go," Étienne mutters.

"But I want to eat real food and watch *Tom and Jerry*!" Ibrahimah whines, slapping the metal gate door with his open palm.

Étienne starts to walk away, leaving Ibrahimah pouting at the door. This is not how Ibrahimah imagined spending his afternoon.

He stomps in protest but Étienne doesn't turn back. Realizing he has no other choice, Ibrahimah follows, turning back every second step in case Aria would appear and beckon them inside with a wave of her hand, and a smile.

"Étienne," Ibrahimah says, catching up with his cousin after a half mile of lagging behind him, "what is cockiness?"

Étienne rubs his chin in thought and then smiles when he remembers. "It means you think you are rich and important like the president or a foreigner."

"Like Moustapha?"

"Yeah."

"What's wrong with being like Moustapha?"

"Nothing. It's just, we're born poor and Moustapha is not. He doesn't have to stay with a marabout. Instead, his marabout comes to him for weekly lessons."

Ibrahimah looks down into his empty red tin can. He would like to leave Marabout and live with Moustapha. A twinge of guilt rises up in his throat; he still loves his mother and father. They turn off of Rue Deux and walk down toward On the Run, even though the gas station and food outlet are normally dead during the afternoon.

"Talibé! I haven't seen you in a long time. *Namanala trop!* Oy! Look at you. All fancy and rich," the manager of the computer shop says, coming out of the store.

Ibrahimah's face lights up at the recognition of his new clothes and status. "Yes."

"Allah has brought you fortune. You continue to be good boys and he will bring you more."

Ibrahimah sits down on the curb, shielding his eyes from the sun. Étienne stands with a hint of impatience in his movements.

"Where are your Talibé brothers?"

"We make more money when it's just the two of us," Étienne replies, looking across the street at the empty shaded porch of On the Run.

"But it's better to be with the group, yes?"

"Look at that car!" Ibrahimah exclaims, pointing to a large yellow Hummer, changing the subject to Étienne's relief.

The vehicle lurches forward, dwarfing all the other cars around it. The driver wears dark sunglasses and a baseball cap. Gold chains lace his neck and wrist. The windows are tinted dark but the driver's window is down, so everyone can see. Begging from that guy would be impossible, Étienne decides, he sits too high up from the ground.

"Sometimes," Étienne says to the computer-shop man, "but we're okay."

"I'll have a car like that one day when I have lots of money," Ibrahimah declares.

"You think you'll be rich enough to buy a car like that?" Étienne asks.

"Yes," Ibrahimah says.

The computer-shop guy laughs.

"Well, if Allah gives you one, little Talibé," he says, turning back to the entrance of his shop, "then I want one too!"

A customer approaches the salesman and they fall into a conversation about setting up a home Wi-Fi network as he ushers the guest inside.

"Why will Allah give you a car like that?" Étienne asks.

"'Cause I'm good. Moustapha is good and he gets everything. Why not me? You said before that Allah loves me."

If God is supposed to love him, and it seems like God loves Moustapha, then he should be able to have nice things and comfort like his friend. His eye catches a boy waving his arm back and forth at them from down the road.

"It's Abdoulaye and Fatik. Let's go see what they're doing," Étienne says.

Ibrahimah follows, still thinking of the yellow Hummer. His yellow crayon has gone missing; if he still had it, he would draw a picture of the Hummer, and himself inside the car. Surely he can get another crayon from Moustapha; he'll ask his friend the next time they visit him.

"There's a football match at the stadium," Fatik says as they catch up to their friends.

Ibrahimah looks up at the stocky boy. Fatik reaches out and tickles Ibrahimah's belly, sending him into a fit of giggles. Ibrahimah scoots behind Abdoulaye, using his wide-faced doe-eyed friend as a shield. They meet up with the rest of the boys from their house in front of the supermarché, Casino Sahm. It's been weeks since Étienne and Ibrahimah have linked up with the larger group of boys during the day, and today they're a rare mass of fourteen bodies—the other seven boys who arrive home late every evening rarely ever link up with the main group during the day. Excited chatter about the football match is lost beneath the noise of the busy intersection. Ibrahimah and Étienne haven't been through here since the car accident. Ibrahimah looks down at his ankle-length pants and the shoes on his feet. He is a miracle. Nothing is impossible for him. He is sure of it.

Avenue Blaise Diagne is crowded with scores of people all the way down to the rough slum, Medina, where the large football field, Stade Iba Mar Diop, encompasses three-quarters of a mile. As they thread through the street, Ibrahimah watches the group of boys from his house and other Talibé boys hit up cars trapped in traffic behind red lights, masses of pedestrians, and moving street vendors. A Senegalese man calls Ibrahimah over to his car and offers him a hundred francs; the child in the backseat hands him a banana. Ibrahimah offers them a prayer and thanks, but does not scarf down the fruit immediately as he would've done not long ago. Instead, he chews the fruit slowly like Moustapha, confidence lacing each step he takes.

They can hear the cheers of the crowd from outside the stadium entrance. Tickets cost two hundred francs each, but the guards slip the boys in free when no one is looking. Inside, they walk toward the farthest end of the stadium to sit apart from the other attendees. Older boys and men will rob them of their money if they are not careful.

"Wow! Étienne! Look at how big the field is!"

He's never seen such a big football field. The match is an amateur junior league of high school graduated boys. Senegal is playing against a team from Mali. The crowd in the stadium is thick and raucous.

"You hungry?" Fatik asks Étienne, holding up a packet of nuts.

Étienne opens his palm and Fatik hands him four peanuts. A Talibé never refuses food. Étienne gives Ibrahimah two. Ibrahimah opens one of the peanuts, dropping the shell on the floor. He looks over at Abdoulaye, sitting next to him, and offers his friend the other peanut.

"You're a good man, Ibrahimah," Abdoulaye says, taking the peanut.

Looking out onto the field, Ibrahimah imagines himself down there in white shorts and a green short-sleeve jersey. He moves the ball expertly from one foot to the other, dodging his opponents with the ease and agility of Thierry Henry or Patrick Vieira. Ibrahimah, the famous football player! People smile at him when he and Étienne walk by. No longer ignored, kicked, or beaten. He is rich and happy, living in a big house, with his own television. His mother brings him as much mango as he wants, along with plates full of mafé and great big jugs of Coca. The sun shines bright through the windows. His sister Fatou tells a funny joke and they all laugh. His father offers him a big piece of meat.

"Ibrahimah!"

Ibrahimah opens his eyes. Étienne, Abdoulaye, and Fatik are looking at him. Ibrahimah looks out onto the football field; nothing has changed. The crowd screams for the Senegalese team to win. Ibrahimah shakes his head to clear it.

"I will be a football player one day and be rich."

Étienne pats him on the back and turns to Fatik. Abdoulaye gets up and says, "I'll be right back," then walks down the bleachers to talk to another boy. The football is kicked up, down, and across the field. The players work hard to score, yet the game sits stagnant at zero to zero. A light-skinned boy trips and clings to his shin in pain. A timeout is called. Someone comes out, talks to him, and then two players help him to his feet and lead him off the field. The crowd screams in support of the fallen teammate. After two hours of neither team scoring a goal, Ibrahimah and the boys grab their cans and make for the exit. It's time to go back to work.

"Where's Abdoulaye?" Ibrahimah asks once they get to the front gate.

Étienne and Fatik look around.

"Maybe he'll meet us later?" Fatik asks.

"Let's wait to see if he comes," Ibrahimah suggests.

The group of thirteen loiters around the entrance of the stadium. Hanging around outside the venue proves to be not such a bad idea, as the traffic builds with tired drivers trying to get home for dinner.

"We have to go," Étienne says at the sound of the bleachers shifting beneath the feet of the crowd inside.

"What about Abdoulaye?" Ibrahimah asks.

"He'll find us. We need to go before the crowd gets out here," Fatik says.

Everyone agrees to head back up, and together they move as one.

Marabout Ahmed's boubou is damp with sweat, he frowns at the boys; most of them made their quota, but that is not the reason for his displeasure. He towers over the children, their heads lowered to the floor. He counts the dirty bodies before him and comes up short.

"Who is missing?"

Silence.

"Someone is missing. Who is it?" Ahmed growls in a low, menacing tone.

"Abdoulaye."

"Where is he?"

"We don't know," Fatik says.

"Who was he with today?"

Étienne, Ibrahimah, and the others look at one another from bowed heads.

"When is the last time you see him?"

"At the stadium after lunch," Caca offers from the back of the group.

"What was happening at the stadium?"

Another bout of silence sits in the room.

"You were fooling around, watching football instead of work-ing?"

Everyone waits for someone else to speak first.

"Answer me!"

"No. W-W-We work," Caca whimpers.

Ibrahimah stands close by Étienne's side. He looks over at Mar-about's wooden cane and wishes he could take it and throw it into the ocean. Forever lost. But he wouldn't dare. The thought of Mar-about's wrath at finding it missing, the mere thought of being caught as the perpetrator, leaves him frozen in fear. The urge to pee is strong and his leg shakes as he tries to hold his bladder.

"You're responsible for each other. Where is he? There is no way not one of you saw where he went!"

"I don't know. We waited for him, but he never showed up."

"You know where he is! I am sure of it. You're lying! You hide something from me!"

Ahmed's face contorts in anger. His dark-brown lips press to-gether into a tight, thin line. In one swift move, before anyone can react, he grabs his cane, steps forward, and begins swinging it down onto the group of malnourished bodies before him. It takes a beat before the initial shock of what is happening sets in, but when it does, the group flees in all directions, abandoning their lines.

Ibrahimah is shoved in the scurry and falls to the ground. Be-neath the trample of feet, he loses the battle with his bladder. After several minutes of terror, the fatigued potbellied man orders the boys to get out. The mangle of bodies contorting in pain looks up at him with confusion.

"Get out!" Ahmed shouts, spit flying across the hot, stuffy room.

"You sleep outside until Abdoulaye returns, and you make up for his daily payment. If not, you will be beat. Now get out!" he yells, composing himself as if recovering from a fugue state.

Ahmed points the cane toward the front door, then goes to his room without another word and slams his door shut. Outside, they scatter across the tiny front yard in search of an inconspicuous place to lie down. Too sleepy to care, Ibrahimah lowers himself down on the bare earth, next to the front door, and goes to sleep. Mosquitoes and gnats attack throughout the night.

The next week is hard. Abdoulaye is nowhere to be found. Étienne calculates that each of them has to raise an extra fifty francs. Against the protest of the other boys Étienne and Ibrahimah continue to split off from the group during the day, but after Ibrahimah and Étienne return to the parking lot several evenings in a row with enough money to cover Abdoulaye's quota alone, Fatik and the others stop complaining.

Every night Ahmed demands the whereabouts of Abdoulaye from each of them and every night the answer is the same: indifferent rumbles of "I don't know."

"The longer you continue this charade, the longer you will suffer," Ahmed growls on the ninth night.

Bruised and bloodied with tears staining their cheeks the boys leave the house to sleep outside, the endless questions of Abdoulaye's whereabouts circling about the group in frustration.

"Where *is* Abdoulaye?"

"Why do we pay for him to run away?"

"I hear he went back to the village and his family says he can stay."

"Étienne, what do you think?"

"No Talibé can go back to the village before his marabout says he can return; it's a disgrace for his family. They can't keep him if he is not fifteen. If Abdoulaye has gone to the village, he'll be back soon; he's only nine," Étienne says.

"I don't know where Abdoulaye is, but it would be nice if he came back," Fatik says dejectedly.

Étienne and Ibrahimah grab their cardboard mats, which they've started bringing outside with them, and lie down at the farthest corner of the yard. Étienne produces a ripped piece of cloth Aria gave them to protect their faces against the biting bugs when they told her about Abdoulaye going missing and Marabout's punishment. Ibrahimah has gotten used to sleeping outside. There is more of a breeze to cool him off as opposed to the stuffy room inside, overrun with bodies. Also, he doesn't have to worry about Marabout beating him in his sleep or making him stay in his room at night. Ibrahimah hangs his head and pouts when he walks out of the house at night, and it's only after he lays his mat out under the stars and covers his face and arms with the cloth from Aria that he allows himself to smile.

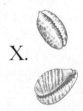

X.

The front page of *Le Quotidien* features a small seedy picture of a shoeless foot with a police officer standing nearby. Beneath the picture is a short blurb.

> *The decomposing corpse of a male child was found two weeks ago with knife wounds to the torso. The police are investigating the situation. No further details are available. If anyone has any information, please contact the authorities.*

All across Dakar people are talking about it. It was someone's uncle, father, brother who stumbled across the body and informed the police.

"It was a grotesque scene."

"It was not a child but a man."

"It was two children."

"No, I heard it wasn't two children but an entire family that was found dead."

Every conversation around the matter draws new imagined details. That afternoon an associate of Ahmed's suggests he go to the police to report his Talibé missing.

"Why didn't you report the disappearance of your Talibé before today?" the officer asks.

"I supposed the boy had run off and would return once he got hungry," Ahmed replies.

"Where did the other Talibé last see him?"

"At the stadium, late in the day," Ahmed says. "There was a football match that day."

"Would you recognize the boy and be able to identify him?"

"Yes."

Two hours later Ahmed is staring at a picture of nine-year-old Abdoulaye. Face bloated, skin ashen and gray; empty eyes stare out past him. Ahmed turns around and looks behind him, afraid of what may be lying in wait for him, but nothing is there. He breathes a sigh of relief. Ahmed gives the officer Abdoulaye's full name, age, village, and parents' names. It is assumed the boy was kidnapped. His liver, kidneys, and heart were cut from his body. Once the criminals took what they wanted, they discarded his body in a field behind some bushes. Ahmed wipes his sweaty face with his hands. There is no air circulating in the room.

"Is the body buried already?"

"No, the International Police of West Africa insisted on conducting an autopsy as part of the investigation."

"I can return the body to the boy's village immediately, if possible."

"The child's parents are alive?"

"Yes. Can I claim the body?"

"That shouldn't be a problem," the investigator says, getting up to talk with another officer.

Ahmed walks out of the station and hails a taxi. That evening he breaks the news to the boys.

"Abdoulaye is not with us anymore. He is with Allah, where he will receive the blessings of seventy-two virgins," Ahmed says.

Ahmed paces across the room in front of them. Sitting cross-legged on the floor, Ibrahimah frowns.

"Abdoulaye is going to starve with all those girls eating his food," he whispers to Étienne.

"Boy, hush!" Ahmed growls. "Let this be a lesson to you all. Dakar is the real world! There are wicked men and women that do not live by Allah's word. They attack me for being a man of Allah. What better way than to kill a Talibé, my very life support! This is war! There has always been a war against the righteous, and it has not gone to sleep. No, the war has not subsided! It is more grotesque than ever before!"

Ahmed's eyes are unable to focus on anything, darting all over the room and across the twenty heads sitting quietly on the floor. Sweat beads line his brow. Every now and again one builds up beyond its capacity, then runs down his nose, where it hangs for a moment before making its descent down to his thin brown lips.

"I leave tomorrow. Everyone is to sleep inside at night. Be mindful of the wicked. They are all around us! Let us pray."

He leads the boys in prayer, then retires to his room, mumbling to himself. The room is quiet and somber as the boys lay out their mats. Étienne and Ibrahimah lie down on the floor facing each other.

"Let's sleep outside," Ibrahimah says.

"No, let's stay in tonight. I don't want to make Marabout angry."

Ibrahimah is quiet a moment. "Abdoulaye is in the sky?"

"Yeah."

Ibrahimah looks over to the small window; there is no moon out tonight.

"He doesn't come back, like Aisatu?" Ibrahimah asks.

"No. Who's Aisatu?" Étienne asks.

"My sister. How'd Abdoulaye die?"

"Someone killed him with a knife."

"Did it hurt?"

He assumes a knife would hurt the same or perhaps worse than Marabout's stick.

"Yes."

"Is he still in pain?"

"No, because he's dead now."

"Abdoulaye never has to work again. He'll never get beat again and he is not in pain anymore. He's better off dead."

Ibrahimah's sleep is deep that night as he dreams of dying and leaving the life of a Talibé in an airplane. The next evening Ahmed's associate Imam Farad from the nearby mosque pays little attention to the boys as he collects their three hundred francs. He doesn't wake them for prayer and he does not care to beat them for being short. A feeling of ease washes across Ibrahimah. Freedom tastes sweet.

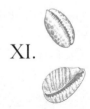

XI.

Islamic tradition insists that a corpse is buried within seventy-two hours of death. In the best-case scenario, the body is buried within hours of the death. It's not like a Talibé has never died under the care of a marabout, but everyone is talking about him and watching his every move, and word has already traveled down to the family. Ahmed would prefer to bury Abdoulaye's body in Dakar, limiting his costs, but expectations are high.

Ahmed arrives in the wee hours of morning and the boy's body is prepared and laid to rest later that afternoon. There is no tradition of open caskets and wakes. Abdoulaye's mutilated body is washed and wrapped in white muslin cloth. His father, uncles, and Ahmed go to the mosque to pray before the burial. Villagers pour into the family's small house throughout the day to pay their respects, bringing offerings of food and money. Abdoulaye's mother sits in the middle of the living room, overcome by a fit of uncontrollable sobbing. A woman ushers her into a back bedroom with smelling salts to calm her down. Ahmed eats a plate of fish and rice, glad that his impatient eyes are hidden behind his dark sunglasses. He'd like to be done with all this hoopla and leave the family to their own accord, but if he left too soon, word would move faster than a herd of bulls in flight. So, he sits, dozing off into a dream of boredom. He welcomes night and is given the best bed in the house to sleep in.

The next morning, without taking breakfast, he bids Abdoulaye's family adieu and travels the short hour journey to his own nearby village. Streetlamps and large flowerless trees grace the paved roads, adding to the sense that the tight rows of houses are impenetrable. The inhabitants of the large blood-red, burnt orange, and taupe homes prefer to stay inside, away from the heat that scorches the earth.

"Husband! I need money for the children's school fees and food," his first wife, Hawa, says as she opens the door.

"Greedy woman, is that how you greet me?" he says with reproach, and reaches into his robe pockets to pull out a wad of money. He counts out her monthly allowance of eighty thousand francs.

"Mhhh." She cuts her eyes at him, waddling away, money in hand, allowing him entry.

Hawa is less than a month away from delivering his fourth child. Something she is proud of, given that his second and third wives have yet to bear him any children. His oldest son brings his bags inside and hoists them upstairs without a word. Ahmed walks into the living room; the paisley overstuffed sofa is plush in comparison to his sparse living quarters in Dakar of just a bed and dirty plastic chair in his room, but one must make sacrifices to ensure his name and family line continue. Hawa brings him a heaping platter of thieboudienne, his favorite dish. She turns the television on and places the remote next to Ahmed, and he sits and eats the dry tomato-flavored rice and fish in silence. The maid shuffles around the house cleaning and dusting. The ceiling fan spins quietly up above.

"Papa!" his daughter shouts as she runs into the room, a large smile exposing her missing front teeth. She fixes her green T-shirt, which sits over her brown-and-gold ankle-length wrap skirt.

"Have you been good for your mother?" Ahmed says, not looking up from his food.

"Yes!" She seems like she's about to offer more, but then holds back.

She stands there, close but not touching him. Unsure of what to do with herself, she sits on the floor and gazes up into his face. His second son, more reserved than his seven-year-old sister, follows his sister into the room but lingers by the doorway.

"Eat," Ahmed instructs the nine-year-old boy.

The child takes two timid steps forward and grabs a handful of rice from the plate. The local news blares through the television speakers. Hawa returns with a large cup of bouye for him.

"Your mother is upstairs. She complains you do not come home enough," she says.

Ahmed shoves the last of the food into his mouth before rising from the couch. He walks solemnly up the tiled stairs and down the darkened hall, past the second living room and the shared bedrooms of his children. Perhaps, in a few years Cheikh will be old enough to manage the boys in Dakar so that he can enjoy more time here at home, in comfort.

Inside his mother's room the lights are out and the curtains pulled tight to protect her cataract eyes. At eighty-five years old she is still strong, and gets around on her own with relative ease, but needs her midday naps. He leaves the door open behind him, allowing passive light to enter.

"Mama."

"Ahmed? Is that you, my son? *Alhamdulillah!*"

He walks over to the edge of her bed and kisses the loose, wrinkled skin on her cheek.

"Help me sit up."

"Are you sure?"

"Yes."

Ahmed lifts her back up and stuffs several pillows behind her, then lights the candle on the dresser.

"Sit, my child," she says, tapping the space beside her. "My son, man of God. Tell me of your travels."

She clasps her hands in front of her as she speaks. Ahmed remembers the days she would sit hunched over the fire cooking rice and frying onions for yassa poulet, his father's favorite dish. She would sneak him a taste test of the tangy lime-onion sauce when no one was looking.

"Dakar is good, Mama. The Quran and the words of Prophet Mohammed are my guidance."

"Oh, my baby," she swoons, "if your father were alive to see you now. He did love you. He would be proud. How you've changed. Such a devout man of God. Disciplined, and admired by all."

Ahmed clucks his tongue and frowns down at the floor; he'd rather forget the memories of his father. He fingers the edge of the long, hidden scar that runs from his wrist all the way up his arm.

"How is my wife behaving? I hear you've had problems breathing?"

"No, no, I'm fine. The cleaning products were too strong and I choked a bit but I am fine. Hawa is a good wife."

She taps the top of Ahmed's hand. He misses his mother's tenderness more than he would like to admit. A man doesn't go chasing after his mother; his father would bark at him. His parents would argue over how best to raise him. His father would hit her and lock her in their bedroom for hours on end.

"Where is your mosquito net? I told that woman to put it up!"

He starts to rise from the bed, shouting for the maid.

"No, no, I tell her to take it down. I feel too closed in with it. Leave it. If it gets too bad, I'll have her put it up. Sit down, Ahmed. Keep your poor old mother company."

"I can't, Mama. I have business to tend to, but will come sit with you later. Do you want me to fix the pillows so you can lie down?"

"No, I'm fine," she says, never breaking her gaze, staring off into the shadows of the dark room as if some shiny magical thing lies right beyond her reach. He can't remember the last time she actually looked him in the eyes.

In the bathroom, he takes his sunglasses off to splash water onto his face. He looks into the mirror above the sink and scowls at his reflection.

"My monthly allowance is not enough; your fourth child will be here soon," Hawa says upon Ahmed's return to the living room. The two youngest children sit on the floor at her feet.

Ahmed stares at his nine-year-old from behind the dark sunglasses.

"Children, go play and leave your father be, he's tired from his travels."

"They're fine here with me. I never see them."

Hawa cuts her eyes away from her son and stares at Ahmed.

"Everything is too expensive. Rice, eggs, bread, your children eat more and more every day and the maid is too greedy. And the midwife, I will have to pay her too."

"Woman, shut up and leave me be. I know the cost of everything. Be satisfied with what you have, or perhaps I give you nothing."

Rolling her eyes, Hawa hoists herself up from the couch and walks out of the room.

"These women take, take, take and give nothing back," he says, to no one in particular.

The visual of Abdoulaye's naked body appears, and he imagines himself with the boy when he was alive; heat rushes up his thighs. His daughter hops up onto his lap, grabs his sunglasses, and plops them onto her small face. He snatches them back and pushes her off him. Unable to catch herself in time, she falls to the floor. She looks up, shock painted bright across her face, and runs out of the room, crying.

"Come sit on your father's lap," he instructs his nine-year-old son, who sits on the floor engrossed with the football match on television.

"But *Papa*," he whines, "I'm too old!"

"You miss your father?"

His son walks over to Ahmed, and sits down on the edge of the sofa next to his father. Ahmed strokes the boy's back while he thinks. To support three wives and a growing family he needs to increase the daily quota of his Talibé to four hundred francs. Twenty Talibé is not enough; his children will be educated, not poor farmers or street vagabonds peddling Chinese goods all day long.

"Go play while I work," Ahmed says, patting the boy on his back.

Fifteen more boys would be an additional hundred and eighty thousand francs a month, Ahmed calculates. With that he can give his two other wives a higher allowance, and they will not complain he is frugal, or spend their afternoons with the witch doctor hoping to find a potion to loosen his pockets. The more money his wives have to spend, the higher status he claims within his village. He can bring his eldest son, who is fifteen, to private school in Dakar.

To his surprise, over the course of the next week several families from his village approach him with their sons. Many take the murder of a Talibé as a direct attack on Islam. Ahmed is also offered two young women but refuses them with the claim that although Allah brings him much wealth, he is but a humble leader and makes peace with just three wives.

A marabout can acquire hundreds of wives because they are allowed to have more than the four wives of regular Muslim men. But he doesn't need any more mouths to feed, or any more women demanding sex from him. He rarely touches the other two and plans to keep it that way.

Rotating two days at each of his wives' homes throughout the week, he eats, sleeps, and lazes about while each cooks and fusses over him in her own way. Both his second and third wives are younger than Hawa, and he gives them each forty thousand francs to cover their living expenses for the month, though all three women have a way of finagling additional money from him.

By the end of the week he has five boys committed to return to Dakar with him and receives sixty thousand francs in offerings for prayer and blessings. Realizing the opportunity before him, Ahmed changes his plans and travels south to see how many more boys, and how much more cash, he can accumulate.

II.

XII.

With Marabout away for several days, the boys sleep in late, skipping morning prayer altogether. Ibrahimah watches Scarface rise from the floor, cross the room, and try the doorknob to Marabout's door, but it is locked. The boy shrugs and goes back to his cardboard mat and lies down. Ibrahimah can't imagine why anyone would *want* to go in Marabout's bedroom, voluntarily. The day is fresh on the horizon. Ibrahimah rolls over and thinks of the last time he and his sisters helped his father harvest the vegetables on their farm.

"It's too hot to work," Binta complained.

"But not too hot to eat?" their mother teased his sister.

Ibrahimah ran up to his father. "Papa, I will help you."

His father looked down at him and smiled and tapped the rim of Ibrahimah's straw hat.

"Okay. You can pick the string beans, only the really green ones though, like this one." His father held up a long bean.

Ibrahimah nodded.

"Okay, well, come close so that I can show you how to properly detach the bean. Pull too hard and you can rip the entire root out, which is bad. Pull too soft and it can break, and then you will stay hungry!"

Harvesting string beans was serious work, Ibrahimah thought as he watched his father closely. Binta was always hungry, so Ibrahimah had to make sure his sister had enough food to eat. After watching his father, he tried to do it. He placed his fingers at the base of the bean where it was attached to the vine and pulled, but the bean did not want to come loose.

"You have to pull a little harder," his father instructed.

Ibrahimah tried again and the bean detached from the vine. Elated, Ibrahimah jumped up and down.

"Papa! I did it," he exclaimed, holding up the sturdy string bean.

"You are a natural, my son, and there's an entire row of beans to pick, so let's get going," his father said.

In the musty, overcrowded room filled with Talibé boys, Ibrahimah can feel the warmth of that day in the sun with his father. He filled an entire pail with string beans before he looked up to find his sisters beneath the shade of a tree drinking water and snacking on a baguette with Laughing Cow cheese.

Ibrahimah looks over at Étienne, who is stretched out on his back with his eyes closed. Midmorning hunger soon motivates them to venture out into the city for the day.

"Where do we go today?" he asks as they step out into the daylight.

"We could go to the airport," Étienne says, though he doesn't sound enthused.

They rarely spend any time in the northern part of the city. With thousands of Talibé in the city, they stick to certain neighborhoods. They do not know how other Talibé will respond to new boys in their territory, but they are sure it would not go well. There are more and more Talibé showing up in Dakar all the time.

"I don't like the airport," Ibrahimah says. The one other time they went up to the airport to work, a Talibé he did not know knocked his front tooth out and he is still waiting for the tooth fairy to come.

"Yoff Beach? Today is Monday."

"Okay."

Ibrahimah loves the ocean and yet they almost never go up to Yoff Beach because it is a two-hour walk. But the beach is home to the women's fish market, the best one in Dakar. The fishermen go out to sea while everyone in the city is asleep and by five or six in the morning, they return with what they've caught, and the women are there waiting. They sell the fresh-caught fish on card tables, or on vinyl mats set out on the sand.

Ibrahimah knows about the women's fish market because he hears all about it through the thin wall between Marabout's house and Diatu's family's house.

Ibrahimah opens his sweaty palm; he has two large coins but only the dark-looking ones, not the shiny silver ones that are worth more money. The walk to the beach is long, and a mango would give him the energy he needs to make it. He looks over at Étienne, who seems unfazed by his morning hunger.

"Étienne, how much is this?" Ibrahimah asks, sticking his palm out.

Étienne looks at the coins and does the math silently.

"Fifty."

"What can I buy? I'm hungry," Ibrahimah says. Marabout is gone, so he is willing to spend his money on food.

"Peanuts."

Ibrahimah does not want peanuts. He wants a mango, or a plate of his favorite dish, mafé, or thieboudienne, or even yassa poulet. The more he thinks about food, the hungrier he gets. The cars along the road halt for a moment and he flings his body into the street.

"Food, please," he says, his hand sticking out.

The man rolls his window up. Ibrahimah sucks his teeth and runs up to the next car.

"I'm hungry," he announces to the man who pretends not to hear him. "I don't want money for my marabout. Do you have food? I'm hungry," Ibrahimah tries again.

The man looks at him.

"I don't have any food with me, Talibé," the man says.

Ibrahimah's shoulders drop and he walks away.

"Here," the man says, shoving a silver coin at him.

Ibrahimah takes the coin and thanks the man. He runs up to the next car and tries the same line again, and it works. He gets two brown coins. The traffic begins to move and he gets out of the way and hops back onto the sidewalk.

"Look." He shows Étienne, who is busy counting his money.

"Wow, you work really fast," Étienne says, impressed.

"Yeah, I told them I don't want money, I want food because I'm hungry. And then they give me money!"

Perhaps he has been doing this begging thing wrong the entire time. So far, what he has asked for he does not receive. So, maybe he should ask for what he does not want and he'll get what he wants. Ask for food and people will give him money; ask for life in Dakar with Marabout and perhaps he will get to return to his village and be with his family. When the traffic stalls again, he tries this new technique and again finds himself more successful than usual, the bottom of his red tin tomato can covered in coins clanging against each other, like the way the boys push up against one another over a small bowl of rice.

Two hours later, Ibrahimah's small belly protrudes over the top of his pants, overfull with greasy rice and the small pieces of lamb that swam within the heavy peanut-and-tomato sauce. He is ready to take on the rest of the day. By the time they reach Yoff Beach it is bustling with the energy of the locals and foreigners alike, all of whom seek the freshest seafood in the city.

The boys run down to the shore and jump into the waist-deep water. They bring their red tin cans so that no one steals their money. Large waves shove Ibrahimah's body around and he enjoys having to work to keep his balance. He wades back to shore to sit down on the sand next to Étienne, who stretches his legs out. The sun will dry his khaki pants and green polo shirt quick enough, and now they will be clean again. Senegalese boys and girls walk along the shore or laze about on the beach, enjoying themselves beneath the late-morning sun.

Ibrahimah lies down on his back and looks up at the sky. No planes or red birds in sight. The calm of the ocean's gentle roar mixed with fresh sea breeze and the warmth of the West African sun lulls him into a trance of relaxation. He is ready to drift off into a place of love and laughter when something blocks his light and kicks a tuft of sand into his face. He sputters and sits up to find a man looming above him with two boys who look a bit older than Étienne. Ibrahimah jostles Étienne awake.

"Talibé," the man starts, "you want to make money for your marabout?"

"What do you want?" Étienne asks. His voice is groggy and he has to shade his eyes to get a better look at the man.

The tall man looks down at Ibrahimah with an easy grin. Ibrahimah looks over at the two boys standing beside the stranger.

"Are you a Talibé?" Ibrahimah asks.

"I used to be," the taller boy says.

"What are your names?" the man asks.

"Étienne."

"Ibrahimah."

Étienne stands up and Ibrahimah follows his lead, making a bit of space between himself and the three strangers.

"I ran away from my marabout the other day," the shorter boy confesses.

"Are you all runaways?" the man asks Étienne and Ibrahimah.

"No," Étienne says.

"It's better if you run away," the tall boy says. "No one to beat you or force you to work for them. You keep your own money."

"I'm going home to my family soon. My marabout said after a year, I can go home," Ibrahimah announces.

The man laughs as if Ibrahimah told a joke. The taller boy joins him.

"Talibé, you are young. The world is a wicked place, if your marabout agrees to send you home, I will personally escort you back to your village myself. In the meantime, I have work I need help with back at my house. I will pay you each the daily quota your marabout demands and I will feed you dinner."

"What do you need help with?" Étienne asks, now considering it more seriously.

"The ceiling in one of the rooms in my house has collapsed and I need help moving the debris. Men would cost too much, but Talibé will do it for a day's income and food. It's a win-win for us both. I think four boys will do. I just met these two."

"I'm Demba," says the short boy.

"Lamine," says the taller boy with the long arms.

"Call me Pape," the man says.

Étienne looks at Ibrahimah to gauge how his cousin feels about the prospect. Ibrahimah does not feel they need to spend the day working. They already had a meal, and although they do not have Marabout's quota in full, they are not without money and with his new technique he may be able to raise enough for both of them by the day's end. Also, Marabout is not even in town, so if they come up short tonight, they will be okay.

"What Talibé thinks twice about making enough money for his marabout?" the man asks, laughing at them.

No Talibé who is smart, Ibrahimah thinks to himself.

"Okay, we come," Ibrahimah replies, and the two boys follow the group of three out to the main road.

Pape waves down a Car Rapide, and when it slows down the group of five jump in and he pays the fare for all of them. Stop after stop the large passenger van empties itself of customers. The bustle of inner-city Dakar is left behind and the more rural parts of the country, villages separated by long stretches of empty flatlands sprinkled with baobab trees, paint the landscape.

"Where is your house?" Étienne asks.

"Pikine," Pape says, looking up from his whispered conversation with Lamine.

Ibrahimah looks over at Demba, who sits staring out of the window.

"How long you been with your marabout?"

"A long time," Demba says, looking at Ibrahimah.

"Other boys at your daara run away?"

"A few."

Demba has open wounds on the top of his head, the side of his face, and all over his arms.

"What happened to you?" Ibrahimah asks, motioning to the boy's arms and face.

"My marabout beats me with a rubber whip."

"Not a stick?"

"No."

Ibrahimah cannot say whether a stick or a whip is better or worse, but Demba's wounds look painful.

"You're better off running away," Ibrahimah says.

Demba looks back outside the small window of the Car Rapide.

"Don't worry," Pape says to Demba. "The *Quotidien* says that there are over fifty thousand Talibé walking the streets of Dakar begging for hundreds of different marabouts. No one will miss you."

Ibrahimah looks up at Pape. Something in the man's voice bothers him, but he cannot articulate what he feels. He assumes that since there are four Talibé and only one man they will be fine. They are the last passengers in the Car Rapide when it arrives in Pikine thirty minutes later. They spill out onto the sandy ground; Ibrahimah's feet sink into the road. With the sun at their backs they walk down a side street and pass several small buildings. Short wooden fences and short cement walls surround the cheap houses. Ibrahimah can tell that the city of Pikine is not as wealthy as Dakar; wealthy people have high cement fences with metal doors.

Ibrahimah knows the house they are going to before Pape opens the front gate. The dilapidated wooden fence is taller than him but barely reaches Pape's chest. A mangy white cat walks along the top of it and looks down at the intruders entering its domain.

"Where is the work?" Demba asks, looking up at the house.

The mustard-yellow paint on the front door is peeling; the screen door is rusted and hanging off the hinge. Ibrahimah and Étienne exchange glances. Ibrahimah cannot read his cousin's face but his doubts are mounting. They trudge up the stairs and the man shoves the front door open. He hangs behind the group and once everyone is in, he fastens a padlock on the inside.

"What is that for?" Étienne asks, his eyes darting around.

"Only to keep the dogs out, they roam everywhere and will come right inside."

"No one wants to get attacked by a mad dog," Lamine says.

The house looks abandoned, covered in thick layers of dust and sand. Houses in Dakar need to be cleaned daily as the sand easily makes its way indoors.

"Over here, boys," Pape says, standing in front of the doorway of a room off to the right of the house.

Étienne and Ibrahimah enter the room first, with Demba on their heels; Lamine and Pape follow. The room is dark, as there is no electricity to be seen, but the room is illuminated with the day's natural light. The room is empty of furniture. Off in the far corner is a bundle of what Ibrahimah first makes out as clothes, until he gets closer and sees the legs of what looks like a boy. Flies buzz about and Ibrahimah slams into a wall of stench he has never experienced before. It is foul and rancid, worse than old spoiled meat. He attempts to walk over to the boy, but the foulness is too great for him. The boy is dead. Ibrahimah sees a chain connecting the dead boy's arms to a pipe that reaches from the floor to the ceiling.

Ibrahimah spins around and sees Demba make a dash for the door, but Pape catches him by the arm and they struggle. Pape drags him over to a radiator, where another chain lies in wait. Étienne starts for the door but Lamine grabs him.

"Ibrahimah! Run!" Étienne shouts as he fights with the boy, who is a bit taller than him but not that much heavier.

Ibrahimah wants to help Étienne. He cannot leave his cousin.

"Run!" Étienne shouts again.

With a burst of energy that comes from the pit of his stomach Ibrahimah runs for the door. This is not about protecting his money. These are not boys who want to take his food. This man wants everything. His body goes for the front door only to remember that it's bolted shut. His eyes drop and he notices a panel in the door hanging loose. He drops down to his knees and shoves his red tin can through the hole before he squeezes his body through and tumbles onto the front porch. He looks through the window of the room he was just trapped inside. Pape is chaining Demba to the wall and turns to help Lamine with Étienne, who has the strong boy in a headlock. Ibrahimah starts screaming his cousin's name.

"Étienne!"

Ibrahimah scans the messy porch full of debris, grabs a rock, and throws it through the window. Pape leaves the room and Ibrahimah runs into the yard, finds another rock, and pitches it through another window, all the while screaming.

"Étienne, don't let them kill you! Étienne! Someone, help!"

Ibrahimah can hear Pape struggling with the padlock inside the front door. He throws another rock through the window in an attempt to hit Lamine, and prepares himself to throw one at Pape the moment he gets outside, but before he can do that, Étienne comes flying out of the first window Ibrahimah broke, and lands on the porch.

"Run! Run!" Étienne screams.

Ibrahimah turns and breaks toward the dilapidated wooden fence. When he hits the sandy path, he turns his head and sees Étienne stumbling down the stairs and Pape bursting through the front door. Ibrahimah pumps his legs faster than he has ever worked them. Every ounce of energy, every breath that he possesses, streamlines into his arms and legs and allows his body to fly across the ground as if he has turned into a bird. He can no longer feel his legs; they don't struggle against the sand. His mind focuses only on the task at hand. He has to trust that his cousin is behind him. He knows that if he turns around, he will lose his focus and momentum, and that is all they need to catch him. Missing one beat would put him back in that room, chained to the floor, his body soon decaying as it gives up and releases itself from the pain and ill that these people hope to exert onto him.

Once he reaches the main road, he takes a left and does not stop. Up ahead he sees a Car Rapide facing toward Yoff. It's at the first and last stop, and is about to take off. Ibrahimah jumps onto the back of the van just as it begins to accelerate.

"Just in time, boy," the change man in the bright-red T-shirt says as he helps him up onto the seat.

Ibrahimah turns and looks back as the old Car Rapide gains momentum, its exhaust sputtering and complaining as the driver presses the stubborn vehicle to move.

Étienne is running toward the van with both Lamine and Pape on his heels.

"Étienne, run!" Ibrahimah screams, his voice cracking.

The change man stands on the back of the Car Rapide, holds on to the side of the van with one hand, and leans his body out long to Étienne. Ibrahimah feels the Car Rapide skip a beat before it finally wakes and begins to gain speed; the driver is a world away and disconnected from what is transpiring at the back of his vehicle.

"Come, boy," the change man shouts, "you can make it!"

Lamine stretches his long arms out and touches Étienne's shirt-tail, but it slips through his fingers. Étienne pumps his legs harder in a last burst of energy, leans forward, and grabs the change man's hand. The man hoists Étienne high and swings him toward the van, directly through the open door. Étienne lands on his feet, drops down to his knees, and tumbles along the floor. Lamine slows his run and stares after the Car Rapide, with Pape lingering behind him.

Étienne flops onto his back, clutches his chest, and heaves for air. Ibrahimah looks down at his cousin, who is bleeding from the side of his head and arm.

"They were trying to rob you?" the change man asks Ibrahimah.

He does not know how to explain what just happened, or why there was a dead boy chained to a pipe, or why they were trying to chain him, Étienne, and Demba. He looks back out the door, but Pape and Lamine are gone.

"Where you boys going?" the change man says.

"Ouakam," Ibrahimah says, uncoiling the palm of his hand to reveal the two coins he managed to keep through his escape.

"What are you doing all the way out here?"

"The man said he had work and would pay us."

Ibrahimah pays the man.

"You will need one hundred francs more for your brother to get all the way back to Ouakam."

That was all Ibrahimah saved from his can.

"Étienne, you have money?"

Étienne sits up and hands the man fifty francs. He approaches a woman with her daughter for the rest of his fare and she pays it for him. Étienne thanks her.

Ibrahimah pats the seat next to him and Étienne sits down. Both boys are quiet.

"Dakar is a dangerous place. You boys should stay closer to your marabout. What if the Car Rapide was not here? You could have been left there. Take this as a lesson," the man says.

Ibrahimah knows being out on the streets is dangerous, but he thought Marabout was worse than anything else the world could ever offer and that if they ran away, they would be able to keep their money for themselves; that they did not need Marabout. Perhaps this is why Étienne never ran away, and why his cousin believes Marabout is not so bad. Maybe he is not.

"What about Demba?" Ibrahimah says.

Étienne doesn't respond.

"We'll get new cans from Marabout," Ibrahimah says.

"Sure."

"You saved us, Étienne."

"No, I didn't. You did. If you didn't break that window, I wouldn't have had a way out."

"I love you, cousin," Ibrahimah says, his eyes wet.

"I love you too."

That evening when they tell Marabout's associate Imam Farad what happened that afternoon, he does not believe them. But they insist they are telling the truth and show him the cuts on Étienne's head and arm from the broken window. In the morning Farad calls the police. Étienne and Ibrahimah relay their story again.

"Would you remember the house?" the heavier cop, Officer Ba, asks.

"Yes," the boys say in unison.

The two officers, Ibrahimah, Étienne, and Imam Farad drive in the police car to Pikine.

"We know the way from the last stop on the Car Rapide," Étienne says.

Thirty minutes later, Ibrahimah finds himself retracing his steps from the day before, but this time with the security of men who are not trying to hurt him or Étienne.

"There." Ibrahimah points at the window he broke.

They lead the men through the wooden gate, its resident cat missing. Étienne pushes the front door open and the smell of the dead boy's body meets them at the door this time.

"You boys, stand back," Officer Ba says, stepping inside the house.

"They tried to keep us in the room there." Étienne points. "That's where the dead boy is, and the other boy."

"Stay outside," the skinny officer says as he follows his partner.

Moments later, Officer Ba runs outside and rummages through the trunk of the police car until he finds what he is searching for, then rushes back inside with a large metal object in his hand. Moments later Officer Ba carries Demba outside. The boy is dehydrated and exhausted, but alive. When he sees Étienne and Ibrahimah on the porch, he begins to cry.

"I thought you had left me," Demba says.

Imam Farad ushers Étienne and Ibrahimah through the gate and to the street.

Officer Ba exits with them and goes to his car to radio for backup and the coroner.

"Are the boys finished here?" Farad asks.

"Yes, we took their statements at the daara. If we need anything more, we'll reach out." Officer Ba looks down at Étienne and Ibrahimah. "You boys were very brave to escape and then report what happened to you and the other boy; you should be proud of yourselves. Allah smiles down on you."

Ibrahimah does not feel particularly proud of himself. He cannot put into words the terror he felt when he realized there was a dead body in the corner of the room, and that Pape and Lamine had tricked them into entering the house. He doesn't understand what they wanted. His mind struggles to make sense of it all.

"Were they going to cut out my organs like they did to Abdoulaye?" Ibrahimah asks.

"You are safe now, Ibrahimah. There is no need to think about that," Farad says.

Ibrahimah looks over at Étienne, who does not look so convinced.

"Young Talibé, you have to be careful and pay attention out here," the officer says.

Imam Farad takes them down the road and they catch a Car Rapide back down to Ouakam. There is a different change man on the Car Rapide today; he wears a navy-blue shirt and brown rust-colored pants and is not as chatty as the younger man was yesterday. When they reach Ouakam, they get out of the van and stand looking up at Farad, but he sends them on their way. They have a lot of work to do to make up for the lost day of income yesterday.

 XIII.

"Maimouna!"

"Yes, Idrissa?" Maimouna asks, looking up from studying the fine cracks on the tile floor.

"Did you hear that?"

"Hear what?"

"Marabout Ahmed lost one of his Talibé to murder in Dakar," Idrissa says a little too loud, his eyes filled with worry.

Madame Touré says, "I would bring my child home. Dakar is not as safe as it used to be. Before you could leave your rams to walk themselves in the evenings for exercise. Try that now and someone will steal them!"

"Dakar is fine! Our boys are fine. Allah will protect them," Maimouna's brother-in-law says.

"Humph, like that young Talibé whose organs were stolen? Do you even know it wasn't your son? I hear the marabout is passing this way in a few days," says Madame Touré.

"It wasn't either of our sons," Idrissa says. "Ahmed has already brought the boy to his family and buried him. Allah is protecting *my* son."

"What do you mean? You believe Allah protects only certain

children? I thought all Talibé were sacrificing for Allah. Why should one be more protected than the other? It could have well been Ibrahimah," Madame Touré's husband says.

"Please, please. Everyone, calm down. This isn't the time for argument," Idrissa says.

Maimouna wishes she were not present for this discussion. If she closes her eyes and allows her body to become very still, she can feel his small body leaning up against her thigh, his big almond eyes inquiring for more milk. It was a horrible idea to send him away. They should have never done it.

Later that evening, after the last of their guests have gone and the gunpowder tea is finished, Maimouna gets in bed beside Idrissa.

"Husband, what if it *was* Ibrahimah?"

"Ibrahimah is still too small. His organs would never support an adult. It's usually adult organs needed."

"Everything in this world is for sale. The wicked would steal their grandmother's heart and put it up for sale," Maimouna says.

"Allah will protect Ibrahimah. I know it in my heart. Have faith, my love."

"I want him back. The safety and well-being of our son comes before anything else in this life. Marabout Ahmed said he'd teach Ibrahimah for a year and then bring him home. The year is almost done."

"I know, my love. My heart is with our son, and I pray for his speedy return just as you do." Idrissa rolls over and wraps his arms around her. Neither of them sleeps well.

Fatou enters her parents' bedroom at first light, Idrissa's side of the bed cool to the touch, as he has left for work more than an hour before dawn. "Mama, I saw Madame N'Diaye this morning while fetching water and she needs an order of fifty patties for this afternoon," Fatou says.

"We'll need more water," Maimouna says.

Fatou grabs two pails and heads down the hill; her sisters are nowhere to be found at the moment.

Maimouna catches a glimpse of a woman walking toward her; the woman is a shadow with the sun sitting behind her tall hourglass figure. She drags her sandaled feet through the hot sand; a platter filled with peanuts, dates, and fruit lies on top of her head. Maimouna has all but lost her motivation to breathe the fresh morning air. Puffy bags cup her eyes and the thought of food makes her nauseous.

When the woman arrives at her door, Maimouna sees an infant is tied to her back.

"Did you hear about the Talibé who tried to return to his village?" the woman asks.

In a small village everyone knows which families have Talibé in Dakar.

"You mean the boy who was murdered?" Maimouna corrects her.

"No, this is after. An older boy ran away from his marabout and returned to his village. He was from Rufisque, just a few hours away from Dakar. He was able to get himself home."

"Well, what about it?"

"This boy was so afraid after the news of the dead Talibé that he returned to his village. His marabout searched all over for him and quickly went to the police for fear it might be another kidnapping. The marabout called his family to report him missing, but instead learned the boy was home."

"What happened?" Maimouna asks, her interest piqued.

"The marabout demanded the boy back, said the code of the Talibé brotherhood demands the boy to remain with the marabout until he is fifteen, if a marabout deems so. The boy refused to return."

"And?"

"The boy's father brought him back to Dakar, of course, and whipped him in front of his marabout for being a coward."

The woman's story seeps down deep into the pit of Maimouna's stomach.

"The boy only has two more years until he turns fifteen and then he can leave his marabout. It made no sense to run away," the woman says with a slight shrug.

The woman takes her leave and continues down the sandy path looking for customers. A dark fog descends upon Maimouna. She moves blindly through the morning and when the patties are done, instead of having Fatou deliver them, she cleans herself up and walks them over. While Madame N'Diaye quickly fetches the money to pay her, Maimouna offers a graceful smile and inquires about the occasion.

"You didn't hear? Marabout Ahmed is passing through sometime this evening and we've requested a special audience with him. You should come with an offering and receive blessings."

Maimouna offers a curt smile. "How are your daughter and her husband?"

"Oh, they are wonderful. She loves being a wife. She and the first wife get along just fine. She's hoping to be pregnant soon."

"That's wonderful. I wish them many blessings," Maimouna says, folding her hands in front of her.

"Thank you! Look here, my daughter sent me a new flat-screen television!"

"Did you hear about the Talibé that ran away back to his village?"

"Oh, yes! What an ungrateful child! In the name of Allah, what a disgrace." She clucks her tongue.

Maimouna remains silent as her neighbor flails her arms in the air to emphasize her point.

"People say his mother allowed him to stay with his grandmother without her husband even knowing! What a wicked woman; her husband should beat her for the deception. Some people cannot be taught righteousness and virtue. They will behave like fools even with Allah looking right at them."

Maimouna clears her throat. "I have to go now, but will pay a visit later."

Back at home, Maimouna begins preparing dinner but anxiety grips at her chest. Ibrahimah's situation is different from these other boys. It was one of Marabout Ahmed's Talibé that was murdered! She lights a fire to boil the potatoes. Would Ahmed go back on his promise to return Ibrahimah?

"Mama! Watch out, your arm!" Fatou screams from the doorway.

Maimouna's body jerks at the disruption, the sleeve of her shirt on fire. The flames lick at the air, trying to catch anything else within their vicinity. She snatches her arm back and Fatou, moving quickly, douses several cups of water on her mother's arm while Maimouna smacks at the flames with the dishrag. Overpowered, the small fire dies.

"Mama, are you okay?"

Fatou comes closer to her, arms outstretched in an attempt to view the wound without touching her mother.

Maimouna stares down at her arm, blinking several times before she can find her words.

"I'm okay, it's just a surface burn," Maimouna says. She walks out of the kitchen to her room.

Fatou follows.

"Mama, is there anything I can get you?"

Maimouna sits down on the edge of her bed and shakes her head no.

"Mama, we need to take care of your arm."

"Daughter, I worry only about Ibrahimah."

Fatou sits down beside her.

"Will he be able to come back home like the marabout promised?"

"I should hope so. Marabout Ahmed said one year," Maimouna says, looking out the window.

"Well, me, Binta, and Aisha have been praying every night for Ibrahimah to return home safely."

Maimouna looks at her daughter.

"I have the best children in the world," she says, touching Fatou's cheek with her wounded hand.

"Stay here, I will get a bandage," Fatou says, hopping off the bed.

Her eldest reminds her of herself; mature and responsible beyond her years; smart, loving, and resilient. Fatou treats her siblings with the same care Maimouna treated her younger cousins, but instead of being the family workhorse, Fatou is full of pride and loves her role as the big sister.

"You constantly remind me of myself," Maimouna says when Fatou returns.

"I want to be like you," Fatou says, dropping her head.

"Like me? No. You will be better. You will finish school, go to college, and become a doctor or lawyer."

"I want to be a schoolteacher," Fatou says as she wraps her mother's forearm.

"You'll be the best teacher in America."

"Africa," Fatou corrects her mother. "I want to live close to you and Papa. You mean too much to me to ever go so far away."

Maimouna smiles and thinks of her own mother and how little time they have spent together over the span of her life. She runs her fingers across the bandaged arm. The pain doesn't compare to the agony she feels in her heart for Ibrahimah.

"We will get Ibrahimah back, don't worry. I feel it in my heart," Fatou says, getting up and leaving the room after planting a kiss on her mother's cheek.

When Idrissa gets in later that evening, her bandaged arm is the first thing he notices. Maimouna waves her hand. "I'm fine, just a small accident while cooking. Marabout Ahmed will be in Saloulou this evening."

"I know," he says, placing his hat onto the dresser.

"Did you hear about the Talibé that returned back to his village?"

"I did."

"It's time for Marabout Ahmed to return Ibrahimah home," Maimouna says. "The year is almost up. He should send him back early. Wouldn't that be nice? Ibrahimah reunited with his sisters. He is too young to be a Talibé."

Idrissa runs his hands along the length of Maimouna's back in a soft caress. After dinner he visits the N'Diaye house while Maimouna waits for him at home.

She braces herself for the joy she'll feel when Ibrahimah comes bounding through the door into her outstretched arms, in the same manner she did when she and her mother were finally reunited after her years in Dakar. She wonders why Idrissa is taking so long. Unable to busy her mind any longer, she retreats to bed, where she lies awake praying, her body trembling with nervous anticipation. Hours pass before Idrissa returns. When she hears his footsteps, she pops up from the bed.

"So," she says, searching his face, "when is our son coming home?"

"My love"—Idrissa takes a deep breath—"he's not."

"What?"

"Ahmed says Ibrahimah is his best student and there's no way he can relinquish custody of him now."

"But it's been a year!"

"I reminded him of our agreement, but he says Allah cannot allow such a travesty to happen."

"What does that mean? Ibrahimah can never come home?"

Idrissa sighs loudly. "When Ibrahimah is fifteen, he'll let him go."

Idrissa sits on the edge of the bed and drops his head into his hands.

Maimouna throws the pillow across the room.

"No!" she shouts, dashing from their bedroom, through the house and out the door. Her feet sink into the thick, soft sand, but she doesn't feel anything except the thunder inside. Rage boils within her stomach, rises up through her chest, and explodes into the back of her throat. Shocked by her outburst, Idrissa lags behind her; he calls to her as she runs toward Madame N'Diaye's house.

Bursting through the front door, Maimouna heads straight into the living room.

Ahmed looks up from the chair, where he is eating his second dinner. Madame N'Diaye sits to his left, her husband to his right. Without a moment's hesitation Maimouna rushes across the room, flinging herself at Ahmed. The table tips to the side against the force of her body and the food flies across Ahmed's lap. Maimouna's arms flail in attack.

Madame N'Diaye's husband stumbles to the floor as Ahmed tries to push Maimouna off to no avail. She digs her fingers into his face and eyes.

"Give me my son back!"

He screams out in pain. She spits in his face, clawing deep red valleys into his black skin.

"Get. Off. Me. You wretch!"

"I'll kill you." Maimouna bites his face. Ahmed's scream morphs into a shrill wail as he struggles beneath the weight of her anger. Maimouna feels hands grabbing, pulling at her but she clings to Ahmed and digs her nails into his skin. Scratching. Tearing. He will feel the pain she does. She will not let go.

The effort to pull her away creates a small space between herself and Ahmed. He takes this opportunity to free his arms and pulls his left hand back, fingers balled into a fist. He punches Maimouna dead center in the face. Pain screams through her eyes and nose. He punches her again. Maimouna's grip on his neck loosens. She screams and flails her arms blindly in front of her, unwilling to give up, to be defeated once again. The two men behind her lift her up and away. Ahmed now takes this opportunity to get up and hits her again.

"Stop hitting my wife!"

Idrissa pushes Maimouna to the side, and rushes up to Ahmed with balled fists. Madame N'Diaye and her husband stand in his way.

"Go home, my brother. Help your wife calm down!"

"Give me my son back. Give him back to me!" Maimouna screams from behind Idrissa. Blood gushes from her nose and mouth. Idrissa pushes past Madame N'Diaye and shoves Ahmed back down into his chair. Ahmed throws his arms up above his head in fear.

Madame N'Diaye and her husband overpower Idrissa and pull him away before he can take another step forward.

"This is uncalled for! How dare you come to my house behaving like an animal!" Madame N'Diaye screams.

"Animal? He's the animal. He's a liar!" Maimouna shouts.

"You will never get your son back. You hear? You crazy whore! The day he returns to you, he'll be wrapped in muslin cloth. I'll make sure of it. Get these wicked people out of my sight!" Ahmed growls. He raises his hand to his face and winces in pain when his fingers land on the bleeding rivers etched across his face.

"Ibrahimah is my child! He doesn't belong to you!" Maimouna sobs.

"Do as I say! Get them out!" Ahmed barks at his hosts.

"Brother Idrissa, please go home. I don't want to have to call the police. You have other children to think about. Please. Go."

Madame N'Diaye starts toward Maimouna, but her husband holds her back. Idrissa turns around, gathers Maimouna into the fold of his arms, and walks her out of the house.

XIV.

The rain is falling so hard that Ibrahimah can't keep his eyes open. It comes in thick sheets and his eyelids are not strong enough to bear the weight of the downpour. So, he walks with his eyes closed, opening them every few seconds to gauge where they are walking. The streets of Point E are flooded up to the middle of his calf, the water rushing in the direction he and Étienne are walking, insisting on getting there faster than them. The sky is dark, making it seem as if night has fallen, but Ibrahimah knows that it's not even lunchtime yet. The intensity of his hunger pains marks the time of day. Étienne taps his shoulder and motions for Ibrahimah to follow him. The streets are empty, its middle-class inhabitants tucked inside warm houses. Not even a taxi passes by, the weather is so bad. Ibrahimah shivers as rivulets of rain fall down his face.

"At least we get a bath," Ibrahimah chatters.

They go inside a computer café, and Étienne approaches the young guy at a small desk in the empty shop, dripping the whole way. The man walks out back for a moment, returning with a small frayed towel that has been cut from a larger one. Étienne dries himself off as best he can and then hands the towel to Ibrahimah, who follows suit.

"Come over here," the young man instructs the two boys.

They cross the room to find a small heater on behind his desk and huddle near it. Ibrahimah looks over at the three phone booths lined up on the opposite side of the store. His family does not have a phone, and he does not remember seeing his neighbors with phones. He has only seen one in Moustapha's house and in his village's telecentre, where his mother would go to call his *Maam* sometimes.

"How would I call my village?" Ibrahimah asks the shopkeeper.

"Do you have a phone number?"

"No."

"You need a phone number to call anywhere, little Talibé. Where do you live?"

"Saloulou."

"Is that in the south?"

Ibrahimah pauses a moment; does he live in the south? He knows he lives farther from Dakar than he had ever traveled before. His *Maam* came and visited them once, but he has never gone to visit her in Guinea. He always wished she would stay and live with them in Saloulou but his mama said *Maam* liked her own home too much to leave.

"Yes, we are from the south," Étienne says.

"How do you know?" Ibrahimah asks. Étienne always knows the answer to everything, like Fatou.

"Because I asked Marabout one day and he told me."

"When was this?" Ibrahimah asks, surprised that a boy could have an actual conversation with Marabout.

"This is before you came. I would sometimes come home early and Marabout would let me pray with him in the evenings," Étienne says, looking away.

Ibrahimah's mind races trying to make sense of what his cousin is saying. This was not the marabout he knew at all.

"Marabout used to be nice?" Ibrahimah asks.

"Not all marabouts are bad, little one," the shopkeeper says.

"I don't know, maybe," Étienne says, answering Ibrahimah's question with a shrug.

The shopkeeper looks at Étienne and then back to Ibrahimah.

"Well, sometimes there is a price to pay for kindness, little one. Do you bring gifts for your marabout?"

"I give him all my money. Why am I supposed to also give him gifts?"

The door of the shop flies open and a gust of wind brings a rough spray of rain. The young man hops up to shut the door. Ibrahimah shivers at the thought of going back outside. His clothes are still wet and uncomfortable.

"What is your name?" Étienne asks the shopkeeper.

"Baba. And yours, little Talibé, what are your names?"

"Étienne."

"Ibrahimah," he says, and looks out the door. "How long do you think the rain will last?"

Étienne looks at Baba, curious to see what he thinks.

Baba pauses a moment. "I think most of the day. Look at how heavy and steady the rain is. This is not a passing storm. It's here till evening."

Ibrahimah's shoulders drop. He is pleased to be inside from the rain but to lose the entire afternoon is not what he had hoped to hear. He looks down into his red tin can and sees only two small coins. He needs big coins. The shopkeeper does not look rich enough to give him what he needs, and the rain is too assaulting to get over to Moustapha's house. Plus, if his friend is not home, they'd be stuck farther away from everything with no refuge. He looks at his cousin and finds Étienne quiet, more than likely calculating what it is they need to do to make this day successful. But the spirits must have heard Ibrahimah's wishes, because after two hours the rain halts, to their amazement. Within minutes Baba receives several customers needing to make phone calls.

"Local calls are twenty-five francs a minute," he tells a girl, pointing to the sign above the booth. "International calls are more. Where are you calling?"

"Mali," the girl says. She turns to Ibrahimah and sees his hand open. "After," she tells him.

"Okay, that is fifty francs a minute."

"Okay, give me twenty minutes," she says, handing the young man five hundred francs.

Baba looks over at the boys.

"If you want, I can look to see if I can find a telecentre in your village. Some villages only have one. If that is the case, you could call it and talk to your parents."

Ibrahimah never thought talking to his mother or father was possible. Baba walks over to his desk, opens the large plastic binder, and flips through it for several moments. He scours a page, flips to another, and then flips back to the page he looked at before. He shakes his head in disappointment.

"This binder has numbers for many villages across Senegal, but usually just the most frequently called villages. I don't see yours on here. Do you know any of the villages nearby?"

The boys shake their heads no.

"Well, if you ever do, come back and we can try to see if the nearby village has a telecentre."

Ibrahimah's shoulders drop.

"It would have been too easy," Étienne says.

"Yeah," Ibrahimah says.

"Boy," the young woman says, tapping his shoulder.

Ibrahimah looks up and she hands him a coin. Étienne looks into his can. Sitting in the shop was worth something. If they were not so hungry, they would stay at the shop longer, but instead they head out to find food. Walking along the side streets in Point E, the city feels cleaner, the trees appear greener, and the air is fresher. Ibrahimah takes a deep breath and wonders what his sisters are doing.

"Let's go to the ocean," he says. The sea always makes Ibrahimah feel closer to his village. He is aware that, at some point, the ocean meets the shore of his home. All of the ocean is connected, and so he really is not that far away from his family.

They walk over to the On the Run parking lot and find Fatik and their other Talibé brothers. It's the magic that happens after a monsoon: the humidity is gone, it's cooler outside, people pour out of their homes, traffic magically reappears, and everyone is in good spirits. They take advantage of this short window of opportunity.

"Boy," Étienne says, turning to Fatik. "You coming?"

"Where?"

"La Corniche."

"Aye," Fatik shouts over to Caca and the others. "La Corniche!"

They walk down the Rue de Ouakam and take a right, toward the coast. La Corniche is the westernmost tip of Senegal. Open land and beach greet both traffic and pedestrians traveling down the smooth paved road from Ngor, the northern tip of Dakar. Cliffs tumble onto narrow sandy beaches below; rough ocean waters kiss the rocky shores that dominate the coastline. Only a few scattered beaches are swimmable.

The boys walk over to the edge of the cliff and sit down amongst a smattering of boulders. It's a clear hundred-foot drop onto the narrow strip of rocky black sand below, and the incoming tide crashes violently against the bowels of the cliff. Salty sprays of ocean water ride the determined winds and brush against Ibrahimah's face. He looks across the water, arms open wide, and leans against the never-ending gusts of wind.

"Look at me! I fly. Brrrrrrrr! Brrrrrrrrr!"

Étienne laughs.

"What sounds like brrrrrr?" Fatik asks, frowning in confusion.

"Airplane! Brrrrrrr! Boom!"

"What goes boom?"

"Look! Airplane there! Listen. Brrrrrrrrrr. Boom!"

The sound of Ibrahimah's voice is overtaken by the low-flying Air France jetliner heading toward the airport in Yoff, less than three miles away.

"I go to Paradise in the sky with Abdoulaye!"

Ibrahimah's lips are moving rapidly but no one can hear him. He can't even hear his own voice. The ground vibrates beneath his feet. He's sure he will take off into the skies any moment now. Two minutes later Fatik concedes the "brrrrrr" is the ground shaking and the "boom" is the airplane's engine.

Étienne searches the ground for rocks and begins tossing them out into the sea. Ibrahimah abandons his game of airplane and follows suit, his small arms barely clearing his rocks off the edge of the cliff.

"I can throw more far than you," Scarface challenges. When he smiles, the scar across his cheek becomes more pronounced. Ibrahimah always has to look twice to make sure he's smiling and not grimacing in anger.

"Let's have a contest," Étienne suggests.

All six boys line up side by side.

"Together, we throw rocks and see who can throw the best," Étienne instructs.

Ibrahimah is excited to be included.

"One, two, three, go!"

The rocks glide through the air.

Ibrahimah pouts as his rock hits the edge of the cliff and tumbles down along the sloping wall, never making it down to the water.

"Mine wins!" Fatik shouts.

"Let's go again!"

The boys move a bit closer to the edge of the cliff to get a better look at the distance of their rocks. Again, and again, the boys search out stones around their feet, count to three, and fling them as hard as they can. Twice, Ibrahimah's stones make it into the water, making him feel like one of the big boys.

Down at the other end of the beach they spot wrestlers running with an entourage of twenty-five to thirty dusty-looking boys and girls. Wrestling is the second-biggest sport in Senegal, after football. The matches bring men, boys, and women alike to the stadium and the large athletes are regarded with much admiration. They train on the beach, next to the natural air conditioning of the ocean, and scores of children and adults will watch them and sometimes join in on the exercises. A few glances are exchanged and Étienne offers a simple "Let's go," and the group seeks out a manageable path down to the water.

Once they hit the sand, the wrestlers are quite far down the coast. Instead of trying to catch up they begin their own wrestling match. Fatik grabs Ibrahimah and slips him into an easy headlock, then flings him onto the sand. The group cheers for Fatik as he raises his fists in victory. Grinning from ear to ear, Ibrahimah stands with sand stuck to the side of his face and takes off full-speed toward Fatik, catching him from behind and mowing him down face-first.

"Ohhhhhh!" the group shouts as the underdog takes the champion down.

Ibrahimah does a little victory dance, swaying his narrow hips from side to side.

"Aye! Boys. Get off the beach! The tide is too dangerous to swim here. See that sign?" A man appears and points to the small sign.

XXX PAS DE BAIGNADE XXX

"We're not swimming," Fatik yells back.

"Well, it's too dangerous. The tide is coming in quick, off the beach."

As the man approaches, Ibrahimah can see that he is a lifeguard. Ibrahimah remembers the last time he was at the ocean too late in the day. Marabout found him. He grabs his can and starts marching off the beach and back up the hill without a word. Noticing he is leaving, the others follow suit. They spend the next two hours searching for more money and food before heading to Ouakam. When Marabout is traveling, they come home earlier than usual and hang out in the neighborhood with the local kids.

"Étienne, will you tell me a story like you did last night?" Ibrahimah asks, approaching the stairs to Marabout's house.

"What story do you want to hear?"

"When the warrior climbs the mountain with the elephants."

"Okay. There was once a great African warrior by the name of Hannibal, and he was feared by many. He promised to conquer Rome, and to do that he climbed the Alp Mountains with many elephants and soldiers, because that is what no one would expect him to do."

Ibrahimah walks into the house and starts to yawn, but he spots a group of fifteen boys sitting on the floor. His yawn is disrupted and lost in the most dissatisfying way.

"Who are you?" Fatik blurts.

Quiet eyes peer up at the group of dirty, barefoot boys standing before them. The boys at the back of the group who have yet to see the strangers are still talking but are hushed quickly by those in front.

"Where did you all come from?" Caca asks.

"Who are you talking to? Shut up and come here with my money!" Ahmed growls from his bedroom door.

The boys fall quiet; laughter ceases, smiles fade. Ibrahimah's heart begins to race and he forgets to breathe.

"You! Come here."

Ibrahimah looks behind him and then back at Marabout, who looks very strange with bloodstained scabs and welts crisscrossing his face. Marabout Scarface.

"I'm talking to you, you ungrateful, wicked boy. Ibrahimah," he snaps, "come to me now."

Ibrahimah's eyes drop to the floor; he should have stayed at the back of the group. He'll never walk into the house first again. Dragging his feet across the tiled floors his sandals make a scraping sound that causes Ahmed to scowl at him.

"Your mother"—spit flies from his mouth onto Ibrahimah's head—"is dead. Your parents are dead. You'll never see them again, and if you do, you won't be breathing. You belong to *me*. Do you hear?"

Ibrahimah is frozen. His parents are dead?

"Mama and Papa are dead, like Abdoulaye?"

Someone puts their hand on his shoulder and he turns around. Étienne looks him in the face with sad eyes.

"Yes. They're dead because you've been wicked. You're disobedient and think you are better than the others with your shoes and Western clothes. Did you think I would send you back home after a year? This is your home. Give me my money and get out of my face. The sight of you makes me sick. I should beat you." Ahmed pulls a dirty white plastic chair from the corner of the room and sits down, palm facing up.

Ibrahimah begins to cry. Étienne grabs the three hundred francs out of Ibrahimah's red tin can and hands the money along with his own over to Ahmed. He takes Ibrahimah's hand and pulls him toward the far side of the room. The other boys line up and begin the epic procession to turn their money in; weeks before, when he first left, they discussed saving three hundred francs specifically for the day Marabout returned. Even if they were short other days, the day Marabout did return would offer nothing less than a horrible fate if any of them did not have the correct amount of money.

"Mama's dead?" Ibrahimah whispers to himself, struggling to fully comprehend the news as they stand against the wall waiting for the others to finish. The new boys steal glances at him, afraid for themselves.

"Shut up about your whore of a mother!"

Étienne hugs Ibrahimah and wipes his face with the bottom of his shirt. Ibrahimah does not know what to do or say. How did his parents die? Where were his sisters? Were they okay? To whom would he go home to? Fatou? As the last boy hands in his three hundred francs, Ahmed offers a rare smile and looks out across the quiet room.

"You all have my money. This is good, because it confirms you can easily collect more. You will bring me four hundred francs starting tomorrow. Do you know how much that is?"

Thirty-five sets of eyes stare at Ahmed unblinking, the new boys stare in sheer fright, the veterans are stoic.

"Four of these," Ahmed says, holding up four one-hundred-franc coins, "eight of these, sixteen of these, and lots of these. If you're not sure you have enough, ask one of your older brothers who knows how to count. If you do not bring back four hundred francs, you will be beat and sent to sleep outside. It is expensive to take care of you. You each have to hold up your end of the agreement or I will not hold up mine."

One of the new boys begins to cry.

"Stop sniveling like a girl before I beat you with this stick. You are a Talibé. A man! Men do not cry for their mothers!"

Ahmed waves his cane at the boy, who quickly inhales his snot and stifles his sobs.

"These are your new Talibé brothers," Ahmed says to the veteran twenty boys, waving his cane at the group of newcomers.

"I'm tired. The journey has been long. Make any noise to wake me and you will answer to my wrath. Now go to bed!"

Ahmed goes to his room, slamming the door behind him. The boys sit, quiet. The sound of Ahmed climbing into bed fills the space and then a deeper silence follows. When they are sure he is asleep they begin to whisper.

"Four hundred francs is too much," Caca says.

"How are we to do that?" Fatik asks.

"Too much money."

"Marabout is greedy. All he wants is money, money, money. Now he brings more boys and wants more money!" Fatik growls.

In small groups they fetch their cardboard mats and lay them down, weaving through the new boys as if they were just one more obstacle. The fifteen newcomers watch them and then two get up to grab a mat and find a place to lay them down. The others move too slow.

"There are only three mats left," a tall boy complains.

"Shhhhh!"

The others don't offer help to the newcomers, but they put their mats closer together to make space. Étienne sucks on his teeth.

"How these boys leave the village to come to Dakar and live this life? They're crazy."

Ibrahimah does not care about the new boys. His parents are dead and maybe even his sisters. He will never survive living with Marabout the rest of his life; begging for money, getting beat on a whim, being forced to stay in the room with him. Now Marabout wants an extra big coin, the coin that he would use for a Coca. He sits up, folding his arms across his tiny chest.

"Do you want to hear the rest of the story?" Étienne doesn't know what else to offer his cousin.

"No. I hate Marabout!"

"Shhhh! No noise. You'll wake him."

"I don't care! I want to leave this place."

"Cousin, go to sleep. We talk tomorrow. Think of your mama and papa in heaven with Allah."

Ibrahimah lies down. He had planned to tell Marabout about the two men and the dead boy, but now all he wants is his mother. She would hold him and make things okay. She would know what to do and make Marabout stop being so mean and wicked. A waterfall filled with grief and sorrow forms an ocean beneath his head. The next morning Ahmed doesn't come out of his room. He sleeps late into the afternoon and when he wakes, the house is empty.

 XV.

It has been three weeks and the swelling of her eye has yet to subside, a small black ring sits below the puffiness. Idrissa worries about her; she has no strength. In the evenings she doesn't join him and the girls for dinner. It started with severe headaches and malaise. Idrissa thought perhaps Maimouna was pregnant. She eventually stopped giving an excuse for staying in bed.

"Wife, what can I get for you?" Idrissa asks, leaning against the entryway of their room.

"Nothing." Maimouna rolls over and sets her back to him.

"Why don't you join me in the living room for tea?"

"I'm not well. I prefer to stay here and rest."

"But my love, I have news I want to share with you. A friend of my father stopped by Marabout Ahmed's house in Dakar. He said both Ibrahimah and Étienne are healthy and well."

The scene of her lunging at Ahmed replays over and over in her head. She should have brought her cooking knife.

"Did you hear me, Maimouna? Our son is doing well."

"Which friend was it of your father that went by, do I know him?"

Idrissa falls silent.

"You're a terrible liar," she says, closing her eyes. Nothing short of Ibrahimah standing by her bedside will soothe her. She closes her eyes and goes to sleep.

The next morning Fatou walks into the room and pulls the curtains aside, allowing the harsh light inside.

"Close the curtains!" Maimouna covers her eyes.

"But Papa said—"

"I don't care what your father says. You are my daughter and will do as I say. Shut the curtains now."

Fatou pulls the curtains shut and sits down on the edge of the bed.

"People in the village say you've gone crazy. I tell them you are ill with fever. Fever makes people do things they don't want. My friends say you attacked a marabout. Madame N'Diaye says she should have called the police and had you arrested."

Fatou pauses for a moment.

"On Friday, the imam talked about the weakness of the mind and how following the teachings of Allah can save a man. He also talked about when a man's wife commits a wrong it is up to the husband to be a good Muslim and practice his faith diligently to ensure she makes it to heaven."

Maimouna listens to Fatou with disgust but cannot help her curiosity. When her neighbor next door doused her sleeping husband in acid for marrying a second wife, the imam gave the same talk in the weeks following the incident. Rumor is, the woman's family whisked her off to Côte d'Ivoire before the police could get their hands on her. She remembers waking up out of her nap that Sunday afternoon to the sounds of desperate screams as his body burned, layer after layer, the acid tearing through his skin, muscle, and bone. The wife also poured acid in a large puddle around his bed, making it impossible to get to him without taking precautions. He died on that bed before anyone could save him. Everyone talked about it for weeks, not because of the weapon she used, but because she used it to kill her husband and not the second wife.

"Do you want me to go on?" Fatou says.

Silence.

"Uncle says Papa should divorce you and take us girls away. He and Papa have been arguing about it every Sunday. Papa says you need time and that it's not your fault because Marabout lied to him. He says Marabout should be in jail for keeping Ibrahimah. Uncle gets upset when Papa says that."

Fatou takes a deep breath.

"I brought you some tea from Auntie. She says it will help."

Maimouna sits up and sips the pungent drink from the cup. She gags on it and pushes the cup back to Fatou and drops her head heavy against the pillow. It tastes like metal.

"What else?"

"Nothing much else. Many people don't speak to us anymore. Others scowl at us down at the well. Madame Diop's daughter claimed I shouldn't be able to fetch water like everyone else because you're a disgrace to our village. But Madame Touré told her to stop and I was able to fetch the water after all."

When Maimouna hears what the village is saying, it feeds her disgust.

"Oh, and Papa says we should go to Guinea to be with *Maam* until things settle down."

"I'm not going anywhere until Ibrahimah is back here with me."

She had suggested leaving in the beginning. Not giving Ibrahimah to that wicked liar of a man. Idrissa said no. Now he wants to suggest leaving. She will die before she leaves this country without her son. That wretched woman Madame N'Diaye should be cast out of this village for her stupidity, revering such a vile man and bringing him into their village.

"Madame Diop is a fool, and so is her daughter. Ignore her. She is beneath you. She gives her body up to any boy who gives her attention. She will never marry. Fetching water for her mother is what the rest of her life holds for her."

"Do you want anything to eat?"

"No, bring me some water."

Maimouna closes her eyes and drifts back off to sleep, only to awaken a few hours later by the shaking of her bed. The wind whips and howls outside and forces its way through the cracks around the windowsill. The house whines and creaks beneath the force of nature. She gets up and goes to check on the girls; the house is too quiet. A quick survey convinces her the girls must be outside. She goes out back to find the laundry threatening to take flight the moment a clothespin fails to hold on to a sheet.

Where are the girls? she asks herself as she runs across the yard and takes the clothes down before they can fly away, draping them over her shoulder.

Back inside she sets the laundry down and heads out to the front of the house. The girls are not there either. Perhaps, her mind is playing tricks on her. She goes to check the calendar, but she is correct, it is still July and school is, in fact, still on summer recess. She has not left the house since the incident with Marabout Ahmed three weeks ago, but something tugs within the pit of her stomach. She grabs her scarf, slips a pair of sandals on, and ventures out the front door.

She checks the well, but the girls are not there. She goes down to the shore, but her children are nowhere in sight. Maimouna, not interested in speaking to any of her neighbors, treks back up the hill, ignoring the stares and whispers that swirl around her, poking at her, antagonizing her. She does not hold on to them and instead allows them to wash over and away from her as she enters her father-in-law's house. There, in his living room, she finds her three daughters sitting on the floor at the feet of their grandfather as he weaves stories of himself and their grandmother. Idrissa's mother died before they were married and so all they have are the remnants of memory to hold on to.

"Papa Yoro, tell us how beautiful Grandmama was?" Aisha asks.

"She was as beautiful as a thousand suns, shining down on mankind. Her heart was made of gold, her smile could calm the most frantic child in the village, her voice lulled all the children in the village to sleep in the evenings as she sang the songs of our ancestors. All of the women in the village came to her for advice and guidance, as her wisdom transcended the ages."

Papa Yoro points to the chair across from him and Maimouna sits down. She does not know why she did not assume the girls were with their grandfather or uncle.

"I want to be like her when I grow up," Binta says.

"A woman has a lot of responsibility. Life is not easy. Many of the women today think it is, but they soon find out that it is not. Isn't that right, my daughter?" Papa Yoro asks, directing his question to Maimouna.

She searches for the words to express her anger, her feeling of betrayal at not only Marabout Ahmed, but everything. How could a man of the old tradition even begin to understand?

"You think you are alone but you are not. Grandmama lost three of her sons all before Senegal gained its independence from the French. Colonialism left us in extreme poverty, our crops were not for us, but for exports. And do not think we were paid fairly. We were not."

"How did you survive? What they did was wrong. How can you accept something that is being done to you unfairly by someone else?" Fatou says.

"That is a question that we will all have to ask at some point in our life. Mankind is not very good at its humanity. It is as if the word itself was created for humans to strive towards, because they so often fail. For centuries, man has raped, pillaged, and bullied one another."

"So, it's better to be bad?" Binta asks.

"Only if you believe that this life is all that there is, and if you do, then you will waste your lifetime trying to take from others what does not belong to you, for fleeting moments of victory, only to find yourself losing, again and again."

"So, it's not better?" Binta says, her head cocked to the side in an effort to make sense of Papa Yoro's puzzle of an answer.

"Only if you find joy in being the last to realize you are the fool," he says.

Maimouna lets go of her thoughts and allows Papa Yoro's voice to soothe her as he reminds her that she is not at war with everyone. Her family loves her, and God willing, Ibrahimah will return home, safe and very much alive.

XVI.

Today is the first day of Ramadan. Children who haven't reached puberty are allowed to eat, but Marabout says as Talibé they have to set an example and fast like the adults. They can break their fast at sundown. Just the thought of not being able to eat during the day causes panic to rise up into Ibrahimah's throat. Étienne says they can eat whenever they find food.

"Marabout sits in the house all day, he has no idea what we do; he just wants his money," Étienne says.

Ibrahimah feels doubtful.

"Don't worry," Étienne says, patting Ibrahimah on the back. "You'll get food and money without even trying. We just need to find a place to hide the extra."

That seems like a good idea. Étienne always has a good plan. Ibrahimah pulls a packet of cashews from his pocket and starts to eat them. The nuts taste so good, he stuffs several in his mouth at once.

"Where did you get the nuts?"

Ibrahimah looks up at his cousin, his big almond eyes full of guilt.

"I took it."

"From the old lady down the road?"

Ibrahimah purses his lips in defiance.

"Ibrahimah! You don't steal from women. She works hard to earn money for her family. Next time, ask!"

"But I'm so hungry!"

"So am I, but we'll find food. We don't steal!"

Ibrahimah scowls at Étienne. His cousin doesn't understand. What is the point in being good when he is forced to live with Marabout and his parents are dead? There is nothing to look forward to. There is no Paradise for being good boys, so why bother?

"I feed myself!"

"Yeah, but Allah doesn't like a thief. Are you a thief? If you get caught, they will cut off your hand!"

"Other Talibé steal all the time. No one cuts off their hand."

Étienne doesn't understand. Who will take care of him if Étienne dies too? He has to learn to take care of himself. Étienne opens his hand and Ibrahimah pours the nuts out for him. They sit down on the curb watching traffic and pedestrians pass by.

"They're good," Étienne concedes, popping another cashew in his mouth.

Ibrahimah smirks as a man approaches them.

"Talibé! Come! I have *zakat* for you."

The boys pop up to their feet, their cans out in front of them. The man drops money into each of their cans, pats Ibrahimah on the head, and walks off with a smile.

"It begins," Étienne says.

A sense of ease washes over Ibrahimah. He arrived right at the end of Ramadan last year, and all he could think about was returning home to his family; he didn't think there was ever a good time to be a Talibé, but Ramadan is when all Muslims follow the text of the Quran more purposefully. Like when he behaved extra good and extra nice to his sisters to ensure his mother would give him a Coca after dinner. He wonders if Christians have a time when they have to be extra nice to other people.

"Where do we go today?" Ibrahimah asks.

Étienne squints against the sun as he thinks. "Maybe we go visit

Moustapha for lunch and football. When the sun goes down, people will buy fresh dates to break their fast and will give us money. We should be close to a boutique or patisserie."

Ibrahimah looks into his can. Two big coins sit at the bottom. He needs two more coins for Marabout, but going to Moustapha's house first sounds like a better idea. They haven't seen their friend for some time now. A car stops in front of them. Ibrahimah gets back up from the curb and walks over to the driver. The woman hands them five hundred francs each.

"*Merci,* ta-ta," they say in unison.

Ibrahimah begins reciting a prayer Étienne taught him.

"Those who spend their money in the cause of God, then do not follow their charity with insult or harm, will receive their recompense from their Lord; they have nothing to fear, nor will they grieve."

Ibrahimah follows Étienne and cups his hands over his face several times. The woman in the car smiles and bows her head in reverence before driving away. The traffic behind her is patient as they perform their ritual. Ibrahimah can't help but smile. If only he could keep the money for himself and go find his sisters and take care of them.

"Étienne, do you think my sisters are still alive?"

Étienne looks over at him.

"My mama would know if your sisters are okay."

"You think Marabout killed my mama and papa?"

Étienne shrugs, with a solemn face. His skin looks burnt beneath the stinging rays of sun. Ibrahimah sighs deep and walks up to another driver beckoning at him to come over. Once Ibrahimah is unable to ignore his hunger pains any longer, they head over to Moustapha's house to see if anyone is home.

"Why, hello, boys! How are you? Oops!" Moustapha's mother covers her mouth with her hand. *"Pardonnez-moi. J'ai oublié que vous ne comprenez pas l'anglais! Bonjour, Étienne et Ibrahimah!"*

"Bonjour, madame," Étienne says.

Ibrahimah looks up at the woman with his eyebrows raised. Her dark, curly hair is pulled back into a ponytail and her shirt is made from Senegalese material but in a style Ibrahimah has never seen before. Her skirt is short and fans out at her knees. Her purple shoes have a very high heel, and make her even taller than before.

"Moustapha, you're going to have to teach your friends English!" his mother gushes. "Aria!"

"*Oui, madame.*"

"*Baignes les garçons et lavez leurs vêtements. S'il vous plaît. Ils sont tellement sales.*"

Ibrahimah looks down at his hands and shirt. He's not that dirty. But a bath at Moustapha's house is always a welcome experience.

"My mother has been taking French lessons." Moustapha snickers. "Now she talks to Aria in proper French, unless she gets stuck."

Étienne and Moustapha slap hands.

"*Namanala trop!* Where've you been?" Étienne asks.

"Where have *you* been! We went on holiday. My parents took me to Paris two weeks before school ended. My father had a big conference there. Then we went skiing in Switzerland, but I don't ski. I prefer snowboarding."

"Snowboarding? What's that?" Ibrahimah asks.

"It's like skiing but both your feet are on one board, like skateboarding."

Ibrahimah is mystified.

"I'll show you how to skateboard later," Moustapha says.

Ibrahimah has no idea what these things are, but he is always interested to discover new things at his friend's house. Upstairs, the warm water envelops his scrawny legs and he leans back in the tub and exhales. His feet are not raw like the last time, since he's been wearing his shoes. Aria hands him a bright-yellow toy.

"Do you know what this is?" Aria asks.

"No."

"It's a duck," Étienne interjects.

"Do you know what sounds a duck makes?"

Both Étienne and Ibrahimah are silent.

"Quack-quack!" Aria blurts, sending Ibrahimah into a fit of giggles.

Ibrahimah lets the duck go and it buoys across his chest to the other end of the porcelain tub. He picks it up and squeezes it. The duck sprays water at Étienne. Ibrahimah remembers that day he couldn't find his sisters and friend Moussa on the beach, the high tide crashing against the dune. The fear he felt right before he saw Ahmed looming before his eyes. He begins to cry. Maybe if he hadn't lost his sisters that evening, he would still be in his village and his parents would be alive.

"Ibrahimah, my chou-chou, what's wrong? Did I hurt you?" Aria looks at him.

"Marabout killed my mama!" he erupts.

"Don't cry, cousin."

"Is this true?" Aria asks Étienne, the duck now floating unattended through the water.

"We don't know. Marabout says Ibrahimah's mama and papa are dead and Ibrahimah will never leave Marabout. He has never said that to any Talibé before."

Aria strokes Ibrahimah's back and shushes him quiet.

"I know you all are from the south. Do you know your village?"

"Saloulou," Étienne says.

"I'll see what I can find out. Ibrahimah, don't cry. If your parents have passed, then they are in heaven with Allah. But let's find out if that is true before you mourn their deaths. Okay?"

Ibrahimah looks into Aria's eyes; she reminds him so much of his mama. She leans over and kisses him on his forehead.

Bathed, with clean clothes, a full belly, and a new outlook on his future, Ibrahimah sits on the edge of the sofa in the living room, dangling his feet.

"My mother says I should teach you English."

"Yes, teach me English. Then I'll be fancy like you, Moustapha," Ibrahimah says.

Ibrahimah thinks of all the Americans he will be able to speak to in English; so many of them walk away when he approaches them. If he knew English, they would have to stop and listen, which should make them give him more money.

"Teach me now!"

Étienne has stopped watching the television and is looking at Moustapha, ready.

"Okay. The first word I will teach you is 'hello.'"

Ibrahimah looks at him, waiting.

"Repeat the word."

"What word?"

"Hello. Say, 'Hello.'"

"Ello," Ibrahimah says.

"No. Hhhhello."

"Ello."

"No, no. The *h* says *hhha.* You have to breathe heavy."

"Hhhhello."

"Yes! Hello means *bonjour* in French or *nangadef* in Wolof."

"Okay, another word."

"Uhmm, *bonjour* is 'good morning.'"

"Good morning," Ibrahimah and Étienne both say together.

"*Bonne nuit* is 'good night.'"

"Good morning. Good night. What about *l'argent*? How do I say it in English?"

"Money."

"Moneee moneee moneee moneee. *Je veux beaucoup moneee!*"

Étienne and Moustapha laugh. Bugs Bunny runs across the screen with Elmer Fudd chasing after him with a shotgun.

The rest of the afternoon is spent learning as many words as he and Étienne can remember. They can watch cartoons another day. Learning English is too important. The sun is setting by the time they leave Moustapha's house, and the two boys practice their new English vernacular while they walk down the street.

"Ow much moneee you give me?" Ibrahimah asks Étienne.

"One undred."

"A big coin?" Ibrahimah replies.

Étienne nods.

"Say it in English," Ibrahimah corrects him.

"Yes," Étienne says, in English.

"You are funny," Ibrahimah says, laughing.

Étienne rolls his eyes and chuckles.

"We go Moustapha tomorrow for more English," Étienne says in his newfound language.

"Yes," Ibrahimah replies, his mind drifting off to the land of American treasure and abundance.

XVII.

Fatou walks into her grandfather's living room eating a biscuit. The entire family, including Maimouna, has been spending a lot of time with their elder since the incident with Marabout Ahmed almost two months ago, now.

"You can't eat that, it's Ramadan," Aisha says accusingly.

A music video of Coumba Gawlo plays quietly on the small television while the two younger girls lie stretched out on the sofa.

"Yes, I can, I have my menses," Fatou says, chewing the biscuit extra slow in Aisha's face.

"Papa!" Aisha calls out, running from the room, the grumbling of her hunger pains echoing throughout the house.

Binta laughs and motions for Fatou to give her a biscuit. She has not reached puberty yet, and no one in the family expects her to fast if she does not want to.

"Not fasting today?" Fatou asks, giving her youngest sister a cookie.

"No, seeing you eat is too hard, but I fasted for five days with no problem. I think Aisha will cheat."

"She's still a baby. She will cheat for sure, and I plan to catch her," Fatou says with a devious twinkle in her eye.

Binta laughs.

"If you don't practice the years before, the first year you are required is really hard. I practiced since I was eight, and by the time I was ten I could fast the entire month. When my menses arrived, at twelve years old, it was a breeze for me."

"Why don't girls have to fast during their menses?"

"Mama said all women are expected to eat during their menses; it's too dangerous if we did not. We could get sick, maybe even die."

"Oh no!"

"I know. In the Quran, Mohammed says women are to eat, so there is no question about it. This biscuit is good. Want another?"

"Yes," Binta says with a smile.

The two girls migrate into the next room, where their father sits in discussion with their ninety-year-old grandfather.

"I've lived a long life," Papa Yoro says.

Aisha sits at her father's feet, leaning up against his leg. Fatou and Binta sit down at the base of their grandfather's bed.

"But Papa, is there nothing I can do? He lied."

"The tradition is older than everyone in our village. He will have to answer to Allah. The moment he walked away with Ibrahimah you granted him legal custody of the child."

"What does that mean?" Aisha blurts out, looking up at her father.

Idrissa pats her on the head, his eyes glistening.

"Child, it means that if your parents went to Dakar today to get Ibrahimah, they could be arrested. Marabout could file kidnapping charges. He is now Ibrahimah's legal guardian."

"But Ibrahimah is my brother. We can't kidnap our own family member."

"Aisha, you and your sisters should go find your cousins. I'll be along soon. This is an adult conversation," Idrissa says, frowning.

Papa Yoro coughs into a handkerchief.

"She might as well stay; she needs to learn the traditions of our culture. The Talibé tradition dates back hundreds of years, young girl. Neither you nor I are bigger than tradition. That marabout will have to answer to God for his lies, but we do not have the power or authority to pass judgment or sentence on a marabout. He stands between man and God."

Idrissa's father is overtaken with another fit of coughing. He points to a cup on the side of his bed, and Aisha pops up to hand it to him.

"Is there anything I can get you, Father?" Idrissa asks the older man.

Papa Yoro shakes his head.

"You know, I sent your older brother to a daara when he was just a boy, before you were born. He worked on a farm, back before so many marabouts moved their daaras to the cities."

"I didn't know that. He's never talked about it."

"The work was hard, I know, but it made him into the man he is today. He spent three years there."

"But, Father, Marabout Ahmed has threatened to keep Ibrahimah until he turns fifteen. That's nine years! How can a man lose his son for a decade? Why am I being bound to a man who is obviously not a man of God?"

Papa Yoro sighs heavily.

"You want me to say what you want to hear, and I cannot. Your brother could disown you from his inheritance and without land to farm, how will you care for your wife and children? Without your community where will you go? Who will protect you?"

"Yes, I'm well aware the firstborn inherits all lands and wealth, but if my brother is taken with this demon, how can I protect my family? I am a man and yet my hands are tied by the old ways. It is not right."

"Everyone has their struggles in this life. You are asking for it to be easy on you because you believe you are right. Yet, everyone else believes they are right also. Take this as a lesson to grow wiser, my son. I will be gone very soon and you will have just your brother left. Ibrahimah will be okay. You have to be strong enough for your family."

Idrissa spends the rest of the afternoon failing to convince his father to take his side in the matter. At dinnertime they go home and the girls set the table for the feast Maimouna has been preparing all afternoon.

"Mama, you don't look so well," Aisha says, looking up from her food.

Idrissa looks at Maimouna and notices her eyes are glassy and her body is hunched over the platter of food that she has yet to touch.

"My love, are you okay?"

Fatou and Binta look up from the food and echo the sentiments of their sister and father.

"I feel hot," Maimouna says, pulling her shawl off her shoulders.

Idrissa gets up and goes to help her to her feet. When he touches her, he pulls his hand away in shock.

"Maimouna! You're burning up."

"Am I?" she says, her body swaying into his arms.

"Fatou, get your mother some ice water. Binta bring me a towel."

Idrissa leads Maimouna into their bedroom and lays her down onto the bed.

"Maybe you have grippe. I don't know," Idrissa says.

"Grippe?" Maimouna mumbles.

"Mama has the flu!" Binta announces when Fatou returns to the bedroom.

"Papa?" Fatou asks, standing in the doorway with a cup of cold water.

"Well, I'm not sure. I will have to go find the doctor. Your mother's temperature is extremely high. It's either grippe or malaria; I don't see how she could fall ill so quickly with anything else."

Maimouna mumbles something indecipherable.

"What?" Idrissa asks.

"Muhhhhhh," Maimouna groans, clutching her stomach as it spasms violently.

"I'll be back," Idrissa announces as he rushes out of the house, leaving the girls with their mother.

Maimouna leans over the side of the bed and vomits onto the floor.

"Get a bucket of water and towels," Fatou instructs her sisters as she goes over to her mother.

Maimouna holds her hand up to keep Fatou back as her body heaves again, expelling from her system any remnants of food and liquid from the day. When she is finished, she curls up into a ball and falls asleep.

When Idrissa returns, he arrives with his brother and the doctor and the men go directly into the bedroom. The girls sit in the living room; having put the food away and already cleaned up the mess beside their parents' bed, leaving just the faint scent of Maimouna's sickness lingering in the air.

The doctor prefers to let Maimouna sleep, since rest is the best remedy for many illnesses. He leaves a tea for her to drink when she wakes and instructs Idrissa to buy acetaminophen for her fever.

In the morning, Idrissa wakes Fatou before leaving for work.

"Keep an eye on your mother. If it gets bad again like last night go find your aunt; she'll know what to do."

Fatou goes into her parents' room and climbs into bed with her sleeping mother. Maimouna sleeps fitfully and when she rises two hours later, she jostles Fatou awake.

"My love, what's wrong?" she asks her daughter.

"You're sick, Mama. Papa told me to watch you."

Maimouna tilts her head to the side in confusion.

"What do you mean sick? I feel fine."

Fatou sits up in bed, fully awake now. She reaches out and touches her mother's face, and finds Maimouna's skin feels normal.

"Mama, you had a terrible fever last night; the doctor had to come. Papa thought it was malaria or grippe. You don't remember?"

Maimouna remembers cooking dinner and then the family gathering together to eat, but then after that her memory goes dark.

"Perhaps it was a fast-moving bacterium," Maimouna says, climbing out of bed, her hunger pains strong and commanding at the moment.

She moves through the day slowly and methodically. The girls clean the house while she starts lunch, and by noon she needs a nap, leaving the girls to eat alone. When Idrissa arrives home at six-thirty that evening Maimouna is feeling refreshed again. She and the girls lay dinner out and the family of five gathers around the platter of steaming-hot food. A few moments later the same thing as the night before begins again. Maimouna sits bent over the platter of food, swaying and seeming to lose her awareness of everything around her. Idrissa touches her forehead to find it hot to the touch and rushes her to bed. Fatou brings an empty pail and sets it nearby in case Maimouna vomits again; at least this time they can catch it. Aisha boils water and brings the tea the doctor left for Maimouna to drink throughout the day.

Maimouna writhes in pain as her stomach spasms. Fatou rushes to the bedside with the pail. A cool rag is pressed to Maimouna's forehead and Idrissa sits her up in an attempt to get her to sip the tea. Maimouna eventually falls into a deep sleep and the rest of the family goes back to finish eating dinner.

"Is Mama going to die?" Binta asks before stuffing millet into her mouth.

"I think your mama is just sick right now, Binta. We will get through this," Idrissa says.

"I hope so," Fatou says.

The next morning, Maimouna wakes as normal again to find Fatou next to her in bed. Fatou recounts the events of the evening again, as Maimouna has no recollection of her fever, the painful stomach spasms, or vomiting.

"The same exact thing, Mama, and at the same exact time as the night before," Fatou says.

Maimouna has never heard of a sickness that arrives in the evening only, and so on the fifth consecutive day of the mysterious illness Idrissa returns home early in the afternoon with a lamb. The lamb cries with fear at its change in environment and tries to pull away from Idrissa as he ties it to a post in the yard. The animal calms down once Binta and Aisha go out to pet it.

"Can we afford this right now?" Maimouna asks.

"Can we not, my love?" Idrissa asks, walking out the door to meet the halal butcher who will slaughter the animal.

The two men go out back and Maimouna watches from the

kitchen window. Idrissa claps his hands to catch the attention of Binta and Aisha and they scurry out of the way. The man takes the lamb by the rope sitting loosely around its neck and leads it over to the large tree at the far end of the small yard. He digs a shallow hole beneath the strongest branch and then takes out a machete. With Idrissa's help they hold the animal down, who by now knows the best of its days are about to come to an end. The lamb bleats in protest, but with the deftness of a man who can do this in his sleep, the man slices its throat in one smooth motion over the hole. Idrissa helps adjust the body of the animal and the majority of the blood is allowed to pour out into the small grave. After a time, the carcass is hoisted up by its hind legs so that it can continue to bleed out before being skinned and cut.

At five o'clock the girls are sent out to their neighbors' homes with cuts of the sacrificial meat. The poorest families are offered the most meat. Maimouna prepares what the family plans to keep for dinner but like the previous evenings, right before the family is set to start eating, Maimouna's affliction arrives again. Once they put Maimouna to bed, Idrissa and his three daughters sit down to eat.

"I love lamb," Aisha says, sucking on a rib bone.

Binta is too focused on rolling the perfect ball of rice to plop into her mouth to pay her sister any attention.

Fatou looks at her father, who is quiet as he eats.

"Maybe the sacrifice needs a couple of days before it can take effect, Papa," Fatou says.

"Only Allah knows," Idrissa says, looking toward their bedroom.

XVIII.

The morning is slow and the boredom of not having anything to do threatens to put Ibrahimah back to sleep. It's nowhere near lunchtime yet, when he and Étienne will go visit Moustapha; now that their friend has returned to Dakar, and school is on summer recess, they can visit for the entire afternoon, watching television, playing video games, learning to skateboard, eating good food, and practicing their English. All before Moustapha's father comes home from work, of course, which is when they take their leave so that he doesn't find them there.

"How much is Magic Land?" he asks his cousin. That would be a good way to fill the morning, and with all the money they have been collecting during the last two weeks of Ramadan, surely they can afford it.

"Too expensive; it's two thousand five hundred francs."

"How much is that?"

Étienne ponders the question for several moments, counting silently on his fingers.

"A week's pay."

Ibrahimah's shoulders drop in defeat; he could justify one day's worth of Marabout's money, but not an entire week. But he deserves to spend a day at Magic Land after all he has had to endure over the last few weeks.

"Are you sure? Maybe we should just try," Ibrahimah says, hope still alive in the pit of his stomach.

"Why you think no Talibé ever goes to Magic Land? Those rich people don't want to be anywhere near us, even if we could afford it. They keep the price high to keep us out."

Ibrahimah knows his cousin is right. He rarely ever steers them wrong.

"Magic Land is stupid anyways," Étienne says.

"No, it's not," Ibrahimah says.

Étienne rolls his eyes and leaves Ibrahimah to sulk alone. Even if he could earn that much money, he knows spending it on Magic Land would be a waste. Food and paying Marabout are his two priorities. He scratches at his arm and discovers a mosquito bite. His dirty fingernails scrape the bump until his skin burns. When he realizes Étienne is walking away, he jumps up to follow him. Ibrahimah drags his can alongside his body, the empty canister bumping into his thigh.

"Where are we going?" Ibrahimah asks.

"We meet the others, over there," Étienne says, pointing to the larger group of boys from their house, "and then we go to the lighthouse."

"What's up there?"

"Doctors who will fix our feet."

Ibrahimah looks down at his feet housed in the blue plastic jelly sandals Aria bought him.

"Why haven't we gone before?"

"We never have the time."

"Are you going to get your feet fixed?" Ibrahimah says.

"I don't know," Étienne says, tilting his head to the side, "it depends."

"On what?"

"On how long they say it takes to heal."

They catch up with the group and Étienne slaps hands with Fatik and the two boys fall into an easy gait. Ibrahimah frowns. His feet were a constant thing of suffering for months. Étienne would try and soothe him with the advice that one day, once his toes healed and got hard, they wouldn't hurt and bleed so badly again. He didn't think the day would ever come, but it did. He would rather not do anything to cause that kind of pain again.

A young girl walks past, dragging her feet in a gait of slow suffering beneath the scorching African sun and the effects of fasting. The ends of her cornrows stick up, haphazardly, around the crown of her head, offering no protection. She wears an old T-shirt tucked into her traditional Senegalese ankle-length wrap skirt and twirls a small black plastic bag that dangles from her wrist.

Ibrahimah would never think to ask her for money, as she is but a maid, a young girl pulled out of school to go live with a family and work seven days a week, with a day and a half off once a month to visit her family in the village. Her entire salary of thirty dollars a month is given to her family back in the village. So, even if she had a five-franc piece to spare, she could not afford to give it to a Talibé.

The older boys at the front of the group push one another in jest and turn around, their eyes watching her narrow hips sashay by like an older woman with curves. A boy clicks his tongue at her but with her chin jutting out she continues on as if she had not heard. The boy's antics fall flat with Ibrahimah. A girl with no money to spare, he does not see the fun in harassing her.

"Have you gone to the lighthouse before?" Ibrahimah asks Fatik.

Fatik shakes his head no. He turns around and glances at the retreating girl.

"Why do they bother the girl? She has no money."

"They're not interested in her money," Étienne says.

"Then why do they tease her?"

"Because they want her to be their girlfriend!" Fatik laughs.

Ibrahimah scrunches his face up in disgust.

"Yuck! I don't want a girlfriend."

Fatik shakes his head. "You're young. Wait till you get older."

"No. I'm fine. I don't need a girl. I just want my mama."

A man dressed in a worn T-shirt and dusty workman's pants, both too large for his thin, angular frame, brushes by Ibrahimah as if he were not there. Some people are not worth the time it takes to ask for money; he knows who will say no from several blocks away. People are not aware that the way they move, the manner in which they regard their surroundings, and their facial expressions say more about them than the words that come out of their mouths or the clothes they wear.

There are some days, though, when his feet hurt, his belly aches, and his skin is so hot from the merciless sun that he would approach a ram for food or money. But today, during the slow but abundant month of Ramadan, he can take a moment and look up at the faces and shoulders of the world around him. He always thought what he really needed was a lot of money, but he has come to realize that what it is he truly needs is time. Time to find food to fill his belly. Time to work. Time to find his way back home. Time to be a boy.

Phare des Mamelles sits in front of the boys. The lighthouse is atop one of two looming hills covered in grass. The story told by the elders is that the twin hills are the remnants of a woman who threw herself into the sea off the coast of Dakar only to be rejected by the sea gods, who tossed her back onto the land, which then grew over and around her. The lasting proof of her existence are the two hills, said to be her breasts, which mark the beginning of the low-key residential neighborhood of Mamelles.

The group starts up the steep and winding hill, but Ibrahimah finds his small chest has trouble catching enough wind to conquer the hill with ease. He stops for a moment, leans over and coughs phlegm, then spits it out onto the ground in front of him.

"Are you okay?" Fatik asks, hitting him on the back.

Étienne is beside him a moment later.

"Cousin, what's wrong?"

Ibrahimah stands up and catches his breath. "I don't know. I'm fine."

"Perhaps you need to drink."

He is quite thirsty now that Étienne mentions it. A Coca-Cola would soothe his cough for sure.

"Come," Étienne says, taking his tomato can and leading him up the hill, "we're almost there."

Seagulls circle above the tall white lighthouse that looms above the city. Ibrahimah shades his eyes against the glare of the sun to get a clear look at the structure.

"The doctors are here?" Ibrahimah asks.

"That is what the others told me," Étienne says.

"How would they fix our feet?"

"They cut the stuff that makes your toes connect and then bandage them separately. When you take the bandage off, your feet will be like normal again."

"I don't want anyone cutting my feet!"

The idea of someone cutting his toes causes the same fear he feels for Marabout to take hold of his body. Étienne touches his shoulder.

"Don't worry; you don't have to get it done."

"Will you do it?" Ibrahimah asks.

"Maybe. I think they give you special shoes so that you can walk. If I get new shoes, I will do it."

Ibrahimah is not excited about the idea of knives and feet but before he is able to communicate his doubt, they are approached by a young Senegalese boy Étienne's height.

"Talibé, what you looking for?"

"The doctor that fixes Talibé feet. We heard they're here at the lighthouse," Fatik says.

"Doctors Without Borders? You're too late. The doctors are gone."

The group comes to a sudden halt.

"How do you know?" Étienne asks.

"I live here. My father is one of the lighthouse watchers."

"Where did the doctors go?"

"They went to Niger, to help with the famine."

"Will they come back?" Fatik asks.

"I don't know. They left right before Ramadan," the boy says, then runs off behind them down the hill.

Étienne plops down on the ground, kicks off his sandals, and stares at his bare feet, toes fused together beneath years' worth of calluses and ingrown toenails. Ibrahimah sits down next to him and lies back onto the grass. The wind atop the hill brings him relief and he plucks a blade of grass, covered in sea salt carried along the ocean breeze, and chews on it. They were too late to get their feet fixed, but that is fine with Ibrahimah, since he would rather spend the rest of his day thinking of all the things he would do if he had enough time.

XIX.

It's been four days since Idrissa sacrificed the lamb for the health and safety of their family and last night was the first night Maimouna did not fall ill with fever and spasms. Instead, Maimouna wakes with a deep fatigue within the pit of her stomach. Fatou tried to comb her hair this morning, but she pushed her away, preferring to sleep until noon. And so now with her braids fuzzy and her dress on backward Maimouna finally emerges from her room and makes her way to the kitchen, to start breakfast.

"Mama!"

Binta runs up to her mother in the kitchen.

"Mama?"

"Get away from me, child."

Binta pauses, stares into her mother's face for several moments, then runs out of the room.

"Aisha! Something's wrong with Mama!"

She needs to get to Dakar. That's what she needs to do. Find Marabout Ahmed, kill him, and bring her son home. Maimouna goes into her room and grabs her change purse, shoving it into her brassiere. Back in the kitchen she grabs the largest blade she can find and hides it in the fold of her ankle-length wrap skirt.

"Mama, are you okay? Is your fever back?" Aisha asks from the doorway.

Maimouna turns around quickly, searching Aisha's face to see if she saw her.

"Go find your sister and help her prepare dinner, my love. I'm fine," she says in a gentle and kind voice.

The sun is blinding and the heat causes her crankiness to rise. The world around her feels foreign and strange. She looks down the sandy path to ensure no one is outside. Her mind is racing, playing out different scenarios of what could happen when she arrives to Dakar. A flood of nausea and dizziness takes hold of her and she holds on to the side of a house for support. Deep breath. Think. Get to Dakar. Find Ahmed. Kill him. Bring Ibrahimah home. But first, she needs to get there. Find transport out of this suffocating little village.

She walks to the main road and hails a horse-drawn wagon. Several trees line the wide road on both sides, creating a shady corridor. The driver slows down for her; the dark-brown horse neighs at the disruption of his gentle gallop. She scrambles up onto the back next to several large bundles of hay, manure, and farm tools. Her shoulders sit hunched over, her eyes blank as she reimagines a scene where she rescues her son from the devil. With the knife in his belly Ahmed will be too slow to catch them. The wagon passes by Fatou walking along the side of the road, carrying a bucket of water.

"Mama!" Fatou yells at the departing wagon.

Maimouna looks past her eldest daughter, who looks at her with confusion and shock.

The wagon stops on several occasions with passengers getting on and off. After the last customer disembarks, the driver parks the wagon, leaves, and comes back to load it with several more bushels of hay. He works around her, never once asking Maimouna where she is going. By now, the high afternoon sun has calmed itself and is setting comfortably on the horizon.

"Maimouna?"

She looks up.

"My love, what are you doing here?"

She looks around at her surroundings. How did she end up at Idrissa's farm, barely an hour from their house? She looks at her husband with accusing eyes. He is trying to trick her. She is supposed to be heading north, toward the Gambia. She frowns as she searches for the driver of the wagon, who has conveniently disappeared. Did he know what she was planning? Idrissa approaches her with his arms open and confusion on his face.

"Leave me," she growls, turning away from him.

"Leave you? Has something happened at home? Are the girls okay? Why are you here?"

"I am going to Dakar," she said, "to bring home our son. Ahmed will pay."

"Maimouna, you will come with me now. Come, we take leave."

He grabs her by the arm and tries to get her down from the wagon.

"No! Leave me. You do trickery to get me here. I'm going to get our son, since you are too much of a coward to do it!"

"Woman, you are burning up with fever again. How are you even here?"

"I don't have a fever!" Maimouna yells.

"Woman, if you don't get down from there and stop this nonsense, this talk of—of foolishness, Allah only knows what I will do to you. Get down, now!"

She tries to scoot back onto the wagon, but Idrissa grabs her by the ankles and pulls her toward him. She tries to kick him away but he's too fast, his grip strong and steady. No amount of strength she attempts to muster can push him away. Her fists fall light against his arms and chest. He half drags, half carries her over to the septplace that is waiting to fill up with passengers. The knife falls from inside her skirt, just missing her foot. Idrissa shoves her into a taxi, climbing in beside her. As the car pulls away, he spots the kitchen knife, lying discarded on the ground. He turns and looks at Maimouna in disbelief. She cuts her eyes at him before staring off into the space before her.

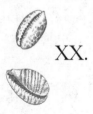

XX.

Ibrahimah looks up at the sky, the sun forcing him to squint hard. He looks for his mother in the clouds, hoping to see her smile, but is met only with blue skies and a blazing orange sun. Since his accident, Ibrahimah has not seen the red bird again. Next to him, Étienne sits on the ground, his legs stretched out. Ibrahimah rests his hand on his hip a moment before joining his cousin against the base of the tree. His skin is sticky with sweat.

"How much money do we have?"

"We did good: five thousand francs."

Ibrahimah's small mouth breaks into a smile; his new teeth are fighting to come in.

"We're rich!"

Ibrahimah has never been that close to that much money before. Étienne says nothing as he sits staring at their bounty.

"Let's buy lots of food! I'm hungry."

"No, we have to save this. Ramadan will end soon. Then it will be hard to get people to give us money. No one gives after Ramadan ends."

A flashback of Marabout thrashing him with that wretched cane pops into his head, followed by the terror of Pape lying about giving them money for a day's work, only to try to kidnap them. Goose-bumps crawl up his arms and he shivers while nodding.

"Let's go to Moustapha's house and put it there," Ibrahimah suggests.

Étienne is quiet a moment.

"Moustapha is rich; he won't ever steal our money," Ibrahimah says, standing up.

When they arrive at Moustapha's house, they find their friend quiet and somber.

"What's wrong, Moustapha?"

"Nothing."

Ibrahimah cocks his head to the side. "You look sad."

Étienne is over on the other side of the yard, looking around at the grounds.

"My father is being transferred for work."

Ibrahimah raises his eyebrows, not sure what transferred means.

"My dad is moving, leaving Dakar for work."

"He'll come back."

"Yeah, I guess. What is Étienne doing?"

"He looks for a place to hide our money."

"Put it in my safe. If he puts it in the ground, it will sink. He'll never find it again."

"Oh?"

"Yeah. Not a good idea. Étienne!" Moustapha waves at Étienne to come over. "I can stash your money inside my safe. My dad bought me one to keep my things secure from the maids. Come, I'll show you."

The boys trample up the stairs to Moustapha's bedroom. Ibrahimah has never been in his friend's room before, just the bathroom, the guest bedroom, and downstairs. Moustapha's room is bigger than the guest room and is brightly lit with a large tall bed abundant with blankets and pillows. A shelf filled with books takes up an entire wall, and he has a flat-screen television with a video-game console below it.

"Is that an Xbox like downstairs?" Ibrahimah asks.

"No, that's my PlayStation. I like the games on it better."

"I want to play," Ibrahimah says, though he's never played such a thing in his life.

"Okay. First come look at this."

Moustapha opens the door to an oversized dark mahogany wardrobe. A mirror sits on the inside of the door and Ibrahimah looks at the reflection of the three of them. Étienne and Moustapha are about the same height, but he is much shorter than the two older boys. Moustapha's light-brown skin is clear and bright in comparison to their dry, dark skin, and his round face is plumper than their drawn, skinny cheeks. Ibrahimah would like to be light and handsome like Moustapha, but he never will be. Étienne is quiet as he waits to see what Moustapha has to show them.

Their friend pulls out a black box from the back of the shelf.

"This is what I wanted to show you."

He presses some buttons, a beeping sound goes off, a click happens, and Moustapha opens the small door. Inside, Ibrahimah spots cards, money, and other pieces of paper.

"I hold my passport and birth certificate, money, and jewelry like my watch in here. You can store your money and come get it when you need. No one will ever have access to it but me."

Ibrahimah is impressed. Étienne hands Moustapha the money they have saved up over the course of Ramadan. Traveling with that much money is not safe. Moustapha counts the money.

"Five thousand francs."

"Yes." Étienne confirms.

Moustapha puts the money on one of the shelves inside the safe and then locks the door. He pulls on the door to make sure it's locked.

"The code is 44-33-22. In case you come by and need to get your money and I'm not home."

The boys stand around a moment before Ibrahimah remembers what was on his mind.

"I want to use the PlayStation."

That evening everything is quiet, like it has been for the last few weeks. Ahmed is slow to swing his cane on any of the boys in the evening, his hunger too intense after fasting all day. On the television, the evening news advertises sunset down to the minute. Ahmed goes out and buys himself a pack of dried dates. He then dives into bowls of rice and fish, rice and meat, bread and eggs, eating his way into a food coma. By the time Ibrahimah and the other boys return, the only thing on Ahmed's mind is sleep and more food.

Ibrahimah and Étienne sit and watch the other boys giving Marabout extra money, gifts, food, soap, peanuts, and more. Ibrahimah is thankful he and Étienne have Moustapha as a friend. Hiding their extra money is the best idea Étienne has ever had. Marabout deserves nothing extra from him. If the man was not so quick to beat them, Ibrahimah wouldn't give him the four hundred francs every night, either. He scowls at the foolishness of the other boys, lies down on his mat, and goes to sleep.

At four-thirty the next morning, Ibrahimah stirs at the sound of Marabout up and about before the morning prayer call rings out across the city. He's getting breakfast before the sun comes up. Ibrahimah closes his eyes for a bit more sleep, but Marabout jostles him awake. Ibrahimah sits up, afraid of what his teacher wants. He motions for Ibrahimah to follow him into his room, where there is another, older, man waiting.

"Come here, boy," the man says.

Ibrahimah stumbles over to the stranger; his fear of what Marabout wants subsides. He has met the stranger before, although he does not know his name. The man only seems to arrive in the early hours of the morning, when all of the other boys are asleep. Ibrahimah gives his hand over to the man, who clips several of his fingernails and makes him spit into a basket where there lie several cowrie shells. The last time the man came, Marabout shaved his head and put his hair in the basket, along with the brushed skin on his arm. Ibrahimah finds it odd but does not mind the attention; he is aware that this is a secret that he shares with his teacher, and Marabout is nice to him when the man is there because the man is helping Marabout Ahmed make the person who gave him the scars on his face pay for hurting him. Ibrahimah looks over at Marabout Ahmed, wanting to ask him what this is all for, but the man dismisses him with a swift movement of his head.

"Shut the door behind you," Ahmed instructs.

Ibrahimah starts toward the door, but his curiosity stops him and he turns around.

"What, boy?"

"What is all this for, Marabout?" Ibrahimah asks.

"For your mother," Marabout says, grinning.

"For my mama in Paradise?" Ibrahimah asks in a small voice.

"Yes, child, for your mother. This is to help ensure she makes it to heaven."

The thought of helping his mother calms his heart.

"Thank you, Marabout," Ibrahimah says, walking out the door.

"No, thank you, Ibrahimah," Marabout says before the door shuts.

Marabout has never thanked him before, or any of his Talibé brothers. Maybe the man is not so bad after all. Ibrahimah lies back down onto his cardboard mat and dreams about his parents in Paradise, laughing and eating.

The next day, by seven in the morning, the streets are packed with people running errands before the noon heat, thirst, and hunger set in.

"During Ramadan everyone feels like Talibé during the day," Fatik jokes.

Ibrahimah finds this quite funny; Étienne scrunches up his face and rolls his eyes.

"Hot, tired, and hungry," Ibrahimah quips.

Fatik slaps his leg, laughing.

Ibrahimah nudges Étienne to join in on the joke.

"Not really funny. Ramadan will soon be over, and then it's Talibé who are hungry and everyone else is rich and happy."

"Ramadan should be all year!" Ibrahimah exclaims.

"I can live with that," Fatik says, chuckling.

Across the street a man gets out of his car and starts waving his hands and yelling at another man, who is trying to stand up.

"What happened?" Ibrahimah asks.

"The driver hit the man on the bike," Étienne says.

The biker pushes the man, yelling at him, and the two get into a shoving match. Several people rush to the altercation in an attempt to calm and mediate the situation.

"Some people go crazy when they're hungry," Ibrahimah says, shaking his head.

Étienne bursts into laughter. Ibrahimah is pleased his cousin is finally joining in on the fun.

XXI.

The approaching afternoon heat leans on the edge of the cool morning air. Maimouna sits in front of a bucket, peeling potatoes, forcing herself to go through the motions of tending to her home as if nothing has happened, even though everything has happened. Fatou continues to report the whisperings of the village. Binta and Aisha run errands and sit at her feet, staring into her face, searching for answers, until she runs them off. Idrissa blames her last delusional episode on a combination of the pungent tea her sister-in-law sent and the illness of fever, but since then she has not experienced the fevers again in the evening, nor during the day.

Frustrated that the lamb sacrifice failed to cure his wife, Idrissa found a different tea concoction at the market that he insists she drink every morning. But it does not matter whether she drinks the bitter tea or the pungent tea, if they work to keep the feverish episodes at bay then she will be content.

This morning, Idrissa kissed her on the forehead before departing for work. She felt a tinge of empathy for him, if only for a brief moment, but then the thought of what Ibrahimah must be enduring in Dakar brought her back to reality.

A skinless potato drops into the bucket with a soft thud, where

Maimouna expected to hear a thwack. She looks down to find she has skinned too many for dinner; at least twenty potatoes sit floating atop the bucket of water, more than double what she needed. She tilts her head to the side and decides to make French fries. The girls prefer them fried anyway. She reaches for the knife from the side of the bucket and the first potato is sliced into wedges in no time. She has skinned and cut potatoes since the age of eight years old and she finds the repetitiveness soothing. Plus, she gets it done much faster since Binta and Aisha are fetching water while Fatou is purchasing fish at the market for dinner. Upon picking up the second potato she cannot say whether it was with intention or an accident, but as the knife comes down to slice the potato, the blade instead cuts through the dark-brown skin of her wrist.

She winces in pain as blood rushes to the surface of her arm. The potato in her hand is now covered in blood. Time stops and she no longer hears the song of birds, or the soft ocean breeze off in the distance. The air around her constricts and she can't move. The blood pools on top of her upturned wrist and when it spills over, she staggers to the ground.

"Mama! What happened?" Fatou drops the black plastic bag onto the floor and runs in a circle. Maimouna begins to laugh, and then begins to sob. It would be funny if the situation were not so dire.

"Fatou!" Maimouna cries as she climbs back to her feet, using the back of the chair she was sitting on for support.

Fatou stops, then dashes off, returning a moment later with a pile of torn rags Maimouna keeps washed and folded in the hall closet.

Maimouna winces in pain as the puddle of blood gathers around her feet. "Get the cornstarch."

Fatou rushes off again. When she returns, in a more calm and focused state Maimouna points to a large tin bowl.

"Rinse my wrist first," she says.

Fatou fills the bowl with water from a bucket that was to be used for boiling the potatoes and pours it over Maimouna's wrist. For a brief second, she can see where the skin is separated, but then the blood replenishes itself. Fatou then sprinkles cornstarch onto the wound.

"Do I wrap the wrist now?" Fatou asks.

"No. See the blood has stopped running?"

"Yes."

"Now rinse the wound again to get the cornstarch off. Then we wrap the wrist, but not too tight, as we don't want the bleeding to begin again," Maimouna instructs.

It takes Fatou two tries before she gets it right, but once the wrist is wrapped properly, she sighs heavily with relief.

"Does it hurt badly?"

Maimouna shakes her head no.

"Mama, what happened?" Fatou asks.

Maimouna shakes her head, unable to vocalize her thoughts as the water surges up from the core of her belly, into her lungs and chest, rising up past the backs of her irises and cascades down her cheeks to her very toes.

"Mama, why are you crying?"

Maimouna cannot explain why, but the floodwaters have been released within her and she has no control over them whatsoever.

"I'm going to lie down," Maimouna sobs, walking away, leaving her daughter sitting alone with a bloodstained lap and a bucketful of potatoes swimming in a river of blood.

The moment Maimouna's head hits the pillow, the dark veil of sleep arrives and her forty-one-year-old body floats into the dream and nightmare of memories both recent and past. There she stands, in the body of her twenty-three-year-old self, eighteen years ago, as she pleaded with her uncle to bring her back to Guinea to the mother whose bosom she yearned to hug and nestle for too long.

For fifteen years she did the bidding for her uncle and his Senegalese wife, and the years had worn her down to her last thread of sanity; she had lived more years of her life with them than she had lived with her own mother, and yet she had never felt like a daughter or even a tolerated distant member of the family. Her aunt treated neighbors and strangers alike better than she treated Maimouna, and at twenty-three years old she was one more cruel word or un-provoked whipping away from losing her hold on life.

"Uncle, you cannot keep me here any longer. I am a woman and want to marry!" she exclaimed.

She couldn't have cared less about marrying, but it was a good enough excuse. Her uncle was no longer her legal guardian. She could leave and return of her own accord, although it would not be the best scenario for either of them, as she did not have the first clue as to how to get to Guinea and traveling alone as a young woman was not safe. Her uncle dropped his head in regret.

"We will leave in a week's time. Do not mention it to your aunt or cousins," he said in a weary voice.

Her heart skipped a beat of joy, but she knew to temper her happiness. He had made so many false promises, yet this time felt different.

"Maimouna!"

Her eyes flutter open with a start. Idrissa's face looms over her. He is unable to mask his fear.

"What happened?"

Her lips part to respond, but no sound rises up from her chest. She really does not know what happened. One minute she was slicing potatoes and the next, her arm.

"I don't know, it was as if someone else was doing it," she whispers, the floodwaters rising again.

A look of anger crosses his face. "Did someone do this to you? Are you covering for someone?"

Idrissa stands and drops his bag to the floor, then looks around the empty room. Fatou is standing in the doorway but does not enter.

"No, no, it was me." Maimouna shakes her head, unable to hold back the tears.

"My darling, I'm not angry at you. Please, don't cry," Idrissa pleads.

Maimouna shakes her head. She cannot explain what she does not understand. Idrissa sits down on the edge of the bed and lifts her up into his arms. She sobs into his arms for what feels like eternity.

"She began crying right after we bandaged her wrists and then she came to bed," Fatou says to her father, handing him a cup of bouye, the chalky sweet drink made out of the fruit from the baobab tree.

He looks at his watch before taking the cup and finishes the contents in three large gulps.

"My love," he says, "it has been more than an hour. Do you think you can calm your tears?"

Maimouna sits up on her own.

"I'm trying," she says between sobs, "but I cannot. I will . . . go back to sleep."

"Are you sure?"

"Please," she cries.

Idrissa gets up from the bed and follows Fatou out of the room. Maimouna lies back down and falls back into a slumber of reprieve.

XXII.

"Wake up!" Marabout Ahmed barks. He hits several boys with his cane as they pull their tired bodies up for prayer. Ramadan ended ten days ago.

"Everything is back to normal," Étienne mutters beneath his breath as he and Ibrahimah scamper out of the house.

Walking down Avenue Cheik Anta Diop, Ibrahimah and Étienne approach a nightclub, Just 4 U. The club is hopping every night of the week. The clinks of glasses and the aroma of good food float from inside along with music from live performances that range from local hip-hop bands to international megastars such as Youssou N'Dour. The club draws large diverse crowds of locals and expats alike, a perfect recipe for begging. During the daylight hours though, the space is still and empty.

"Ibrahimah, watch out!"

Étienne yanks his cousin by the arm as a hail of rocks showers the streets, flying above their heads, streaking against cars, and landing at their feet. Dakar University students are commencing an all-out attack on the pedestrians and traffic. A rock sails across the sky and crashes through the passenger-side window of a taxi. Taken by surprise, people run for cover. A short, stocky Senegalese woman is knocked to the ground after getting hit in the head with a rock. Anything the university students can find flies through the air and onto the road in front of them: chairs, wood, stones, pieces of the cement foundation from the dilapidated buildings on campus. Cars parked near the main entrance are flipped. Tires are burned. Avenue Cheikh Anta Diop becomes a war zone of disaster and havoc. Étienne and Ibrahimah run along with a crowd of adults toward the nearest side street.

Students line up inside of the black iron fence that protects them from the repercussions of the outside world. On the far western side of campus another large mass of students has strategically lined up along the inside of the fence facing La Corniche and launches a coordinated attack onto the passing traffic. Anyone foolish enough to try to pass by the university bears the burden of the angry assault. Busted car windows, dented rooftops—bleeding bodies stagger away. Backed-up traffic leaves those unable to maneuver fast enough in harm's way, and the energy of the rioters reignites with the sound of every window breaking or pedestrian screaming out in pain.

Ibrahimah is enthralled by the movement and chaos. It reminds him of the cartoons he watches on television at Moustapha's house, but now the action is right in front of him.

"Étienne! This is better than *la télé* at Moustapha's house!"

He and Étienne duck down behind a car, watching in fascination as a group of eight male students exits the campus gate, eyes darting in all directions. In one deft move the group flips a car over, busts out its windows with their feet, and throws pieces of lighted wood inside to set the vehicle on fire, along with several old tires and a mound of days-old trash waiting to be picked up by the sanitation department. The massive crowd of students lets loose a resounding cry of victory. The perpetrators run back inside the gates as the shower of debris from the other students resumes onto the emptying streets, damaging the business facades directly across from the school.

"Étienne, look there."

Ibrahimah points to a student throwing a chair from the balcony of a dormitory.

"I see. Look!" Étienne points to another student jumping over the fence to return back to the safety of the campus.

"Why are they doing that?"

"I don't know."

"This is fun!" Ibrahimah says.

"It's not fun. They're going to get in trouble. Look!"

Big black Hummers roar down the road and military men in riot gear, strapped with large black guns to match, pour out of the vehicles. The soldiers shout at the small groups of nosy pedestrians to clear the area immediately. Large bazookas are pulled from the vehicles and pointed toward the gates.

A bazooka fires off. Boom! Silence. Boom! Silence. Boom! Large fireballs shoot out over the campus gates toward the massive crowd of students. The students fall back. When the fireballs cease, the students resurge with more stones and debris. A second bazooka is brought to the front line. Boom! Boom! The students scream as they choke and cough, the gas constricting their air passages. The students run away, toward the center of campus, away from the soldiers' line of sight.

"I want a gun like that."

"Me too. That gun is bigger than you!"

"It's not!"

"I'll shove you into the gun and shoot you off into the sky!"

Ibrahimah crosses his arms and pouts at Étienne. "No! I'm big. Don't shoot me!"

"Don't cry! When you get big, you'll shoot a gun like that." Étienne pats his cousin on the shoulder and smiles at him. "Don't be a baby. Look! They're trying to stop the fire."

Ibrahimah forgets his anger as he watches the car burn; fire shoots up into the air from the blaze and disappears before his eyes. He has never seen anything so fantastic. The abandoned road is littered with destruction and debris.

The winds shift and push the tear gas back onto the soldiers, but face masks help protect their eyes and lungs. The invisible gas hits Étienne and Ibrahimah with a start. Ibrahimah begins choking and coughing, his eyes aflame with the burn of poison. He and Étienne's hiding place is no longer a refuge from the violence before them.

"Étienne, it hurts!"

"Let's go!"

They run down Boulevard de St. Louis with other startled pedestrians on their heels.

"What's going on? Why are my eyes burning?" an older woman asks.

"Tear gas to run the students off. The wind pushes it back onto us!" a man says, rushing past her.

The older woman starts to cough and leans over to spit. Ibrahimah and Étienne walk for a while in search of cleaner air to breathe as they wait out the pain in their throats and sting in their eyes. The sounds of rebellion can be heard throughout the neighborhood. When silence washes over the city for ten minutes or more, hearts skip a beat in hope that the students have retreated. Étienne and Ibrahimah pass by a woman selling peanuts and buy themselves two packets. Ibrahimah's heart is still racing with adrenaline. An old man sits with his transistor radio on, listening to the newscast.

"Citizens should stay inside. Traffic is backed up on both the Eastern and Western sides of Dakar. Travel between downtown and the rest of the city is impossible. Reports from the local hospital have estimated more than two hundred and fifty people have been rushed to the emergency room with injuries, several of them severe."

"Those troublemakers should be shot! Business has to go on! People have lives. Those students create a ruckus over every small issue there is to complain about," the old man says.

"I hear they were fed rotten meat and many students got sick," the peanut lady says.

"So, that makes it okay to throw food into the streets and attack innocent people? The military should be allowed to go on campus. That would immediately end this charade." The man scoffs and waves his fist in the air.

The woman shakes her head. "Before the law was enacted the police brutalized the students. It is right the president does not allow the police on campus."

"But the students take advantage and we are the ones to pay! Remember when they hijacked a bus full of people and kept them hostage on campus? Or when they kept the chancellor hostage in his office for several days? They should be jailed, not given scholarships for their silence."

"I agree, it's a problem. They should just stop giving the scholarships," the woman says.

"Hmph, if it were that easy. These bastards will riot until the president breaks. Police force is what they need."

Ibrahimah looks at Étienne with his eyebrows raised as they walk away.

"Students should be shot!" Ibrahimah mocks.

"One day I'm going to be a soldier. I'll shoot big guns and drive a big car," Étienne says.

Ibrahimah finds this amusing and laughs.

"Why are you laughing?" Étienne says, frowning.

"You'll never drive. You'll crash into the students and they'll go flat!" Ibrahimah doubles over in laughter.

"I will drive one day! But I like the idea of making stupid people flat with big car tires!"

By nine o'clock the students calm down and the boys spend the evening begging and comparing notes with Fatik and the others about what they saw and heard. But by noon the next day, the students commence rioting again and for the next six hours havoc rains down onto Dakar; citizens are caught in the crossfire. Again, the military fires shells filled with tear gas to subdue the rioters.

"The students are stupid. They hurt too many people for no reason," Étienne says as they make for cover.

Ibrahimah learned his lesson when the tear gas hit them the first time, so today, they visit Moustapha in hopes of eating a decent lunch and tapping into their stash of money. With the raised quota of four hundred francs, along with the difficulty of getting money post-Ramadan, and in addition to the chaos of the rioting students disrupting the flow of life in Dakar, the boys have been feeling the pressure more than ever. Many of the boys have been coming back short, and Marabout's wrath has been seemingly at an all-time high, so Ibrahimah and Étienne keep to themselves more than ever. Often, they are the first boys back home in the evenings and have found that this allows them more ease because Marabout is not so angry yet. The radio plays while Marabout Ahmed counts their money.

"In a highly strategic move the students have pushed the bar. Four days of riots, causing millions of francs in damage, cutting off businesses, and causing foreign investors and local NGOs to threaten the president with flight if something is not done to rectify the matter. The word from the president's office is that there will not be a tuition hike. The matter first surfaced when the university's bursar's office, supported by several banks, requested an eighteen-hundred-franc hike in tuition, to a total of sixty-eight hundred francs. The inconvenience for the bursar's office and the burden on local banks to produce the outdated and low-circulated coins twice a year caused a massive and brutal uproar on the campus of fifty thousand students and caused a pushback never seen before from students at the university. The chancellor is in the process of trying to determine who is responsible for the riots, as several dozen students have come forward claiming responsibility, in hopes of the scholarship offers that would allow them tuition at any school in the world outside of Senegal. The—"

Ahmed turns the radio volume down and shuts his door after collecting their money. Ibrahimah and Étienne go outside and bump into Caca and Scarface, who are just arriving back to the house.

"Boy, where you been?" Scarface asks, towering over Ibrahimah.

Ibrahimah looks over at Étienne. "I've been right here. *You're* the one just showing up—where've *you* been?"

"He has no money. Our day is hard just like yours. Someone stole from him earlier," Étienne says, stepping in between Ibrahimah and the older boy.

Scarface puffs up his chest but then dismisses Ibrahimah with a wave of his hand and walks away.

Slow to fall asleep that evening, Étienne overhears Scarface whispering.

"Marabout wants to know why they're never short money anymore."

"How we find out?" Caca asks.

"We'll follow them tomorrow."

XXIII.

Maimouna's crying fits continue. She has lost track of how long she has been in this state and is sure that someone has gone to a spiritual doctor and put a spell on her. Under no circumstances can she stop sobbing; she cannot think of what else could cause such a malady, other than the work of dark magic.

Both Fatou and Idrissa confirm her eyes still produce tears in her sleep, as every morning her pillow is wet. Drinking and eating are almost impossible, as is going about her daily chores—but it is not just the crying alone that is the problem—it is the heaving and deep sobbing that she cannot control. She is thankful sleep comes so quick, or she may have lost every one of her senses by now. Light invades the room and she brings her hand up to shelter her eyes.

"Maimouna, it's me, Idrissa."

She sits up in bed, sobbing.

"I've brought the doctor with me."

A noise escapes from the back of her throat that sounds like a muted howl of pain.

"Young lady, you have a sickness," the old man says.

The old man stands at the foot of the bed, his brown skin wrinkled and leathery, black eyes piercing straight through to her core.

His upper body bends over in a curved arch. He taps his cane against the floor.

"Bring me a chair."

Fatou drags a white plastic chair into the room. "Where do you want it, ton-ton?"

"Just here," by the side of the bed.

He sits down and stares Maimouna in the face. She closes her eyes, wishing for all of this to be over. His presence compels her to open them again. She hopes he does not give her another bitter or pungent tea to drink.

"Bring me my things," he says, turning to his grandson, who's been standing at the door silently.

The boy brings him a sack and then sets several containers on the dresser behind him. Fatou hands the old man a cup of gin-gembre. He takes a long drink before handing it back to her. His stubby fingers fumble with the sack until they find their way inside, retrieving the shells and pieces of animal hair.

"Grandpa, you have everything?"

The man grunts in approval and the boy quietly walks out of the room behind Fatou. Idrissa stands at the foot of the bed.

"You have to open your heart and submit yourself fully. If you don't believe, the magic will not work; it will turn on you like a cancer that eats the body."

She wants him to return the dark magic back to Madame N'Diaye, surely the person who has placed this curse upon her. The old man begins to burn several sticks and sets them aside as smoke fills the space. He reaches over and drops white cowrie shells, along with the separate pieces of animal hair, into a shallow bamboo basket. He reaches into the pouch hanging around his neck and then drops several twisted and gnarled roots on top of the shells and hair. He holds the basket with a torn piece of Maimouna's clothing out to Idrissa, who dutifully places several silver francs into it. The doctor shakes the basket to a rhythm only he knows as he mumbles indecipherable prayer verses. His eyes flutter involuntarily.

A flash of hope washes over Maimouna. She visualizes Ibra-himah coming home to her after breaking free of the chains of suffering as a Talibé. She sees her family together, healthy, with bellies full of food. Her daughters marry good men. Ibrahimah is strong. Her family is proud, God-fearing, righteous. Marabout Ahmed is dying, writhing in pain and distress, and Madame N'Diaye loses all of her children to death and sickness.

"Keep your thoughts pure, my child," the old man says under his breath.

He lights a match beneath the basket. The cloth inside ignites and he blows on it to create smoke. He stands and walks around in a circle with the basket, then places it on the ground between himself and the bed, and stamps one foot. He sits and picks up the cowrie shells and some of the silver coins, then tosses them to the ground beside the basket, looking down at them with deep intent. He repeats this process several times, studying the manner in which the shells move and the positions in which they lie after each toss. When he is satisfied, he places the shells back into the basket. His head falls forward, then back. Within the thick smoke in the room Maimouna sees Ibrahimah appear from behind the doctor.

"My love, you're home!"

Ibrahimah shakes his head no as he stands there looking at her with his red tin can clutched tight to his chest. The old man stands up again, and the image of Ibrahimah breaks apart within the white smoky cloud. He walks over to her dresser, where several unmarked glass containers lie, and grabs a small plastic bottle, mixing liquid from each of the three containers together. He takes powders out of several plastic bags and drops them into the mixture he's concocting.

The old man sits back down and sets the bottle next to him.

"Set five thousand francs into the basket."

Idrissa walks over and places the money inside. The old man shakes the basket while he chants, then spits inside and lights the fire beneath the basket again but not as close. He hands Maimouna the five thousand francs. The money is warm to her touch.

"You are to buy food with this and feed a poor child or family. Also, buy soap and give to someone like the Talibé or those without a home. Then buy two packets of peanuts, in the shell, and give them away."

He hands her the liquid potion.

"This medicine has many functions. Rinse your hands and feet in it while thinking of the well-being of your family."

Maimouna grips the bottle tightly.

"Sprinkle drops throughout and around the perimeter of your home to repel evil spirits from entering."

The old man rises.

"You understand all of my instructions?"

"Yes," Maimouna says, the sobs ceding.

"Where is my grandson? I take my leave now. I am tired."

Idrissa helps the elderly man gather his things and walks him out of the room.

"Fatou," Maimouna calls out in a weak voice, attempting to get out of her bed.

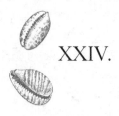

XXIV.

When Marabout doesn't open his door to lead the morning prayer, the boys who wake with the sun stay on the cement floor to eke out more sleep.

"Have you seen Ibrahimah?" Étienne whispers to Fatik, sitting up on his mat.

Fatik gives a knowing look and motions toward Marabout's bedroom just as the door creaks open for Ibrahimah to slide out before it slams shut again. Ibrahimah walks over to Étienne, his eyes sleepy, his face pained. Étienne puts their mats away and rests his arm around Ibrahimah gingerly as they leave the house together. The morning air is thick with dew.

"I don't feel good," Ibrahimah whines.

"Let's find food."

They pass a large rock and Ibrahimah leans up against it, refusing to walk any farther. He has no interest in begging or walking around Dakar today. His mother pops into his mind and he wonders what she is doing. It's too early for her to be cooking yet. He imagines clinging to her leg or drinking her milk but then he remembers: she is dead; his father too. It's like a punch to the belly, sadness grips his body, depleting him of oxygen. He then remembers the man in the morning and the basket. He clings to the idea that his parents are better in Paradise than on Earth, but he still cannot help but yearn for his mother this morning. Just seeing her face would make everything better.

"I found you a mango," Étienne says, coming back to the rock Ibrahimah has made his home for the time being.

Ibrahimah looks at Étienne, then the mango. All is not lost. He still has his cousin, but he cannot stop the feeling of dread that squeezes his body so tight.

"I want my mama."

"I can't steal one of those, so this will have to do." Étienne shoves the mango toward Ibrahimah and drops it into his hands.

"Where's yours?" Ibrahimah asks in a small and pained voice.

"I'm fine," he says, climbing up onto the boulder.

Ibrahimah holds the mango to his chest. He wishes it were his mother. He bites into the skin and pulls it back, his stomach growling at the sweet scent of sugar permeating from the sugary meat. He is tempted to eat the entire thing.

"Here. Take," Ibrahimah says, offering his cousin the other half. Étienne takes it, mango juice spilling onto his hands.

"Thanks," Étienne says as he finishes the fruit.

"I hate Marabout, even if he says he helps my mama in Paradise," Ibrahimah says.

"Me too," Étienne says, between bites of mango.

Ibrahimah looks at Étienne with surprise. He is used to his cousin defending their teacher.

"Marabout is wicked. He does things that are bad," Ibrahimah says, looking into Étienne's face to gauge his cousin's reception.

"Yeah."

With the burst of sugar from the mango in his stomach Ibrahimah finds the energy to walk a bit more until they find a quiet street with a few trees offering scant shade. The tall multi-dweller houses that line the road show no signs of life. The small store next to them is dark; someone inside listens to the latest song by Youssou N'Dour.

"What would happen to us if Marabout died?" Ibrahimah asks.

"I don't know. Maybe we go back to the village or another marabout would take us."

"I hope he dies soon."

Étienne looks over at Ibrahimah.

"Come on. Let's find a better place to rest."

The boys walk slowly through the streets of Mermoz. All is quiet except for the occasional car that races down the hot, sticky asphalt. They stop at a small freestanding boutique with a short bench beside its entrance; several large trees shade the area.

Étienne throws the mango seed into a bush and then turns to Ibrahimah.

"How does Marabout help your mama in Paradise?"

"A man comes in the morning sometimes and Marabout cuts my nails and hair and puts it in a basket for the man. He said it was for my mama."

"I've never seen this man."

"The man comes when everyone is sleep. Marabout wakes me up and tells me to be quiet."

"Like a secret you're not supposed to share with us?" Étienne asks.

"I think so," Ibrahimah says, looking up at his cousin. He wonders if sharing his secret with Marabout was a good idea.

Ibrahimah and Étienne come upon a few men standing and talking amongst themselves nearby, selling grilled corn on the cob. Islands of sunshine force their way through the thick leafy trees, but not enough to conquer the cool shade. A boy recognizes Étienne.

"Hey, boy, how goes you?"

"Babacar. *Namanala!*" Étienne says, slapping hands with the skinny boy with a hunchback.

"I miss you more, my friend. It's good to see you! Eat with us," the boy offers, waving his hand to the group of boys huddled on the ground.

Étienne and Ibrahimah join the group of four boys for a bowl of rice. Ibrahimah eases himself down slowly while watching the boys sit on their heels, talking and laughing. He looks down at his shirt. Aria calls it a peach-hued polo; she took his green one after he shared the story of Demba. Wearing the shirt made him sad. He then looks at the boy next to him, who is wearing dark-brown pants, a blue button-down shirt, and white sneakers. Ibrahimah cocks his head to the side.

"Are you a Talibé?" he asks the boy in sneakers.

The boy turns to him and breaks into a coy, slanted smile.

"I am."

"You don't look like a Talibé. Where is your red can?"

"I lost it. I need to get a new one."

"Why do you dress so nice? Talibé are dirty and poor."

The boy throws his head back and laughs.

"You're a funny boy. My marabout buys us clothes. Not all marabouts are greedy wretches." He pats Ibrahimah on the shoulder.

"My mother and father are dead. If my marabout dies, I want to go to your marabout."

Ibrahimah turns back to the bowl of food and plops the last bit of rice into his mouth. The boy he was talking to stands up and drifts off into conversation with someone else. Ibrahimah lingers on the ground a moment, then crawls over toward the trunk of the nearby tree and leans against it. His skin burns hot. Across the lot the men are eating their grilled corn and drinking café. His eyes fall heavy as he watches Étienne draw circles on the ground with a stick while talking with the hunchback boy. Within moments he is asleep.

"Students fight because they don't want to pay eighteen francs more," Étienne says.

"They should be a Talibé or a cripple like me and then they know what it means to suffer."

"You're not a cripple; your back is curved instead of straight. Look at my finger. It curves like your back." Étienne jostles with Babacar, laughing. "If Talibé fought people for money, they would throw us in the sea."

"Or under a bus!"

The boys laugh.

"Instead, the leaders of the student riots get scholarships to go to any school in the world so that they don't riot again next year, except every year a new batch of troublemakers starts trouble for any stupid reason to get the scholarships!" Babacar says, shaking his head.

"Maybe Talibé should join the students next time," Étienne says with a smirk.

"Babacar, let's go work," the buttoned-down-shirt boy says.

"No. The sun is too hot. Wait."

"What's wrong with him?" the boy asks, pointing to Ibrahimah.

"He'll be okay, he's just tired," Étienne says.

"Well, we're going. We'll meet you back here later."

"Okay, *ciao*," Babacar says to his friends with a short wave.

Moments later a white-haired British woman approaches the two friends.

"Tu veux de l'argent, Talibé?"

Étienne and Babacar give each other a knowing look.

"Oui," they say in unison, smiling at their inside joke.

She hands them three hundred francs each. Walking away she notices Ibrahimah and turns back.

"Est-il malade?"

"Non, fatigué," Étienne says.

She walks over to Ibrahimah and drops several coins into his red tomato can. She turns and waves to Étienne and Babacar. They pass their cupped hands over their faces in prayer for her. After she is gone from sight, Étienne puts the three hundred francs in his pocket.

"Do you collect a lot of money here?"

"Sometimes, but this is luck. I've never seen that woman before. The others missed out; they should have stayed."

"More for us."

The two boys nod like a pair of old wise men.

"How much do you have to raise every day?"

Babacar looks at Étienne, confused. "What do you mean?"

"Our marabout raised our payment to four hundred francs every night. How much do you pay your marabout?"

"We don't have to pay our marabout a certain amount. The five boys who raise the most money every week get a prize. The three boys who raise the most every month get a bigger prize."

"Like what?"

"New shoes"—Babacar sticks his leg out to show Étienne his Nike sneakers—"new clothes, pencils, cookies, and chocolates. One month, all the boys did better and he bought everyone ice cream."

"I never knew that about your marabout!"

"You never asked."

"My marabout beats us and makes us sleep outside when he's really angry."

Babacar nods in understanding. "My marabout says men like that give the brotherhood of Talibé a bad name."

Ibrahimah stirs awake, groggy and stiff. He rubs his eyes while looking around in anxious confusion, then pulls his achy body up from the base of the tree. He drags his feet across the dirt, kicking up a small billow of dust around his knees. Étienne looks at him and turns back to his conversation. Ibrahimah leans up against the bench, frowning as the tingling beneath his skin reverberates from the tips of his toes on up through his entire body. A hen runs past, screaming at the top of her lungs, a rooster hot on her trail.

"Why does the plain chicken always run from the colorful chicken?"

"One is a boy chicken; the other is a girl chicken. The boy chases the girl," Babacar says.

"Why?"

"Because that's what boys do. Chase girls!"

Étienne and Babacar laugh.

Ibrahimah scrunches his face up as he wakes. "What's so funny about chasing girls?"

"The boy chases the girl to make baby chickens," Babacar says.

Ibrahimah yawns big. He's not interested in the rooster-chicken mystery. A man walks up to the store clerk to buy cigarettes and Ibrahimah walks up to the man and begs for money, his voice soft and pitiful; a combination of the grogginess that has yet to wear off and the suffering he wears like a badge. The man hands Ibrahimah a hundred-franc piece. Ibrahimah mumbles thank you and walks away. He drops the coin into his tomato can and it clanks up against something. He looks down and notices four silver hundred-franc coins sitting on the bottom. He cocks his head to the side and stares in confusion.

"Étienne, look! Magic!" he says, pointing into his can.

"What?"

"Money appears in my can. It's magic!"

Étienne laughs and walks over to Ibrahimah.

"No, an Englishwoman put money in your can while you slept," Étienne says, resting his hand on his cousin's shoulder.

"Easy money is the best," Babacar says with a chuckle.

"Too bad we couldn't sleep and money just appears like that every day!" Étienne snaps his fingers in the air.

"Like that!" Ibrahimah says, snapping his fingers, copying Étienne. Maybe the tooth fairy whispered to the lady to give him the money. He looks up at the sky. Or perhaps his mother is now an angel looking after him. He doesn't have to worry about getting beat tonight.

Étienne looks over by the group of men and catches a glimpse of Scarface and his sidekick, Caca, crouched down by the wheel of a car. They've been spying on him and Ibrahimah.

Scarface pushes Caca in anger.

"Why are you mad at me?" Caca yells.

"We waste our time following these two sissies," Scarface says as he walks away, not caring that their cover is blown.

Étienne turns back to Babacar and Ibrahimah and smiles.

XXV.

For forty days and forty nights Maimouna cries, but the deep, guttural sobs cease the day the spiritual doctor leaves, and so every morning and evening thereafter, she rinses her hands and feet in the chalky concoction he gave her. But the tears continue to fall ceaselessly, and so every morning she changes her pillowcase and bedsheets only to soak them afresh, overnight.

The morning her tears finally do stop, Maimouna is overcome with joy. Her appetite returns and she drinks endless amounts of bissap, soda, tonic, black tea, gingembre, bouye, and water with vigor; her body desperate to rehydrate. That evening she prepares yassa poisson for dinner and lights a candle, praying nonstop for five hours in hopes of Ibrahimah's safe return home, and in gratitude for the freedom from the ill will of others. She goes to bed with dry eyes and a dry pillow.

"Mama."

Her eyes flutter open.

"Mama, are you awake?"

Maimouna looks around the room. Light breaks through the parted curtains.

"Is everything okay?" she asks, sitting up. Her body struggles to wake up.

"Grandpa has passed away," Fatou says with wet eyes.

"As soon as one good thing happens, something terrible arrives to replace it," Maimouna says, sighing heavily and getting out of bed.

Idrissa is home within an hour of receiving the news and finds Maimouna in the kitchen with the girls. She looks up at her husband with solemn eyes. He hugs her and kisses her gently on the mouth.

"My father was ill. It was a surprise he held on this long. He has joined my mother, and is now with Allah. May both my parents rest in peace," Idrissa says before leaving to meet his brother at the mosque.

Maimouna and the girls bring food, drinks, and fatayas over to their uncle's house, where family and neighbors are gathered. It is the first time in months that many of the neighbors have seen her.

"Maimouna! *Namanala trop!*" Madame Touré exclaims. "You've lost so much weight! I knew you were not well, but *oh là là! Ma belle chérie,* I did not know just how bad. Why have you not called on me?"

Maimouna responds with pious silence as a tide of whispers swells within the room.

"She is fine," Maimouna's sister-in-law booms over the chatter, "she just needs to have a successful pregnancy."

Maimouna looks over at her sister-in-law. Not this talk again of having another child. She is done with childbirth if she can help it, and having another child so that she can forget about Ibrahimah, her child who is still alive, feels wicked and unnatural.

"Did you lose a baby to miscarriage? Is that what this has been all about? That would make sense, actually. You know, with everything . . ." Madame Touré allows her voice to trail off as she uses her hands to make a sweeping gesture.

Several women in the room move closer to listen, and the whispering ebbs as its inhabitants ponder this new line of thinking.

"A woman's hormones, when she is pregnant, are unpredictable. You become a lion, willing to devour anyone that threatens the well-being of the life you are creating or have created," Madame Cisse says, in a matter-of-fact manner.

"That is true. I was terribly cranky, yelling at my husband and children throughout my entire pregnancy of my third child. It is like I was possessed," another woman says, shaking her head.

Whether her sister-in-law meant to change the winds of discourse or not, it is working, with the help of Madame Touré. She should have called on her friend and neighbor long ago. Madame Touré has been on her side from the start of this disaster with Marabout Ahmed, but one can never know whom to trust fully, so it was best to keep her family's problems as quiet as possible. She cannot deny that it feels good to reconnect with the women in her village, although it is at the expense of her father-in-law, and Madame N'Diaye is glaringly not in attendance; she left before Maimouna arrived, as organized by Maimouna's sister-in-law.

Over the course of the next week, Maimouna visits Madame Touré and her sister-in-law on several occasions; she receives several orders for her fatayas and goes about her days and nights encased in prayers for Ibrahimah, herself, and her family. Maimouna's respite lasts a mere seven days before her desire or ability to participate in the daily ritual of life dissipates once more.

"Get out," Maimouna growls from her bed.

Fatou stops cleaning and stands in the middle of the room, uncertainty draped across her shoulders. This phase is worse than the month-and-a-half-long crying fit. At least Maimouna was trying then. This time feels different to Fatou.

"Go!"

Maimouna watches the thin silhouette of the girl walk out of the room. She lies there with dark pouches of woe encircling bloodshot eyes. Her hair is matted to her head; flakes of dandruff speckle her scalp like cinders of ash above a fire. She replays Idrissa's words in her mind from that morning.

"How long are you going to behave this way, woman? You cannot continue on in this manner! It's been three weeks since my father passed. We are all mourning!" Impatience nestled at the base of his throat.

The room was too dark to see the worry in his eyes, but the disapproval in his voice was clear enough. She tried to explain to him the mountains of hate and disgust she feels for herself and everything around them, but no sound would leave her throat. Even now, her vocal cords fail to express her despair. The relief she had once felt after her fits of crying ended was now a faded memory. Her attempts at getting well seem frivolous and shallow. Leaving her bed is nonnegotiable. Visitors are turned away. She refuses to allow the spiritual doctor to come again or to drink any more variations of bitter, pungent, or overly sweet teas made out of roots, fungi, and dirt. She has lost the energy to fight. She is unable to face the present, and her mind is flooded and tormented with memories of her youth.

After her uncle returned her to Guinea, she never saw him again. His lies and deceit were too much for her mother to endure, and she expelled him and his wife from their lives, which unfortunately included her cousins. Little did anyone know Maimouna had saved two hundred and fifty thousand francs for her mother; she wanted to bring something to her for all the years they had spent apart. A gift to show that even with so much distance between them, she loved her mother dearly and thought of her every day.

"My child," her mother said, holding Maimouna's thin face in her hands, "forgive me for not knowing the evil your uncle would allow around you. Every time I felt something, your uncle would appear with stories of your wonderful life and small gifts he claimed were from you. I thought the feelings of worry I had were just my overactive imagination. I was young and foolish. Please, forgive your mama."

Maimouna would find herself crying tears of joy over a simple meal of chicken and rice cooked by her mother, on her way home from the market, or in the morning upon waking and realizing that she was not in Dakar but in Guinea. In the early morning she would clean the house and it would fill her with pride to do something for the person she loved the most. Some days she would miss her cousins, but it never lasted long enough to cause her too much grief. She would cook for her mother the Senegalese dishes she learned to make so well and she beamed with joy when her mother gushed over the flavorful meals.

She found work cleaning for a French family in the area and doted on her mother. It was at the market that she met Idrissa selling wares imported from France and China. She would visit his stall twice a week, coming up with excuses to buy things like perfumes and knickknacks for her beloved mama. Eventually, he learned where she lived and called on her at home. Her mother could not understand what it was with their family and the Senegalese, but she blamed herself for Maimouna's affection for Idrissa.

"Had I kept you here with me, you would be married to a fine Guinean man by now," her mother lamented.

"Oh, Mama!" Maimouna playfully teased. "You know you love him too!"

Her mother smiled. "I do. He is a good boy and will do right by you."

Their courtship lasted a year before Idrissa came back from one of his trips with the news that he was moving back to Senegal.

"My mother passed away," he announced while they were drinking an evening tea in the yard.

"I'm so sorry," Maimouna said as she cupped his hand into her own.

"My father has told my brother to lend me some of his land for my own. No longer will I work in trade and wares but become a farmer like my father and his father before him."

"Oh," Maimouna said, letting go of his hand.

"I want you to come with me. Be my wife, Maimouna."

"Oh!" Maimouna's eyebrows shot up. Of course, this is the direction she expected their relationship to go, but she never harbored the idea of returning to Senegal. Never in a million years. She dreamt of living in a house next door to her mother and seeing her every day for the rest of her life.

"I promise to never take on an additional wife. You are my only love."

That wasn't the cause of her hesitation, but she was glad to hear he would forego Islam's allowance to marry up to four wives.

"I never imagined moving back to Senegal. I only just reunited with my mother three years ago."

"Your mother can come with us!"

"I'll ask her."

Her mother refused, but urged her to go and create a life for herself with Idrissa.

"You have been blessed with a good man. Your suffering did not happen in vain. It was noted, and you are now reaping, and will continue to reap, your just rewards, my child."

They married, and within two weeks she was living in the village of Saloulou in her very own five-room house.

Maimouna looks around the darkened room. Allah has turned his back on her. Her sufferings of youth were not enough penance to offer lenience in the face of her present crimes: sending Ibrahimah away to live the life of poverty, pain, and hardship. She flips over to lie on her other side, leaving her back to the door. She has no blessings.

Night arrives, concealing all that is wrong in the world. Fatou walks into the bedroom for the second time that day and shakes her awake. Maimouna wrinkles her nose in disgust. She finds the smell of food disgusting.

"Take it away."

"Mama, it's rice and lamb, just like you do it. You have to eat something. Please."

For a moment Maimouna feels bad for her daughter. She is trying her best, but the truth is the effort means nothing. Life is still suffering, pain, and disappointment. She never should have brought these children into this life. She should have known better. What a fool she has been all these years.

Fatou walks around to the other side of the bed and sits on its edge. She places the candle on the dresser and attempts to put a spoonful of rice into her mother's mouth. Maimouna knocks the spoon away and spills rice on the bed. Fatou puts the tray on the dresser, rolls her eyes, and walks out of the room.

Fatou joins her father and sisters in the living room to eat. Gone are the days of family chatter and discussion. Dinner by candlelight casts shadows across solemn faces as the rolling power outages continue. Idrissa looks over at his daughter and sees the pain in her eyes.

"Fatou, the food is very good. Isn't it, girls?"

"Yes."

"Delicious."

Idrissa reaches over and pats Fatou on the shoulder. "You'll make a good wife one day, my daughter."

Fatou hangs her head as she nibbles on a piece of chicken. "I wish Ibrahimah had never been born," she mumbles.

Idrissa looks up with surprise on his face. "Fatou! How could you say such a thing? Our family is going through a hard time, but there is still hope. Allah blesses those who have faith."

"But Papa, how much more can we take? Why is Allah testing our faith? We are good people. Me, Aisha, and Binta are good in school. We do our chores without complaint. You and Mama work hard. Ibrahimah is just a baby and look at what has happened! Nothing we do is working."

"It's not fair," Aisha mumbles, her shoulders slouching in unison with her sisters'.

"Girls, you know your mother has had a hard life. She and I met three years after she had escaped from her uncle and yet I had never met a woman with a more gentle and loving heart. I knew that no matter what life dropped at our feet, we would conquer it, together, with love."

Tears well up in the corners of Fatou's eyes and she struggles to hold them back. "How will we conquer this? Mama has given up. She is too tired to fight. We are tired. And Ibrahimah—is he still fighting?"

"Fatou, you are right. Your mother is tired. I am tired and I know you, my children, are tired. It does seem like your mother has given up hope, but I believe a part of her has not, or we would not be having this discussion right now. She refuses to leave the bed and eat, but she is still in the bed, in the house, with us. I thought perhaps this phase would pass like all the others but you have awakened me to realize that I need to try again. Perhaps I have given up hope these last days because of my fatigue, and I am sorry. I promise you; we will get through this."

Binta, Aisha, and Fatou get up and embrace their father.

The next afternoon Idrissa's older brother visits with his wife and children. Cousins meet one another at the door and run off to play while the adults discuss matters. Fatou serves a drink that is a mixture of sweet bissap and spicy gingembre on ice, and lingers close by, more interested in the adult conversations than playing with ten- and eleven-year-olds.

"How is she?"

"Not good, brother."

"Perhaps she needs to see a doctor?"

"Nothing is working."

"I mean a real doctor, not one of those heebie-jeebie witch doctors. Perhaps she has a tumor or cancer."

"More like cancer of her senses," Idrissa's sister-in-law interjects. "You should have continued to give her the tea I sent."

Idrissa looks over at his sister-in-law with tired patience.

"The teas are not working, and at this point she refuses to drink any more of them, and who can blame her. She's tired. We're tired," Idrissa says.

"*I* should talk to her, woman-to-woman. She needs to stop this selfish nonsense. I know she is not Senegalese, but she was raised in Dakar. We are strong, resilient women. She brings us shame."

Idrissa waves his hand toward their bedroom and his robust sister-in-law hoists herself up out of the chair. She bumps into Fatou along the way.

"Fetch me another glass of that bissap-and-ginger drink. Did you make that?"

"Yes."

"It's absolutely delicious, my dear."

"Thank you, ta-ta," Fatou says.

"You'll have to make me a special batch this week," she says, walking into Maimouna and Idrissa's bedroom.

The brusque woman squints as her eyes struggle in the dark, her nose contorting into various angles at the stench. She walks across the room, pulls the curtains back, and opens the window, allowing anxious sunlight to burst through.

"Close it."

"I cannot see without light and cannot breathe without fresh air." She grabs a chair and drags it over to the window. "It stinks in here."

Fatou returns and hands her aunt the drink.

Ice cubes clink as she takes a long, greedy gulp from the oversized plastic cup. "Go, I'll call you when I need you."

Fatou takes to aimless sweeping outside the bedroom door.

"You plan to lie there until death? Leaving your husband and children to fend for themselves?"

Maimouna turns her back to the window in an attempt to block the assault of sunlight through her closed eyelids.

"You think you are a good woman?"

"I'm not."

"You're right," her sister-in-law scoffs, "you're not. A mother doesn't abandon her children and husband. You have a good husband. He's not taking additional wives or sleeping with other women. He hasn't divorced you and taken the children, though he has every right to do so!"

"Perhaps he should."

"You scorn what Allah gives you. You spit in his face as you lie here refusing to care for your family. Understand that ungratefulness redeems no bounty in this life or the hereafter."

Maimouna scoffs at the intrusion of this pompous woman in her space; her bleached skin gives off a smell of the dead as she attempts to cover it with talcum powder and body spray. Maimouna wishes death would release her this very moment.

"Look at me and my husband. We sent our Étienne away to be a Talibé more than six years ago and Marabout Ahmed says he's one of the best boys in Dakar. Children should not be burdens to their elders once they are brought into this world. They're here to serve their parents, to bring them honor." She pauses a moment and looks over at Maimouna. "I admit, I missed my Étienne dearly at first, but then we were blessed with another child. That new child was a gift from Allah. You disrespect our traditions when you behave this way. People whisper and gossip about this all through the village and the next; you bring our entire family shame."

What does this stupid woman know of honor or tradition? One does not abandon their child for the sake of blessings from a marabout. Death will put her out of this misery soon enough. The question that begs to be answered is when will this old wretch leave and go back to dallying in someone else's business?

"Go ahead, turn your back to me but you cannot make me leave. You'll listen to me. Life is difficult for us all. There's nothing you can do to spare your children the disappointment and pain of life. You dishonor the Muslim brotherhood of the Talibé with your sorrow and self-pity."

"Leave my room."

"Perhaps your guilt has to do more with the distance you have created between yourself and Allah. What woman mourns a child who is alive and well? It's absurd. You have lost your mind for sure."

"Say what you may. You will pay for abandoning your child, as will I."

Her sister-in-law clucks her tongue. "You're an insolent woman. I pity your husband and children, for they're the ones who pay for your stupidity."

She gets up from her chair to leave but stops midstep.

"Fatou!" she calls.

The young girl scurries into the room.

"Yes, ta-ta."

"Help me get your mother up. We'll bathe her and clean this room once and for all. The stench in here is unbearable."

"Na'am."

"Pull these sheets off and go put them in the back for washing. Is there water up here or do you have to fetch some?"

"We fetched water earlier."

"Good. Fill the pail inside with water to bathe your mother."

Fatou begins pulling the sheets back off the bed. Maimouna tries to hold on to them but she is no match for the healthy teenager. Her sister-in-law shoves Maimouna's body to the left and then to the right as Fatou pulls the fitted sheets off. When Fatou returns with the water, her aunt is in her brassiere and underwear, waiting.

"I don't want my clothes getting wet," she says, before turning her attention to Maimouna.

"Don't touch me."

"Shut up, woman. You've caused enough trouble. The least you can do is bathe your body. You're disgusting."

Fatou lowers her head in shame.

"Help me raise her up."

Fatou and her aunt hoist the hard, bony shell that used to house Maimouna's voluptuous and curvy figure. Irritated, she shakes their hands off and walks hunched over in short strides toward the bathroom. The house has no running water, but the drain in the middle of the tiled bathroom floor works fine.

"We'll need more water; her hair needs to be washed also."

Fatou runs outside and instructs her sisters to go fetch more water from the well.

"Why? We're busy. Do it yourself," Aisha says, placing her hand on her hip and pursing her lips.

Fatou grabs the girl by the ear and drives her nails into it. Aisha tries to pull away but is no match for her older sister. Fatou looks over at Binta.

"You want the same?"

Binta shakes her head.

"Then take these buckets and go fetch more water."

Fatou releases Aisha, who steps away frowning and rubbing her ear.

"Auntie is bathing Mama and we need more water. Plus, we have to wash the sheets and cook."

The girls raise their eyebrows.

"Mama's up?" they ask in unison.

"Don't ask questions, do what I say now," Fatou yells over her shoulder, returning to her mother and aunt.

"Woman! Close your eyes. I have to rinse the soap from your hair!"

"Leave me," Maimouna says, her teeth chattering and body shivering beneath the cold water assaulting her skin.

With Fatou helping her aunt, Maimouna eventually gives up her fight and allows the water to flow over her body. She cannot say for sure that what she went through as a young woman, living as a servant, was easier or harder than what is happening to her now. She does not know where she found the resilience to survive such a harsh and unrewarding life. She did love her cousins back then and she often focused solely on them, tending to their needs and desires, so perhaps, it was through caring for them that she found solace. Perhaps life's struggles are easier to bear when one is young. Perhaps God did love her back then and that is how she survived, but she is certain he does not care for her now.

Fatou and her aunt's coordination is sloppy and water splashes in every direction, leaving Fatou and her aunt sopping wet. Fatou hands her aunt a towel and the woman pats herself dry while grumbling under her breath about what a foolish woman Maimouna is, and now look at how wet she has gotten herself doing charity for her husband's brother. Fatou grabs another towel and pats her mother dry.

"Come, Mama," Fatou coaxes. She slips Maimouna into a bra and panties then rummages through her dresser for a wrap skirt and matching top. Maimouna sits hunched over with limp arms on the edge of the bed. Her sister-in-law puts her elaborate outfit back on and sits down in the chair.

"You are going to put her in *those* old clothes?"

"They're clean and comfortable," Fatou says defensively.

Her aunt rolls her eyes and looks out of the window.

"Mama, sit on the floor. Let me braid your hair."

Maimouna slips down to the floor and Fatou sits above, her legs dangling over the side of the bed. Fatou makes neat parts and braids tight cornrows from the front of Maimouna's head to the base of her neck.

Her daughter is such a mirror of herself. If only the love of her children and husband were enough to wake her out of this wicked dream, Maimouna thinks to herself. Fatou wraps her mother's head in a scarf.

"Well, that's better! You almost look presentable again, thanks to me. Let's go sit in the living room with our husbands," says Maimouna's sister-in-law.

Maimouna shakes her head. She cannot bear sitting in a room with her husband and brother-in-law, becoming a spectacle to be discussed, or a problem to be fixed, each seeking to triumph over the other, convinced their solution is the right one.

"It'll be good for you."

Maimouna shakes her head again and slaps at the hand of her sister-in-law. The only reason she tolerates this woman is because Fatou is present, but if she never saw her sister-in-law again, she'd lose no sleep.

"I have to wash the sheets. Mama can sit with me while I do that. She could use the fresh air."

"Sure," she says curtly.

Outside, the sunlight hits Maimouna's eyes like lightning. Her hand rises to shield her face. How'd she ever leave the house in such harsh conditions? Fatou drags a chair over to a shady part of the small yard and Maimouna sits down. She covers her face with her hands before her sister-in-law moves them down to her lap.

"You need the sun," she scolds.

"I have an idea!" Fatou says, dashing inside the house, returning within moments with the straw hat her father wears while working.

She plops the hat down onto her mother's head, grinning ear to ear. The hat sits low on Maimouna's head, the large brim shading her eyes. Maimouna folds her hands into the middle of her lap and sits quietly. Fatou gives her aunt a smile of satisfaction while the woman sucks on her teeth in response. Fatou sits on a small bench in front of the pail with the soiled sheets and blankets and begins the wash. Maimouna's sister-in-law returns to the living room with the two men, her chest puffed out in victory.

"Well, I've got the lady of the house out of bed and cleaned up, and she's now sitting outside to get some fresh air. It's a good idea to take the mattress out and beat it. It holds a wretched stench, if I do say so myself."

The two men look up at the woman in awe. Idrissa jumps up from his seat and obliges the demands of his brother's wife. He grabs the mattress and drags it outside. When he steps out of the back door, he sees Maimouna sitting, wearing his hat. Fatou looks over her shoulder at the sound of footsteps and smiles when she sees her father. He points to the person with the hat and Fatou puts her hands over her heart. Binta and Aisha return in a cloud of noisy chatter as they lug the heavy buckets of water.

"Girls, calm down," Idrissa says.

Raised eyebrows are returned as they look to see why they should be quiet.

"Mama!"

Idrissa rests a stern hand on Binta's shoulder and the girl looks up at her father with questioning eyes.

"Mama, would you like to say hello to the girls?" Fatou asks.

Maimouna does not stir beneath the respite of the large-brimmed hat. Fatou looks closer and notices her mother's eyes are shut.

"I think she's asleep."

"Let's leave your mother for now. Run along, unless Fatou needs you for something else." He turns to his eldest daughter. "Fatou?"

"Aisha, empty one bucket of water into the blue pail, and then put the other over there. I need you all to clean the turnips and carrots," she says, pointing.

"You heard your sister, go over there and start preparing dinner."

Idrissa walks over to Maimouna and rests his hand on her shoulder. Her head bobs up but just as soon settles back into a bent-over position.

"My love, it's good that you're getting fresh air."

Maimouna does not respond. He pats her shoulder a few times and heads back inside. Fatou has the girls hang the sheets in the sun. Within two hours they'll be crisp and dry. Fatou beats the mattress while the vegetables boil on the fire. She glances over at her mother every thirty seconds to ensure she is fine.

Maimouna is awake, and with the brim of the hat pushed back

she watches her girls busy at work. She lifts her hand and Fatou is by her side within seconds.

"I need to lie down."

"Yes, Mama. Binta, watch the pot while Aisha helps me bring Mama inside."

With slow, meticulous steps the girls lead their mother into the house and lay her down onto a mattress in their shared bedroom. Maimouna lets out a sigh. She tells herself that there's nothing wrong with being bathed fresh before death arrives. She wills the end to come quickly and within moments she is sound asleep.

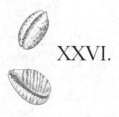 XXVI.

"Why are you always looking up at the sky?"

Ibrahimah averts his eyes from the clouds and looks over at Étienne. "The bird flies where he wants to go. The airplane flies to places far from here. I want to be in the sky, too, free to go where I want."

Étienne looks at the stalled traffic in front of them, black clouds of exhaust fumes spit out of the backs of several Car Rapides. He looks up and sees fat cumulus clouds sitting calmly against the baby-blue background. A black bird zips by, then disappears behind a brush of trees.

"Maybe you're right."

Ibrahimah glances up at the sky one more time. Still no sight of the red bird. "I am."

He and Étienne walk toward downtown Dakar with Fatik and several other boys from their house. Not their usual territory for begging, but Ramadan ended months ago and raising four hundred francs a day bedevils every boy in the house. They walk past the football stadium in Medina, the last place they ever saw Abdoulaye alive. A teenage boy yells at a girl and hits her. She struggles to pull away from him until an older man comes and runs him away. The girl fixes her shirt, her eyes wet, and walks away, shaken. Something cracks below Ibrahimah's foot and he looks down. A piece of broken glass sticks into the thin sole of his shoe. He lifts his foot up and pulls the glass out of the plastic jelly sandal. The edge is sharp.

"Are you okay?" Fatik asks.

"Yes, I'm fine."

"Well, don't kill anyone with it!"

"If I kill someone, they'd go into the sky to Paradise. It's better than here."

"No, if you kill someone you go to hell for being wicked!"

Ibrahimah raises his eyes to Fatik. "Will Marabout go to hell?"

"Maybe. What do you think, Étienne? Would Marabout go to hell if Ibrahimah killed him?"

"Yes."

"So, if I killed Marabout he'd go to hell, and I'd go to Paradise?"

"Who is talking about killing Marabout?" Caca asks.

"No one is talking about killing Marabout," Étienne interjects.

"I am!" Ibrahimah shouts.

Fatik starts laughing and the other boys in the group chime in.

"How would you do it, Ibrahimah, in his sleep?"

"Do it the next time he makes you sleep in his room!"

"Take that stupid cane and give it to him good!"

Ibrahimah looks up at all the older boys laughing and slapping one another on the back when one of them thinks of a cleverer way to kill Marabout.

"Why has no one tried to kill him yet? He's wicked all the time," Ibrahimah says.

The noise and chaos of Sandaga drowns out the boys' mumbled responses. There is no real answer to the question that has passed through all of their minds at one point or another. It is too dangerous even to acknowledge.

The large open-air market is home to the worst traffic bottleneck in Dakar, since the road is the main route in and out of the city. Cars crawl through the narrow alleys that are already crowded by makeshift vendor stalls and slow-moving, sweaty bodies. The asphalt is so hot, it gives way beneath feet and tires. The boys push their way through the tall crowds, sliding up against cars with frustrated drivers leaning on their horns with no resolution in sight. Young women hold their heads up high, backs straight, as they sway their hips from East Africa back to the West. One driver, angry that his honking is being ignored, accelerates. People jerk their bodies from the car's path, hitting at the car and cursing. The driver shouts back from inside his rolled-up windows and air conditioning. The boys break through to the other end of the market and Ibrahimah's eyes light up at the sight of the long lines of stalled vehicles fighting for passage through the ill-conceived junction.

"Be careful, stay close."

Ibrahimah tightens the space between himself and his cousin. Downtown is the beggar's field of dreams for its influx of wealthy foreigners, and for its pedestrian and traffic congestion as far as the eye can see. But the boys don't frequent downtown for a reason. Thieves, bandits, pickpockets, hustlers, adult beggars, families of vagabonds, and all kinds of downtrodden convene there looking for an opportunity.

The boys assess the four-way intersection and decide to head down the shady avenue that wraps around the market. No sooner do they arrive than they realize that they have to compete with the large congregation of albinos and the disabled. This road is one of Dakar's most popular spots for begging, and the people who are stuck in traffic are used to ignoring requests for money and food.

"When does Ramadan come back?" Ibrahimah asks, hopeful that it will be soon.

"Next year."

"How long is that?"

"A long time; the rain leaves and then comes back before Ramadan returns."

"I wish it were Ramadan all the time."

Étienne smirks as he looks around.

"Hey," Étienne says to the others, "there's no good money here. We're going."

"We're going to stay," Fatik says, and the other boys nod in agreement with him.

Ibrahimah and Étienne walk down toward Place de l'Indépendance. The small green promenade marks where a band of people stood and declared independence when Senegal officially broke from France in 1960. The green strip of land, the only public space with grass in the dry desert heat, stands in the middle of a large half-mile roundabout. The boys walk between the tall buildings that hold state offices, HSBC, the Sôfitel hotel, TAP Portugal airline offices, travel agencies, and other businesses representing the bustling West African economy.

Ibrahimah and Étienne turn left off of Place de l'Indépendance and find the block across the street from the popular French pastry shop La Galette to be just the right spot for them. Within seconds Ibrahimah breaks off from his cousin and approaches a statuesque woman. Her bright-orange dress billows behind her with every step she takes. A look of annoyance flashes across the woman's face, but she catches herself as she glances down at him. Dried snot sits on his upper lip, and his khaki pants and peach polo shirt are dirty. He barely reaches the middle of her thigh. She slows her gait, reaches into her Louis Vuitton handbag, and pulls out several coins. Ibrahimah reaches his hand out.

"Your can," she says, pointing.

Ibrahimah shoves his tomato can forward and she drops the coins inside. Ting-ting-ting ting-ting-ting! When he looks back up to say his blessings he's met with the tails of her dress and her long silky black hair.

Ibrahimah attempts to approach every set of legs that walk past. His entreaties are barely audible on the noisy street. Most don't even see him as he finds himself bumped, pushed, and ignored by those in a rush to get to their destination. The women naturally move at a slower pace due to their kitten heels and tight wrap skirts. Through trial and error, he learns it's best to stand close to the wall of the building, then dart in and out of the pedestrian traffic to approach rich-looking women as they click-clack along.

"Give me money for my marabout."

"That's not how you ask an elder for money, Talibé," a Senegalese woman with a bright-red face scolds him.

Ibrahimah strains his neck to get a better look at her. He can't imagine why she is so red. It looks like her face is on fire.

"Well, what do you say?" she asks.

Taken aback by the attention, Ibrahimah is quiet with apprehension.

"Well?"

"Sorry, ta-ta."

"Now, that's better."

The woman flings two fifty-franc coins into his red tomato can and struts off. Her strong perfume lingers, leaving Ibrahimah dizzy. He stands staring after her, confused and amazed.

"Her bleaching has gone bad."

"What?" Ibrahimah says, turning. He stands eye to eye with a man with no legs.

"That's what happens to African women who bleach their skin. They turn red and get all kinds of skin cancer. You can't run from the sun," he says, laughing.

Ibrahimah laughs too; this man is funny. Who would ever try to run from the sun? It's everywhere.

"What's your name Talibé?"

"Ibrahimah."

"You want a watch? I sell watches." The man lifts up his arm to show off shiny gold and silver wares. "I got Rolexes today."

"No, I don't need a watch."

"Hey, kid, everybody's got to know what time it is. I've never seen you around here before."

Ibrahimah shakes his head. "I live in Ouakam. Where are your legs?"

"My legs? I've never had them. Was born without them, but I don't let that slow me down!"

Ibrahimah looks inside his can and pulls out three peanuts from the few scattered at the bottom and offers them to his new friend.

"Thanks, Ibrahimah, you're a good one. You'll get to heaven with no problem."

The man looks down at one of the watches on his arm.

"Well, I've got to go. Take care down here. Downtown is a rough place. Thanks for the peanuts."

"Okay."

The man waves, then uses his muscled arms to propel his torso around the corner. The day continues on with the stream of bodies passing by. Ibrahimah peeks around the corner of the building and spots his new friend peddling his wares to men in business suits exiting the bank.

With the arrival of sunset, the flow of bodies subsides as the workforce flees downtown and heads north of the city for home. Étienne leans up against the building wall to count his money—nine hundred francs. He smiles.

"How much do you have?"

Ibrahimah hands Étienne his red tin tomato can. He's exhausted. His feet are throbbing and his legs tingle with fatigue. Étienne's head is bent over for several minutes.

"Wow," Étienne says, looking up, "you have two thousand, two hundred francs. Five days' worth of money for Marabout. We did good today! We'll take a Car Rapide back tonight."

"Good. I'm too tired to walk."

Étienne suggests they buy a pack of peanuts from a woman breaking her table down and use the plastic to wrap their coins so they don't make noise in their cans.

"Aye, boy! You coming?" Fatik yells out from across the street. The rest of the group is with him.

"Where?" Étienne yells back.

Fatik puts his hand to his mouth.

"Yeah!" Étienne's eyes light up.

Ibrahimah and Étienne cut across Place de l'Indépendance, talking and jostling about with their Talibé brothers; they all made their quota this evening, so their spirits are high. They approach a high white cement wall encased in the aroma of African spices and lamb. One of the boys knocks on the gate and within moments the whine of nuts and bolts in need of a good oiling fills the air around them and a slim, older Senegalese man appears. He has salt-and-pepper hair, a sharp, angular nose, and smooth brown skin. He is dressed in expensive Western clothes.

"Good evening, ton-ton."

"Come," the man says, waving them inside, his nails freshly manicured.

The man leads them along a white stone path lined with two mango trees, an avocado tree, and rows of strawberry bushes. The path opens up to a large sprawling fresh-cut lawn and an in-ground swimming pool with reclining beach chairs along either side. The pool water is crystal clear, with an intricate mosaic design shimmering at the bottom. Ibrahimah feels a sense of anxiety crawl up into his stomach until he notices the most impossible thing to grace his young eyes. Over to the far-left side of the yard sits a large canopy with raised flooring; several groups of Talibé sit before heaping platters of food. More than twice the number of Talibé who live with his marabout are eating together!

"Is this heaven?" Ibrahimah asks.

"I think so," Étienne says, taking in the scene in front of him.

If there is such an abundance of food in heaven, then Ibrahimah does not mind if seventy-two girls live with him; he'd have more than enough to share with his new sisters. Countless young Talibé boys talk and laugh through mouths full of rice. The sight of so much food stirs the hunger pains of the new arrivals. The Senegalese man turns and smiles down at them.

"Hungry, eh?"

"Yeah," Caca says, distracted. Ibrahimah's group is brought to the side of the canopy to wash their hands and then led to two empty spots. Ibrahimah places his can down between himself and Étienne. He wiggles and readjusts himself on the floor with impatience. When the platter of food is placed down between them several boys lunge forward at once.

"There is more where this came from, so be respectful. Patience!" the man instructs.

The boys pull back from the platter in a wave.

"See the others, how they eat and share. If they are still hungry after the plate is empty, there is more. You are not animals."

"Yes, ton-ton," they mumble, in unison.

With calculated pacing, the boys extend their right hands into the platter and gather rice to stuff into their small mouths. The man watches them a moment to ensure they don't tear one another apart.

"Remember to chew!" the man says before stepping away.

Rice to mouth, hand to platter, rice to mouth. Ibrahimah sits in quiet embarrassment looking around to see who is watching as he stuffs the rice down his throat. The platter of food is finished within minutes.

"You ate mine!"

"No fighting. We'll get kicked out!"

As if on cue a woman appears and asks the boys if they would like more. The boys mumble "yes." The next thirty minutes are spent with Ibrahimah stuffing as much food into his small stomach as he can fit. He and Étienne have not stopped by Moustapha's house in more than a week. Étienne advised that they avoid visiting their friend after he noticed Scarface and Caca following them during the day again. They can't go back until Étienne is certain the coast is clear. A big white car pulls into the back and stops where the pavement meets the grass. A white Frenchman and woman get out. Together they walk over to the canopy.

"*Bonjour, Talibé! C'est bon ce que vous mangez?*" the man asks.

Ibrahimah finds it bizarre that these toubabs, a word he recently learned to call white people, care whether or not he finds the food good. During the day they wouldn't have even looked at him.

"*Oui, c'est très bon. Merci beaucoup!*" several of the boys say.

Their smiles gleam in the evening dusk and the boys pause from eating to offer a prayer of thanks and blessings for the couple.

"*Ahh, bien.*"

The older Senegalese man approaches the couple. He bows his head in greeting; they exchange a few words, then retreat to the house together.

"Who are the toubabs?" Ibrahimah asks.

The boys in his circle hush him. "Toubab" is not the nicest thing to call a white person.

"This is their house. They feed Talibé every day," Fatik informs the group.

Ibrahimah looks over his shoulder at the house.

"Why have we never come before?" Ibrahimah asks Étienne.

"We would need money for the Car Rapide. Downtown is too dangerous, and too far to walk home. If Marabout lived downtown, it would be good."

He could see himself walking into the big house of the white couple, sitting on a soft chair, and watching cartoons with Étienne. They'd be his new parents. Moustapha and Fatik would visit, and together they'd eat mafé and tell jokes. His new father would tell him that he is a good boy and he can go to school. In his school bag he'd have lots of crayons like the one the girl gave him, and he'd spend all his days drawing airplanes and big guns, like the ones the soldiers carry.

"We got lucky today," Étienne says. "Now we have to go give Marabout his money."

The trek from downtown to Ouakam after a long day of working would take them at least three hours on the badly lit streets of Dakar.

Ibrahimah dozes as the Car Rapide ambles along in the dark. Unable to resist, he leans up against Étienne's shoulder and dreams of his grandfather. He clings to the old man's hand as they walk across the ocean, their feet making a soft spattering sound with each step. A large airplane flies along beside them, but they talk with ease over the engine. Ibrahimah sees Abdoulaye inside the plane smiling and eating a big piece of meat. Abdoulaye beckons Ibrahimah to come inside. He turns to his grandfather and points to the plane: "Look, Grandpa, it's Abdoulaye! Let's go eat."

His grandfather pats him on the head. "It's not your time, little one."

"But there's food inside the plane and the plane is going to Paradise. I want to get on the plane, Papa Yoro. I want to see my mama."

His grandfather smiles but shakes his head. Ibrahimah tries to pull away, but Papa Yoro won't release his hand. The plane turns and heads away from him.

"No! Come back! Grandpa, why don't we go too?"

Ibrahimah turns to his grandfather and screams. Marabout squeezes his hand, leering down at him. A red feather falls from his mouth to his chest as blood oozes from the corners of his lips.

A rooster screams and Ibrahimah jolts awake. His body is soaking wet, making a little puddle of mud beneath him He doesn't remember getting off the Car Rapide or paying Marabout. He scratches at his cheek and sits up. The morning prayer call rings out across the neighborhood. He has no idea how or why he slept outside in front of the house, but other than the annoyance of multiple mosquito bites, he shrugs it off; it's better than being inside with the devil.

 XXVII.

A thick fog climbs the hill from the shore and wraps itself around the house. Fatou inhales deeply. The rain will arrive within moments. She rushes to take the clothes down from the line, and leaves them in a pile inside the house for her sisters to fold when they return with the baguettes. She looks over at the pail of vegetables waiting to be washed and cooked. There are three large barrels and every other pail they own in the yard waiting to catch fresh rainwater for cooking, drinking, and laundry, saving several trips to the well at the bottom of the hill. The barrels were an inheritance from Grandfather.

Fatou looks at the empty white plastic chair and sighs. Things had gotten a little better after her aunt came. She and her sisters were getting their mother up in the mornings, bathing her without a fight, sitting her out in the back while they cooked and cleaned. Today Maimouna opted to go back inside and sleep after her morning bath, though, leaving Fatou wary of just how long this reprieve would last. She looks up at the sound of heavy footsteps moving through the small house.

"Papa?" Fatou calls out, confused as to who it could be.

Idrissa walks over and pats her on the head.

"Yes, yes, it's just me," he says.

Her father has aged much in the last few months. His hair has begun to turn white around his ears.

"You're home early. Is everything okay?" Fatou asks.

Idrissa grunts in the affirmative while searching out a cup and pouring himself some water.

"Okaaaaay," Fatou says, turning on her heels to go back outside.

"We have a visitor coming today. Is there anything to drink prepared?"

They haven't accepted a visitor in weeks. The story Idrissa came up with was that Maimouna had come down with a terrible flu, worse than grippe, and to prevent contaminating others they've quarantined themselves as much as possible. The whispers throughout the village have risen again, but no one dares to barge in on them.

"We have bissap. I'll be done with lunch soon. I'm making fish with the vegetables you brought home yesterday."

Her father goes into the living room to watch television. Aisha and Binta walk through the door, wet, but not quite drenched.

"Is the bread wet?" Fatou asks, exasperation in her voice.

"I'm not stupid, Fatou," Aisha says with a roll of her eyes, dropping the dry bread, wrapped in a plastic bag, onto the counter.

"I'm just saying—"

"I was seven years old then! Ya Allah, get over it. I'm not a baby. I'm eleven, only two years younger than you." Aisha rolls her eyes and turns to walk away.

"I was just making sure, because there's a visitor coming this afternoon."

Aisha stops in her tracks; Binta looks up from the cookie she just unwrapped.

"Who?" Binta asks.

"I don't know," Fatou says. "Papa says someone is coming to visit today."

Aisha frowns, her eyes disbelieving. "You lie," she accuses.

"I'm not. Go ask Papa. He's home early, in the living room, waiting."

"Who do you think it is, a doctor for Mama?" Binta asks.

"Peel the potatoes," Fatou says, pointing to the bucket. "It'll help pass the time."

Aisha and Binta plop down in front of the bucket of potatoes, whispering between themselves. Fatou hears the approaching footsteps before anyone else and dashes to the door. When the knock comes, it's a normal knock, like someone who just happened to be in the neighborhood; a knock that suggests that you should come out and enjoy the gay afternoon. Bracing herself for the worst, Fatou swings the door open and her mouth drops in shock.

"Grandmama!"

The seventy-five-year-old woman doesn't look a day over fifty, her smooth dark skin elastic against the laws of gravity and age. Her thick black hair shows no signs of gray. Two long braids hang down her back, her petite frame sturdy and strong. She's completely dry, as are her shoes and luggage, though behind her the drizzle has morphed into a full monsoon that rages without mercy, whipping and bending the trees.

"Oh, my, my, look at you! What a beautiful young woman you've become."

Fatou's smile threatens to overtake her entire face. "Come in, come in, before you get wet. This is the best surprise! Papa didn't tell us it was *you* coming."

Idrissa greets his mother-in-law inside the living room with a warm embrace.

"Thank you," he whispers into her ear.

She pats him on the back.

"Maam, Maam, Maam!"

Aisha and Binta rush toward their grandmother, almost toppling her over in an excited embrace; hugs, kisses, and a sense of relief wash over the space. Their grandmother will know what to do.

"Sit, you must be tired from your travels," Idrissa says, waving his hand toward the living room.

"No, I'm fine. Where is my daughter?"

XXVIII.

Ibrahimah scratches without mercy at his arms, hands, and face. Of all the people and animals in Dakar the savage mosquitoes seemed to attack only him through the night.

"Ibrahimah, come!"

Ibrahimah frowns at Étienne, refusing to budge. "No."

Étienne walks over and puts his arm around Ibrahimah's shoulders. He tries to coax him forward, but Ibrahimah brushes his cousin's arm off and steps back. Étienne lets out an exasperated sigh. "What's wrong?"

"I'm hungry and tired," Ibrahimah says, still scratching. Fresh blood mixes with the caked dirt beneath his fingernails.

"Ibrahimah, please come. We'll find food."

He doubts it. "I want cake!"

Étienne throws his hands up in the air, grabs his can from the ground, and walks away. The air is thick and unmoving. The sun sits above, its tyranny slowing everything down within its grasp. Ibrahimah's legs feel like lead, his knees hurt, his feet are tired, and his back aches like that of a grown man working the land. His head spins and he's unable to make sense of anything around him. His body loses its strength, his knees buckle, and he collapses as the world goes black before his face meets the hot earth.

"Boy!" a woman calls from across the street.

Étienne looks over to her and the Malian fruit vendor. They're both pointing behind him. He turns around to find his cousin crumpled to the ground.

"Ibrahimah!"

Étienne runs over to Ibrahimah and tries to jostle him awake. The Malian fruit vendor pulls Étienne back and drops his head down to Ibrahimah's face.

"He's breathing."

The man gently rocks Ibrahimah.

"Call his name," he says, looking over at Étienne.

"Ibrahimah. Ibrahimah! Cousin, wake up!"

Tears spring into the corners of Étienne's eyes.

"Have you all eaten today?"

Étienne shakes his head no.

"He wanted cake," Étienne cries.

The man picks Ibrahimah's limp body up and carries him over to his fruit stand nestled beneath the shade of a tree. He places Ibrahimah down onto a bench, grabs a cup of water, pours some onto a rag, and dabs it across his face.

"It may be hunger and heat exhaustion," the man says.

Several passersby have stopped to see if the boy is all right.

"The Talibé boy passed out from hunger," the woman informs the small crowd.

Eyebrows shoot up in the air. A woman shoves a sandwich, wrapped in paper, toward Étienne.

"For him," she says, pointing at Ibrahimah.

Étienne takes the sandwich and touches his stomach while looking at Ibrahimah.

"Ibrahimah!" the man says.

Ibrahimah's eyes flutter open. Disjointed by all the faces leering down at him he closes his eyes again.

"Am I in heaven with my mama?" Ibrahimah asks.

The Malian man looks down at the little boy, confused for a

moment, then chuckles. "No, you are alive, my child. Can you sit up?"

Ibrahimah holds his hand to his head as the Malian man gently sits him upright. He is dizzy and feels like he did whenever he tried to hold his breath underwater longer than his sisters. Fatou always won. This feeling is much worse, since there is no way for him to quit and come up for air.

"Eat this," Étienne instructs, shoving the sandwich at him.

The fruit vendor takes the sandwich from Étienne. Ibrahimah watches with big eyes as the man opens the paper, splits the sandwich in two, and hands a half to each of them. He motions for Étienne to sit down next to Ibrahimah on the bench and gives them a cup of water to drink. There in the shade they nibble the sandwiches self-consciously, thankful to be eating. Ibrahimah's stomach gurgles and feels a bit queasy with the taste of food, but he'd rather be eating than not.

Seeing that the child is okay the crowd returns to its lazy gait.

"You boys be careful. You have to drink water in this heat," the woman says. Satisfied with herself she walks off.

"Drink water?" Ibrahimah repeats.

Étienne glances after the woman, then returns his attention to the matter at hand, his sandwich.

"Drink water," the Malian man grumbles. "How do children drink enough water if they've got nowhere to get it?"

Ibrahimah finds it soothing to watch the short, slim Malian man with the long fingers sell fruit. He could sit on this bench, beneath this tree, eating sandwiches forever. When his sandwich is finished, the man hands Ibrahimah a banana. Ibrahimah obliges without argument; with food in his belly his eyes are coming back into focus and the wooziness begins to fade.

"The other boys must be far by now," Étienne says. "We can visit Moustapha today."

Ibrahimah's face lights up as much as it can, the dull throbbing in his head holding his joy at bay. Maybe Aria has medicine so he doesn't fall down again. The passing traffic slowly builds in front of them.

"One day we won't have to beg anymore," Étienne says.

Ibrahimah smiles at this grand idea.

"People will lay down gold and silver on the ground for us to walk over when we return to our village."

"My mama and papa will come down from heaven and be there with lots of food," Ibrahimah says.

"Don't forget your Hummer," Étienne says, looking at his cousin.

"And big guns to shoot stupid people!"

"No shooting, Ibrahimah. We're good."

"Okay, I'll drive over stupid people with my Hummer!"

Étienne laughs and looks up to find the pleasant-faced Malian man standing above them. The man hands Ibrahimah a packet of cookies, and within seconds he has stuffed two in his mouth.

"I feel better," Ibrahimah sputters, cookie crumbs flying across his lap.

"Sit for some time," Étienne says, looking over his shoulder at the cars piling up behind him, due to the out-of-sync traffic light a quarter mile up the road. He approaches the cars with a tempered calm.

Ibrahimah dangles his legs over the edge of the bench. Cars idling in traffic exude black, curly smoke from their bottoms. Drivers with scrunched-up faces stick their heads out car windows in search of answers. A tall, slim security guard, dressed in a black uniform and black cap, walks a large black-and-tan German shepherd. Several drivers stare at the man and dog. It's rare to witness someone walking a dog, much less one so big. A woman and two girls cross the street to avoid walking past the pair, yet both man and dog move with ease, unfazed by their spectacle. Right as they're passing by Ibrahimah, the dog turns his large head and looks straight at him. Pulling away from the guard, he licks Ibrahimah's hand.

"Down, boy."

Ibrahimah has never seen a dog so big, but he doesn't flinch, just like he was not afraid of the lion.

"Little Talibé, you aren't afraid," the tall, skinny security guard says, chuckling.

Taking advantage of the lax hold on his leash, the dog moves in closer to Ibrahimah and licks his cheek. His hair tickles Ibrahimah's neck and sends him into a fit of giggles.

"A brave Talibé you are," the guard says.

Étienne approaches the dog from behind and touches the hind end of his back. The dog turns his head, acknowledges Étienne silently, and then turns back to Ibrahimah, who beams with delight at the attention.

"Okay, Oscar, let's go," the guard coaxes. The dog pulls against the guard, exhales loudly, then succumbs and slowly walks away.

"You boys doing better?" the Malian man asks, turning away from the departing customer.

"Yes," Étienne replies.

"That's good."

Étienne cups his hands in front of his face.

"Thank you for your kindness, may Allah bless you, ton-ton," he mumbles.

The Malian man with the cocoa-brown skin folds his hands in prayer over his chest and bows in appreciation. The boys take off to the streets again.

"I'm hungry," Ibrahimah complains, his patience waning as people continue to ignore his requests for money and food.

"We just ate an hour ago!" Étienne exclaims, looking at his cousin in disbelief.

"Well, I'm hungry again!"

Ibrahimah's plastic jelly sandals are looking worn; a strap has broken on one foot. He grips his stomach with his hand. Spotting a woman selling peanuts, Ibrahimah approaches her.

"May I have some peanuts, please?"

She motions for him to take a small packet.

"Thank you, ta-ta," Ibrahimah says, stuffing the peanuts into his mouth without a thought of saving some for later, or sharing any with Étienne.

"You said we'd go see Moustapha," Ibrahimah says.

"I know," Étienne agrees, "but first let's see if we can find some more money."

"Don't we have money in the safe at Moustapha's house?" Ibrahimah asks. He needs a break.

"We do, but never let the luck of finding more money pass you by. Let's go."

They walk over toward the gas station in Mermoz, next door to the bookstore, Librarie IV, which is in the exact opposite direction of Moustapha's neighborhood. The shaded station and food market are busy as cars pull in and out of the parking lot.

"Get two big coins and then we'll go see Moustapha."

Ibrahimah falls into action. He approaches a rich-looking Senegalese woman in a heavily starched pink-and-purple boubou.

"Talibé, I'll give you money when I finish inside."

Ibrahimah turns to the next set of legs approaching, a man in a black crisp suit and shiny black leather shoes. Ibrahimah scores two small fifty-franc coins from him. Clink, clink, they fall into his red tin tomato can.

"*Aye, petit garçon. Comment ça va?*"

Ibrahimah looks up to see a light-skinned black man smiling down at him. Étienne runs over, bumping into Ibrahimah as he greets the man.

"*Vous êtes ici. Je ne vous ai pas oublié tous les deux.*"

"What does he mean he doesn't forget us? Who is he?" Ibrahimah asks Étienne.

"He's the American man that bought us Coca a long time ago at the boutique. Remember? He's sure to give us money today."

Ibrahimah's eyes light up.

"Mooneh, please. Tank you," Étienne says, looking up at the American man.

"Whoa, little Talibé! You speak English now?" The man's eyes pop open wide. A grin spreads across his face.

"Yes, please give me mooneh," Ibrahimah says, with his practiced English, palm open wide, waiting to be blessed with riches.

The man laughs out loud.

"Why is this man laughing? He doesn't understand me?" Ibrahimah asks, sucking his teeth, reverting back to Wolof.

"I think he's in shock." Étienne says in Wolof before turning to the man. "We are angri, please buy us food."

"Angry?" the man repeats, his head turned to the side in confusion.

"Yes, *beaucoup* angri," Ibrahimah adds, touching his stomach.

"Oh! You're hungry? Damn, times are changing when Talibé start learning English," the man says, laughing.

"What did he say?" Ibrahimah asks. The man spoke a bit too fast for him to catch everything.

"He thinks Talibé speaking English is funny," Étienne says.

Ibrahimah cracks up laughing, joining the man and Étienne. A Senegalese woman passes by and stares at the foreign man like he is crazy.

"What do you want to eat?"

"Food," the boys say in unison.

"Okay, stay here. I'll be back," the man says, walking away while shaking his head in disbelief.

"I can't wait to tell Moustapha. We need to learn more English," Ibrahimah says, reverting back to Wolof.

"Imagine how much money we can get from Americans if we could speak perfect English," Étienne says.

Ibrahimah's eyes light up. The exchange has infused him with a burst of energy. They linger by the door, when four Talibé boys about Étienne's age run over to them.

"Aye. You get lots of money here?" a boy asks.

"Not really," Étienne says, pointing toward the cars pulling up to the gas pumps. A driver in the queue sticks his head and arm out of his window, gesturing to the taxi driver in front of him to wrap it up. The taxi driver sucks his teeth and turns his back to the impatient man.

Ibrahimah sees the woman from earlier coming out of the store first and runs up to her in hopes that she gives him the money she promised. When the other boys see the large Senegalese woman in the bright expensive outfit, they rush up alongside Ibrahimah, pushing him out of the way.

"Watch your manners!" she yells at them.

"Money!"

"Give me money!"

"Money for me."

They stumble over one another, shoving dirty hands up toward her face.

"Back away from me, Talibé! Back! I give money to whomever I want, and not to boys who have no manners!"

"Come, baby," she says to Ibrahimah.

She plunks down several one-hundred-franc coins into his hand and saunters away with a cut of her eye at the others. The four boys glare at Ibrahimah. He scoots back over to Étienne.

"Should we go?" Ibrahimah asks.

"No, we wait for the American man."

Ibrahimah watches the rowdy group of boys vie for money and attention. A foreboding feeling circles the insides of his stomach. The American man walks out of the market and the group of boys rush him, almost knocking him over.

"Whoa, *calmez-vous!*" he shouts, raising his hands up in the air.

Several people look over at the scene. He drops a coin in each of their cans as they shove and push. Once free he walks up to Étienne and Ibrahimah and gives them money, boxed apple juice with the straw attached to the side, bananas, and the thick, sweet yogurt with the millet on the bottom. Ibrahimah's eyes light up at the sight of his bounty. He needs to learn more English from Moustapha. The other boys see what is happening and rush over, demanding more.

"Hey, boys, *la prochaine fois, d'accord?*"

"Greedy American," the boy in the green T-shirt says, spitting on the ground and stomping back over to the entrance of the store.

The other boys press the American further, but he puts his hands in the air, showing them he has no more to give. Étienne and Ibrahimah thank him quietly but linger, curious to see if the man will succumb to the boys' pressure. He doesn't, and walks away with a wave. Étienne grabs Ibrahimah's arm and pulls him away.

"Give me your drink," the boy with the torn pants demands.

Étienne doesn't turn around, and drags Ibrahimah behind him.

"No!" Ibrahimah yells, his legs doing double time to keep up with Étienne.

"I said give me your juice, stupid!"

Étienne turns just as the boy swings at the back of his head. The boy's fist brushes his cheek. Étienne drops his tomato can to the ground and throws a punch at the boy. Ibrahimah picks up his cousin's can and steps away from the brawl. Confusion and anxiety rush through his body. He doesn't know what to do. The memory of the brawl with Scarface and Caca outside the nightclub comes rushing to the forefront of his brain. They can't afford to lose their money.

"Stop!" Ibrahimah yells, taking a step forward, then a step back.

The other three boys rush over with grins on their faces.

"Beat him! Show him a lesson!"

A second boy rushes over and jumps in on top of Étienne. The two boys drag Étienne to the ground, kicking and punching him in his head, torso, and back. Étienne grabs the boy with the torn shorts by the calf and pulls him to the ground. Ignoring the blows to his body he throws his weight onto the slim boy and bites his ear, breaking the skin. The boy screams out in pain.

Foreigners walk by with trepidation on their faces. Several drivers standing at the gas pumps look away. In the excitement of the brawl the other two boys hadn't paid any attention to Ibrahimah.

"Aye, boy! Come here, give me your food."

Just as the two boys start toward Ibrahimah two gas-station attendants approach them, shouting that they stop.

"Fuck you!" the tallest of the boys shouts over his shoulder.

Ibrahimah doesn't know whether to run and hide or stay, but the station attendants are on the group within seconds after the tall boy's retort. The tall, slim attendant rushes toward the three-way brawl, with the short, stocky attendant close behind.

"Stop this at once!"

He yanks the two boys off Étienne. The boy with the torn shorts, and bleeding ear, backs away but then comes up and hits Étienne in the head. The man tries to grab the bleeding boy, but he hits the man in the arm and then attempts to run behind him to get at Étienne again. The man catches the boy by the bottom of his T-shirt. In the boy's struggle to get away, the man ends up pulling the T-shirt up over his head and beats the boy in the head, back, and torso. The other boys watch. Their twelve-year-old bodies are no match for the adult men.

"You think you're tough! You little shit." The man hits the boy once more before letting him go.

"Fuck you!" the boy yells, tears in his eyes, blood running down the side of his neck.

"What?" the man says with a start, but the boy runs away.

"Get out of here and don't let us see you again!"

"Étienne, you're bleeding," Ibrahimah says.

Étienne gives his arms a once-over, dismissing the superficial scrapes he finds. He wipes his mouth with the back of his hand and finds his bloodied lips are the source of Ibrahimah's worry. He takes the tail of his shirt and wipes his mouth again.

"I'm okay."

"You all get out of here too. Get!"

"Come on, Ibrahimah, let's go."

Étienne picks up his drink from the ground and brushes the dirt from the straw. He takes his red tin tomato can from Ibrahimah, ensures his money and food are safe, and the two of them walk in the opposite direction of the four boys.

"You got your money?" Étienne asks.

"Yes."

Ibrahimah looks around the vicinity of the area, wary of bumping into the boys again.

"Don't worry. They're gone."

In the afternoon heat, time stands still, no breeze dares show itself. Ibrahimah watches the ants scurry across the earth in search of food, then give up and run back home. The rumble is faint at first but increases with each step. When the ground begins to shake, Ibrahimah raises his eyes to meet the large Alitalia plane overhead, shaking everything awake beneath its flight path to Yoff Airport. With it comes a gust of thick, hot air that encapsulates the two boys.

Ibrahimah raises his arm in an attempt to touch the belly of the aircraft as small round faces look out of the windows and down at the streets below.

"Maybe one day you'll fly the plane and take us far from here," Étienne says as he watches the tail end of the plane disappear over the neighborhood of Mamelles. "I want to see the world far away from Dakar."

"Paradise is outside of Dakar for sure."

Ibrahimah sucks the last of his juice, then frowns at the empty carton, not ready for the drink to be finished so fast. He pulls the straw out and chews on the plastic. He drops the carton into his tomato can and walks along with the straw sticking out of his mouth.

"I like this drink," Ibrahimah says.

Clear blue sky stretches on for eternity except for a scatter of featherlight strokes of cirrus clouds. He has not seen the red bird in a long time. He wonders if the bird has left him, like his parents.

Ibrahimah and Étienne pass a group of women lined up along the wall of the Danish embassy, sitting on cardboard boxes. Plump babies suck from limp exposed breasts. Ankle-length wrap skirts are pulled up to their knees in hopes the stagnant air decides to adjust itself and offer them relief. Bodies bent to the side in fatigue, the women quietly watch the backs of the boys as they walk down the hill. Ibrahimah scratches at his butt.

Another plane passes overhead, its massive wings blocking the sun's rays from kissing his face. The temporary shade feels good. Walking through the soft earth, he kicks at the hot sand, causing a cloud to billow up around him. He feels invincible within the fog until the earth finds its way into his mouth and eyes, causing him to cough and gag. He rubs at his eyes, making things worse.

"Meow."

Ibrahimah spins around in an attempt to follow the source of the sound.

"Meow."

"It's a cat," Étienne says.

"Where?"

Ibrahimah spins around in another circle.

"Meow. Meow."

"Here," Étienne says, walking over to a mound of sun-scorched shrubs and weeds. Ibrahimah runs over, excited to see the animal. The boys move the dead wiry shrubs around but don't find anything.

"Meow."

"I think it's here!"

Ibrahimah runs over to a rusted red pickup truck parked next to the shrubs. Below, two tiny white kittens spotted with black are huddled together. Their fur matted to their emaciated bodies, they shiver in the shade away from the unbearable heat. Étienne finds a stick and begins poking one of the kittens. Each time the stick connects with its small body, the cat cries out in pain. On the fourth poke the angry kitten gives a scathing hiss and scurries out of reach. The other kitten continues to cry. Ibrahimah tries to pick it up, but the kitten retreats toward its sibling.

"Why are they here alone?" Ibrahimah asks.

"People throw the babies away. They don't want them."

Ibrahimah looks up at his cousin. "Why?"

"I don't know."

Ibrahimah turns back to the scared kittens.

"I'm hungry," Ibrahimah says.

"Let's go."

After one final glance at the kittens Ibrahimah grabs his red tin can and stands. With each step he takes, the cries of the two kittens increase tenfold in an attempt to get the two boys to return.

The street lies still. No birds flutter about. No cars amble down the uneven road leaving thick clouds of fumes and dust behind. No young, hungry Senegalese men drag their sandaled feet across the ground selling Chinese goods.

Approaching the familiar address, Étienne walks up to the big metal door and rings the bell. The high cement walls loom larger than usual and the bell echoes throughout the compound. Ibrahimah looks out across the street. Something sparkles beneath the sunlight and catches his eye. He walks over as a faint breeze washes

over him and the smell of the Atlantic Ocean rushes into his nostrils. The faces of his sisters flash before his eyes, eclipsing his sight
for just a moment. "Fatou," he mumbles under his breath. The shiny
object sparkles again. He bends down and picks up the flat, round
silver object. It's bigger and flatter than any of the coins he's received. He flips it around in his hand. The surface is smooth on one
side and has etchings on the other. Excited, he brings the metal
piece over to Étienne.

"Look, money."

Étienne looks at the silver coin in his cousin's hand. "That's not
money."

"No?" Ibrahimah asks, frowning.

"No. Money has numbers to tell you how much. That has no
numbers, just lines and circles. See," Étienne says, comparing a
hundred-franc piece to the silver object, "not money."

Ibrahimah frowns and puts the shiny metal object into his can.
It's too shiny not to be important, Fatou would know if it were really
treasure.

"I don't think anyone is home." Étienne says.

"Ring the bell again."

Étienne reaches to press the doorbell again when the sound of
metal fighting against metal takes center stage.

"What do you want?" someone grumbles.

To the right of Moustapha's house, a short, sleepy-eyed Senegalese man sticks his head out of a metal door, annoyance in his eyes.

"We're looking for our friend Moustapha."

"The family is gone to America," the guard says. "They left a few
days ago. The father got a new job in New York."

"New York?" Ibrahimah asks.

"Yes, America," the man says.

"Thank you, ton-ton," Étienne says.

The man retracts his head and slams the door shut.

"America?" Ibrahimah asks.

"Come, let's go," Étienne says, walking away.

Ibrahimah's legs are frozen.

"Moustapha went to America?!" Ibrahimah exclaims.

"Yes, let's go."

"What about our money!" Ibrahimah cries, meeting his cousin's pace, his legs taking two strides for every one Étienne takes.

"We'll figure something out," Étienne says, squinting against the sunlight.

"Will Moustapha come back soon?"

Étienne stops abruptly and looks down at Ibrahimah.

"Probably not," Étienne says, biting his bottom lip.

Ibrahimah pictures the map on the wall of the bedroom he shared with his sisters but can't remember where America is in relation to Africa anymore. "Where's America?"

"Far away from Dakar." Étienne starts walking again.

Ibrahimah is quiet a moment, his thoughts run through his brain too fast for his mouth to articulate; English, money, food, baths, clothes, cartoons, air conditioning, PlayStation, Xbox, Moustapha.

"How do we get there?"

"We have to take a boat across the water, or a plane."

Planes that go to America and Paradise cost a lot of money because that is how the rich people come to Dakar. Ibrahimah drops his head. They pass a boulangerie and the smell of fresh bread baking engulfs him. His stomach screams with hunger.

"I need food."

"Why do you keep complaining? We're used to being hungry all the time!"

Customers rush in and out of the boulangerie with barely a glance at the unmistakable looks of hunger. Those who do notice walk faster in an attempt not to see. Étienne suggests they go find food somewhere else.

"We'll go over there where they sell dibi to try. It's better, maybe."

"No. I need food now!" Ibrahimah demands.

Ibrahimah sees a woman approaching and rushes up to her. She waves him away. He continues asking and lurks close to her leg. With one sweeping move she swats him upside his head.

"You listen when an adult tells you no, you little ingrate. Now go away!" she scolds.

Ibrahimah's mouth settles into a pout of disappointment and anger.

"I told you we should go. You don't listen," Étienne says.

"But I'm hungry," Ibrahimah whines.

"Rich people want to keep everything for themselves. They don't care about Talibé."

Disappointment sits on Ibrahimah's face.

"Come, let's see how much money we have; with the extra we'll buy food, okay?" Étienne says.

They crouch down in a spot hidden behind a car. Ibrahimah leans his head up against the vehicle. Moustapha didn't steal their money, but how could he forget about them? He was the best friend Ibrahimah has ever had, besides Étienne. He stands up and the ground spins beneath his feet. His stomach gurgles in anger and he lurches forward; a mixture of blood, undigested peanuts, and bile spills out of his mouth.

Ibrahimah wakes with a start. The room is devoid of color and his skin is roasting. The open window brings no air from the moonless sky into the crowded room. The rhythmic sound of forty boys breathing deep within their sleep fills the space; Ahmed returned with five new boys from a recent trip to Mali.

A thousand pins and needles prick him over every inch of his body. Hot liquid escapes his butt. His stomach spasms. He tries to sit up but instead vomits all over himself before he collapses onto his cardboard mat. He whimpers in pain but none of the other boys stir. Ibrahimah grips his stomach and rocks onto his side. He vomits again. Étienne wakes up and helps him to the hole behind the house. He fails to control his bodily functions and diarrhea runs down his bony legs.

Étienne searches out an old ripped piece of cloth and attempts to clean Ibrahimah using the day-old water from the pail in the back. He's still tending to his cousin when the prayer call sounds at five o'clock and Marabout appears. Étienne rushes toward their teacher.

"What do you want?" Ahmed dips his hands in the pail of water.

"Ibrahimah is sick."

"Sick how?"

"He has diarrhea and vomits. It won't stop."

"Let me see him."

Ahmed walks over to find Ibrahimah squatting over the hole, convulsing and vomiting between his legs, crying out in pain, and clutching his belly. Ahmed walks out of the foul-smelling space.

"Stay with him," he growls over his shoulder, walking back into the house.

"Cousin, what do you need?" asks Étienne.

Ibrahimah whimpers in response. Étienne goes to fetch more water from the pail. When he returns, Ibrahimah is curled up next to the hole, sleeping.

"Ibrahimah, wake up."

Ibrahimah replies with a pained moan.

"Let's go back in the room to sleep on the mat. It's dirty here."

Étienne tries to move him, but Ibrahimah protests. Why is Étienne being so mean to him? Who cares about the mat inside the house? It's better right here.

"You will make Marabout mad. Come, you don't want a beating."

Ibrahimah allows his cousin to drag him to his feet and they stumble back into the room, where the rest of the boys are in prayer. Ibrahimah's mat is wet with a cocktail of bodily fluids. Étienne guides Ibrahimah to lie down on his own clean mat and drags Ibrahimah's soiled piece of cardboard outside. The other boys wrinkle their noses at the smell. With their prayers complete and the sun shining brightly through the window, the roomful of boys prepares to go out to work. With mats put away, they grab their empty tomato cans and file out of the door.

Ibrahimah lies in the middle of the room, on the floor, curled into a fetal position. Étienne hangs next to his cousin for a while and then goes to Ahmed.

"Teacher, Ibrahimah's too sick to work."

"Where is he?"

Étienne points to the bundle of boy on the floor. Ahmed sighs. He walks over to Ibrahimah and pokes him.

"Leave him. You go to work. He'll sleep and should be fine to work tomorrow."

Étienne hesitates to leave. Ahmed slaps him across the side of his head, hard. "Go!"

Étienne walks away but turns back to look at Ibrahimah one more time. Ahmed goes to his room and slams his door.

Ibrahimah sleeps fitfully and dreams of his village. It seems only moments have gone by when conversations suddenly disturb his slumber.

"Come close to me. Are you lying?"

"No, Papa, I would never lie to you."

"You love your papa, don't you?"

"I do."

"We'll be together forever, yes? You won't ever leave your papa, will you? Tell me you will never leave me."

"Never. We will always be together."

Ibrahimah's eyes flutter open. Is he back in the village with his father? No one loves his father more than he does. But his eyes dart across the room and he catches sight of Marabout and two of the boys from his house, Scarface and Caca. Ahmed wraps his arm around Scarface and the boy leans over and kisses him on the cheek.

"You two are my special boys."

The boys look at each other with tepid smiles.

"You take care of your papa, the way these other boys cannot."

"Yes, sir," Caca says.

Ahmed punches the boy in the back and he yelps out in pain.

"What did you call me?"

"Papa, I called you Papa!"

Caca looks up at Ahmed with fear in his eyes.

Ahmed's demeanor eases as he watches them eat; they stuff handfuls of burnt rice and chicken into their mouths.

"After you finish eating, we'll take a nap together. Are you tired? Would you like to take a nap with your papa?"

Scarface offers Marabout a tight smile. "Yes."

Caca leans over the plate, and shoves more food in his mouth.

Ibrahimah closes his eyes. His throat is parched but he dares not utter a word. His body too weak to budge, he allows the sounds of their voices to fade before drifting back into a slumber. His mother appears before him with a tall glass of bissap to drink. The sweet sugary drink washes through his body and he jumps to life, running down the hill to the shore of the beach. The waves roar loud and thunderous and he jumps into the ocean.

His body moves without effort through the water as he dips below the surface, swimming deep down into the belly of the sea alongside sharks, sea spiders, eels, and squid. Jellyfish drift by, their bodies folding and unfolding in their slow, beautiful dance. Flat-faced fish shimmy across the ocean floor. The water becomes colder and the valleys darker the farther down he goes, but he is not afraid. A shimmer of light flashes off in the distance and he swims toward it; the light never gets brighter or larger than the small dot it appears as, but it beckons him all the same. So he swims with confidence that he will reach it, but once he gets right in front of it he realizes there is no place to go but through, and so that is what he does, swims straight through and finds himself facedown on a thick bed of grass, arms caught in the air with no water left to manipulate. He turns around to see the wall of water leading back to the sea, standing free on its own. Ibrahimah stands up and shakes the drops of seawater off of his body.

"Ibrahimah!"

He looks over to see Abdoulaye, Demba, and Aisatu eating strawberries and mango beneath a tree with bright-purple flowers. Aisatu's small two-year-old legs are chubby and short compared to the two older boys.

"Is this Dakar?" Ibrahimah asks, looking at Demba.

With a coy smile etched across his mouth, Demba shakes his head no.

"Heaven," Abdoulaye says, sweet strawberry juice running down his chin.

The three children jump up and run down a grassy, tree-lined passageway. Aisatu's giggles sing out amongst the trees.

"Wait! Come back!" Ibrahimah runs down the winding path, his feet sinking into the thick, damp grass. The air is soft and fresh; a warm breeze strokes his skin, just as his mother would when she was soothing him.

He runs down a row of short blue-leafed trees, but stops after a while to look to his right. There he sees the boys waving for him to follow. He runs toward them but instead of waiting they run away again, laughing with joy. Ibrahimah stops and looks up. Fat red apples hang low enough for him to reach and he pulls one down and bites into it. The sky above is a deep violet, yet the space around him is bright with the illumination of a hundred suns. The sweet nectar bursts with flavor inside his mouth and he sits down. He takes a deep breath filled with freedom and joy. He chews slowly and closes his eyes as he listens to the sound of a dragonfly flap its wings nearby.

Large raindrops fall so slowly that he can see images within them before they hit the ground. He sticks his free hand out and catches one. Within his palm he can see a man bent over crying. In another raindrop is Marabout and the man that would come in the morning. He instantly understands that his teacher was not helping his mother—but hurting her. Another raindrop falls within his palm and he can see Étienne running away from something, afraid. Ibrahimah jumps up and tries to catch as many raindrops as possible. The apple falls from his lap and the sound of Aisatu's giggles fades. Something shifts in the air and his eyes flutter open.

Ahmed holds a naked Caca by the neck; the boy's face contorts in pain. Ibrahimah clamps his eyes shut and wills his brain to return to the place below the sea, with Abdoulaye and his sister and the images of those who love him, but he does not return. Instead he is left trapped in the room filled with the sounds of suffering and evil.

"Ibrahimah."

Someone is touching him, he tries to push them away, and pain shoots through his body.

"Marabout, no," he cries.

"Ibrahimah."

He opens his eyes. Étienne has returned home early. Ibrahimah is wet with excrement, and dried bile lies next to his head. Étienne looks over at Marabout, who listens to a local radio station while eating his dinner. Étienne takes the piece of bread he begged from a woman earlier and tries to get his cousin to eat, but Ibrahimah refuses to open his dry, cracked lips.

"Ibrahimah, you have to eat something," Étienne says, his voice a quiet whisper.

The thought of eating food makes him want to vomit again.

"I brought you Coca."

"The man in the morning hurts me and Mama," Ibrahimah mumbles before losing consciousness.

"What are you doing?" Ahmed barks from his bedroom door. A grain of rice falls from his chin.

"I'm trying to get him to drink something."

"What?"

"Ibrahimah is thirsty."

"What are you giving him to drink?"

"Coca."

"You bring *him* Coca, but not your marabout. You boys do not respect me."

Étienne looks up at the large man with a dubious expression.

Ahmed scoffs. "He doesn't need Coca, leave him. Bring it to me."

Étienne hands the soda over to the large man.

Ahmed grunts. "Now get out of my sight."

Étienne lies down next to his cousin. He had a strong feeling that Marabout wasn't helping Ibrahimah's mother in heaven. He sleeps fitfully as Ibrahimah whines and writhes in pain throughout the night. Étienne wakes to the sounds of coughing and finds Ibrahimah sitting up bent over his lap. Ibrahimah heaves as if he is going to vomit, but nothing but a dry, painful cough comes.

"Ibrahimah, you okay?"

Étienne puts his hand on his cousin's back. Ibrahimah is still hot with fever.

"I . . . hurt."

"I'll get you some water."

Étienne walks quietly to the back of the house and grabs a cup of water from the pail.

"Drink this."

Ibrahimah shakes his head, but Étienne insists. Ibrahimah takes the water and sips.

"Are you hungry?"

Ibrahimah shakes his head no and lies down. A few moments later Étienne looks on as Ibrahimah grips his stomach in pain and vomits. When the last of the water and bile has exited his system Ibrahimah rolls over to his side, closes his eyes, and goes back to sleep. It is up to Étienne to save his cousin.

 XXIX.

Morning sunlight bursts through the parted curtains. The air smells fresh and the room feels more spacious than usual. Maimouna lies unmoving, meeting her mother's unwavering gaze.

"When did you get here?"

"Is that how you greet your elder? I've been here three days. The rain is heavy. The spirits are discontent," Maimouna's mother says, sitting down on the chair by the window and gazing up toward the sky.

Her lips continue to move, but without sound. A string of wooden beads lies in her lap. She touches each bead with her thumb and pointing finger before grabbing the next one.

"I don't see any rain."

"You've slept through most of it, but it will come again; nothing lasts forever."

Maimouna watches her mother's hands.

"Why did you not send for me?" her mother asks, still looking out the window.

"I don't know. I wanted to get better on my own. I'm supposed to be the mother to my children that I always wanted. It's so hard, though," Maimouna says, looking away.

Her mother turns and looks at Maimouna just as a miniature red bird lands on the windowsill; its small body is no bigger than the wingspan of a butterfly. Her mother reaches out and touches its head. It sings out in response, then flies into the room and lands on the edge of the bed, looking into Maimouna's eyes. Head cocked to the side, it comes closer to get a better look. Maimouna holds her breath.

"Am I dreaming?" she whispers.

"Would you like this to be a dream?" the red bird asks.

Maimouna blinks several times and then looks over at her mother, who has lighted a pipe. Her mother inhales deeply then exhales the smoke in tight swirls that spread out like a hungry fog. Maimouna looks back at the tiny bird and reaches her hand out. It steps back, spreads its tiny wings, and flies out of the window. Maimouna drops her hand onto the bed and looks to her mother.

"How long will you stay?"

"As long as I am needed."

Maimouna sighs. "Nothing can cure me, Mama. We've tried everything. The devil is too strong."

She looks over toward her mother, the light fading around her. Her mother rises, touches her head, and walks out of the room. Outside, Fatou follows her grandmother around.

"Fatou."

"Yes, *Maam.*"

"Bring me a bowl and spoon, I need to mix these herbs together."

"Yes, madame."

Her grandmother bends over the bowl and burns several roots and twigs inside. When the flame has fizzled out and just the burnt ash is left, she sprinkles a green powder over it and mixes it with tree bark and a dark liquid. Fatou watches intently.

"This will make everything right again."

Fatou's shoulders slump, her eyes sad. "Nothing works, *Maam.* Nothing."

The older woman looks at Fatou, fire burning in the center of her jet-black eyes. "The magic practiced against your mother is dark, and it is strong, but sacrifices have been made. What I do is permanent. There is no going back."

She points to a canister. Fatou picks it up and hands it to her.

"But how will Mama get well without Ibrahimah?"

"Your brother will return home, and when he arrives, he will stay."

Fatou raises her eyebrows in surprise. Her grandmother opens the canister and pulls out a paper bag. The bag rustles in her hand as it rises and falls. Fatou takes a step back. Her grandmother motions for her to grab the paste as she heads back to the bedroom with the paper bag. While Maimouna sleeps, the older woman scoops the paste up with three fingers and spreads it across Maimouna's forehead and down the bridge of her nose. She mixes a smudge of it into a glass of water next to the bed, then reaches into the paper bag and pulls out a heart, still beating all on its own. She sits it in a woven straw basket surrounded by several cowrie shells and slides it beneath Maimouna's side of the bed. On the windowsill sits the tiny red bird.

"Watch her," Maimouna's mother says over her shoulder to the red bird as she leaves the room with a wide-eyed Fatou in tow.

Heavy rains fill the pails to the brim and allow the girls laissez-faire afternoons once they are done with their morning chores. Binta and Aisha arrive fresh out of breath, their legs wet with the salty ocean water, caked beach sand falling from their ankles in small clumps. They bump into Fatou.

"Why do you follow *Maam* around the house all day?" Binta asks.

"To help her with anything she needs," Fatou says, sweeping fallen leaves and other debris into a small pile.

"The beach is more fun," Aisha says, slurping on a cup of Fanta orange soda.

"To show my appreciation. I'm happy that *Maam* has come to help us."

"Why are you so appreciation?" Binta asks, putting a hand on her waist and jutting her hip out to the side.

Fatou sighs with exasperation and leans on the broom. "*Appreciative.* Because, now that *Maam*'s here, you and Aisha do your chores without me having to yell at you!"

Fatou pulls at one of Binta's braids. She smacks at Fatou's hand and rolls her eyes.

"Roll your eyes if you want, but it's true. You and Aisha know *Maam* will do juju on you and make you grow a hunch on your back if you misbehave. You'll walk around like this all your life!"

Fatou bends over and scrunches her face up, dragging her left leg behind her across the floor. "You'll be ugly like a witch. All the boys will run from you, and you'll never get married or have children."

Binta's eyes open wide with fear.

"Don't listen to Fatou, *Maam* would never do that to us." Aisha sucks her teeth. "Anyway, I don't care to be married. I want to be a singer."

"Oh no? I'll call *Maam* right now. She'll burn the other roots and powders she has in her pouch, just for you!"

"No, no!" Binta cries, frowning at Aisha. "We'll be good. Aisha, shut up and listen to Fatou!"

Fatou clicks her tongue.

"Binta is smart," Fatou says, looking at Aisha and cutting her eyes. "Now clean those potatoes! You've had enough fun for the day."

Fatou skips off into the house with a wide grin on her face as her sisters sit down in front of the pile of root vegetables.

Dinner is quiet that evening, a sense of calm reverberates amongst them all. Binta smiles every time she sticks a French fry in her mouth.

"I hate peeling potatoes," Binta says with a grin, "but I *love* French fries."

Aisha rolls her eyes while Fatou sneaks glances over at her grandmother. Idrissa hangs his head low, brooding and absent. They all hold tight to the belief that *Maam* will fix it.

That evening Maimouna sits up, a surge of energy rushing through her body. Her bare feet are cool against the tiled floor. The rhythmic sound of her mother's breathing is comforting in the dark room. She walks past the girls' bedroom and the sound of Idrissa sleeping in the living room. Outside, the sandy floor feels cool at first then turns warmer as her toes sink deeper. The full moon illuminates the navy-blue sky, and fluffy cumulus clouds race by in search of the sun. She holds her wrist, feels her scar.

She walks past the houses of her neighbors. A lamb picks its sleepy head up to look at her. She remembers Ibrahimah running down this hill with his sisters. Down at the shore, the roar of the ocean's breath is calming; it never changes its manner, never tells a lie, never claims to be something that it is not. She sits down on the sand and rakes her fingers deep into the earth until she finds the dense, wet layers beneath. She stares out across the dark sea.

"What are you looking at?" she asks.

The moon looks back, silent and without bias.

"It's not right! Where are you now, Almighty Allah? Where is my son?"

A star glistens in the distance and she closes her eyes. She thought a family of her own would eclipse the pain and anger that had planted itself and grown so wild and abundant within her during her childhood. She looks down at her hands, the same hands that have lovingly cared for her children and husband. The same hands that had violently attacked Marabout Ahmed, and wished to tear him to shreds. There is too much wickedness in the world to escape.

Rising, she walks down the shore; the warm ocean water caresses her ankles, the hem of her nightdress catches salt and seaweed, and the wind slaps against her skin. She takes a step forward and a rush of excitement surges within her belly. She takes another step. And then another. This feels right. Submerged up to her knees, the strong current pulls and pushes her frail body about. She'll walk out until the water reaches her neck and then she'll let go. It will be easy. Her grief will subside and her sorrow will wash away. She takes another step forward but this time the tide pushes her back. She tries again but is met with an even stronger wave that pushes her back even farther; she has to catch herself from falling when suddenly someone grabs her arm.

"Mama, what are you doing?" Binta asks.

Maimouna spins around. "No, this is the only way."

"Mama, you can't do this again! You can't hurt yourself."

Maimouna stands there, unmoving, the waves licking at her thighs.

"Mama! Papa! Papa! *Maam!* Help! Help!"

"No one can hear us down here," she says, wrenching her arm from Binta's grip.

"I don't care. Help! Ibrahimah, tell Mama to stop! Fatou, Papa!"

Maimouna looks past Binta as if someone is calling her name in the far distance.

"Mama! Wake up!" Binta yells, pulling and shaking on her mother's arm.

Maimouna blinks several times and then looks down at Binta as if seeing her child for the first time. She looks out into the dark, roaring sea, its mystery looming within the night, then turns back and pulls her youngest daughter into a hug.

"I'm sorry, my baby. Come, let's go."

She does not need any more of a sign. Binta's eyes are wild, tears streaming down her cheeks. Maimouna takes Binta's hand and allows her youngest daughter to lead her away from the beach and up the hill to the house. Inside, Binta finds a dry nightgown and helps her change. Maimouna climbs into bed next to her mother, who is still asleep.

"Don't tell anyone about this," Maimouna whispers.

Binta curls up on the end of the bed at Maimouna's feet. The red bird returns to the windowsill and snuggles down into his feathers. Maimouna drifts back to sleep but then awakens within minutes because of the brightness of the moon. She opens her eyes, ready to get up and shut the curtains, but the bedroom wall is missing, along with Binta, her mother, and the tiny red bird. The turquoise sky glimmers behind a bright-yellow sun. No wonder she can't sleep. It's daytime. Small eruptions of red fire burst forth from the sun's surface and streak across the heavens. She reaches up and catches one of the flaming eruptions. It's cool. Her heart settles down. The fire isn't here to destroy her.

She floats up from the bed into the sky. A single tear escapes the corner of her eye and drops below. Her gaze follows it to the row of small houses lined up along the desert sand. When the teardrop reaches the surface, a small pond appears.

The cliff that the village sits upon, which saves them from plunging into the sea when the tide rises, looks small and insignificant. The steep hill they walk down is barely an incline. Maimouna frowns. She hates everyone in the village. She grabs at her wrist, but something is different. She looks down. The scar is gone. Her ascent comes to an abrupt halt and she begins to free-fall. The sea, black and stormy, crashing up against the cliff, rises higher than she's ever seen before and threatens to engulf the village.

"No! Wait! Don't let me go!" she screams.

Her hands grasp at air and she lands on a cloud. Her body lies deep within its cottony folds, bundles of softness enveloping her. The misty, cool air washes away her tears, the village below hidden beneath layers of condensation. She reclines her head and closes her eyes. She sees a small window ahead; she looks down at her feet but she cannot see them, as she is no longer in the cloud. This space is dark, dry, and without an up or down. The only way out is the window, and she wills it to come nearer until she is at its edge. The light inside is dull and yellow. The cement walls are painted tan and several cracks run the length of it. The faint whisper of a radio plays off somewhere in this world, so foreign to her. On the brown-tiled floor lies a thin blue foam mattress and on top of it lies the small body of a boy.

Maimouna leans forward to get a better look at the person. She tries to climb through the window but she cannot get the bottom half of her body to appear. She reaches her arms into the room, but the boy is too far to reach.

"Ibrahimah!" she calls.

The boy sits up, his back erect. His eyes pop open wide and his mouth opens wide in a silent scream. It is her child! She fights to get through the window, but something holds her back yet again.

"My baby, come to Mama. Come, let me take you home," she cries.

Ibrahimah's eyes fill with water and it spills over onto the floor, flooding the room. His mattress floats over toward the window, but not close enough for her to reach him. Ibrahimah reaches out his hand and opens his palm. In it lies a small tooth. In his gaping mouth, she sees his front tooth missing. She takes the tooth and then tries to grab his wrist, but the water begins to recede and the bed floats back out of reach.

Ibrahimah's eyes close and with his hands reaching toward her he lies down in a fetal position, his lips trembling in a silent whimper as he sleeps.

Maimouna is engulfed in the black void, and when the light reappears, the cloud beneath her dissipates, leaving her once again in a free-fall. She screams, falling backward with her arms flailing about in the air. She reaches for the window, but it is gone and so she stops fighting, screaming, flailing, and allows her head to fall back and her arms to reach up toward the heavens and she lands on her bed with a soft thud. She turns her head toward the familiar sound of her mother's steady breathing, the red bird looks up from the windowsill but is silent, and Binta is curled up into a ball at the foot of the bed. Maimouna attempts to replay in her mind what just happened, but she cannot fight her fatigue and, within an instant, returns back to a deep, dreamless slumber.

In the morning, Maimouna wakes up clutching her body, her brow furrowed. Her mother and Binta are gone. The morning sun paints the room in gold tones, bringing warmth and softness, easing her tight muscles. She unfolds her limbs and stretches. Something drops to the floor. She hangs her head over the edge of the bed and notices the basket of cowrie shells and roots sticking out from beneath the bed. The doing of her mother, of course. She searches the floor further and notices a mysterious object. Frowning, she picks it up and turns it around in her hand. It's a baby tooth. She cocks her head to the side before her eyes light up and it all comes rushing back to her.

Ibrahimah lying sick and dying on that foam mattress on the floor. His tears. The water. Ibrahimah handing her his tooth.

"Are you ready?" the red bird says from the windowsill.

"Yes. Are you?"

"I'm going to him now," the bird says before flying away.

After the bird has gone, she rises from her bed and puts the tooth in the pouch she wears around her waist, stuffed with herbs and cowrie shells for protection and longevity. She sits by the window and takes a deep breath. Butterflies dance by while their colorful avian neighbors sing sweet ballads filled with happiness. She doesn't remember hearing the birds and the crickets before. She had almost lost faith, and with it, her son and her family.

In the living room Maimouna finds her mother sipping a concoction of life-sustaining root tea. Fatou and the girls are busy with their morning chores before the heat makes it impossible to exert the energy to do a sufficient job.

"Do you want anything?"

Her mother looks up at Maimouna and smiles.

"No, my child, I'm just fine."

"I'm sorry I didn't call you." Maimouna's shoulders drop in shame. "My husband shouldn't have had to contact you for me."

"There is no need to be sorry. Your burdens are real, but so is your ability to free yourself from their chains, but we all need a little help at times. You are my daughter and as long as I have breath in my body, I will be here for you. Just like you are for your children."

Her mother opens her arms and Maimouna finds herself nestled within a cocoon of love and strength.

"We are a family that survives the worst of trials. If you were not strong, you would not have survived those years of being treated like a slave and I would not have survived the truth of your experience."

Maimouna looks up at her mother.

"To fail is not something to be ashamed of. Life is a series of failures, my child, and the greater the failure, the greater the spirit to rise up from the ashes."

"But what of the evils in this world, it seems they search out the innocent? They seek to devour what is good. Like parasites."

"It is true. There are parasites that roam every inch of the Earth. They're greedy and ravenous and do not care for anyone but themselves. You have to find the courage to turn your head from them, even if you cannot remove yourself from their midst, physically, at first. But at some point, you will have to find faith, that you can free yourself both physically and spiritually, for as soon as you do the parasites will soon begin to devour themselves."

Maimouna pours herself a cup of her mother's tea and sips the hot, spicy drink as she ponders her mother's wisdom. She was too afraid as a girl to run away from her aunt and uncle, even after she got older, because she did not know where to go. So, she waited until she could convince her uncle to bring her home. There are many paths to freedom, some quicker than others.

"Do you have something?" her mother asks.

Maimouna reaches into her pouch and pulls the tooth out.

"Am I crazy?" Maimouna asks.

"Would you prefer to believe that?"

Maimouna shakes her head no.

"That magic done to you has spilled over onto Ibrahimah and would have soon spread to your entire family, and village. You've witnessed more than most people can ever imagine. There are more layers and doors than we can count. Give me the tooth. I have something I need to do, before I give it back to you."

She can be a victim or a warrior. She hands her mother the tooth. She will keep fighting.

 XXX.

The morning prayer call fills the room. Oblivious to the noise and movement around him, Ibrahimah doesn't stir.

"What's wrong with him?"

"I don't know."

"What if we get sick too?"

Caca and Scarface look at Ibrahimah with distrust.

"You get sick yet?" Étienne barks.

Caca smirks and walks off. Étienne doesn't want to leave Ibrahimah another day.

"Teacher, Ibrahimah is sick. He needs medicine."

"Medicine," Ahmed scoffs, "after all I do for you. Provide you with a home, clothes, and lessons of life. Now he sleeps all day and I lose money. And you say I need to buy medicine. Get out of my face. He'll get over his laziness once he gets hungry enough."

Ahmed returns to his bread and café. Four sugar cubes to a cup or he's annoyed for the rest of the morning. Étienne shifts from one foot to the other.

"Teacher, Ibrahimah is not getting better. He can't eat or drink. He throws up. His skin is hot."

"You talk too much. Now, you'll bring back your money and his. Go, before I whip you."

Étienne looks on at the man with his balding head and greasy face. Disgust and anger set into Étienne's expression.

"You're still standing there?"

Étienne grabs his can and stomps off.

The next morning, Étienne picks his sore body up from the floor.

"You're back in my face again. Last night's whipping not enough for you?"

"Ibrahimah's dead, he's not breathing."

Ahmed looks up with a start.

"What! What are you talking about, you little fool?"

Étienne stands motionless without expression.

Ahmed bolts out of his room, pushing past him. "Where is he?"

The boys move out of the way like the parting seas of Moses, creating a direct path to Ibrahimah's crumpled body. Ahmed drops down to his knees and puts his ear to the boy's nose. Shallow breaths can be felt, but just barely.

"He's alive." Ahmed wipes the sweat from his brow. "Boy, get up!"

Ahmed shakes Ibrahimah, but not even a whimper rises from the boy.

"Go next door and get Madame. Tell her a boy is sick and come immediately."

Étienne runs next door. Diatu has her baby brother strapped to her narrow back. She sweeps the floor while her mother sits over a pail of dirty laundry.

"Madame, Madame! Come quick. A boy is dying!"

The older woman wipes her hands on her lap and follows Étienne next door, with Diatu on her heels. When they enter the room, all eyes turn to the intruders. The boys are not used to seeing women inside their space.

"Let me see."

Ahmed moves to the side and allows the woman to look at Ibrahimah.

"How long has he been like this?" she asks, frowning at the pile of skin and bones on the floor.

Everyone looks to Étienne.

"Three days."

"Three days! Has he eaten or drank anything?" the woman asks.

Étienne shakes his head no.

"You should have said something to me sooner! You stupid, stupid boys. I can't afford this!" Ahmed yells.

Confusion washes across the room while Étienne's angry gaze bores a hole in the back of Ahmed's head.

"Well, what's done is done. We know now. The boy needs a doctor immediately. Diatu," the woman says, turning to her daughter, "go to your uncle and tell him to fetch the doctor, quick!"

"Étienne, go with her, make sure she relays the message properly," Ahmed instructs with authority.

Étienne and Diatu walk in silence, weaving down several streets in Ouakam before coming to a small shanty. The hovel is fastened together with thick fisherman's rope tied thoughtfully through drilled holes in the aluminum material.

"Uncle! Uncle!"

Diatu's little brother wakes up and begins to wiggle on her back. He stares at Étienne.

"Uncle!"

"What?" a sleepy voice grumbles from inside.

"Mama needs the doctor quick. A boy is dying!"

Étienne stands quietly next to the girl. She's the same height as he is, and just as skinny, but a year older than him.

"I'm coming."

A man in his mid-fifties sticks his head out of the curtained entranceway and looks at his niece. His skin is leathery and wrinkled; his thick hair is not combed.

"Who is this?"

"Talibé."

"I'll go fetch the doctor now."

Diatu's uncle dips his head back behind the curtain and within several moments exits his place dressed in dark-blue pants, a dusty brown shirt, and old weathered leather sandals. The children watch as the man walks off in the opposite direction they came. They are sure to be asked whether he actually went or not. Étienne and Diatu hang outside the shanty.

"Should we wait for him to return?" Diatu asks.

"No."

"Ahhh!" the baby shouts from Diatu's back, reaching his fat little hand toward Étienne.

Étienne looks at the baby and pokes his finger at it.

"Ahhh!"

"Hush!" Diatu shakes her body from side to side.

The toddler frowns at Diatu then plops his head down against the nape of her neck while staring wide-eyed at Étienne. They start back toward home in a slow, easy manner. Without the doctor there's no need to rush.

"Do you think he'll be okay?" Diatu asks.

"I don't know."

"My mother says your marabout is no good. We hear you tell him the Talibé is sick, but he just yelled at you to go to work."

Diatu looks at Étienne with expectant eyes, but he stares straight ahead.

"If that Talibé dies it will be your marabout's fault, just like the other one. Everyone knows your marabout didn't look for that boy while he was getting his heart cut out of his body. My mother says Marabout Ahmed might as well be killing the Talibé himself; he treats you all so bad. Why do you stay with him? I would run away. Anything is better than that."

"Shut up! You talk too much."

Étienne pushes the skinny girl away from him. The baby starts crying as she stumbles, catching herself just in time before falling.

"Stupid Talibé! I could have fallen. You all deserve to die!"

She folds her arms across her chest and doubles her pace, walking up ahead and looking back every once in a while, to make sure Étienne isn't coming after her. She makes it back to the house first and the room is cleared of the other boys. Her mother is bent over Ibrahimah.

"Did you find your uncle?"

"Yes. He left to fetch the doctor."

"Good. Talibé, get your marabout. We'll move the boy to my house, where I can look after him while I finish my business and wait for the doctor."

Étienne goes into the bedroom of his teacher and the man grunts at him in acknowledgment.

"Madame says—"

"I heard her. Help her move him."

Étienne returns to the crumpled mass on the floor.

"Help me lift him up," the woman says.

Ibrahimah is light enough for the large woman to pick him up, but Étienne sits his cousin upright, then hoists his small body up. The woman makes a big to-do about balancing Ibrahimah, but her dramatics create more chaos then help, causing Étienne to almost topple over under the weight of his cousin.

"Come this way."

Étienne follows the woman to the back of her house, taking each step with caution.

"Put him here."

She points to a pail of water.

"I was going to do laundry, but the boy is disgusting. He needs to be bathed. Hold him up while I pull this shirt off him."

Étienne does as he is told. She grabs a bar of soap and lathers Ibrahimah up. His head flops to the side like a newborn, his breath faint.

"Boy, grab that towel from over there. Diatu, when I'm done here, dump this water, refill the pail, and start the wash."

Thirty minutes later, Étienne sits down on the edge of the blue foam mattress on the floor, staring at the wall, Ibrahimah lies unconscious behind him. Étienne's mind wanders toward memories of his family back home in the village, the images of his parents and siblings fading more and more with each passing year—he nods off to sleep.

"What's happening in there?" Diatu's mother yells from the back of the house.

Étienne opens his eyes and looks around him.

Diatu stands in the doorway, her hands on her narrow hips. She rolls her eyes. "It was that ugly Talibé screaming. He's crazy."

"Girl, shut up and wash these things here like I told you to do earlier. Talibé! Come here," the woman demands.

Within seconds Étienne is in the doorway.

"Tell your marabout I need to use you today to help me."

Étienne lingers in the doorway.

"Diatu, go next door and tell the marabout what I just say."

"Talibé, what is your name?"

"Étienne."

"Okay. Étienne, I need you to take this down the road past the big tree and over the bridge. At the boutique, take a left and go past the restaurant; it's the third house down with the yellow door. There is only one house with a yellow door on that road. Only a fool can miss it. Ask for Madame Aminata. Tell her I need two sacks full. You hear? Two sacks! Don't come back with no less. Now go."

Outside he sees Diatu bouncing back toward her house. When she spots him looking at her, she sticks out her tongue. He looks up at Marabout's house and walks off down the street. The sun illuminates the black asphalt and he can feel its heat through the soles of his plastic jelly sandals. The paint on old cars glistens, tricking the eye for a moment, causing one to think they are new. He follows the directions Diatu's mother gave him, and when he arrives Madame Aminata looks down at him, heaves a large sigh, and rolls her eyes toward the heavens.

"Now she has someone else coming to fetch my goods with no money in hand. Are you her son?"

"No."

"Nephew?"

"No."

"Who are you then?"

"Étienne."

"Who do you belong to?"

"Marabout Ahmed."

"A Talibé, eh?" she says with raised eyebrows.

"Yes."

"Talibé don't run errands in the day for women, what are you doing here?"

"My cousin is sick."

"He a Talibé too?"

"Yes."

"What is he sick with?"

Étienne shrugs. Madame Aminata is tall and thin. She wears a slim ankle-length dress, her angular face glistens in the sunlight, and her wig is on backward.

"Is he very sick?"

"Yes."

"That is why she sends you. Come."

Étienne follows her inside. A small skylight three stories up lights the dark, cool hallway leading into the kitchen. The fragrant scent of burning incense fills Étienne's nostrils. The woman disappears behind a door and emerges twenty minutes later.

"Here, take these. Tell her I'll give to her today but next time she pays me my money or nothing."

She hands Étienne the sacks, now filled to the top. His long, skinny arms struggle with the weight.

"Swing one across your shoulder, then the other. Here, let me show you."

The woman swings each sack over one of his shoulders and onto his back.

"Better?"

"Yes."

Étienne walks out of the door hunched over beneath the weight. With the heat gaining momentum and no tree coverage, sweat dribbles down every porous area of his dry skin. He concentrates on putting one foot in front of the other and wills his body to make it back.

"Étienne!"

He looks over and sees Fatik standing in front of a boutique.

"Come! Help me with this."

Fatik runs over and takes the second sack from Étienne.

"Put it on your back, it's easier."

Fatik swings the sack a few times and it lands awkwardly onto his back. He leans forward to balance it while he walks.

"Why are you carrying these big bags?"

"I'm helping the madame next door. Ibrahimah is there waiting for the doctor."

"He's alive? He looked dead this morning."

"Maybe. The doctor comes soon."

"Good."

"Where are the others?"

"On the main road but I'll meet them after. I wait for a man I met yesterday, he told me to meet him at the boutique today and he'll give me money."

"Oh." Étienne raises his eyebrows in curiosity.

"He hasn't come yet, but I'll wait a bit more."

Fatik stops at the edge of the dirt yard in front of Diatu's house.

"Bring the sack inside."

"It's okay?"

"Yes, come."

Fatik follows Étienne around the back of the house into the small backyard, where they find Diatu and her mother. The boys heave the sacks onto the ground with relief.

"What did Madame Aminata say?"

"She is still waiting, and won't give to you again."

"Yes, yes," Diatu's mother says as she waves her hand dismissively, "this will last a month for sure. I will have something for her then."

The boys stand waiting for further instructions, but the woman waves them away. Étienne leads Fatik into the room with Ibrahimah. They stand side by side staring down at the unmoving body.

"Well, I'm going," Fatik says, breaking the thick silence. "I don't want to miss that man if he returns with the money he promised."

"See you later."

They slap hands. Étienne sits down on the floor and leans his back up against the wall. He wakes with a start to the sound of a man's voice.

"Boy, get up and move for the doctor."

An old wrinkled man hobbles over to Ibrahimah. Diatu's uncle helps him sit down on the floor and the old man puts his face close to Ibrahimah's nose to listen to his breathing.

"Has he vomited or had diarrhea in the last hour?" the old man whispers into the space.

Étienne shakes his head no.

"No, the boy hasn't eaten in days. He's been like this for some time, as far as I can see," Diatu's mother says, clicking her tongue and giving her brother a knowing look.

"Bring me my sack. Also, I need a bowl and some water in a cup."

"Diatu," her mother says.

The old man feels Ibrahimah's stomach for a while then turns Ibrahimah over, pulls the oversized T-shirt up, and examines his rectum.

"He has worms."

Once he has the bowl and cup from Diatu, the old man takes a mixture of ground powdered herbs from several plastic baggies and puts them into the bowl. He mixes them together, then drops several small twigs inside, lights them on fire. When the flame dies, he waves his hand over the bowl so that the roots and herbs smolder. He places the bowl next to Ibrahimah's head; a mixture of familiar and foreign scents fills the nostrils of everyone in the room. Whenever the smoke starts to die out, he relights the mixture.

"Bring me another bowl."

"Diatu."

He digs through his sack and pulls out an old dirty plastic container. He pops the lid off, and a thick black substance that looks like bread dough sits inside. He scoops out a bit with wide, gnarled fingers and lops it into the second bowl. He opens two bottles of brownish dirty liquid and mixes the substances together into a heavy dirty gray shake.

"Hold him up a bit; he needs to drink this over the next five days until it's gone. Just one sip for now is sufficient to get things started."

Diatu's uncle sits Ibrahimah's lifeless body up as the old man puts the liquid into Ibrahimah's mouth. They tilt Ibrahimah's head back and the liquid slides down his throat.

"Turn him over," the old man says.

With a different plastic bottle, with a long thin nozzle, he squirts something into his anus. Ibrahimah groans.

"Find something to put under him. The worms will come out and we need to kill them."

Diatu walks away with her face scrunched up in search of something to catch the worms. The old man reignites the fire and waves the smoke into Ibrahimah's face. Everyone begins choking.

"It stops the vomiting and spasms," the old man says.

Within minutes something begins to move around Ibrahimah's butt. The old man flips him over and bends his short legs in toward his stomach. Several live worms wiggle and squirm out, looking for a refuge. The worms are scooped up into a plastic bag. Bile escapes, along with several more worms. The process goes on for another fifteen minutes until nothing else comes out.

"Will the boy need more?" Diatu's mother asks.

"No, but if there are any more worms, nestled deeper in his system, the liquid will kill them. In another day begin to give him the milk from rice and mix this powder in it and make him drink a little like we just did. He has to rest for some time before he is strong again."

"He will stay here with me."

"Good," the old man says.

"Doctor, please sit in the living room a moment while I fetch you something from the boy's marabout."

The doctor follows Diatu's uncle into the living room.

"Talibé, go to your marabout, tell him we need to pay the doctor now. Ibrahimah is very ill. Close to death. We also have medicine for other boys, to ensure they don't get sick like Ibrahimah. Go now, the doctor waits."

Étienne finds Ahmed on his knees in prayer.

"The doctor gave Ibrahimah medicine and now he waits."

Ahmed grunts at Étienne. After several silent minutes he reaches under his mattress and pulls out the long black stocking. He hands three bills to Étienne, puts the stocking full of money down beside him, and returns to his prayer. Étienne folds the money into his hand and walks away. Before walking out of the house his eye catches both his and Ibrahimah's red tomato cans sitting up along-side the wall alone. He peers inside his can but it's as empty as he expected it to be. Inside Ibrahimah's can the lone little baby tooth sits. Étienne grabs the tooth. Next door he gives Diatu's mother the money. She looks down at the franc notes and sucks her teeth. She pockets two of the notes and walks into the living room and hands the other to the doctor.

"Thank you, Doctor, for everything; we'll call you if the boy gets any worse."

The old man bows his head in thanks and struggles to get up from the sunken couch. Diatu's uncle offers the older man his arm and they walk out together.

"That cheap bastard, he should be stricken down by Allah him-self . . ." Diatu's mother mumbles under her breath, and walks out of the back door.

Étienne stands over his cousin and watches him. Ibrahimah's brow is furrowed in pain. He takes the tooth from his pocket and places it into Ibrahimah's hand, closing his cousin's fingers tight around it.

"Keep the tooth for good luck," Étienne whispers.

"Talibé!" Diatu's mother calls out.

With one last look at his cousin, Étienne walks away in search of what it is that the large annoying woman wants now.

XXXI.

The days flow in and out like a hazy dream. Ibrahimah still hasn't woken up and Diatu's mother doesn't seem quite as optimistic as she was before about his condition. It's been three days since Étienne has seen Ibrahimah, as every time he returns in the evening all the lights are out in Diatu's house.

Étienne squints against the sunlight. He stands waiting for a petit Gambian to decide whether or not he's going to give him money. He would rather be in Ouakam with Ibrahimah.

"How long have you been a Talibé?"

Étienne shifts from one foot to the other.

"You like being a Talibé?"

"Are you going to give me money or not?"

The guy searches through his pockets and offers him a fifty-franc coin.

"Thanks."

The man hooks his fingers into his suspenders and settles back on his heels. "You know, young man . . ."

Étienne walks away. La Corniche, the coastline that runs the length of Dakar, has recently been sold off to the highest foreign bidder to raise money for the country. The beach, which is open to everyone, will soon to be fenced off for the exclusive use of the new hoteliers' wealthy clientele. Étienne cuts his eye away from the construction and spits on the ground. Everything is falling apart. If you don't have money, then you are nothing in this world. If this is the price he pays to go to heaven, he would rather go to hell.

"Étienne!"

He doesn't look up.

"Let's go get lunch."

"I'm fine, go ahead without me."

Fatik puts his hand on Étienne's shoulder but he shoves it off. "Come on, I think there's lots of traffic over by Casino Sahm." Fatik looks around at the empty coastline barren of traffic and people.

The sight of the tattered group of boys angers Étienne. He slows his pace, wanting to make distance between himself and them, but Fatik slows down too.

"Marabout wants five hundred francs now? It's impossible!" a short boy in the group squeaks, his voice going through the change.

Fatik shakes his head. "Marabout is greedy. He's worse than the rich people. At least they *give* us money sometimes." He turns around. "What do you think, Étienne?"

Étienne kicks at a stone on the ground; he looks over toward the ocean, but his eyes meet a half-erected building, its innards showing signs of halting construction. He scowls.

"Marabout cares only about himself," the squeaky boy says.

Several boys voice their agreement. Something catches the eyes of the group and the boys take off running, leaving Étienne behind.

Walking by a street vendor, Étienne snatches a large bag of cashews while the woman is not looking. The creamy taste of the five-thousand-franc bag of nuts satisfies something inside him. He walks along, staring at the people ignoring him; walking the streets day after day to feed Marabout and make Marabout rich. Ibrahimah had been right all along, but Étienne had convinced himself that this life of a Talibé would be worth it in the end because his parents would be happy and there was a real reward waiting for him. Allah would bless his sacrifice. He knew boys who were tied with chains at night like dogs for being short their money, or who were locked out and forced to sleep in the street every night and beaten even when they weren't short, or touched in bad places all the time, every night. He and Ibrahimah had it bad, but not as bad as it could be. Plus, he had no other choice. No place to go. The old man who was his friend, and teacher, made the evenings at Marabout's house bearable for all those years, and when Ibrahimah arrived to Dakar, he had someone to think about other than himself. But now the old man is dead, Moustapha has left for America, and Ibrahimah might die. He is right back where he started when he came to Dakar, alone. He has been asleep all these years, it's time for him to wake up.

"Where'd you get those?" Caca asks him as Étienne approaches the group.

"I bought it."

"Can I have some?"

"No, get your own"—Étienne pauses a moment—"or pay me. How much money you got? I'll give you some for fifty francs."

Caca assesses the few coins he has in the palm of his hand. The cashews look really good and even the smallest packets, at five hundred francs, are too expensive to buy. He hands Étienne the money. Five cashews drop into his open palms. With the first bite of cashew the smile on Caca's face proves it was worth it. He runs off to the others in the group up ahead.

"Étienne! Give me some," several boys demand eagerly.

"If you have money, then yes. But if you've got no money, then no cashews."

The boys wave their hands dismissively, grumbling to one another. Étienne sets the bag of cashews in his can. He looks around at the people walking up and down the sidewalks, and in the street. A foreign woman walks by and the boys pounce on her with fervor. Étienne watches as they run up to the woman begging for money while she walks with her head held high so as to pretend she does not see them. The boys give up after she crosses the street.

"You look like animals begging," Étienne says.

"Shut up. We're working. What are you doing? Eating your nuts and doing nothing like Marabout," Ousmane shouts. He is one of the new boys Marabout Ahmed has recently brought back to Dakar.

"Shut up!"

"Étienne is like Marabout!"

All the boys turn and look at him, their faces set in disgust. Étienne pushes the tall, lanky boy.

"Take it back!"

"Étienne is a greedy, dirty marabout!"

Étienne hits Ousmane in the face as his anger boils from the pit of his stomach and explodes into his chest.

"Stop!" Fatik yells, inserting himself between Étienne and Ousmane in an attempt to break them apart, but he gets knocked to the ground and trampled on. He screams out in pain as the two boys tumble over him, out into the street, in the way of moving traffic.

A driver screeches to a halt and the driver behind him slams on her brakes, her tires skidding across the asphalt. A heavyset man jumps out of the first car and pulls the boys apart.

"You want to get killed? I could have run you over!"

The cars piling up behind the ruckus begin to honk their horns. The boy attempts to throw another blow at Étienne but misses.

The man grabs Ousmane by the back of his neck and jerks him to the side. "You listen to me or I'll whip you worse than your friend here!"

The boy wrenches his body away from the man, his lip bloody, shirt torn. Ousmane grabs his tomato can and walks away with squared shoulders.

"You're not out here to act like fools," the man says, still holding onto Étienne's arm.

Étienne stares at the ground, pouting. The man releases him, gets back in his car, and takes off ahead of a wave of angry horns and shouts. The group looks from Étienne to the other boy to make sure they don't try to go at it again. Once it is safe to assume the battle is over, the boys pounce onto the stalled traffic with renewed energy. The heavyset man backed up more than twenty cars.

"Étienne, where are you going?" Fatik asks.

"I have other things to do."

Étienne wanders through the streets, his thoughts far from the noise and heat of the city. When Ibrahimah wakes up they will run away, maybe go to America or back to their village, anywhere but in Dakar with Marabout. At thirteen years old he's old enough to take care of them both, and he knows better now than to go off with people like Pape and that liar of a boy, Lamine.

Car horns scream in the background as he steps out into traffic; people scowl at him when he bumps into them without an apology. His legs feel heavy, his chest tight. Unable to take another step he sits beneath a tree, places his can between his bent legs, and rests his head on his knees. Several birds sing a melody amongst themselves in tune with the sounds of passersby. The world is slipping away, but he has to hold on until Ibrahimah wakes. His cousin will not die. He cannot die. The five o'clock evening prayer call fills the air and Étienne picks his head up, eyes bloodshot. Taxi drivers pull over to the side of the road, rinse their feet, hands, and head with bottled water, then lay their rugs down to pray.

A tiny red bird lands near his feet. Étienne is tempted to kick it away, but the way the bird looks at him causes him to pause. The bird searches its wings for ticks and dirt. Étienne looks down into his red tin tomato can. Six hundred francs sits at the bottom, not enough to cover both his and Ibrahimah's daily payment. There is no way he can raise a thousand francs a day. Only crippled kids, little girls, and Talibé under five make that kind of money, and Marabout is quite aware of this fact. Maybe he'll stop by the neighborhood of Liberté Trois, though he wonders if showing up with enough money every night will make Marabout suspicious. Perhaps he'll just take the beating tonight.

"Hey, boy."

Étienne looks up to find an older man glaring at him; spit dribbles down the man's chin and open sores litter his neck and face.

"Come here," the man growls.

"Get away from me," Étienne says, jumping up.

The man lunges toward him, grabbing his arm. Étienne kicks him and tries to wiggle out of his grasp. The man digs his long black fingernails into his skin. Étienne turns and bites down hard into the man's forearm, causing him to yelp in pain. The man loosens his grip for a split second and Étienne wrenches away, running down the tree-lined street.

Running out of steam Étienne slips into a quiet alley between two houses and tries to catch his breath. He turns to see if he's lost his pursuer and is shocked when his eyes meet the disfigured face of the man. He tries to shout, the sound traveling from the base of his belly up to his larynx, but it gets caught at the back of his throat.

The man bares brown, slimy teeth at him. How was he so close that Étienne didn't hear him? Afraid to move, Étienne drops his eyes down to see the long black handle of a knife protruding from his body. He tries to cry, to breathe, anything, but only the rush of warm blood escapes, spilling out the corner of his mouth. His can drops to the earth. He reaches out to push his attacker away, but the man gathers Étienne's falling body into an embrace. The little red bird appears behind the man's head and it screams out in pain, fluttering its wings wildly, but the sound of its voice is too small to attract help.

Images of his village appear. The ocean hums somewhere in the background. The forever-luminescent sun above fades to dark. His last thought screams inside his head—Ibrahimah!

III.

XXXII

Gaining consciousness, Ibrahimah finds Diatu propped up on her elbows, staring at him.

"You whisper in your sleep."

He raises his eyebrows at the interesting news.

"What are you whispering about?" she asks.

"Heaven," he says.

"Do you know what it looks like?"

Ibrahimah smiles. Diatu's face perks up.

"Tell me."

"The sun shines like a fire, deep down below the sea. That is where we are from, and when we die, that is where we return."

"You're strange. Everyone knows heaven's in the sky."

"It's not. People are too afraid to go deep where the light does not seem to exist. If they didn't run away so fast, they would understand that they can see in the darkness."

Diatu raises her eyebrows with intrigue.

"And what is in the darkness?"

Ibrahimah curls his lips into a small smile.

"Light."

"I thought you just said it was dark," Diatu says, rolling over onto her back to stare up at the ceiling.

"It is. But people can't see the light because it's so small. You have to stay in the darkness until you can see the light."

"And what is the light?" Diatu asks, turning back to look at Ibrahimah.

"Heaven."

"Can I get there without having to die?"

"Yes."

"Tell me."

Ibrahimah looks at Diatu, and for the first time she realizes that his eyes are jet-black.

"Did you know your eyes are black?" she asks, forgetting about his answer to her question.

"My papa calls them his black pearls," Ibrahimah says, his chest filling with warmth at the thought of his father.

"Everyone wants blue and green eyes, but your eyes are beautiful."

"I know," Ibrahimah says.

Diatu laughs. "You almost died; did you know that? And now you're awake with the same cockiness of all the other Talibé boys; you're a true Senegalese man."

"Do you want to know the answer to your question?" Ibrahimah asks. He can feel the fatigue of talking creeping up on him.

"Yes. Wait. What was my question?"

"How to find heaven. Do you still want to know?"

"Yes, yes. Tell me."

"Don't be afraid of the darkness."

"Like evil?" Diatu asks, incredulous.

"In the dark you can't see what is there, or what is coming, but if you run away then you will never know. You will never see the light. When you stop being afraid, you will find the path to heaven."

Diatu falls silent as she thinks about what Ibrahimah has just said.

"Mama didn't believe me when I told her you would wake up," she says, and gets up from the blue foam mattress on the floor.

"I almost died."

Diatu turns before walking out of the room. "I know."

Ibrahimah takes a deep breath; the air filling his lungs feels good. He stretches his stiff arms and legs, then rolls over and closes his eyes with exhaustion. When he wakes again the late-morning sun paints a golden river across the wall above him. Little flecks of lint waltz in the air. He stretches again, and this time his body is a little less stiff, then he squeezes his legs tight to hold his pee. He gets up and hobbles through the house like an old man, his muscles weak and unconditioned. In the bathroom he aims for the toilet but a thunderous sound frightens him and he misses. He adjusts his grip, moves his hand an inch, and tries again; the stream returns to the porcelain toilet bowl. He doesn't like these fancy toilets; aiming for a hole in the ground is much easier. The loud sound thunders again and he walks to the backyard, where he finds Diatu, alone, bent over a pail of wet laundry.

"What's that sound?"

Diatu looks up. "Gunfire."

Multiple shots go off, one after another.

"Who's shooting?" he asks.

"The police."

"At the students?"

"No. The vendors at Sandaga refuse to shut down and go back to the village."

"Why do they need to go back to the village?"

"Because the president wants Dakar to be more like Europe, and less like Africa."

Ibrahimah is quiet a moment. Diatu picks up the transistor radio that was sitting at her feet and turns the volume up.

"Several government offices have been ransacked and destroyed by rioters. The president has decreed a state of emergency. Citizens are advised to stay inside until further notice. Sandaga Market is officially closed. The army has arrested hundreds of market vendors."

The sound of the radio is too much for Ibrahimah; he walks over and turns the volume down. "It's better in the village."

"But you can't make money in the village. Anyway, what do you know, you're just a boy."

"I know a lot."

Ibrahimah looks up at the blue sky, then squats down on the back of his heels to rest.

"Where would we buy clothes and things we need for the house if vendors can't sell their goods in the markets?" Diatu asks.

"The tailor makes clothes."

"I *like* American clothes. Gucci, Prada, Nike. Those brands are too expensive at the stores."

"Your clothes are fine," he says. "You don't need clothes from America."

Diatu smirks at him.

"I'm tired," Ibrahimah says.

"You know where the bed is."

"Where's Étienne?"

Diatu looks up with surprise in her eyes, then lowers them to the ground.

"I don't know."

"If you see him, tell him I said to come," Ibrahimah says, rising.

Inside, he lies down on the thin foam mattress that feels luxurious in comparison to the cardboard mat he has slept on for so long in Marabout's house. The smell of tear gas drifts across the city and into his nostrils. Hopefully Étienne is okay.

Later that night, as if reading Ibrahimah's mind, Étienne steals into the room, bringing with him a bag of nuts and soda.

"Étienne!"

Étienne puts his finger to his mouth and points to Diatu, her breath even and steady. Ibrahimah's smile fades.

"I don't want to work for Marabout anymore. He cares only for money, and he lies," Ibrahimah says.

Étienne hands the nuts to Ibrahimah.

Ibrahimah puts two cashews in his mouth and chews. The creamy nut mixed with salt melts on his tongue and coats his throat on its way down. Étienne hands him the soda and he washes it down, the fizz burning his tongue and the roof of his mouth. Dissent screams outside the window. The people of Dakar riot through the night.

When Ibrahimah wakes the next morning Étienne is gone, but Diatu's mother is standing over him with a wide grin on her face.

"Little Talibé, you've awakened!" she says, arms folded across her chest, clutching her large bosom.

He offers her a tepid smile, not sure if the fact that she is aware of him being awake is a good thing, or bad. He hopes he hasn't done a bad thing, but he didn't even hear her so there was no way to know that she was standing at the door. Perhaps, she came every morning to stare at him, or perhaps Diatu told her mother that he had awakened, though he somehow doubts this. He'll just have to be brave for what is to come, because he can't go back and undo any of it at this point.

Next door, the boys are busy putting their cardboard mats away when Diatu's mother enters the house. The room buzzes with whispered conversation and nervous glances toward Ahmed's bedroom door. He has yet to show himself this morning.

"Marabout Ahmed!" she calls out in a singsong voice. "Good morning!"

Several moments pass before his door swings open, his body drenched in sweat.

"Why, there you are! What a beautiful day today will be, yes? I think so. Yes, yes. I've come to let you know I will need five thousand more francs." She puts both hands on her hips and leans back on her heels. "That little Talibé sure has an appetite on him! I had to get him more medicine. I just *knew* he was going to wake up sooner or later."

Smiling big, she looks around at the boys scattered across the room. Large, quiet eyes look back at her and then to Ahmed. Within a vacuum, void of air, light, or sound, Ahmed moves across the room and slaps the woman hard, across the face, the sound bouncing off the bare walls of the room, cracking the paint and shaking the cement foundation. She stumbles down to one knee and screams in shock, the shrill pitch piercing through the two-room house, threatening to break the glass of the lone window in the room. The boys move in a single motion, making space between themselves and the scene before them.

"Where is it? Who has taken it?" Ahmed roars, barreling past the woman on the floor into the mass of boys quivering before him.

His turban is missing, exposing a bald, tiny, egg-shaped head. Blank eyes stare at the raging madman towering over them, waving a long silky black sock.

"Who? *Who* has taken my money?"

The boys turn to one another, their eyes pleading that the guilty give themselves up and take the blame. Ahmed's face swells with rage.

"I-I don't know," Scarface says quickly, looking around the room.

"Not me," several voices mumble over one another.

"Someone knows. Yes, yes! You know, all right, because one of you *stole* it!"

"How dare you hit me!" the woman cries, rising from the floor.

"You!" Ahmed spins around. "You know who has done this! Who is the wicked dog that stole five hundred thousand francs from me? Five hundred! Who is it? Tell me, whore!"

He runs up to her, his bare feet slapping against the cold tile floor, grabs her by her hair, and drags her across the room. She screams out in pain while she tries to regain her balance. Fatik runs outside, and within moments several men enter the house just as Ahmed takes his cane and cracks Diatu's mother across the back. She howls out in pain as the wood crashes into her body. Several women run into the house. The men bark orders to take Diatu's mother out.

"How"—she struggles to catch her breath—"h-how dare you accuse me? After all I've done. You crazy fool!"

"You greedy whore! Give me back my money!"

Spit flies out of his mouth as Ahmed lunges toward Diatu's mother. She screams in fear and stumbles back, falling to the floor. The two men closest to Ahmed grab his shoulders. The women hoist her up and rush her out of the house.

"Let go of me," Ahmed growls, "and get out! All of you. Get out!"

Fatik and the other boys trample out of the house before he can say another word. Back home, Diatu's mother shouts with fury.

"Never again! If another of these boys dies, it will be *him* to pay!" A scream bursts from her lungs, hands clenched tight, body stiff as it releases. "They should lock him up! Diatu! Fetch my brother, quick!" Another scream slips from her chest.

"Ibrahimah, it's time for you to return to your marabout!"

Ibrahimah looks up with sunken cheeks from the floor, where he's playing with a bottle cap. He wilts at the woman's words.

Diatu's mother's eyes roll to the back of her head.

"That man is the devil!" she screams.

"But Mama," Diatu intercepts, "he's still not well."

"You shut up and stay out of this! You know nothing! I want him out of my house. Out!"

The women, having backed off for a moment, usher her through the house toward the living room.

"Leave the boy for now, you're angry. Shhhhh," the elder woman of the group says.

"He had murder in his eyes! That man is evil; I don't want to have anything to do with him! He probably killed those two Talibé of his. He's a monster!"

"Let the men calm him down first. If he did hurt the other two, could you live with yourself if he hurt this one? You saw his rage."

Ibrahimah stops playing as he listens. Of course Abdoulaye has died, but who is this second boy they're talking about?

Diatu's mother doesn't respond but obliges the older woman by sitting down. Diatu's uncle arrives within the hour, along with Marabout Sa'id, who lives nearby, and Imam Farad, Ahmed's associate from the nearby mosque. Sa'id is hunched over with age, but is still taller than everyone in the room at an even six feet. He has a long, gentle face and droopy eyes. Imam Farad is light-skinned and slim. He wears a kufi on his head and holds his wooden beads, constantly moving from one bead to another in succession.

Diatu brings a platter of rice and fish and three oversized cups of orange soda to the men. The elder woman relays her secondhand version of what transpired next door. The men listen in silence. Diatu's mother is brought to lie down in her room and within moments is asleep. The men talk in hushed tones, long after the food is gone, before venturing next door.

"*Salamalaikum,* brother," Imam Farad says, entering the house first.

Ahmed's bedroom door is open but he doesn't get up to greet them. He sits on the floor, his shoulders slumped, chin on his chest.

"Brother," Imam Farad says again, clearing his throat. "*Salamalaikum.*"

"*Malaikumsalam,*" Ahmed mutters.

The men stand around waiting for something more, but Ahmed doesn't lift his head. Marabout Sa'id, who is blind in one eye, resorts to sitting on the edge of the bed. Imam Farad grabs the lone chair in the room, sets it in front of Ahmed, and sits. Diatu's uncle stands close to the wall, his hands clasped behind his back.

"We come to you in good tidings, my brother. To offer you support. Djibril's sister tells him you are in distress. That you've been robbed."

Ahmed lifts his head, his puffy face painted in defeat. It takes a moment before his eyes adjust and he can see the men in front of him.

"Yes, my brothers, I have. Five hundred thousand francs. My entire month's salary. I am a man of meager means to care for my family in the village"—he pauses a moment—"and my Talibé. Only bad omens have come upon me for my servitude."

"Brother," the imam says, "you cannot speak in such ways."

Ahmed closes his eyes, the rising and falling of his chest the only movements he makes. The three men exchange glances.

"Allah is good and looks after his sheep. These are bad times for all."

"What does this have to do with *me* and my money?"

"My brother, what I'm trying to say is, prices are rising to levels never seen, families unable to buy rice, eggs, or bread. Petty theft and break-ins are spreading fast and wide throughout the city. The riots," Farad says.

"But who would steal from a marabout? A teacher of Allah! *Allahu Akbar!*"

The elder marabout agrees. "God is the greatest."

Imam Farad sighs heavily.

"Times are changing rapidly, my brother. Dissent cries out in our streets as hardworking men are pushed out of the city. Rumors are spreading fast of a long list of laws, created on a whim to appease foreign outsiders, being cast down from the president. The wicked do not offer a marabout exception in these times. We are all at Allah's mercy."

Ahmed looks into the faces of the men sitting in front of him, his eyes darting back and forth. "What? What are you talking about?"

"The Talibé will be no more, sent back to their families," the elder marabout says. He leans forward, wagging his finger at Ahmed and staring hard at him through his good eye. "It's said that they will try the marabouts in court for *harboring* Talibé. Arrest *us!*" He starts coughing and wheezing. Diatu's uncle, Djibril, steps over and pats him on the back.

"Arrest us? For *what*?! For teaching the words of Prophet Mohammed? *Alhamdulillah,* have mercy on those who do not see, for I cannot!"

Ahmed gets to his feet, his breath coming fast and quick. He waves his hands about, pacing in the tight space.

"When the winds shift toward the wicked, chaos prevails. The righteous have always suffered, my brother," Imam Farad says.

Ahmed stops pacing and narrows his eyes at the three men in front of him. Sa'id looks at Ahmed with the fatigue of a man who has seen and heard it all. Imam Farad continues to move the beads through his fingers and offers no reaction at all.

"You lie! You try to distract me! That no-good whore next door has fed you these lies! She has stolen my money and is trying to get more. No marabouts will be arrested, and what does that have to do with my stolen money? Nothing! It has nothing to do with it. Get out! Get out of my house!"

"No? You must not read the paper, because everyone is talking about it. Look here at today's *Quotidien*. Front page!" Djibril pulls the paper from his back pocket and hits it several times to make his point. "There are foreign organizations, NGOs, supporting this new faction against our traditions and yet you scoff at us. You call my sister a whore. *You* should be the first to send your Talibé back to the village!"

"I shall call the police and report you and your sister! I'm sure you were in on this scandal against me."

"Call the police! I will ensure they take your Talibé and charge you with human trafficking. That's what the foreigners are calling the marabouts now, human traffickers!"

"Trafficking? This is nonsense. I'm calling the police now. Get out!" Ahmed says.

"I would advise not," Imam Farad interjects, standing up between the two men. "If this is all true it's best to stay quiet, at least for now. You've already had two of your Talibé attacked, Ahmed. You would be a perfect example for the courts if these rumors prove to be true. Don't give the devil fuel for his fire."

Ahmed shakes his head, mumbling to himself. This cannot be. The floor is moving beneath his feet and he cannot catch his balance, he cannot seem to get enough air to fill his lungs.

". . . but then it could be just talk. Every so often there's an article in the paper claiming the Talibé suffer. They are boys! A boy needs a stern hand and a life that teaches him to be a man. Without the daaras these boys would sit in the village with no education, barely enough food to eat—burdens to their families! Our government cannot disregard hundreds of years of tradition because some foreigners, outsiders, are asking them to do so. It's absurd!" the elder marabout says, his voice giving out, the anger too much for his frail nature.

When Ahmed's attention returns to the roomful of men, the sun has bid adieu and night has fallen upon the landscape outside his window. Tired of the conversation, the elder man yawns.

"Well, it's getting late, we must leave you with the blessings of Allah," Marabout Sa'id says.

"I agree," Farad seconds.

"Well, what about my sister and this madman?"

"It is you who is the madman!" says Ahmed.

"Brothers," Imam Farad interjects once more, "can we agree that this is not the way to go? The enemy is not within this room."

Ahmed grumbles under his breath.

"He should apologize to my sister!" Djibril says.

"Brother Ahmed is very sorry for his rash actions; he should not have struck out and hit an innocent woman," Imam Farad says, looking Ahmed in the eyes.

"If your sister did not steal from me, then I apologize," Ahmed says, looking at Djibril.

Djibril shifts from one foot to the other, and with his face set in a scowl walks out of the two-room house, slamming the door behind him.

"Can we leave you in peace, Brother Ahmed?" Sa'id asks, rising from the edge of the bed.

"Thank you, my brothers," Ahmed mumbles. "May Allah guide you in all that you do."

"*Alhamdulillah,*" the two men reply in unison.

With the visitors gone, the boys file into Ahmed's room with their day's earnings. He barely notices them as he reads the article in the *Quotidien* again and again.

 XXXIII.

The glare is blinding. Everything spins into a massive kaleido-scopic vision, causing Ibrahimah to grab hold of the fence for balance. His heart pounds hard and fast; he feels weak.

Several cars drive by, bald tires dipping and scrambling over the uneven road. The air stinks like sewage, exhaust, and sweat. A young man walks by yelling out the inventory of the cheap imported kitchenware he carries slung over his narrow, sweaty back—the president's ban on street vendors has failed. A baby screams with colic from a house nearby, its voice strained and hoarse. A plane flies overhead, shaking the ground beneath his feet.

Ibrahimah looks back. Diatu stands there with sadness on her face as she blocks the entrance to his refuge. Her mother, still traumatized from yesterday morning, has made herself clear. He walks out to the sidewalk, his focus solely on placing one foot in front of the other. Not noticing the boys next door, spilling out from Marabout's house, he sits down on the curb.

"Ibrahimah!"

Fatik is standing over him, smiling, and a moment later Étienne joins them. Ibrahimah's heart skips a beat at the sight of his cousin.

"What are you doing out here?" Fatik asks.

"I have to go back to Marabout." A heavy sigh escapes his chest. He rests his chin down onto his knees.

"Ibrahimah, we thought you weren't going to make it. Allah blesses you with life, boy! You escaped death two times now!" Fatik says, patting Ibrahimah on his back.

Ibrahimah looks up at Étienne and then over to Fatik. Their clothes are dirty, their skin rough and scarred. The straps on Étienne's jelly sandals have broken, the soles worn down. Ibrahimah remembers the day Aria bought them their shoes. How new they looked. How good he felt. Étienne's big toe sticks out of a hole at the front of his sandal. Ibrahimah looks down at his own bare feet; he grew out of the jelly sandals before he fell sick. He has no idea what happened to his pants, sweater, or polo shirt. He pulls the oversized T-shirt down over his naked knees. Ibrahimah looks up with doubt in his eyes. He had hoped things would be different, but they seem worse.

"Well, let's go before anyone sees you and tells Marabout," Fatik says, looking over his shoulder. A few boys look their way but then take off in the opposite direction toward the Rue de Ouakam.

"I can't do it. I can't go back. I hate Marabout."

"Shhhhhh, don't say that here." Fatik looks over his shoulder.

Fatik grabs Ibrahimah's hand and pulls him up. They walk in the opposite direction, in hopes of avoiding the other boys. Ibrahimah knows he's alive because of his mama, but he can't understand why he's still in Dakar.

"I have to go find breakfast. You coming?" Fatik asks.

Étienne shakes his head and leans up against a tree.

"No, we'll stay here," Ibrahimah says.

Fatik cocks his head to the side. "We?"

"Yeah, me and Étienne," Ibrahimah says, motioning toward his cousin.

A somber look falls across Étienne's face.

"Ibrahimah. Are you feeling okay?" Fatik asks.

"Why do you ask that?"

Fatik pauses a moment, a look of pain on his face. "Étienne is gone."

"No, he's not, he's right here," Ibrahimah says, pointing.

"He's not. They found him a few days ago."

"What do you mean?" Ibrahimah's voice rises. He looks over at Étienne, but his cousin's face is like stone.

"Étienne, tell Fatik he's crazy. You're right here."

"Étienne is gone, Marabout said so. If you see him it's because he's come back to watch over you."

Fatik looks at the empty spot Ibrahimah keeps pointing at and takes a step back.

"Étienne," Ibrahimah cries, "tell him you are here, alive!"

Étienne shakes his head.

"But you brought me Coca last night."

"You dreamed of your cousin, Ibrahimah. Étienne was killed."

"You're lying!"

Tears run down Ibrahimah's face and he finds it hard to breathe. He bends over and grabs his legs to brace himself. "Étienne is not dead. He's not!"

Fatik stands there awkwardly. He looks around, but the street is deserted. Ibrahimah walks over to Fatik and hits him. Fatik grabs his hand and holds it tight, then pulls Ibrahimah's sobbing body into a hug. The sun disappears behind large storm clouds, returns, and disappears again before Fatik releases his embrace. When Ibrahimah turns to talk to Étienne, his cousin is gone.

"What will I do?" he sobs.

Fatik looks at him.

"Is Marabout taking Étienne back to the village?"

"No, he said he put Étienne to rest the same day they found his body."

Ibrahimah lies down on the ground and curls up into a fetal position.

"Ibrahimah"—Fatik bends down and shakes his arm—"let's go back to Diatu's house; maybe her mother can help you."

"She doesn't want me. I need *my* mama."

A woman walking by stops. "What's wrong with him?" she asks.

"He's okay, I think," Fatik says, sounding less sure than he would like to believe.

The woman walks closer to Ibrahimah. "*Petit,* are you okay?"

"Étienne is dead. I can't . . . Mama!" Ibrahimah sobs.

"Come, help me with him, he can't stay here like this," the woman says.

Fatik helps to lift Ibrahimah, but his legs won't work and he falls back to the ground. The pain in his heart is too great. He doesn't belong here. Étienne and Abdoulaye were good but now they are dead. Marabout is wicked and he is alive. He cannot understand why Allah would let this be. He scrunches his eyes shut, squeezing them tight, hoping this is all just another one of his bad dreams.

Ibrahimah sits up and brushes away the small pebbles and dirt from the side of his face and looks over at Fatik, who is eating a banana. The woman is gone. He must have fallen asleep.

"You want some?" Fatik asks.

Ibrahimah doesn't have an appetite but takes a bite anyway.

"We should go to work soon," Fatik says, looking down the empty street, the midmorning air still cool. "Marabout wants five hundred francs now."

"I want to go back home to my family," Ibrahimah says.

"Do you know how to get back to your village?" Fatik asks.

"I go to the depot and take a sept-place south to the Gambia and cross the river," Ibrahimah says with authority in his voice. "After that I don't know the way. You should come with me."

Fatik looks over at Ibrahimah. "You're crazy. Marabout would kill us if we tried to run away."

Ibrahimah looks up at the sky; its intense blueness looks foreign to him. He remembers the tears in his mother's eyes and touches his hand to his lips.

"You ready to work?" Fatik asks.

"I have no other choice."

Approaching the house, they see Ahmed dragging a suitcase out the front door.

"Marabout," Ibrahimah yells out, but the man doesn't turn around and instead climbs into the back of a taxi that immediately takes off. Ibrahimah's face falls. A man is walking toward him but Ibrahimah doesn't recognize him.

"*Salamalaikum*, ton-ton," Fatik says.

"*Malaikumsalam*, Talibé." The man looks at Fatik quizzically.

"Where is Marabout going?"

"Well, I was going tell you boys this evening once you returned. He has to go to his village and then Mali. He'll return in two weeks."

"What about Étienne?" Ibrahimah asks.

"Who?"

"The boy who was just killed," Fatik says.

"Oh, what about him?"

"He is my cousin." Ibrahimah's eyes burn with tears.

"Well, he's with Allah now in Paradise."

"Thank you, ton-ton. May God be with you." Fatik bows and pulls Ibrahimah away.

"Address me as Marabout Sa'id. Be sure to have your money tonight," the older man calls out after them. "Marabout Ahmed gave me specific instructions on how much I should have by his return. I'm to beat any boy who returns short." He pauses a moment. "I plan to bring my nephew to do the whippings. I don't have the energy for it. Warn your brothers," he says, and wags his finger.

Ibrahimah turns to glare at Marabout Sa'id. He's done with the beatings.

"Marabout is traveling to get more boys," Fatik says.

Ibrahimah glowers in the direction of the departed taxi.

XXXIV.

"Pssst."

Ibrahimah sits up and finds Étienne sitting crossed-legged next to him.

"Étienne, you've come back!"

Étienne puts his finger up to his lips and motions for Ibrahimah to follow him. Everyone, including Marabout Sa'id, is still asleep. Ibrahimah's eyes light up.

"What is it? Where are we going?"

Étienne shakes his head. He is not going to tell him in advance. Ibrahimah rubs his eyes; he is happy to have Étienne with him— even if no one else can see his cousin, Ibrahimah knows he is real. They fall into a comfortable silence as they walk along the dark streets. A rooster screams off in the distance.

"Will you always come back to be with me?"

Étienne shrugs.

"What happened to you? How did you die?"

Étienne shrugs.

They walk along an abbreviated section of the coastline that is not yet overtaken by construction as the sky turns from midnight blue to a cool gray. The city slowly comes alive with the rising sun, on cue. Ibrahimah looks into the cars both old and new along the road. A female passenger tosses her head back in laughter. A young girl in the backseat of a car presses her round face against the window. The colors of the ensembles the women wear jump out at Ibrahimah in bright blue, purple, pink, yellow, gold, and red. He drinks in each color, his palate alive with the different textures and varieties. How long had he been asleep? Walking past the high fence of the French-Senegalese Bilingual School, the period bell rings and the rustle of students rushing to class floats into his ears. He imagines himself in the midst of their carefree chatter. He has so many questions for Étienne but he doesn't know where to begin; his mind is overwhelmed with the bustle of movement going on around him.

A warm breeze passes by and he opens his palms and pushes his hand against it. Following Étienne into Liberté Trois, they stop in front of a small dark makeshift restaurant filled with the aroma of rice, tomatoes, peanut oil, and fish. Inside, the woman working at the register greets him with a smile. Ibrahimah doesn't look up into her face until she walks over and strokes his cheek.

"Ta-ta!"

He can't believe his luck. He thought he'd never see Aria again.

"It's been a long time, Ibrahimah. I miss you too much, my chouchou," she gushes as she bends down and scoops him up in her arms. "How did you find me? Are you here all alone? I heard you were very sick."

"Where's Moustapha? Did he come back from America?"

Aria clucks her teeth. "No, I don't believe he and his parents will be back for a long time."

"Oh," Ibrahimah replies, dropping his head.

"No matter, we have found each other again. That is good, yes?"

"Yes!"

Ibrahimah smiles up at the gentle older woman who reminds him of his mother. She leads him to the back of the restaurant and sets a platter of food in front of him, along with a cup of Fanta orange soda. Ibrahimah's eyes pop open wide.

"For me?"

He never thought he would eat Aria's delicious food again.

"Yes. So, you can get strong again."

"I have no money." Ibrahimah frowns with worry.

"You are my baby," Aria says, placing her hand to her chest. "Whatever I have is yours. Having you near me is a blessing from Allah. Eat!" She heads back to the register to attend to her customers.

Ibrahimah cups his hand over his face and prays for Aria. He is sure his mother sent her to him. He sits down and puts a small amount of rice in his mouth. His appetite is not what it used to be.

"This is a good surprise," he says, smiling.

Étienne pushes a piece of fish to his side of the platter.

"I'm okay." Ibrahimah looks around. Inside the small dark room of the restaurant sit a long table and eight chairs where customers can eat. The restaurant space is attached to a small house and opens up into a backyard; the tiny unpaved area has a single patch of grass surrounded by arid earth. A big luscious mango tree sits in the center, keeping the space cool and shady, and a ram stands nearby eating the lonesome patch of grass for its lunch. Ibrahimah puts a piece of fish in his mouth and chews it slowly and steadily. There is a lull in the restaurant and Aria returns.

"Ibrahimah, I asked around about your parents," Aria says.

"My mother is alive," he says, not looking up from the food.

"Oh? How do you know?" she asks, her head cocked to the side.

"She told me when I saw her."

"When did you see her?"

"In my dream. She's waiting for us in the village."

Étienne looks at Aria and then Ibrahimah.

"Us?"

"Me and Étienne," Ibrahimah says, motioning to his cousin.

Aria raises her eyebrows.

"Ahh, I see. Étienne has come back for you?"

"Yes."

"Well then, after you eat go inside the kitchen; beneath the sink something waits for you."

A customer rings the bell at the counter and Aria heads back.

Étienne stands up and beckons for Ibrahimah to follow him.

Ibrahimah stuffs a piece of fish into his mouth and follows Étienne into Aria's kitchen. Étienne points to the cabinet door.

"What?"

Étienne rolls his eyes in exasperation, pointing. Ibrahimah falls to his knees, swings the door open, and finds a small black box inside. Ibrahimah stares at the box a moment, then like the switch of a lightbulb, it all comes back to him.

"Moustapha!"

Ibrahimah enters the code their friend taught them, and the safe clicks and the door flies open. On the top shelf sits a small green man. It's the G.I. Joe Ibrahimah used to play with while they watched cartoons. A rush of love and joy fills his chest.

"Moustapha left this for *me*?" Ibrahimah laughs in delight and surprise. "I thought he took our money to America."

They had close to five thousand francs left in there from the bounty of cash they had raised during Ramadan. He won't have to work so hard for a while. When Ibrahimah looks back inside the safe, he bends down to look at the back of the bottom shelf. Expecting to see five thousand francs he's shocked to see a multitude of ten-thousand-franc bills, neatly stacked. Before he can process the weight of the situation, Ibrahimah slams the door shut and shakes his head, as if trying to wake from a dream.

"Étienne . . ."

Silence fills the space around him.

"But Étienne"—Ibrahimah struggles to catch his breath—"we're rich! Did Moustapha leave us all this money?" Ibrahimah squeals.

Étienne shakes his head no.

"Where did it come from?"

Étienne is quiet, a dark shadow falling over his eyes.

"Well, I can go home to my mama now," Ibrahimah says, and stands up straight. He pauses a moment and thinks of going to see Moustapha in America. He looks over at Étienne, but his cousin frowns at him. No, Étienne is right. He needs to see his family first, and then they can go to America. Ibrahimah opens the safe again and stares at the money; when he looks back up Étienne is gone.

"Étienne."

Ibrahimah gets up and looks around the neighboring rooms for his cousin.

"Étienne? Étienne!"

He returns to the kitchen and sits expressionless on the floor of the kitchen until Aria comes searching for him.

"You found your surprise?"

"Yes."

"Moustapha was so worried about giving you boys this safe when he was leaving. There was little time to prepare before they left. I searched around for quite some time but finally found who your marabout is and that's when I learned you were sick, and found Étienne."

"Oh."

"What's wrong, little one?"

"I want to go home, but with Étienne."

"You'll see your family again soon. Don't you worry. And your cousin will always come back to look after you. Death cannot break the bond of a love so deep."

Ibrahimah nods, though he questions everything that has happened.

"I will give you a bath later. I have some clothes that will fit you."

"Pants?"

"Yes, pants, my chou-chou."

The bell rings again, signaling another customer. He'll ask Fatik tonight to go with him; there's no way his friend can refuse him once Ibrahimah shows him the money. He can do anything as long as he has money. Money fixes everything. Ibrahimah searches out a piece of cloth and wraps the bills in it. Étienne did good. Ibrahimah leaves a stack of ten-thousand-franc notes on the kitchen counter beneath a carton of eggs for Aria. Tears blur his vision as he walks back to his plate of food. His G.I. Joe sits on top of the bounty of money inside his red tin tomato can. He can already taste the ocean air of his village.

XXXV.

His bags are heavy, his black boubou soaking wet, his feet covered in mud, and his face is set in a scowl when he discovers the door is locked. When he bangs on it, green paint chips fall to his feet. Hawa swings the door open, the baby strapped to her back. Her eyes open wide with surprise.

"What are you doing here?" she blurts.

Ahmed barrels past her. "Get my bags," he growls, motioning behind him.

Upstairs he pulls his clothes off and steps into the shower. The cold water does nothing to calm him down. Towel-dried, in a plain blue ankle-length dashiki, he lies down and goes to sleep. The sound of the rain outside the window rages through the night.

The smell of eggs and café wakes him in the morning. Downstairs, the contents of his suitcase are drying on the clothesline in the sun. His wife arrives with breakfast, her eyes nervous. The house is quiet; no birds sing outside the window, no fresh ocean air sweeps through the room.

"Your mother went out for a bit to visit friends. The maid is at the market. I have to go to my papa. He is having pain. The kids are

at school." Hawa pauses a moment and then adds, "Hassan is upstairs in bed, he has a fever."

She stands over him, twisting the hem of her shirt, and glances
up at the ceiling. Ahmed grunts at her and stares at the black television screen. He stuffs the food into his greedy mouth; a smudge
of butter sits on his bottom lip and bread crumbles down to his
chest.

"If I had known you were coming, we could have prepared. How
long are you here?"

Ahmed's heavy breathing fills the air.

"Well, we'll make your favorite tomorrow for dinner," she mumbles to herself. The baby strapped to her back stirs. She swings her
hand behind her and caresses its bottom.

"I'm going. The maid will return any moment."

Beads of sweat sprout up across his forehead. The heat taunts
everything within its midst before the late-afternoon rain. A spider
crawls up the wall behind the television. Changing its mind, it turns
to the window and exits in one swift move. A copy of *Le Quotidien*
sits beside him, crispy and warped.

Ahmed is sitting in the same spot when the afternoon heat arrives; the food residue on his plate has hardened and his robe is
drenched in sweat—the open window brings no relief. The sound
of a thud above his head catches his attention. He walks upstairs,
slow and meticulous, and pokes his head into Hassan's room.

"Papa! I didn't know you were home."

"I am. Why are you home?"

"I have a fever."

Ahmed steps into the room. Hassan sits on the floor playing
with a toy truck Ahmed brought home last Ramadan. His sons are
no less deserving than the president's children.

"You like your truck?"

Hassan smiles big, his two bottom teeth missing. Ahmed sits on
the edge of the twin-sized bed and stares at the boy. His breath
deepens, heat rises from his groin into his chest.

"Who do you love more, me or your mother?"

Hassan looks up at Ahmed with a quizzical look. When he sees the look in Ahmed's eyes, he lowers his gaze.

"You, Papa, I love you the best."

The afternoon sun has been replaced by clouds and Ahmed steps into the shower a second time that day. The water rains down on him, mixes with sweat, and washes away the evidence. There's nothing to worry about; he'll recover his lost money with more boys. Later he will calculate how many more Talibé recruits he needs to make up for the lost income. With his towel wrapped around his waist he walks into his bedroom.

"Mother!" Ahmed says.

She stands in the middle of the room, body straight as an arrow, face frozen as stone.

"What are you doing in here? Are you okay?" Ahmed looks around the room for something to cover his body.

"I would like a word with you."

"Yes, madame," he says to her, retreating.

Downstairs, he finds his mother in the living room, a kettle on the coffee table with two cups, sugar, and milk. She motions for him to sit down next to her.

"Why are you here, my son?"

"I have some business to attend to. I'm only here for a few days."

"I see," she says. "I had a dream. I wasn't sure what it meant, but now you are here."

She reaches for the kettle and Ahmed tries to do it for her but she waves his hand away. She pours the hot water, the instant Nestlé café already sitting at the bottom of each cup. She drops four sugar cubes into his cup and none into her own. With a splash of milk, she takes a sip. She motions to the other cup and Ahmed obliges.

"Hot drinks in this heat will cool the body down," she says.

Ahmed looks over at the window, his breath calm and even.

"The rain will cool things down," he says.

"For you, it will not rain today."

Ahmed finishes his café in two greedy gulps.

"Mama, I will have to leave you. I have to attend appointments this afternoon."

"Your father told me something was wrong with you when you were a boy, but I never wanted to believe it."

Ahmed looks away.

"How could you be so wicked?"

"I don't know what you mean."

"Hassan."

Unable to look his mother in the face, he rises.

"You must be mistaken," he says. "Perhaps you're going senile."

He towers over his eighty-year-old mother, a sneer forming across his face.

"Sit down," she commands.

"No, I have t—" He leans over, then falls back onto the sofa, clutching his stomach. He looks over at his mother then down at his empty cup.

"Mama?"

Hot fire sears through his body and he doubles over again. A cry escapes his lips as his body heaves for air. His mother looks him in the eye. He stares dumbly into her dark, steely gaze, writhing in pain, and falls to the floor. Drool falls from his lips and dribbles down his chin. His eyes open wide and then nothing. No movement, no sound, no breath. Ahmed lies strewn across the floor. His mother rises, picks up the tray, and walks out of the room. When she returns to the living room with a pot of tepid water filled with herbs, she walks up to Ahmed's motionless body and dumps the concoction onto him. Her heart beats once, twice, thrice as she sits down onto the sofa and waits.

Ahmed spasms with the same violence as before, gasps for air, and clutches his chest. He lies on the floor for several breaths before he sits up, one hand still on his torso while the other holds on to the edge of the sofa. He hoists himself up and takes a tentative step forward, wobbles a bit, stops, takes a deep breath, and then straightens his body erect. Several beats later he walks over to his mother and bends down to give her a kiss on her forehead like his father would do.

"I gave you life, and I can take it away," she says.

"Only if I let you," he whispers into her ear, his hands circling around her throat.

She looks him in the eye as her life hinges on the breath she cannot claim as her own. Ahmed leers down at his mother's aging body and meets her hardened stare. She does not blink, nor does she stir beneath his assault.

He tightens his grip, clenching his teeth in determination. The clock on the wall screams with every tick. His fingers overlap one another as he wrangles her neck. Sweat rolls down his arms.

Ahmed lets out a soft cry and releases his mother. He takes a step back and looks at her in confusion. She raises her cup to her lips and takes a sip, never breaking her gaze with his own.

Ahmed sits down in the chair across from the woman he just tried to murder, his hands shaking as he searches out his handkerchief to wipe the sweat from his face.

"As you were saying," his mother says.

XXXVI.

Someone knocks hurriedly at the front door, followed by a thunder of footsteps barging into the house. Maimouna looks up to see the stricken face of her sister-in-law looming at the living-room door.

"Maimouna!" she cries.

"Sister!"

"My Étienne. Ya Allah! My Étienne," she says, coming across the room and grabbing on to Maimouna for support.

"Sit, sit, please," Maimouna says. She brings her sister-in-law over to the free chair across from her mother and Madame Touré, and sets the distraught woman down. The three women had been discussing Maimouna's dream, and the rumors coming from Dakar about another Talibé.

"How could he do this?" she asks with eyes that are red and weary.

"So, it is true. We just learned the news moments ago, but were not sure it was really Étienne," Maimouna says.

Madame Touré clucks her tongue. "He is a wretch, and makes all marabouts look bad. I don't want to say I told you so, but I told you he was no good when he refused to return Ibrahimah!"

"Madame," Maimouna says pointedly, looking over at her friend.

"I want to blame you, but how could I? With all the dark magic against you, how could you cause this to happen to my Étienne? Perhaps you are a curse because you are not Senegalese. A curse to this family," Maimouna's sister-in-law spouts, "but he left my son in Dakar without giving us a chance to bring him here to bury him, or go to Dakar. My son! He is a monster!"

She leans her elbow onto her thigh and holds her head in her hand; quiet tears wet her palm. The women sit in silence. There are no words that can soothe the initial shock of learning your child is dead.

"I did not want to send Étienne, but my husband was adamant. A woman cannot defy her husband's wishes. I got pregnant again, and lost the baby. And then a second pregnancy failed. On the third attempt I had little Fili, but he was always so sickly. I prayed for God to grant me strength. We sacrifice a lamb once a month. I give to the poor. I keep cowrie shells beneath my bed. I pray. I go to mosque. I've tried to do right for my family. What more can a woman do?"

"There is no right way to be a mother. You will fail, and in that failure you gain wisdom to pass down to your daughters so that they may not make the same mistakes as you," Maimouna's mother says.

Fatou walks into the room and replenishes everyone's cups with ice and bissap.

"Maimouna, you are blessed with such a good girl," her sister-in-law says, taking a long drink from her glass.

"I know."

"Dear, make me another batch of the bissap and gingembre, when you can."

"Yes, ta-ta," Fatou says with a small curtsy before leaving the room.

"Maimouna, I couldn't allow myself to agree with you about Ibrahimah, or I would have lost my strength and fallen apart over Étienne going to Dakar. I had to believe, but it was selfish of me."

Maimouna looks at her sister-in-law and realizes that they are all the same. Lying to themselves, pretending things are fine when they are not.

She sighs. "Sister, Ibrahimah is coming home."

The woman looks up, confusion clouding her face.

"What do you mean? You cannot have your son back. There is no one, other than God, who would dare question the authority of a marabout. You are without power, unless the marabout himself decides to do right by you and we know he will not."

"Ibrahimah is coming home. That I can promise you, and no one will take my child away from me again under the guise of religion, or the old ways."

The four women sit in the silence evoked by Maimouna's statement.

"Did you hear a marabout approached Madame Keita about taking her two sons and she staunchly refused, with the full backing of her husband? More people are refusing to send their boys to daaras, and good for them. These marabouts are abusing our traditions for their personal profit. There are no blessings in suffering for someone else's gain," Madame Touré says.

"The tides of change are coming. It is time that women take their suffering and use it for the good of all, not just to promote their own agenda," Maimouna's mother says, rising.

Maimouna stands up and offers her hand to the older woman, who brushes her help away.

"I may be aging but I'm not dead yet! I can get myself up, young woman. I'm off to take a nap; sleep is the elixir to a long, youthful life. Cheat yourself on that and nothing in this life matters, as you won't be around long enough to see it!" she exclaims.

"It is good your mother is here with you, Maimouna. No woman, or man, can find the strength to conquer the wickedness in this world without family," her sister-in-law says.

"I am fully aware of my blessings," Maimouna says, looking at her sister-in-law.

The women spend the rest of the afternoon talking, and by the time she takes her leave, Maimouna's sister-in-law seems to be in a more peaceful place.

Over dinner that evening the girls cannot contain their excitement.

"We should have a big party for Ibrahimah when he gets here," Binta says, her cheeks puffed out with millet.

"I think your brother will be very tired," Idrissa says.

"Why can't we just go get him? How is he coming home, and with whom?" Fatou asks.

The desire to go find her baby tugs at Maimouna, and her mother pats the top of her hand.

"It doesn't work that way, my love," Maimouna's mother says. "He has to come home on his own so that he can stay. Your parents are still beholden to familial and cultural tradition."

"Papa, will you let Ibrahimah stay?"

Everyone knows the rules. Talibé are not allowed to return home, and if a boy should return home, even if the marabout relinquishes the boy early, it is the responsibility of the father to send him back or find another marabout who will take the boy as a disciple.

"We will find a solution," Idrissa says, looking over to Maimouna.

"I don't think it will be difficult," her mother says.

"I am surrounded by the strongest women on Earth. How did I find such blessings?" Idrissa's eyes fill with tears.

Maimouna grabs Idrissa's forearm and squeezes it gently.

"You are a lucky man, Idrissa, and smart enough to know that strong women are a blessing and not a threat," his mother-in-law says with a chuckle.

"We love you too, Papa," Fatou says.

"Me too," Binta says, her mouth full.

"Me—" Aisha spills rice onto her lap.

"Girls!" Maimouna scolds.

"Mama, did you hear that Madame N'Diaye's daughter has returned home?" Fatou asks, changing the subject.

Maimouna looks over at her eldest, forgetting Aisha's mishap. "No. Isn't she just visiting?"

"No, she arrived this evening. The women were talking about it at the well. She ran away from her husband. His two other wives treat her bad. One threw acid in her face and cut her cheek with a blade. The husband does not believe it was his second wife that did it to her and accuses that she did it to herself for attention."

"Madame N'Diaye may be a fool, but her daughter does not deserve that," Maimouna says, clucking her tongue and looking over at Idrissa.

"Well, my husband is not going to take additional wives. I want a husband like Papa," Aisha announces.

"It's terrible, they say. Her husband sent her home and says he wants a divorce. They say she is distraught."

"Madame N'Diaye was too caught up with her own self-righteousness to realize her daughter needed her," Maimouna's mother says. "Take this as a lesson. Women are just as dangerous as men, even more so at times. A woman who is jealous or insecure will attack you, maim you, hurt you physically, spiritually, or emotionally if she feels threatened."

"The world is under a constant siege of wickedness," Idrissa murmurs.

After dinner, while the girls clean up, their grandmother takes a tuft of herbs and roots and burns them throughout the house.

"How do we protect ourselves when *Maam* is not here?" Aisha asks Fatou.

This is something that has been on Fatou's mind for months.

"I think it's important to learn the old ways. It's why I follow *Maam* around, to learn how to use the roots and spells. Not for dark magic, but for protection. Look at how she has helped our family."

Aisha and Binta contemplate their older sister's wisdom.

"A powerful woman knows how to protect herself," Fatou says.

"And when to ask for help," Binta adds.

"No one will ever split us apart. We will always protect and help one another, even if we do not always agree," Fatou says to her two younger sisters.

"Including Ibrahimah?" Aisha asks.

"Yes, including our baby brother. We will never let anyone take him away from us again," Fatou says.

Fatou sticks her hand out and the other girls place their hands on hers.

"And we will never break this bond," Fatou adds.

"Never," Aisha says.

"Never," Binta replies.

"Girls!" Maimouna calls out from the living room.

"*Na'am,*" Fatou replies.

"Come! Your papa is going to read to us."

The three girls trample into the room to find their parents nestled together on the sofa and the Quran open on their father's lap. Idrissa opens the Quran to where he left off the night before.

"O ye who believe! It is not lawful for you to inherit women against their will; nor should you detain them wrongfully that you may take away part of that which you have given them, except that they be guilty of a flagrant evil; and consort with them in kindness; and if you dislike them, it may be that you dislike a thing wherein Allah has placed much good."

The girls form a half-circle on the floor in front of their parents, excited for the future that lies in wait.

XXXVII.

Ibrahimah walks out of the sanctuary of Aria's yard and back into the streets of Dakar. The fingernail-shaped moon dominates the starless night. He feels comfortable in his new pair of pants and sandals. He hugs his red tin tomato can to his chest with one hand while the other rests inside his pocket clutching the green toy. He walks down the street brooding about his next move; find Fatik and ask his friend to go with him, go to Marabout's house and sleep, then first thing in the morning set off for his village.

It is too late in the day to try to leave now. Aria told him it will take fifteen hours, an entire day, to get there. "You'll have to take a Car Rapide to the depot and ask for the sept-place that will take you south, cross the Gambian border, and take a van to the ferry to cross the Gambian River, and then another sept-place to the southern side of the Gambian border to cross back into Senegal, and then a sept-place from there to your village. Do you think you can do this by yourself?" she asked.

"I will go with an older boy from my house," Ibrahimah said.

"Do you want me to write it down?"

"Yes, please."

"Give this paper to any elder lady if you get lost along the way."

A Car Rapide passes by and honks its horn; a thin young man hangs off the back of the van, looking for passengers to pick up. The ride would get him to Marabout's house faster, but there are so many pickpockets among the passengers at night that he wouldn't be safe by himself. Ibrahimah hugs his riches closer to his body and thinks about what he will buy for his family with the money. The dark evening sky and broken streetlamps veil his body from inquiring eyes. Two men walk by, immersed in their own discussion, unaware of his small, silent footsteps moving past them. To be ignored in the day is much different from the anonymity of the night. He imagines Étienne walking beside him.

At the end of the street he steps back into a sea of streetlamps and passing cars. Approaching the On the Run parking lot, the area is filled with the smell of food cooking, the sound of music, drivers filling their cars with gas, and Talibé scattered amongst customers and the downtrodden. A Mauritanian woman with smooth, light-brown skin and high cheekbones carries a baby on her hip with her free hand stretched out, begging. Across the street several adults lay their cardboard mats down alongside the computer store, where they sleep until just before the shop opens in the morning. Ibrahimah spots Fatik and rushes up to his friend.

"Aye," Ibrahimah says, tapping him on the shoulder.

"Ibrahimah!" he says, turning with surprise, "where were you all day?"

"I went to see my ta-ta."

"Oh," Fatik says, not caring who this ta-ta is in particular.

"What are you doing?"

"Looking for food and money, what do you think?"

Ibrahimah digs into his tomato can and hands Fatik a five-hundred-franc coin.

"Here," Ibrahimah says, "take this."

"Thanks!" Fatik says, turning the coin around in his hand before it disappears into his own can beneath a dirty, torn cloth. "Where'd you get the money?"

"I'm going back to my village in the morning," Ibrahimah says, ignoring Fatik's question.

"South?"

"Yes. Come with me."

Fatik's twelve-year-old body stiffens and he takes a step back.

"I don't think so. Marabout will kill us if we try to run away."

"He won't know for at least two weeks. He went to find more boys. My mama waits for me in the village. I have to go. She will let you stay, if you come."

"Your mama can't protect us from Marabout. No one can. Not even Allah," Fatik says, shaking his head.

"There's nothing good here for us if we stay."

"But Marabout will punish us if we run away."

"Marabout is wicked, that's why Abdoulaye and Étienne are gone. We'll die too if we stay."

Fatik looks around to see if anyone can hear them, but the scuffle for money and food distracts the other boys and adults.

"If you don't like it with my mama, you can say you want to go back to Marabout. You know the way better than me. You *have* to help me."

Fatik rolls his eyes up toward the midnight-blue sky and then looks at Ibrahimah with doubt on his face.

"I don't think this is a good plan. If it was, Étienne would have run away with you a long time ago."

"We didn't have money before."

"What? Five hundred francs? That's not enough."

"I have more."

Ibrahimah pulls the cloth back and tips his can so Fatik can peek inside. Fatik looks up at Ibrahimah, his mouth formed into a small circle.

"Wow! How much do you have?"

"A lot."

"Where did you get it from?"

"Allah."

Fatik is silent for a moment.

"Okay," Fatik says after a beat, "I'll go with you, but first let me find food."

Ibrahimah looks across the parking lot of On the Run. The same evening crowd of Talibé and women begging plays out like the cartoons he would watch at Moustapha's house. Elmer Fudd chasing Bugs Bunny, again and again. This is the last evening he will spend scavenging for food and the leftover change in someone's pocket, or being afraid to return to Marabout's house because he is short his daily quota. He is the rabbit and he will finally get away.

Once Fatik tires of searching for food, they return to the safety of Marabout's house to get a good night's rest before embarking on their journey, but instead of sound sleep Ibrahimah is restless throughout the night. The mosquitoes buzzing around his ears go unnoticed as he imagines the moment when he walks down the sandy road to his family's house, the smell of his mother when she wraps him into her embrace and the sound of his sisters' voices. He's had to smother his desire for home for so long, now he can hardly breathe in anticipation. He clutches his red tin can to his chest.

Dozing off somewhere in the wee hours of the morning, he awakens before morning prayer. He looks to his left where Fatik lies, ready to wake his friend, but instead of Fatik's sleeping body resting next to him his eyes are met with an empty cardboard mat. Not wanting to wake any of the other boys, Ibrahimah grabs his can—it must have slipped out of his hands while he slept—and rises to see if Fatik is at the hole out back, but before he can maneuver through the sleeping bodies he notices how light his red tin can feels. Fear turns to desperation as he rummages inside with his hands to feel nothing but a packet of peanuts and his toy.

This can't be. The money he was going to share with Fatik and use to return back to his village is gone. Ibrahimah looks around the room, but Fatik is not there. He runs to the rear of the house and then out front, looking up and down the street. Fatik is nowhere to be seen. Ibrahimah's eyes glisten and a wail threatens to spring forth from the innards of his belly with each step he takes back to his mat. His body crumples to his mat in defeat and his hand slips on a piece of paper. He picks it up and notices a single ten-thousand-franc note—the bill must have fallen out. Ibrahimah looks into his can again, unable to comprehend how his friend could have done this to him. The G.I. Joe figurine sits at the bottom, standing at attention, ready for battle. Ibrahimah flips the toy around in his hand.

"Étienne," Ibrahimah whispers, "where are you?"

But Étienne doesn't come. The room is filled with the sound of sleeping boys wishing the night would never end, because the day brings nothing but hardship and pain. Ibrahimah knows his mother is waiting for him. He has to be strong. He will be eight years old soon. If his friend Moustapha were here, he would figure out a way to find his village. Moustapha was really smart, just like Étienne.

Ibrahimah stands up, puts the money in his right pocket with the directions from Aria, and stuffs his G.I. Joe in the left pocket. The morning prayer fills his ears just as he steps out of the front door with his empty red tin tomato can, and the determination to find his village on his own.

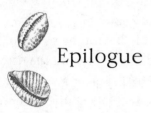

Epilogue

The veil of night is thick and the ocean roars loud and unforgiving. He is afraid to walk to the edge of the cliff, where the sea crashes up against its bowels, but this is his only escape from the terror that is sure to meet him in the morning. The creature will want more before first prayer. Afterward, it will oust him from the bed back into the roomful of boys, who will avert their eyes at his shame. As they know why he limps, each step more excruciating than the last, killing off a bit more of who he was before.

He cannot tell if the ocean is calling him or threatening him, but tonight, he will do it. He will walk to the edge and jump onto that wave that will wash him ashore to his home, cleanse his memory of the devil, and end his descent into peril. He takes a step forward, but a gust of wind rises up and pushes him back. He looks around but he is there alone. There is nothing to stop him. He can do this. He steps forward again. No wind. He takes another step. Nothing again. Good, he thinks to himself. Taking a deep breath, he raises his arms up to his chest and pumps his legs into a bolt of fearlessness. At the wall of darkness that lives at the cliff's edge, the outline of his village appears. His mother's fish patties cook in the oven, the sweet and spicy aroma intertwining and looping upon itself as it stumbles up into his nostrils and lingers.

Just as his foot touches the edge of the cliff, his body is yanked back by his neck with a force so violent, he falls down onto his back. Before he can regain his composure, his body is dragged across the sandy terrain, back across the Rue de Ouakam, the uneven earth, and the pebble-covered road, to the front of the creature's house.

He has no time to open the door, and so his body is pulled through the solid wooden object, leaving millions of tiny splinters piercing every inch of his soul, dragged back up onto the bed, and slammed down into his body. The creature hovers above him, dripping with sweat.

"You're not going anywhere," it spits into his face.

The creature leans down, its breath hot with the smell of a rotting animal, its teeth yellow, gums inflamed. It licks Ibrahimah's face, then shoves its hand into his neck before lying back down and falling into a sleep, deep enough to satisfy, but light enough that anything more than a tepid breath from Ibrahimah's body will stir it into action. The wet sheets beneath his body are cold and uncomfortable, but he dares not move. The moon quietly departs to illuminate someone else more deserving, leaving the room in complete darkness.

Ibrahimah opens his eyes, his chest bereft of air. He peeks over to his left and sees nothing but gravel and the wheels of the car he slept behind. He steals a glance over to his right and is met with a thorny shrub pricking at his skin. He breathes a sigh of relief. A dream. It was just a dream. He is no longer at the mercy of the devil, but a half-day's journey away from Saloulou, and his family.

Finding the correct transportation depot in Dakar, and getting a driver to sell him a seat in a sept-place took half the day, and then the eight-hour drive down to the border took more than twelve hours, according to the other passengers, because the station wagon broke down on the uneven dirt road that led to the Gambian border, and they had to wait for a new vehicle to come and fetch them. The passengers argued for a refund, but it did not happen. By the time they got to the Gambian border, Ibrahimah was exhausted but he managed to slip past border control by walking close to an elderly woman and hiding behind the folds of her large boubou. By the time she realized he was next to her they were on the Gambian side of the border, where he scooted away in search of a place to sleep for the night, hidden from any and everyone.

The sound of Earth's creatures waking weighs heavy on his shoulders; the night is so much more peaceful, and safe. He closes his eyes for a brief moment, to go over the next set of steps in his journey, when someone kicks his foot. He jumps up ready to fight, but is surprised when he finds who it is standing idly across from him.

"Étienne?" Ibrahimah cocks his head to the side, then rushes over to the boy with open arms. Holding his cousin in an embrace, he catches a glimpse of a tiny red spot off on the horizon. He wonders if that is his bird, but the thought leaves him as he tears himself away from the body of his lost friend and confidant. He approvingly looks Étienne up and down.

"You found me!"

Étienne offers a coy smile.

"Where've you been?"

Étienne uses his hands to make a sweeping motion.

"Are you back for good?"

Étienne nods.

"They said you were dead, but you are here again and we can touch each other," Ibrahimah says, throwing his arm up across his cousin's shoulders.

Étienne does not respond.

"Do you remember when I couldn't touch you?"

Étienne nods again.

"Can you talk?" Ibrahimah asks, eyeing him suspiciously. His arm falls from Étienne's shoulders.

Étienne lifts his neck and points to the wound that has been sewn up rather badly.

"What happened?"

Étienne makes a stabbing motion into his neck.

"Are you staying for good this time?"

Étienne nods in the affirmative and the two boys fall into their old familiar stride along the dirt road.

Ibrahimah's mind is overcome with a deluge of questions of who attacked Étienne and was he really dead, but something stops him and he becomes somber. The last time he met someone who was in a place he was not supposed to be it turned out to be the devil himself, and his life took a terrible turn because he was too trustful. Ibrahimah glances over at the boy that looks like his cousin but wonders what it is that truly walks alongside him. Étienne could be an angel sent back to him, or another version of the devil in sheep's clothing. Once he makes it home, he will decide what needs to be done. He is not a child, like he was that evening on the beach so long ago. He knows better this time.

Author's Note

According to Human Rights Watch, "More than 100,000 *talibés* living in residential *daaras* across Senegal are forced by their Quranic teachers, also known as *marabouts,* to beg daily for money, food, rice or sugar. Thousands of these children live in conditions of extreme squalor, denied sufficient food and medical care. Many are also subject to physical abuse amounting to inhuman and degrading treatment."

I encountered Talibé daily during the four years I worked and lived in Dakar, and was profoundly affected by the boys I got to know. What I learned of their joys and their pains has never left me, and I am grateful that fiction allows me to share some of those feelings with readers, many of whom may have never traveled to magnificent Senegal.

For more information, see "'There Is Enormous Suffering': Serious Abuses Against Talibé Children in Senegal, 2017–2018," Human Rights Watch, June 11, 2019, https://www.hrw.org/report/2019/06/11/there-enormous-suffering/serious-abuses-against-talibe-children-senegal-2017-2018.

To donate and learn more about work being done to help Talibé children in Senegal, check out the following organizations:

Maison de la Gare at mdgsl.com
Empire des Enfants at empiredesenfants.sn/en
Samu Social Senegal at samusocialsenegal.com/en

Acknowledgments

I am thankful to have had the opportunity to live in West Africa, for the friendships I forged while there and the discovery that we are a global village, connected in more ways than one. To the Talibé boys in Senegal who bravely forge ahead each day, unwilling to give up hope for a world that will allow them to be children, and see them for the beautiful deserving beings that they are.

I am forever indebted to John Reed, who saw the potential in this story in its very rough first draft, and who helped me realize my own potential as a novelist. You are my hero. To Luis Jaramillo, who has been there for me over the years with kindness, understanding, good advice, and patience. To John Freeman, who has been that person I can always turn to, regardless of where he is in the world. I want to send a special thank you to my agent, Ryan Harbage, who allows me to be myself and who believes in me without waver—we make a great team and I would not be here without you. To my editors extraordinaire, Chayenne Skeete and Caitlin McKenna, who took me in with love and helped me to realize that there are genuine and nice people in the world and that this process does not have to be painful; thank you for your generosity and openness. To Susan Kamil, who would not let this book fade to the sidelines, and who moved literal mountains to ensure this story would have its day, you will be forever missed—may you rest in peace.

To the entire Random House team, who brought this story to life in the midst of a global pandemic. You are amazing. Thank you.

To my early writing group: Natalie Rogers, Minette Greenberg, Joyce Jacobson, and Lenore Grandizio, who listened to me read the very first pages as I wrote them; and to the many friends who have heard me talk about the story over the years, who have read various iterations, who printed hard copy drafts when I had no printer and no money, who motivated me to push outside of my box, and who have loved me even when I may not have been at my best, I appreciate you. There are many names but I'd like to offer special thanks to Fatma Abdullahi, April Jackson, Anna Konte, Duarte Geraldino, Olivia Newman, Chanelle Elaine, Zelle Bonney, Wandie Bethune, Alexandra Boggs, Leia Menlove, Andreea Scarlat, Betsy Ho, Erin Shigaki, Justin Sherwood, Lori Lynn-Turner, David Lehman, Gina Sharpe, Wilson Hughes, Michael Vincent Miller, Cindy Spiegel, and Emi Ikkanda.

I'd like to thank the Tyrone Guthrie Centre, the Virginia Center for The Creative Arts, Vermont Studio Center, the Lower Manhattan Cultural Council Workspace Residency, and VONA, with a special shout out to David Mura and Junot Diaz, for offering me space and time to write and rewrite drafts of this story. I also thank The New School for being a mecca of support for its students, and the creative writing program staff for the relentless work that they do to support budding writers.

To my mother, Lunita, and my siblings Kalimah, Keith, LaDawn, Walid, and Salim. And to my great-grandmother, Mary-Ann Ebanks, who unwaveringly watches over me and who is always present in my heart.

KEISHA BUSH was born and raised in Boston, Massachusetts. She received her MFA in creative writing from The New School, where she was a Riggio Honors Teaching Fellow and recipient of an NSPE Dean's Scholarship. After a career in corporate finance and international development that brought her to live in Dakar, Senegal, she decided to focus full-time on her writing. She now lives in East Harlem.

Twitter: @KeishaB

This book was set in Celeste, a typeface that its designer, Chris Burke (b. 1967), classifies as a modern humanistic typeface. Celeste was influenced by Bodoni and Waldman, but the strokeweight contrast is less pronounced. The serifs tend toward the triangular, and the italics harmonize well with the roman in tone and width. It is a robust and readable text face that is less stark and modular than many of the modern fonts and has many of the friendlier old-face features.